`Praise for Penelope Blue

"A sexy, fun, cat-and-mouse chase that hooked me from page one!"

—**Jennifer Probst**, *New York Times* and *USA Today* bestselling author of *The Marriage Bargain*

"The minute I finished reading...I started it over. That's how good this book is! I laughed, I cried, and I fell totally in love with Grant Emerson and Penelope Blue, one of the most fascinating book couples I've ever read."

—**Sandra Owens**, author of the bestselling K2 Special Services series

"Tamara Morgan has masterminded the perfect heist of the heart."

—**Katie Lane**, *USA Today* bestselling author

"A rollicking romp that packs a surprising emotional punch."

—**Jenny Holiday**, author of *The Engagement Game*

"This sexy cat-and-mouse game between an FBI agent and a jewel thief had me furiously flipping the pages until the very end."

—**A. J. Pine**, author of *The One That Got Away*

"Morgan opens her Penelope Blue series with an utterly unique, compelling, and surprisingly touching romance, full of snarky commentary and blistering chemistry."

—*RT Book Reviews*

SEEKING MR. WRONG

TAMARA MORGAN

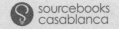

sourcebooks casablanca

THE HEIST

"I'M TELLING YOU, IT'S THE ONLY WAY WE'RE GETTING IN." I stab at the blueprints spread out on the table in front of the two of us. "You can set up as many detonations as you want, but that steel is impenetrable. All you'll do is make a lot of noise and announce yourself to every single person within a two-block radius. Is that what you want?"

Federal Agent Simon Sterling—a man most noted for his ability to freeze the happiness out of every human heart—crumples the blueprints in a fit of pique.

"Fine," he says. "You want to spend ten hours crouched inside a ceiling panel on the off chance the security guard will take an extra undocumented break that day? Be my guest. I'm not going to stop you."

"Thank you," I say and grab the wadded-up papers from the floor. I make as much noise as possible as I lay them flat again, which serves to infuriate my husband's partner further. He doesn't like that I'm right—hates even more that of the two of us, I'm the one behaving most like a professional.

Penelope Blue: former expert jewel thief turned FBI consultant by day, loving and totally underappreciated FBI wife by night. My talents know no bounds.

"And it's not as if the guard's going to *randomly* take an extra break," I explain in a level voice. One thing I've learned working with Simon over the past few months— he's a lot easier to go up against if you make yourself sound as much like a robot as possible. "We'll make sure he's indisposed beforehand."

His interest gets the better of him. Although I wouldn't go so far as to say his icy exterior *cracks*, it does thaw a little. "How will you do that?"

"Oh, there are lots of ways. I'm sure Jordan can think of something." I wave my hand. "Eye drops in the coffee will do in a pinch, but that approach lacks a certain savoir faire, don't you think?"

I take his annoyed exhalation of breath as a yes.

"Okay, so he's out of the way, and you can slip down and grab the amulet from above," Simon says. "What then? The guard's going to notice that it's missing the second he returns. How do I extract you before he sounds the alarm?"

"Aha! That's where things start to get interesting." I lean closer to the page, but I don't get a chance to outline the details of my plan. Before I so much as point out the drainage duct my team and I uncovered during a routine walk-through, a *real* alarm sounds.

I look up, startled, as an intermittent flash of red and the screaming whir of a fire alarm fill the conference room Simon and I share. To the best of my knowledge,

I haven't done anything to warrant an office-wide panic. In fact, the heist I'm outlining isn't even real. It's part of an exercise Simon and I are devising to help beef up the Major Thefts training program.

"What did you do?" Simon asks, his own thoughts taking a similar turn. Like me, he doesn't bolt at the sudden alarm, even though we can hear several people in the hallway starting to evacuate. "What are you trying to steal from the FBI this time?"

"Nothing!" I protest. "And I resent the implication that I'm involved in *every* alarm that goes off around here."

For one, I haven't stolen anything in almost three months. Ever since I became a consultant for the New York field office of the Federal Bureau of Investigation, I've been a model citizen in every sense of the word. I don't steal, I don't lie, and I even pay my own taxes now—real IRS taxes. Did you know the government takes almost twenty percent of everything you earn? And people think *I'm* a thief.

For another, I would never do something so clumsy as set off an alarm like this. Full-scale fire alarms are great if you want to bring every police and fire official in the city running—but that's something that rarely works in a thief's favor. The idea is not just to get the goods, but to get *away* with them. The less involved the authorities are, the better.

In fact, the only reason I can think of to set off an alarm would be because someone wanted to create a distraction. If, for example, there was an event taking place inside this building that I wanted to interrupt…

My head snaps up. "Oh, no. It can't be. He wouldn't dare."

Simon's questioning gaze meets mine.

"Simon, what time is Grant's physical?"

"Four thirty," he says without hesitation. He has a computerlike memory for schedules and lists. It's infallible most of the time, but don't bother asking him to remember a girl's birthday or where she prefers to order lunch, even when you know the answer will never be the sushi place around the corner.

"And what time is it right now?" I ask.

He doesn't have to look at his watch, either. Clocks are programmed into his android brain. "Four thirty. Why? You don't think—"

No, I don't think. I *know*.

"That sneaky, lying bastard," I say as I bolt out of my chair and head for the door. Normally, making sudden movements around Simon isn't a good idea, as he enjoys pulling out his handcuffs on any pretext he can find. For once, however, I have nothing to worry about. My husband's partner and I are in perfect unity. "I thought it was weird when he scheduled the meeting for so late on a Friday. I should have known he was up to something."

I dash out of the conference room with Simon on my heels. With a quick glance up and down the hallway, I scan for evidence that we're all going to die in a fiery blaze. I don't see or smell smoke coming from either direction, nor is anyone evacuating at a pace other than an annoyed walk.

Just as I thought—a false alarm.

"What's the standard protocol for an alarm like this?" I ask, mentally calculating the time it will take for the building to go on lockdown and open back up again. I don't like my odds.

Simon hesitates, which goes to show how little he trusts me even after all this time. We spend almost twenty hours a week together now, planning fake heists and advising foreign nationals on the safest way to transport their jewels, but he'd still happily consign me to the trunk of his car, should the opportunity arise. Fortunately, he's the one person who knows Grant better than I do, and he eventually reaches the same conclusion as me: *we've been duped*.

"They'll evacuate the civilians, close off the floors at each end, and post a team at every exit," he says, his tone clipped. "As soon as the all clear comes through, they'll open it back up again."

"And how long will that take?"

"Long enough for him to get what he wants." He sighs. "I don't know, Blue. He's awfully determined. Maybe we should just let him—"

"No way." I take off for the emergency exit. The medical offices are located five floors down, and they're five floors I intend to take at a flying pace. Forget the teams at the exits and metal fire doors coming to a close—I'm light on my feet and nimble enough to squeeze through any open space. And I will, too.

My husband might be able to send the entire FBI building scattering, and he might be able to push even Simon beyond the limits of his patience, but there's one person he can't order around—no matter how hard he tries.

That person, as he well knows, is *me*.

As expected, I find my husband flashing his most disarming, crinkly eyed smile at the doctor trying to exit the medical office in accordance with standard evacuation protocols.

"But, Dr. Lee, I need a quick signature here at the bottom, and I'm good to go." He hands her a slip of paper. "I'm afraid I won't see you again today with all this going on. Would you mind skipping the exam just this once?"

Dr. Lee, who's both far too young and far too unmarried to withstand a smile like Grant's, takes the piece of paper. "I don't know, Agent Emerson. This is highly unethical."

"You know as well as I do that this is only a formality. I passed the physical test last week and have never felt better. Please? For me?"

"Don't do it," I warn from the doorway. It's difficult to hear me over the sound of the alarm still clanging in the distance, but I can make myself heard when I set my mind to it. And my mind, to put it mildly, is set. "He's lying through his teeth. He passed the physical, yes— and reinjured himself to the point where he can't even stand up straight."

I can't hear Grant's low, muttered curse, but I can imagine it just fine—I've heard it plenty enough times in my life for that.

"Look at him," I add. "He's not fit for anything but another round of therapy."

He turns to me with a scowl. He also stands up incredibly straight, though I don't miss the grimace of pain that crosses his face as he does it. That one is going to cost him.

"The building is under evacuation, Penelope," he says. His voice is easy even if his stance isn't. "Civilians are supposed to be outside by now."

Yes, which would explain why he pulled the alarm in the first place. Step one, get rid of the wife. Step two, flirt with the doctor to get his way. Step three, return to work against the advice of countless medical professionals and the screaming pain of his own body telling him to slow down.

"I'm not going anywhere until you give me that release form." I fold my arms and firm my stance. Grant's eyes brighten with the self-satisfied gleam of a man who thinks he's found a loophole, so I hastily amend my command. "That *unsigned* release form. Believe me—I'm not a woman you want to cross right now."

Dr. Lee looks at the form in alarm.

"Don't listen to her," Grant wheedles as he hands the doctor a pen. "She'll do or say anything to get what she wants."

Ha. Talk about a man willing to go to any means to achieve his ends. I don't know how illegal it is to fake a fire at an FBI building just to harass a doctor into signing a medical release, but I can't imagine it's looked upon with favor. Not that he cares about any of that. I've never met a man so dishonorably honorable as my husband. Sure, he fights crime and locks up bad guys for a living, but you wouldn't believe the kind of rules he breaks to do it—and without so much as a twinge of conscience.

Behold, our marriage in a nutshell.

"And he's trying to trick you into clearing him for a job that he's in no way, shape, or form ready for," I reply. "Give it to me, or I'll have to report you both."

Grant narrows his eyes. "Penelope, so help me…"

I narrow my eyes right back. "Grant, so help *me*…"

"Maybe I should give you two a minute," Dr. Lee says with a nervous laugh. "I get the feeling this isn't really about a release form."

I ignore her. This is too important to lose focus. See, three months ago, my husband was shot in the line of duty. A bullet entered his back and emerged through his abdomen, barely missing his spine and all major internal organs. He's lucky to be walking—luckier still to be alive—but to hear him tell the tale, his injury is nothing more than a scratch that needs a kiss and a bandage.

The thing is, I *have* kissed him, and I *have* changed his bandages—and still I've watched him struggle for the past ninety days to reconcile the body he once had and the one he's stuck with now. He's not healing the way he's supposed to. He pushes too hard and tries to do too much. His greatest goal in life is to get cleared to return to field duty, and he's worked single-mindedly toward that goal since the day he was discharged from the hospital, common sense be damned.

But he's not ready. I know it and Simon knows it and, yes, even Grant knows it. Getting him to admit that out loud, however, is an exercise in head-against-the-wall futility.

"Poke him," I suggest with a gesture at Grant's stomach. "Go ahead. Stick a finger out and jab him right in the scar. See what happens."

Grant's scowl lightens to a half smile, his lips turned up at the corners. "Is that a challenge, my love?"

Despite the fact that I would like to poke this man into full-on obedience, I can't resist that smile or the playful way his coffee-black eyes twinkle in the flashing red alarm. There's nothing he loves more than turning our arguments into a game. He thinks he has a better chance of winning that way.

"Sure, if you want to call it that," I concede. "Let's make it a challenge. If Dr. Lee pokes you as hard as she can and you don't flinch, I'll let you keep your stupid form."

"And if I do flinch?"

"You don't return here until *I* decide you're ready." I hold his gaze. "You're not the only one who can be stubborn, you know."

He extends a hand, holding it steady until I slip my palm against his. The rough texture of his skin is warm and familiar, as is the way he lingers over the perfunctory handshake a second too long.

"Then it's a deal." He turns to Dr. Lee. "You heard my wife. If you poke me and I don't move a muscle, you can go ahead and sign the form. We'll be on our way and won't bother you again."

Dr. Lee blinks at him, her green eyes owlish behind their frames. "That's, um, not how any of this works. You guys know that, right?"

"And if he does move a muscle, you need to prescribe him at least four more weeks of physical therapy," I counter, ignoring her. "You might also want to throw in psychological counseling, because the man clearly needs it."

Grant takes a step in my direction. "I beg your pardon," he says, low voice grumbling. "There's not a damn thing wrong with my brain, and there never has been. Except for maybe the day I married you."

I match my step to his, drawing so close we're practically chest to chest. "If that's not clear proof you're out of your mind, then I don't know what is. A *fire* alarm, Grant? Really? Have I taught you nothing?"

As if on cue, the siren turns off, plunging the three of us into a ringing silence. I pause a moment before I move, allowing myself time to adjust to the sudden alteration in my surroundings.

"Huh," Grant says. He casts a glance at the clock on the wall and frowns. "That didn't take nearly as long as I wanted it to."

"Probably because I sent Simon to go call in the false alarm," I say and turn to the doctor. "Does this mean you'll have time to do a full exam now? I wasn't kidding before—he's good at hiding it, but he's in a lot of pain."

"No way." She holds up her hands. "I'm not doing anything except maybe sending you *both* down to psych."

"Hey, now!" I protest. "There's no call for drastic measures."

"Yeah," Grant agrees with a laugh. "I'm probably okay, but you can't send my wife down there. She'd never make it out again."

Grant and I turn toward the doctor as one, aligning together to defend ourselves against her. The way we conduct our marriage may be unorthodox, but there's no denying that we work best when we work as a team.

Unfortunately, there's no time for me to convince the doctor to perform her test after all, because Simon appears at the door, breathless and red-faced.

"Oh, good. You're both still here." He nods in Grant's direction. "I was up in the section chief's office calling off the alarm, and you'll never guess what just got the all clear."

"No way," Grant says, his eyes lighting from within. "They actually approved it?"

"I've got the paperwork signed, sealed, and delivered." Simon rubs his hands together. "Complete that release form, Doc, and let my man get back to the field. We've got work to do."

"Simon!" I cry. I thought he was supposed to be on my side.

"Sorry, Blue," he says, sounding like the least apologetic man of all time. "But you're going to want to get in on this one, too. Leon called an emergency meeting up in his office. If all goes according to plan, you two ship out Monday."

THE MISSION

As it turns out, Dr. Lee *can* be persuaded to sign a release form without the requisite medical evaluation. One quick phone call upstairs, and Grant is suddenly fit to return to duty, no questions asked.

"But what about the Hippocratic oath?" I demand. "What about the fact that he pulled a fire alarm to avoid his appointment today?"

"You don't have proof that was me," Grant points out.

"And he *did* pass the physical test last week," Simon adds.

"Sorry, but this one's over my head," Dr. Lee says with a hunched shrug. She's the only one in the room to sympathize with my plight, but even she's unmovable. "Hippocrates has nothing on the director of the FBI."

I swear, I'd be amused at how quickly they all turned if I wasn't so outraged. For these people, the job *always* comes first.

I treat both men to a barrage of insults on their intelligence and dubious moral code until we make it back up to their floor. I continue as they lead the way to the office of Christopher Leon, Grant's half brother and the agent who currently heads up their department. I especially don't stop when we're all seated at the table and the proposed mission is finally laid out before me.

"Are you freaking kidding me?" I cry. "No way. It's a death trap. It's not happening."

"Penelope, I don't think you understand—" Christopher begins. His booming voice is cut short by an almost imperceptible shake of Grant's head. Even though Christopher is technically Grant's superior, he's not his equal in terms of either experience or wisdom, so he has a tendency to defer to my husband's wishes.

It's part of what makes my attempt to slow Grant down so difficult. Few people are willing or able to stand up to the full weight of his charisma—Christopher included.

"But if she'll just hear us out, I know she'll come around," Christopher protests. "She must have misunderstood the details."

"As she is neither an idiot nor a child, she understood just fine." I push back from the table. "Thank you for inviting me, gentlemen, but you're clearly deluded—every last one of you. The answer is no."

I doubt many people have said no quite so forcefully when confronted with Grant Emerson, Simon Sterling, and Christopher Leon, their massive shoulders crowded in a row, but I'm not scared of them. I've faced firing squads of this caliber plenty of times before. In fact, I've faced this *particular* firing squad more times than I care to count.

"But Penelope—" Christopher begins again, his voice even louder this time.

In case it isn't obvious, there's a strong family tendency toward obstinacy running through his and Grant's shared bloodline. The two men might not have grown up together, their father being the sort to stick around only long enough to leave his DNA behind, but their ability to hold fast to one dogged path is nothing short of miraculous. And annoying.

"We aren't asking you to *play* in the poker game," Christopher says. "We only want you to be on the boat where it will take place."

The specs for the game he's talking about are spread out on the table in front of me, glossy page after glossy page of carefully snapped photos arranged like a brochure meant, I assume, to entice me. Most of the photos are of a cruise ship gilded to the hulls and equipped with every modern convenience known to mankind.

According to Team Shoulders over there, it's the site of an upcoming poker tournament between some of the most cunning card players in the world. And by *cunning card players*, I of course mean criminals. Known criminals, suspected criminals, criminals who are wanted in every single one of our world's 196 countries... The stack of dossiers in my hands reads like Facebook for Felons. For one full week, they're going to gather and mingle and cheat at poker together.

In theory, I have no objections to all this. I like ocean views, and I like people who break the law, and if you're going to hold a giant illegal poker game, why wouldn't you put it on what amounts to a floating casino?

Unfortunately, few things are as simple as they seem—especially where the FBI is involved. According to the ridiculous plan they've been putting together behind my back, they'd like to send someone under-cover on that boat. More specifically, they'd like to send my *husband* undercover on that boat.

Alone. Without backup. Protected by no one but me and anyone from my team I can convince to come along.

"We've looked at every scenario, but nothing else is viable," Christopher says.

I'd say he's being purposefully obtuse, but I'm never quite sure with that man.

"It's a small ship, and everyone buying a ticket is being thoroughly vetted ahead of time, so there's no way we can land a full team without detection," he continues. "It's going to be a stretch just to get Grant on board."

I throw my hands up in annoyance. "Of course it is. In case you weren't aware, criminals don't enjoy having their illegal activities monitored by the feds. We're picky about that sort of thing."

"But, Penelope—"

"Enough!" I cry. "It'll never work. Even if I *could* convince my team to hop aboard the—what, *Shady Lady*?—there's not going to be much we can do to pro-tect Grant out there on open water. We're thieves, not thugs. Have you asked my dad's opinion?"

"We tried." Simon casts a sideways glance at Grant. "He hasn't proven himself to be particularly helpful."

"That sounds ominous."

"No, not ominous." Christopher stumbles over his words in his rush to reassure me. "He's planning on attending the cruise to try and win the tournament for himself. He feels a federal presence would interfere with his plans. He suggested we, ah, abandon the project."

I laugh out loud at that. In other words, my dad told them exactly how high they could stick their interfering badges.

"He's not wrong," I point out. "One whiff of the men in black, and everyone on that ship will jump overboard. Either that or they'll shoot Grant and leave his body for the sharks. Why do you want to go so bad? You can hardly arrest *everyone* on the *Shady Lady*. It says here the boat holds six hundred people."

"I don't plan on arresting anyone, actually." Grant leans across the table and pushes one of the dossiers at me. The name at the top reads Johnny Francis, and there's a list of suspected crimes underneath that makes my head swirl—armed robbery, extortion, racketeering. The list is impressive enough on its own, but in the place where there's supposed to be a picture, there's a question mark instead. "All we want is to track down a potential contact. We got a tip that he's going to surface for a chance at winning the tournament. I want to be there in case he does."

"Who is he?"

Simon snorts his disgust. "You don't know who Johnny Francis is?"

The name, I'll admit, is familiar, but so are a lot of the people Grant arrests. It doesn't mean anything. Just because I once belonged to the union doesn't mean I'm automatically plugged in to every bad guy out there. That's like assuming all plumbers know each other.

I glare. "You don't either, or you'd have a picture of him."

Grant laughs. "She's got you there, Sterling." To me,

he adds, "Unfortunately, most of what we know at this point is speculation. We've been trying to get eyes on this guy for three years, but he's not easy to find. Even though he knows everyone, no one seems to know him. He has no associates and no aliases that we're aware of. He's a ghost. This poker game might be our only way of putting a face to the name."

I'm still not buying it. "So you want to go undercover at an elite illegal poker game in hopes this Johnny Francis character will sit down next to you and introduce himself?"

"Well, no," Simon admits. "But between Emerson, you, and any other members of your team you can convince to come along, we can narrow the pool of potential candidates. You guys can ask questions and move around in ways we can't."

He has a point. I might not be as firmly rooted in the criminal world as, say, Johnny Francis, but the name Penelope Blue means something. I hate to brag, but I'm kind of famous.

"I should also mention that you'll need to find your own way on board," Christopher says. "That includes making contact and covering the entrance fee. There can't be any ties back to us, or Grant's safety will be compromised."

"Gee. How enticing. How much does a ticket aboard this ship of fools cost?"

"To attend as a spectator? I'm not sure. But the buy-in to play is set at an even million."

A *million* dollars? "Are you kidding?" I ask as my gaze skims from one determined male face to another. "What prize are they offering for *that* price tag? A trip to the moon?"

Grant is the first to respond. He lifts a hand to his mouth and emits a sound that goes something like, "*D*coughcough*monds.*"

My incredulity morphs instantly to interest. "I'm sorry—what did you say?"

"*D*coughcough*monds*," he repeats, fake cough less pronounced this time.

"Okay." I sit up straighter and fold my hands on top of the table. "I'm listening. You may proceed."

Grant's chuckle, deep and rich, fills the room. "I told you we should lead with that."

I ignore his gentle mockery, directing my attention to Christopher and Simon instead. "What kind of diamonds are we talking? I want specifics—cut, weight, quality. Leave nothing out."

"Calling them diamonds might be misleading," Simon says. "There's only a single gem in the center of the tiara."

My pulse picks up. I can think of a few tiaras of that design. "Go on," I urge.

"There are also a few sapphires affixed to the setting, which I believe is solid gold. The scrollwork is—"

I hold up one hand, stopping him short. "Say no more. It's the Luxor Tiara, isn't it?"

"Yes." Simon's brows come up in mild surprise. "How did you know?"

Because I'm an intelligent woman with eyes in her head and carbon in her blood, that's how. Even though I've never seen the Luxor Tiara in person, I can fully picture the two-hundred-carat diamond in its center, the approximate size of an egg.

I'm starting to feel dizzy, though I can't tell if that's

caused by outrage or interest. Most likely it's the second. *Luxor* and *tiara* were the first words I spoke out loud. I drew pictures of myself wearing that tiara in elementary school. My dad had a mobile of it hanging over my crib.

Okay, so that's not strictly true, but I *can* remember drifting off to sleep at night with my dad sitting by my side as he recited a list of the most valuable pieces of jewelry in the world. We weren't a *Goodnight Moon* sort of family, and my father isn't the greatest story-teller, so recitations of this sort were common. I could still probably name the estimated value of all the crown jewels in descending order.

The Luxor Tiara isn't one of the crown jewels—at least not for a crown that has any real claim to it. Although it once belonged to Spain, it's most famous for having been lost and buried deep under the Caribbean for most of its history, nestled alongside pirate plunder in shimmering shades of silver and gold. Recovered by treasure hunters in the early 1980s, its ownership has been disputed ever since it hit dry land. Governments want it, museums want it, archaeological experts want it, and most important, jewel thieves want it.

Jewel thieves want it really, really bad.

Christopher's brow furrows in concern. "She's not saying anything. Why isn't she saying anything?"

"Give her a moment." Grant leans back in his chair, a smile playing on his lips. "She'll come around."

I do, too, but it takes me a minute. An offer like the Luxor Tiara doesn't pop up every day.

"I don't understand," I say as soon as my faculties are back online. "The ownership of that tiara has been con-tested for decades. How can it legally be up for grabs?"

"Legally, it's not." Simon's tightly pinched nostrils indicate his continued disdain for all things underhanded and shady. "But the man currently in possession of it—a smuggler by the name of Peter Sanchez—doesn't care. The cruise departs from Cuba and sticks to international waters from there on out, so no one has any jurisdiction to stop him."

"Not that we want to stop him, anyway," Grant puts in. "All we want is to find Johnny Francis and bring him in for a chat. No one is going to get in trouble, and no one is going to get arrested. I'll be there merely as a player and an observer. There will be no physical strain whatsoever. In fact, it's practically a vacation."

Despite my reservations—of which I have many— I'm starting to get excited. I've seen my husband play poker before, and he's not half bad.

"If you win, will you get to bring home the tiara?" I ask.

"Er, I'm afraid I can't do that," he says with an apologetic air. "Convincing the government to lay out a million dollars for this was no easy task. They'll claim any of my winnings."

"Stupid greedy government," I mutter. And then, after a few greedy calculations of my own, "Wait—at a million a player, it'll only take, like, twenty entrants for this Peter guy to get the full value of the tiara. How many people will be there?"

"We estimate around fifty players total, not counting the five hundred or so additional guests and crew," Grant says. "That's the reason we're asking for your assistance. I can't realistically sift through that many people on my own in just one week, especially since I'll have to play in the poker game to protect my cover."

"And you can't bring Simon?"

"You think Simon could blend in with that crowd?" Grant asks with a laugh.

Simon just shrugs; we all know he couldn't.

"It's too risky to bring anyone else. It's too risky to bring *you*, but I don't see what other choice I have. It's you or no one, Penelope. You're all I've got."

His words hit me exactly where they're meant to—right in the heart. I can count the number of times Grant has asked me for help on two fingers. He's not the kind of man who likes to show his weaknesses, as today's events have proven, and he's especially not the kind of man who likes to ask his wife for help in protecting them. In fact, not too long ago, *he* was the one trying his damnedest to take care of *me*.

"If I say no, will you still go without me?" I ask.

Grant's dark eyes lock onto mine. "Yes. I have to. It's my best chance of finding this guy. My fake identity *should* hold no matter what, but…"

I don't need him to finish. If it doesn't hold and he's trapped out in the middle of the ocean with a blown cover and a weakened body, there's no saying what will happen.

No. Scratch that. There *is* saying what will happen. I might not know who this Johnny Francis guy is, but I do know what men like him are capable of. If my husband isn't killed outright, then he'll be tossed in some dark, dank hold and tortured until he reveals everything. I wasn't kidding when I said that criminals don't take lightly to being duped by federal agents. Torture would be the least of his worries.

The dizzy feeling returns, although this time, it's accompanied by a surge of excitement strong enough to have me gripping the edge of the table to balance myself.

"This is a terrible position to put me in, and you know it," I say.

"We're sorry," Grant says. Of the three men he's apologizing for, I'm sure he's the most sincere. "It's not ideal to spring this on you at the last minute, but we didn't think the plan would get approved. We're as surprised as you are—apparently, Major Thefts is only one of several departments interested in Johnny."

"Then why can't another department send someone in?" I ask.

"Because," he says simply, "we're the only department that has *you*."

Oh, dear. Arguments don't get much more compelling than that.

"Besides, you did say you wanted to be more involved at work," he adds. "It doesn't get much more involved than this."

Nor, to be perfectly honest, does it get much better. Despite the dangers, this undercover plot has all my favorite things—intrigue and diamonds and my friends and family gathered under one roof. This kind of job is exactly the sort of thing I wanted to take on when I first joined the FBI. Until now, there's been a lot less action and a lot more sitting behind a desk than I was hoping for.

"Fine," I say and sigh. "But I want it stated for the record that I'm only agreeing under extreme duress."

"Noted."

"Also, I'm not going as some stupid spectator. I'm playing in that poker game—and if I win, I'm keeping the tiara."

"That's a pretty big *if*." Now that he knows he's hooked me, the smiling crinkles around his eyes come out in full force. "The last time we played poker, I beat the pants off you."

He means that literally. He beat the pants off me, as well as my shirt, my bra, a lacy wisp of underwear... You get the idea.

"Yeah, but that's because I let you," I reply with a mild flush at the memory. I think I can safely say we *both* won that particular poker game. "And I can't speak on behalf of Riker or Jordan or Oz. The decision of whether they want to participate is entirely up to them, especially since Riker..."

My husband winces an apology. What I didn't say, what I don't need to say, is that Riker and games of chance aren't the best mix. He's been doing really well with his gambling addiction recently, but this kind of temptation won't be easy.

"This mission is strictly voluntary. If he feels he's not up for it, just say the word." Grant rises to his feet in a single, authoritative movement, his hand extended across the table to where I sit. Unless you're looking for it, it's impossible to see the way he favors his right side. "Do we have a deal?"

"You're a sneaky, underhanded, manipulative bastard, you know that?"

"I'll take that as a yes."

I slip my hand into his, the familiar warmth of his grip almost enough to make me forget how angry I am at him for putting me in this position in the first place. *Almost*.

"I don't like it, but I'll do it," I say. "And only because our life insurance policy doesn't cover acts of supreme idiocy."

"*Only* for that?" he asks with one lift of the brow.

Okay, and for a once-in-a-lifetime glimpse at the Luxor Tiara. But I refuse to give any of these men the satisfaction of hearing me say so out loud.

THE SUPPORT 3

As usual, I'm the last to know about anything and everything even remotely cool.

"Um, Riker?" I ask. "Why are you wearing a wet suit in the middle of your living room? I swear, if this is a kinky sex thing, I'm walking out the door and never coming back. Not even if you catch on fire."

Riker, who is not only wearing a wet suit but also has a swimming mask over his eyes and flippers on his feet, turns to me and grins. Well, he grins as much as a person *can* grin with a snorkel shoved into his mouth, but the idea is the same.

I scan his apartment for signs of further deviation— namely Tara Lewis, the woman he's been seeing for the last few months—but he appears to be alone, thank goodness. Not that I'm complaining about his social life. Far from it. *I* might think that dating my blond bombshell of a stepmother would be one small step above stabbing forks in my eyes, but she's been weirdly good for him.

I think it's because they both like to complain about the same things: honesty, legally earned income, me.

"Wait a minute. If this isn't a sex thing…" I whirl back to him, the snorkel suddenly making perfect sense. "Oh, my God. You're getting ready to go to the Caribbean. You're getting ready to go to the Caribbean on a gambling cruise, and you weren't going to invite me."

He pulls the mask down from his eyes, leaving a ring of red around his forehead. It makes him look demented but not contrite.

"Oh, I'm sorry," he says. "Would you like to uproot your life for the next seven days and go on an illegal vacation with me? I won't tell your husband if you don't."

I glare. "Yes, actually, I'd love to. In fact, I was on my way home to start packing, but I needed to stop here and invite you first. That's what friends do. They tell each other when they plan glamorous criminal adventures."

"Wait—seriously?"

"Yes, seriously." I pause. "Well, I'm serious about the going home to pack part. *And* about the inviting you part—but it's not because I'm your friend. I'm here as an ambassador of the FBI."

Riker seems to recognize how ridiculous it is to hold this conversation while wearing flippers, because he reaches down to unsecure his feet. He also unzips his wet suit halfway to reveal the smooth, hard lines of his chest. What my stepmother sees in that flat, hairless musculature is beyond me.

Well, that's not fair. There was a time, many years ago, when Riker and I were more than friends, and I seemed to like his flat, hairless musculature just fine then. And if I'm being honest, he's filled out considerably since we were younger—there are dips and swells and honest-to-god shadows peeking out from the folds of his wet suit. The problem is that in comparison to the hard wall of a chest I get to sleep with every night, there's no contest.

Poor mankind. With guys like Grant in this world, no one else stands a chance.

"They can't arrest me for playing in a private tournament," Riker says in a defensive tone. "Not unless they arrest all the other people who will be playing. And the FBI has no jurisdiction over me outside the United States—I checked. They'd have to bring in the CIA or Interpol, and I haven't done anything to warrant *their* interest in at least a decade."

It's in my power to reassure him that he's not in any trouble, but I'm pleased to see that he's still capable of showing remorse, so I don't. This trip is a bad idea for more reasons than I care to count, but as far as Riker is concerned, there's only one worth noting.

"Riker," I say.

"Pen," he returns flatly.

"Gambling?"

"It's just one poker game."

"It's always just one poker game."

He lifts his chin in a belligerent angle. "You said that money was mine to do what I want with. No strings, no rules. This is starting to feel an awful lot like strings and rules."

The money he's talking about is a bus locker full of cash I saved up from my pre-Grant days. My half is still carefully tucked in hiding—and a good thing, too, with all these new expenses looming—but I gave Riker his share a few months ago along with the promise that I wouldn't interfere in his life anymore.

Stupid promises. Between Riker and Grant, all I seem to be doing these days is the exact opposite of what my instincts urge.

"Well?" he asks. "Go ahead. Tell me how stupid I am, how I'm fucking up my life and you won't always be there to bail me out. I'll wait."

I sigh instead. As much as I might want to fall back into the roles of our youth—a fierce, bickering loyalty that was sometimes the sole thing keeping us alive—I've recently learned better. We're semifunctional adults with our own semifunctional adult lives, and that means backing off sometimes.

"At least this one requires you to pay your full entrance fee up front," I say, resigned. "One million all in, right? Do you need any help with it?"

"Between what you gave me and a few odd jobs Jordan and I picked up, I've got it covered." He eyes me askance, as if waiting for the catch. "You aren't mad?"

"Of course I'm mad. I'm furious. I spent the better part of twelve years trying to keep you away from this exact situation." I don't give him a chance to argue. "Is Tara going?"

Now he's really starting to look at me with suspicion. "Ye-es. She's the one who told me about the game in the first place. She's playing, too, in case you're wondering."

Of course she is. Tara would never pass up a chance to win that tiara. She's the one person in this world who might be more diamond-crazy than I am—and she'll wear it, which is the funny thing. If given a chance, she'll place that goddamn crown on top of her platinum locks and go grocery shopping in it.

She could totally pull it off, too.

"I'm glad," I say and mean it. Not only is Tara way more effective than me at keeping Riker out of trouble, but more bodies on our side means more support for Grant. Together, we might—*might*—be able to get him out of there alive. "That makes you, me, Tara, and my dad at the tables, and hopefully Oz and Jordan, though they'll probably come as spectators."

Riker cracks a laugh. "*You're* playing poker? Against that crowd? Pen, you'll be out in five minutes. No, scratch that. Four minutes. You might as well throw your money from the top of the Empire State Building and watch it float away."

Irritation pricks at the base of my spine, causing me to straighten. "Please. I can play poker. It's not like it's hard. All you have to do is match the colors and shapes."

He groans, passing a hand over his eyes. "Colors and shapes? For fuck's sake. You're going to make me a laughingstock."

I ignore him. "There's also the luck of the draw, which I've always been better at than you."

That's true, and Riker knows it. Even though his best bet would be to lay off gambling for good, there's something to his infallible belief that the luck will turn his way if only he keeps playing. By the law of averages, it *has* to. No one has worse luck when it comes to a bad run. I saw a man once bet Riker that he couldn't roll a single seven out of thirty throws of the dice—something he later said was so rare, it was practically a statistical impossibility. But Riker somehow managed it.

And, I should note, almost lost his fingers in the process. It was a good thing I was carrying a bag of loose diamonds in my shoe at the time.

Riker opens his mouth to protest, but I stop him before he manages to inflate his lungs all the way. "I didn't come to argue about my poker-playing skills or lecture you about gambling," I say. "I came to ask a favor. There's one more friend of mine who plans to join the game."

"Who? You don't know anyone else."

"I know Grant."

It takes a second for that one to sink in, and Riker almost chokes once it does. "*Grant* is playing? As in, your law-abiding husband? As in, the man who brushes his teeth every morning in the reflection of his FBI badge?"

"Yes. He's going undercover."

"Why?"

"To find a bad guy."

"He'll have plenty to choose from. Is this a general dragnet, or does he have someone specific in mind?"

"He's after someone named Johnny Francis. Have you heard of him?"

Instead of answering me like a normal human being, Riker just laughs.

"Are you finished?" I ask after a full twenty seconds of his unchecked mirth. He's going to give himself an aneurysm.

"Almost." He draws a deep breath. "I'm sorry. That was rude. I thought I heard you say Grant is going to try and find *Johnny Francis*."

"I didn't."

"Okay, phew. He'd have better luck finding Jimmy Hoffa wrapped up in Amelia Earhart's skeletal embrace."

"I didn't say he was going to *try*. I said he was going to do it." I pause. "And we're going to help him."

He stares at me, unblinking. "I think maybe you should start this one from the beginning, Pen."

So I do. I do a good job of it, too, only voicing my displeasure over the plan twice. Two and a half, if you count that aside about all the stupid men in my life and their stupid inability to recognize a bad idea when it's staring them in the face.

As soon as I'm done, Riker's laughter is nowhere in sight. "You weren't kidding, were you?" He lets out a low whistle. I can tell from the sound of it that he's as intrigued by this plan as I am. "It's a hell of a stretch, but never let it be said that I denied a man his chance at beating the long odds. I don't know what makes the FBI think I'm going to be any help, though. I've never met Johnny Francis—never even been in the same city as him, as far as I can tell. I couldn't pick him out of a lineup."

"Me either, but the alternative is for Grant to go in without any kind of backup. They can't get any other agents on board without drawing suspicion, so we're taking the place of his usual support team. Oz can provide technical assistance, I'm sure Jordan could manufacture a bomb out of her dinner should the need arise, and you and I can sneak around behind the scenes. It's not ideal, but it's better than sending him in solo."

Of course, that's half the story. The other half is a much darker, much less pleasant tale.

"You know what these guys are like," I say, unable to keep the quaver from my voice. "You know what they're capable of when they've been crossed. What do you think is going to happen to him if he's discovered out there on his own?"

Broken kneecaps. Dismemberment. The complete and methodical takedown of everyone he holds dear. Riker has been on the receiving end of these kinds of threats far too often not to recognize how much danger Grant will be in the second he boards the *Shady Lady*.

"Please say you'll help," I beg. "He needs you. *I* need you."

Riker pauses, and I can practically see the cogitations of his weaselly little brain. I don't mean that as an insult. Riker might be sneaky and underhanded, but he's sneaky, underhanded, and *smart*. It's not a bad combination when life hasn't exactly been generous with the handouts.

"If I do this," he says slowly, "if I agree to put my own life at risk so your husband can play cops and robbers, what do I get in return?"

"I don't know." Strange it hadn't occurred to me to ask that. Normally, I'm all about the monetary compensation, but I've been too worried about Grant to care. A living, breathing husband is all I ask for. "What do you want?"

Although I used to have him pretty well figured out, I have no idea *what* Riker wants anymore. I've already given him quite a bit; as loath as he is to admit it, he's been granted more leeway than regular criminals thanks to his association with me. I'm valuable to Grant, and Grant is valuable to the Bureau, and that's been an equation that's worked well in our favor so far. But beyond that?

"I want the Luxor Tiara," he says.

"Well, obviously," I reply. "We *all* want the tiara. Why do you think I agreed to this in the first place?"

"No, I mean it. I want a guarantee the FBI won't interfere with my attempts to get it. If I walk off that boat with the tiara in my possession, I want your husband's solemn vow that no one will come after me. It's mine, free and clear."

I'll have to ask Grant to be sure, but I doubt he'll raise much of a fuss. The chances of Riker winning a poker game against a room full of hardened criminals and cardsharps is slim, to say the least.

"Done. Is that all?"

He tilts his head. "How much more do you think I can ask for?"

"Honestly? Whatever you want. I'm not sure what the FBI plans on doing with this guy once they find him, but a million dollars to board a ship where he *might* be present isn't exactly a small investment." Not to mention the fact that they're sending in an agent who should, by all medical accounts, be sitting on the sidelines. "They want him, and they want him bad."

Riker's grin lifts the left side of his lips, turning his whole demeanor downright sunny. I assume that means he's in.

"You shouldn't have told me that, Pen," he says and rubs his hands together. "There's nothing I love more than seeing a team of federal agents beg."

"You could just help out of the goodness of your heart, you know."

"No one has ever accused me of having a heart before," is his quick retort. "And don't look at me like that—I'm much better off without one. If finding true love means turning into the honorable, law-abiding citizen you've become, I want no part of it."

I agree with a sigh. He's right. As much as I love my husband, having to become the *responsible* one in our relationship does seem like an awfully high price to pay.

THE JOURNEY

4

"You don't know me. You've never met me. You aren't even sure you like me all that much." Grant holds out his hand. "You're also very modest and won't walk around in that scrap of a bikini Tara gave you."

I slip the wedding ring off my finger and place it in his waiting palm. His fingers close around mine, holding me tight. Grant might be playing the role of suave, commanding federal agent right now, but I can tell he's starting to get nervous.

And no wonder. My dad was able to get me in on the poker game at the last minute, but he made it abundantly clear that I'm to sever all public ties to the man I call husband for the duration of the trip. My marriage to an FBI agent hasn't been widely advertised, but it also hasn't been kept a secret, and gossip in the thieving circuit is worse than in a high school. I have to give every appearance of being the same carefree thief I've always been, up to and including publicly renouncing the man I love.

I balked at that last part, but my dad put his foot down. *It's not being married to Grant that's a problem for these people, baby doll*, he said. *It's that you seem to like it.*

Which sums up my life pretty succinctly. My friends and family don't mind the times when I use Grant to get ahead. It's all those times when I'm *not* using him that trip them up.

In an effort to reinforce my carefree status, our staterooms are located as far away from one another as we can get, and we've sworn a solemn oath to have as little to do with each other as possible. Grant might be adept at going undercover—and he's sporting a shorter, darker haircut to prove it—but I'm a terrible liar. I always have been. Anyone seeing the two of us interact on board will be sure to sense something. The best thing we can do is keep those interactions to a minimum.

"Hey." Grant chucks me under the chin so I'm forced to look up at him. It takes me a moment to adjust to the sleeker, barbered style, but his smile will always be recognizable. It's practically cemented in my soul. "It'll be okay. You won't be alone out there. All your friends will be on board, and your room adjoins your dad's, so he can be your first recourse in any kind of danger."

"It's not *me* I'm worried about," I say with a scoff.

"My room is right next to Tara and Riker's," he replies lightly. "And Riker promised to protect me with his life. Well, he didn't say those exact words, but I slipped it in his contract when he wasn't looking."

I'm not as amused by that as my husband wants me to be. Riker has some pretty decent moves—when he can be bothered to use them—but he's not going to be around all the time to bail Grant out of trouble. For the bulk of the trip, Grant's going to be wandering around alone and unprotected.

"Not that I expect there to be any danger," he adds, as if reading my mind. "All this is standard operating procedure for going undercover—something I've done countless times before. My cover story is in place, and my support team—you—is prepped and ready. All I have to do is ID this guy and make first contact. I'll be in and out and no one will be the wiser."

His words don't make me feel much better. Not when I caught him examining his scar in the bathroom mirror this morning, wincing as he prodded the edges. Around me, he's always careful to put on a strong, brave face, swaggering around like he's king of the castle, but those rare, unguarded moments have a tendency to slip through.

He hates being in a weakened state, I know, but what bothers him even more is letting me see it. He's my protector, my guard dog, the man who would lay his life on the line for my safety—and no amount of bullets in the back will ever change that.

I'd love him for it if it didn't make me so *mad*.

"You'll keep a low profile?" I ask. "You promise?"

"I promise to pull the plug the second I feel like you're in danger," he says, evading my question with neat precision. "Or if, at any moment, I feel unequipped to extract myself. You have to trust me on this, or it will never work. We're a team now, remember?"

I remember. Being on Grant's team is like getting picked first for dodgeball. The glory never fades.

"Grant, before you go—" I begin, just as he says,

"Penelope, I know we haven't always seen eye to eye, but—"

Curious, I gesture for him to go first.

"It's nothing big," he says. "I was just thinking how nice it is, you being a part of my professional life like this. I know I fought it at first, but I'm glad we've been able to make this work. With the exception of Simon, I can't think of anyone else I'd rather have watching my back."

Well, crap. I shouldn't have let him go first. That might be one of the nicest things he's ever said.

"Turns out I really like working with you, Penelope Blue," he adds, adopting his favorite playful rhyme. There's no sound I like better, and he knows it. "I've always believed an agent is only as strong as his field operatives. The way I see it, having you out there makes me damn near invincible."

When I don't respond right away, too busy blinking around the sudden tears in my eyes, he asks, "What was it you wanted to tell me?"

Oh, nothing. Just that instead of having the same faith in him that he seems to hold for me, I'm ninety-nine percent sure he's going to get himself killed out there.

"It's nerves," I lie. "You know me—I always get jittery before a big job."

He looks suspicious at that. I can't say I blame him. I've never shown myself prone to anxiety or self-doubt before. Grant has always felt that my biggest asset is the fact that I refuse to acknowledge danger of any kind—at least when it comes to myself. Confidence, he claims, is half the job.

Since the success of our mission depends on our

keeping things that way, I toss my hair and distract him with a dazzling smile.

"So is this it?" I ask. "We're officially strangers? From here on out, it's nothing but sunshine and poker and a big, empty bed all to myself?"

The dark glint in his eyes indicates he's been doing some hard thinking about his own empty bed, but there's not much we can do about either one. The couple that spies together doesn't always lie together.

"This is it," he agrees. "From now on, Oz is going to serve as our go-between if we need to communicate. Otherwise, you and I have never met."

"You'll keep an extra eye on Riker and make sure he doesn't do anything stupid? I know you'll have your hands full, but I'm worried about him."

"Yes, Penelope. I promise to take care of Riker."

"I know he's not your favorite person, but—"

"I said I'd take care of Riker, and I mean it." He sighs. "I don't like putting him in this position any more than you do, and if there was any other way…"

I nod, forced to accept his reassurance for what it is. Even if there was any other way, it wouldn't matter, because Riker would still be on that boat. There are few things more difficult in this world than stepping back and watching the people you love make mistakes, but short of tying Grant and Riker up and begging them to see reason, there's not much else I can do.

"It's only seven days. Less if we can pin down Johnny Francis sooner than that." He gives my hand a yank, pulling me into his arms and holding me there as if we're going to be separated for a year instead of a week. "You'll remember what I said about that bikini?

It's practically indecent, and I'm going to have enough to worry about as it is. What was Tara thinking, giving you that?"

A smile curves my lips. She was thinking the same thing as me, I expect. My stepmother and I might not always see eye to eye, but she knows as well as I do how damnably attractive Grant is—especially if he's going to be sauntering around in tuxedos and swim trunks under the gleaming Caribbean sky. His pecs alone are enough to bring the average woman to her knees—literally—and I know what goes on at these kinds of things. Cruise ships are practically floating orgies.

"We'll see," I say coyly, unwilling to give him any more than that.

And it's a good thing, too, because even the mention of me in that bikini has him getting carried away with our embrace. He's suddenly all hands and lips, both of them moving over my body as if it's the last time he'll ever be granted such a pleasure. Despite the fact that we both have a plane to catch, I allow myself to be swept up along with him.

Don't judge. When you're married to a man like Grant, a week is an awfully long time.

"Penelope, stop fidgeting this instant." My father doesn't look at me as his voice crackles through the headset. "I *will* turn this plane around if you don't get control over yourself."

There's just enough dad-threat in his voice for me to still my nervous shifting. Although turning the infinitesimally small Cessna around and traveling back the way we came might have sounded good about half an hour ago, we've since passed the halfway mark across the Florida Straits. At this point, it would take longer to get home.

"Thank you," my dad murmurs.

I'd like to repay his calm civility with a casual murmur of my own, but we hit a patch of bumpy air before I can draw a breath. All pretense of me being a calm, rational adult vanishes at once. The plane lurches, the nose dips so far downward I'm tossed against the seat belt, and I can no longer hold back a scream.

"For God's sake, Penelope." With a sigh composed of the same granite as his profile, my dad steadies the plane and tosses me his in-flight bag. "You're acting as though you've never done this before. Have some of my sleeping pills."

I move just enough to shake my head. Pharmaceuticals and undercover espionage go together about as well as pharmaceuticals and jewel theft. In other words, not at all.

"You should take something," he says. "We still have two hours to go."

"I'll be okay," I manage. "I have breathing techniques I use instead. They're how I'm able to hide in small spaces for so long during a job."

"Breathing techniques?" he echoes in disbelief.

Demonstrating the shallow, silent breaths is easier than explaining them, so I give myself over to the cyclical task of filling and emptying my lungs. At first, I'm not sure it's going to be enough—the rapid in-and-out is a poor distraction from the tiny metal walls crushing us at five thousand feet—but my dad's too-casual voice soon brings all thoughts of imminent and fiery death to an end.

"So," he says. "Tell me about your friend Riker."

I pray for another patch of bumpy air. My dad is technically still married to Tara, even though they haven't been together in years. I don't know why they won't just buckle down and get a divorce like normal people, but I suspect there's more at play, emotionally speaking, than just a fair division of assets.

"I'm worried about him." I doubt that's why my dad brought Riker up, but I say it anyway. Mostly because I *am* worried about him. "The poker game itself might be okay, but being around that many hardened gamblers, all those bets and side bets and promises of more... I'm not sure. He's never been good at knowing when to stop."

My dad grunts. "He seems like a man who's capable of handling himself."

That's because my dad has never seen him in the middle of a winning—or losing—streak before. "Maybe, but he's not going to be of much use to Grant if things start getting out of hand. He could end up hurting him more than he helps him."

"Your husband also seems capable of handling himself. Crashing a cruise ship full of notorious criminals was, after all, his idea. I warned him how it would be."

When I don't respond right away, my dad casts me a quick look and sighs. He dislikes being forced to take sides—especially when one of those sides belongs to the FBI—but that's something he's had to do a lot lately.

"I wish you wouldn't look so worried," he says. "These people will pick up on it and use it against you without a second thought. It's not like you to be so anxious."

"I'm not anxious," I protest. "It's the adrenaline of being trapped in this small cabin, that's all."

His long pause carries with it a sense of disbelief, but when he speaks, it's not to chastise me for losing my nerve. "As long as your husband keeps his head down, I'm sure he'll be fine. It's not as if this is his first time going undercover. He knows how to keep a low profile."

I find myself nodding along. That's exactly what Grant said to me before—that he knows what he's doing, that the two of us will be fine as long as we work together as a team.

"You're right. Of course you're right," I say. "I mean, he caught you, and you were once considered the most elusive jewel thief in the world."

My dad's *harrumph* could be taken as an assent or disagreement, but there's no denying the facts. The FBI has him on speed dial these days.

"And you don't, um, mind that Tara invited Riker to go on the cruise with her, do you?" I ask. My dad and I aren't close—not in a way that makes talking about sexual partners anything but awkward—but I have to ask anyway. "It's not weird?"

He keeps his gaze trained on the horizon, the bright blue sky separated from an even brighter ocean by a single hazy line. "Of course not. How your stepmother chooses to entertain herself is of no concern to me."

"She must have known you'd be coming, though."

"One would assume."

"And that a lot of your old friends and associates would be there."

"It promises to be a regular reunion. I can hardly wait."

I don't believe him—his tone is too flat, too even—but since delving into his psychology to work out the kinks of his love life isn't on my bucket list, I let the subject drop. My primary fear is that my dad is plotting some way to kill Riker and dispose of his body while out at sea. Both the opportunity and temptation will be there, especially if Tara packed any bikinis as small as the one she gave me.

Hopefully, murder isn't part of my dad's itinerary. Even though he can be scary sometimes, he's not *evil*—at least, not to my friends. I try not to think too much about what he's capable of doing to people outside his immediate circle, but I know his hands aren't exactly clean. My husband might be the most noble and honorable man in all creation, but my father is not.

"So," I ask lightly, hoping to turn the conversation to calmer, less complex waters. This is going to be an awfully long flight otherwise. "What do you plan to do if you win the Luxor Tiara?"

"*When* I win it, I'm going to do what any self-respecting man under close surveillance by the FBI would do."

"I…" *Huh.* I don't know what that is. "Bury it and leave a treasure map for posterity?"

He sighs, deeply disappointed, as he so often is, by my lack of ingenuity. "In case you didn't check the docket, the ship ports at the Cayman Islands at the end of the seven days. Several of the banks there have been in contact to offer a secure vault to the winner, no questions asked. Isn't that where you keep your money? Or do you prefer working with the Swiss?"

I prefer to squirrel my money away underneath

mattresses and inside bus lockers like most petty bur-
glars, but I don't say so. It hurts my dad's feelings. Since
he abandoned me for most of my adolescence, the gaps
in my criminal education are a constant source of guilt
for him.

In fact, the only reason he helped me secure passage
on the *Shady Lady* and buy a place at the poker table is
because I claimed a wish for family bonding time. Well,
that and the fact that I swore I'd sneak inside one of his
suitcases if he didn't. He knows I'm good for it.

"Switzerland is nice this time of year," I say eva-
sively. "Maybe next time we can take our undercover-
sting-operation-slash-family-vacation there."

Mentioning the sting operation causes him to frown.

"Next time," he drawls and speeds up the plane, "I'm
leaving the entire sorry lot of you at home."

THE *SHADY* LADY

5

MY DAD MAKES GOOD ON HIS WORD AND ABANDONS ME AS soon as we board the *Shady Lady*.

After the traumatic flight from Miami, he suggested I change into something more comfortable before we boarded the ship. I assumed he meant that literally, but he took one look at my cutoff jean shorts and slouchy tank top and renounced all intentions of claiming me as his own. In honor of this vacation-away-from-vacation, I discarded my usual cat burglar chic in favor of a breezier, beachy feel. I thought for sure my flip-flops and high ponytail would fit right in, but apparently I misjudged my audience.

These people are *fancy*. Women navigating the observation deck on high heels, men in loose-fitting linen that billows in the clean-scented Caribbean breeze, jewels and glasses of champagne sparkling in every hand... This is much less *Gilligan's Island* and more *Titanic* than I was expecting.

Though I guess neither one of those stories ended particularly well. I should probably find some new metaphors.

"There you are!" Jordan's voice hails me from across the deck. She, apparently, got the note about Dressing for a Gambling Cruise 101, because she looks flawless in a shimmering gold halter top and tiny white shorts that make her legs seem fifteen feet long. She even has matching gold bangles all up one arm, which glint against the dark, lustrous hue of her skin. "I was afraid you'd miss the boat. We launch in less than ten minutes."

"My dad likes to make an entrance," I say by way of apology. He was also probably hoping to avoid boarding the same time as Tara, but I doubt he'd appreciate me saying so out loud. "Here, give me a hand, will you? These bags weigh a ton."

She does, but with a perplexed frown. "Why are you carrying them yourself? Someone should have taken them to your room for you. There are some pretty strict rules—apparently, the guy running this boat designed every detail according to his exact specifications."

"I tried to ask someone, but I ended up carrying someone else's stuff in addition to my own." I gesture at a black leather bag slung over my shoulder. "The lady must've thought I work here—she gave me a fifty-dollar tip and everything. Speaking of, I need to find room 506."

She laughs, the throaty trill drawing the attention of several of the classier-looking men in our vicinity. "It's your blue top. The crew is wearing the same color."

A quick glance at my surroundings proves her to be correct. Several people in a similar shade are moving neatly through the crowd, carrying bags and delivering drinks. It's nice to note for future reference, but I wish I didn't look *quite* so convincingly menial. If you count the inheritance I'll get from my father someday, I'm probably one of the richest people on this boat—and that's saying a lot. I'm pretty sure that lady over by the gangway is wearing a dress made of real gold chainmail.

Jordan hefts the bag. "Do you want me to rifle through and see if there's anything worth taking?"

"I already did. It's mostly suntan lotion and condoms." I sigh, thinking of what a great combination that is. Relaxation and sex—two things I won't be having much of in the near future. "I guess I should be glad *someone* is going to enjoy this vacation."

"Uh-oh. Sounds like you're missing your dear old hubby."

Sadly, I am—and it hasn't even been twenty-four hours yet.

But "That stuffy bore?" is the response I give, loud enough for anyone eavesdropping to overhear. "No way. After spending two years in that man's company, the only thing I want to do is enjoy this vacation. *Alone*."

This time, it's the less-classy-looking men in our vicinity who turn in interest.

"Oh, yeah. I forgot how excited you are to be rid of him for a spell," Jordan says quickly, an apology in her lifted brows. She knows the rules—from here on out, we have to play this thing night and day. There's a strict no-weapons-and-no-surveillance-equipment policy aboard the boat, but you never can tell what a crowd like this one will do. Some of the tech these guys have access to is next-millennium scary.

"The less I think about that man, the better," I say with complete honesty. "Right now, I mostly want to find my room and take a nap."

"You do look awfully tired," Jordan agrees. She leans in to poke at the bags under my eyes. "When was the last time you got a full night's sleep?"

It's been so long, I can't remember. If I had to guess, though, I'd put the date right before Grant's accident.

Sighing, I do my best to shake off my foreboding sense of doom and gloom. The sun is shining, there's a twenty-million-dollar diamond somewhere on this boat, and I don't have to get on another tiny airplane for seven more days. Things could be worse.

"I'm fine," I say and swat her hands away from my face. "Let's just go find my room."

"Aye, aye," she replies with a laugh. She bustles me off the main deck, which is comprised primarily of the swimming pool and an outdoor bar, to find someone to assist us. She does, too, much quicker than I expect. My initial surprise at her efficiency fades away when I notice the man in the royal blue polo, khaki shorts, and sailor-style hat bears a not-so-remarkable resemblance to Oz.

Oz is, as always, a bland and comfortable vision—and I don't mean that as an insult. He has one of those faces everyone has seen before but no one bothers to remember. It's one of my favorite sights in the whole world. He gives me a tight salute and clip of his heels, causing me to almost blow my cover by laughing out loud. I don't know *how* he got himself hired on to the *Shady Lady*'s crew—if he even is an official part of it— but I know better than to question his methods. Nothing could make it easier for him to deliver messages and eavesdrop in places we can't go.

"This one's headed for 506," I say and hand him the bag along with the fifty-dollar bill. "But I can take my own, thanks. I'm sure you have enough to keep you busy as it is."

He salutes again, and this time, I give in to my urge to laugh, shaking my head as I watch him depart. I'm almost certain that, like me, he'll take a look inside that bag as soon as he rounds the corner. He's probably searching all the luggage he carries and finding a heck of a lot more than prophylactics in the bargain.

"Damn. For a laugh like that, I'd have volunteered to deliver it myself." A deep voice hails us from behind, and I turn, expecting to see one of Jordan's admirers. But the owner of the voice falls into the "less classy" category, his expression difficult to read behind his aviator sunglasses.

Like most of the men I've noticed on the cruise so far, this one oozes power without making a mess of it. I don't know what the trick is, but it has something to do with the way they carry themselves. I mean, this guy looks more like a gym rat than an elite poker player, what with his deep bronze skin, closely shaved head, and too-tight microfiber shirt, but there's no doubt in my mind he's here to play. Not spectate, not hang on the outer edges. *Play.* Confidence is part of it, the way he's looking at the pair of us as if sure of his welcome, but there's also a kind of gritty suavity that can't be denied.

Riker has it, too. He's got the hard edge of a man who's not afraid to fight with his fists—and win—but he's also a pretty boy who knows all he has to do is smile and the ladies will come running.

This man tries a smile on me now. "Since I can't be your errand boy, can I at least help you with those, ah, are they suitcases?"

I look at my suitcases with a frown. They're not *that* bad. Okay, so the duffel bag I threw my wadded-up underwear into has seen better days, but I love my weathered and slightly frayed hard-shell case. It has a secret X-ray-proof compartment built into the frame for quick and easy jewel smuggling. They don't make them like this anymore.

"No, thanks," I say in as repressive a tone as I can muster. "I've got arms."

"I noticed. And legs and a head and everything. The full package."

I strongly suspect him of mocking me. "I'm sorry, is there something I can do for you?"

"Yeah. You can hand me a tissue. I'm going to cry."

I look to Jordan to see if she has any idea what this guy is talking about, but she just casts me a helpless shrug.

"Handkerchief?" he suggests when his plea fails. "Napkin? Ah, no. I forgot. How about a pair of gloves? You never used to leave home without them. Didn't want to leave any messy fingerprints behind."

My eyes flare as I once again survey the man. All the parts are still there and still the same, but once I mentally add a crop of sleek black hair and drop fifty pounds of muscle, realization hits. "Oh, my God. Hijack? Is that you?"

"Penelope Blue." His arms open, and before I know

what's happening, I'm falling into them. "Guess I won't be needing that tissue. You *do* recognize me."

His hug is a familiar one, though it feels weird to have any arms except Grant's wrapped so possessively around my torso. It's a feeling that's magnified when Hijack pushes me back enough to plant a firm kiss on my mouth. Romantically speaking, it's not much of a kiss—more of a friendly smack, really—but I pull back, startled at the strange taste and texture of another man's lips on mine.

"I can't believe it's actually you," I say, making a big show of reconciliation to cover for the awkwardness of the embrace. Also to cover for Jordan's inquisitively raised brow, which doesn't fail to notice the kiss or my reaction to it.

"I thought you fell off the face of the earth," I add. "It's been, what, six years?"

"Six years, eight months, and I'd say around two and a half weeks, but who's counting?" He shakes his head before I can answer. "You haven't changed at all. I saw the hot strawberry blond in cutoff jeans and couldn't believe my luck. I thought I'd gone back in time."

My heart gives a dainty flutter at the compliment, even as my brain recognizes it for the ham-handed flattery that it is. That's what happens when your nearest and dearest gang up and tell you how haggard you're looking lately—every sweet word is like manna.

"Oh, please. You're the one who looks amazing. I didn't recognize you with all that"—I make a vague motion over his body, sleekly outfitted from head to toe and probably aerodynamic to boot—"athleticism."

He glances down at his biceps and grins. "Super fruit and protein powder. Who's your friend, by the way?"

"Oh! I'm sorry. This is Jordan. She's an amazing chemist and one of my favorite people on the planet. Jordan, this is Hijack—who, if you can't tell from the name, is something of a whiz when it comes to vehicle acquisition. Riker and I knew him eons ago."

"You didn't tell her the best part." Hijack smiles again, and even with the sunglasses covering the upper half of his face, it's hard to imagine how I could have mistaken him for anyone else. Crooked eyeteeth and wide lips give him a charming, if slightly lopsided, grin. "Penelope was the love of my life. At least, she was until she broke my heart one rainy Brooklyn afternoon."

He places a hand over his pecs as if to prove it.

"Please," I scoff. "It was Queens, and it was ninety degrees outside. You're thinking of some other girl."

"Spoken like a true heartbreaker. It took me years to get over her, and now here she is, as gorgeous and cruel as ever." He turns to Jordan. "I hope you don't plan to treat me the same way. I couldn't handle being rejected like that again."

I feel myself coloring up, unsure how I'm supposed to respond. While it's true that Hijack and I were once a thing, it was a very brief thing, neither one of us all that serious or committed. He was my post-Riker boyfriend in my pre-Grant life. Although there's no denying he's got his good qualities, I remember him mostly as a scrawny hustler with a wandering eye and the ability to hot-wire a car in under twenty seconds. If it wasn't for the latter, I doubt I'd have put up with the former.

"What have you been doing with yourself all these years?" I ask. "When we parted ways, you were heading to Germany to join up with a bank crew."

"I did. You should've come with me. Germany is amazing—so much old money, so many old buildings. You can carve through some of those vault walls with a spoon. I won't tell you my net worth now. It'll make you jealous."

"You know I wanted to stay stateside," I reply, not nearly as jealous as he'd like me to be. Money, though nice, has never been my root evil. Depending on who you ask, that would be willful self-sufficiency and/or a tendency to flippancy. "Besides, the buildings in the U.S. aren't that hard to get into the normal way."

"Only if you're the great Penelope Blue. Your talent is the stuff of legends."

I can't help it—my shoulders come up. I've always wanted to be a legend.

"Speaking of, I heard you got married." He casts an obvious look at my left hand, his smile widening when he sees no sign of a ring. "Ha! I knew it couldn't be true. Especially since they said you married a fed."

"Oh, um." My shoulders move back down again. "Actually…"

"You didn't."

"It's not as bad as it sounds, I swear."

"A fed? Come on, Pen. That's consorting with public enemy number one."

"I know, but he's a lot handier to have around than you'd think." It's not a lie. Federal clemency is a real boon in my line of work. "And you wouldn't believe the kind of inside access he gets me." Also true. Just look where I'm standing right now.

"Shit. You're serious, aren't you?" He doesn't, as I'd feared, appear to be alarmed by that revelation. If anything, he looks intrigued. "I refused to believe it until I heard it from your own lips. Is he here?"

"Are you kidding?" I squeak. "A federal agent on this boat?"

"This is our annual girls' trip," Jordan says. "I'm just here for the sunshine and booze, but Pen wants to try her hand at the Luxor."

Hijack's interest picks up even more. "Is that a fact? I never took you for much of a gambler."

"I'm not, but I'd kick myself for the rest of my life if I didn't at least *try* to win it," I admit. "A girl doesn't get a stab at the Luxor Tiara every day. Besides, I'm no worse than half the people I know are playing. Have you seen it?"

"No one has. Word is they're going to reveal it tomorrow at the opening ceremonies." Hijack hesitates, choosing his next words carefully. "When you say you're no worse than half the people playing, does that mean Riker is here, too?"

Poor Riker. His terrible reputation precedes him. "Yeah. I haven't run into him yet, but he should be around here somewhere. Man, he's going to be happy to see you again."

"No, he won't. I know all his tells."

I laugh. I know all his tells, too. Riker is unable to hide his glower when he's dealt a bad hand—which is just about always. Riker's foul moods are probably why I was so drawn to Hijack back when we first started dating. Every other word out of his mouth is a lie, and he'd sell his own soul for a few hundred dollars, but he's so charming, it's hard to fault him for it.

As if he's also remembering the good old days, Hijack reaches over to tweak my nose. It's an affectionate yet condescending gesture. I'm glad my husband isn't here to see it.

"Do you have dinner plans yet?" he asks. "If you do, cancel them. I want to walk into the restaurant with the two most beautiful women on this ship."

I hesitate, unsure whether I should commit myself before I receive any instructions from Grant, but Jordan answers for the both of us. "We'd love to."

"Perfect. I'll swing by your room to collect you around seven." He turns to me and stares for a drawn-out moment, as if memorizing my features. "I can't tell you how happy I am to see you again, Pen. Leaving you behind was my biggest regret. We were good together, you and I."

Until he appeared on the deck of the *Shady Lady*, I hadn't given Hijack more than six minutes' worth of reflection over the span of six years, but I find myself nodding all the same. We *had* been good together, if only because of how simple it was—casually dating, planning small jobs, enjoying opportunities the moment they knocked. Those were my carefree days, when my biggest worry was whether or not I could remember where I stashed my latest take and then deciding it didn't matter, since I could always steal more.

"Life sure was easy back then, wasn't it?" I agree. "We had some fun times."

He holds his hand up in a mock toast as he bids us goodbye. "Here's to hoping we have a few more."

Jordan waits until the back of Hijack's shorn head disappears around a corner before turning to me with one carefully raised brow. "Well, that certainly was interesting."

That's Jordan for you—always discreet.

"If by interesting you mean a big problem, then, yes, it was." I sigh. I'm going to have a hard enough time lying to strangers. Lying to my ex-boyfriend? That's a whole different level of complicated. "Why did you agree to dinner?"

"Because we have to eat. Besides, if you're going to know every single person on this boat, we'll find you-know-who in no time. All you have to do is cross off the names of everyone you're related to, have helped commit a crime, and/or slept with. That's half of them right there."

"I can't help it if I'm criminal royalty," I tease, but a nagging worry settles in the pit of my stomach. The idea was to keep our heads down and our profiles low. Hijack isn't exactly a low-profile sort of guy.

He's also not a very helpful one. After all his smooth words, he never actually lifted a suitcase and made good on his offer. Jordan and I are left alone to hoist my bags and head in the direction of the elevators, pushing past people who don't take kindly to being jostled, well-versed as they are in the habits of pickpockets.

On the way, I notice and am noticed by three more familiar faces—two bruisers who have worked with my father before and a woman I recognize as Riker's favorite fence—and that nagging worry hardens into a rock.

I might not be criminal royalty, but I *am* a lot more recognizable than I realized. These are people I know, people who know me back, people who would never forgive me if they find out my federal agent husband is lying in wait somewhere on this ship. We're playing a dangerous game here, and I don't mean poker.

Oh, how times have changed since my carefree Hijack days.

THE SURVEY

6

BEING DESCENDED FROM ONE OF THE WORLD'S MOST successful jewel thieves sure does come in handy sometimes.

No sooner does Jordan leave me at the door of my stateroom than I find myself facing what has to be the most luxurious six hundred square feet I've ever seen. Enough of my life has been spent residing in hotel rooms that I'm fully aware of how many creature comforts can be packed into a small space, but the *Shady Lady* architects outdid themselves.

As soon I set foot inside, I notice the foyer divides into two neat halves. One side is taken up with a living room done up in white and beige—admittedly not my favorite shades, but understandable when set against the floor-to-ceiling glass doors at the back, where the ocean provides a dazzling burst of color. The second half of the stateroom is a bedroom, complete with a king-size bed that stretches forever and—oh, how magnificent—a bathroom with a marble whirlpool tub. I'm not normally one for long soaks, but there's something about that cool slab of white stone that calls to me. My proposed nap, which sounded so heavenly before, pales in comparison to the idea of submerging myself in water and refusing to come out until I'm shiny and new again.

"Thank you, dear Dad, for being so formidable and rich," I say as I head toward that bathtub. I'm pretty sure I have the person on the other side of the adjoining door leading out of the living room to thank for the extravagance of my current surroundings. Little old Penelope Blue might warrant a window—and *maybe* she could manage to finagle an extra bar of soap in the shower—but this full royal treatment isn't something people extend my direction very often. Nor am I averse to taking advantage of it when I can.

The tub is a quarter of the way filled and I'm out of my clothes when I hear a knock at the door.

"Go away!" I call. The running water must muffle my voice, because the knock sounds again. "I mean it. I'm busy!"

"It's room service," comes the equally muffled reply. They're the sole three words in the English language— with the possible exception of *Grant needs you*—that could get me to abandon those enticing wisps of steam. With a halfhearted grumble, I shove my arms into the provided robe and unlock the door.

But on the other side there are only lies. And Tara.

"How dare you?" I accuse. "You don't have any food."

"It got you to open the door, didn't it?" she asks as she pushes past me. Like Jordan, she's dressed to impress, her short, tennis-style dress ideal for giving the impression of wealth and athleticism. Or so I assume. I mostly see the back of it as she takes a survey of my new digs.

"Well done, Pen," she says with a whistle. "This room is incredible."

"Gee, thanks. Why don't you make yourself at home?"

My stepmother casually ignores me, as she almost always does, opening closet doors and helping herself to a sparkling water from the minibar. "Our room is half the size and doesn't have nearly the same view—your dad must have pulled some heavy-duty strings to get you in here. Is that what you're planning on wearing?"

I cinch my robe tighter. It's soft and white, and I fully intend to smuggle it out of here as soon as the cruise is over. "Yes. I was just about to take a bath."

"No, you're not. Put something else on. Something pretty. You look like a crazy cat lady who spent the night with her head under a sink."

Honestly, this is just getting *cruel* now. "I don't look that bad! I swear, between you, Jordan, and my dad, I'm developing a complex."

Instead of taking back the insult, she purses her brightly painted red lips and tries not to look at the door leading to the adjoining stateroom.

"When a man like your father is moved to comment on your state of dress, it's time to take action." She hesitates, and I can tell from the way not a single muscle in her face twitches that it's a calculated pause. "Is he in there right now?"

"My dad? I don't know." Nor am I sure I care to be having this conversation with her. "I doubt he and I are going to be doing much in the way of bonding on this vacation. He thinks I cramp his style."

"You cramp everyone's style."

Surviving the world's youngest—and most beautiful—stepmother requires a thick skin, and I like to think I've developed a good one. Still, her words needle me more than usual. Once upon a time, before I got all straight and narrow and worried about Grant, I was considered the fun one of the group. I swear.

"Why do you care what my dad's doing, anyway?" I ask. "You're supposed to be vacationing with Riker."

Her pursed lips pull down in a frown, the expression so brief that had I blinked, I would have missed it. But I didn't blink, and I didn't miss it, and I don't like it. There's something more going on here than a pair of estranged spouses taking separate vacations on the same thirty-thousand-ton pleasure cruise. Something a lot more. Take it from a woman who knows what it's like to be in a constant battle of one-upmanship with her husband.

"Tara..." I begin, but her rare unguarded moment is over. She opens my hard-shell case in the middle of the living room and pulls out one of the outfits she let me borrow for the trip. It's an orange romper that looks halfway comfortable, which is rare for one of Tara's loaners. Most of them are made of Lycra.

"Put this on."

I look longingly back at my tub. It's no longer steaming. "But I was hoping to unwind before dinner."

"Too bad. You and I have work to do."

"*Real* work, or you-want-to-scope-out-the-competition-and-need-me-to-go-with-you work?"

"Both." She tosses the romper at me. "There was a message in my towel swan. His Majesty would like us to make a survey of the boat's layout and commit it to memory."

She loses me at *towel swan*.

"On the bed," she says. "Or didn't you notice?"

I shake my head. "I was too blinded by the luxury of my surroundings."

With a muttered "brat," Tara heads toward the bedroom, returning with a white bundle in her arms. From the looks of it, that's no swan—I think it might be a frog—but the idea is the same. The terrycloth has been twisted to resemble a creature that, when unfolded, regurgitates a slip of paper covered in my husband's signature scrawl.

Go over the boat with Riker and memorize every last inch, especially hiding places and emergency exits. And lifeboats. Always lifeboats.

Aw, how sweet. Grant's been dwelling on the *Titanic* metaphors too.

"It's pretty genius if you think about it," Tara says as she leans in and reads the note, oblivious to a little thing called privacy. "No one will think to look for messages in the towel animals. I had no idea Oz was so talented."

"Me either, but how am I supposed to respond? By folding my bras into monkeys?"

"That's what I intend to do," she says breezily—and unhelpfully, I might add. What if I have an emergency? What if I have information that will save Grant's life? An army of towel animals won't save him then.

"You'll want to destroy that note so it doesn't fall into the wrong hands," she adds and stands there watching me until I make an effort to do so. My instinct—composed, admittedly, of spy movies and cartoons—tells me to shove it in my mouth and swallow, but I end up ripping it into pieces and flushing them down the toilet instead.

Since bath time looks to be out of the question, I drain the tub and follow Tara's orders to get dressed. The sleeveless top and loose shorts combo is as comfortable as it looks, and there's something to be said about the simple elegance of it. Especially when Tara commands me to bow my head and clasps a chunky gold necklace around my neck before loosely ruffling my hair around my shoulders. The woman knows fashion, there's no doubt about that, but she also knows me. In a matter of seconds, I go from street rat to swanky cat burglar—no complicated undergarments required.

"There. Now you're fit to be seen in public with me."

"How generous of you," I say dryly. "How come you're the one coming with me, anyway? The note says I should go with Riker."

"No real reason. Riker had other things to do." She moves toward the door, ready to embark on our mission, but I don't follow right away. It's an action she interprets with alarming accuracy. "Don't worry. I didn't throw him to the loan sharks just yet. He wanted to go over the passenger list to see who else might be playing in the tournament, so I flirted with the captain and stole a copy. I figured it might also help in the search for Johnny Francis."

"Oh." I blink at her. "That was good thinking."

A toss of her hair is the only acknowledgment she

gives of my compliment. Tara would kill anyone who said so out loud, but underneath her sex kitten exterior lies a heart that might not be made of gold but is certainly plated in it. Even though it's the last thing she wants, I can't help but let her know how much I appreciate it—her willingness to take care of Riker, to support Grant's mission, to put herself out there for no reason other than it being the right thing to do. There aren't a lot of kind-of-but-not-really-stepmothers out there who would do the same. I place my hand on her arm and give it a gentle squeeze.

"You're good for him," I say. "And for me. Thank you for doing all this."

"Don't be so sappy, Pen. I didn't come down here to chat about your feelings." She shudders over the word *feelings*, her nose wrinkling in disgust. "The sooner I fulfill my obligations and escort you around, the sooner I can focus on getting that tiara."

"If all you want is to win the tiara, why are you helping me?" I ask. I hate to look a gift horse in the mouth—or in this case, a gift jewel thief in the eyes—but there's no reason why I can't make a survey of the ship on my own. "You don't have to, you know. This was supposed to be your vacation. No one would think anything of it if you just ignored me and had your own fun."

Instead of answering, she turns the question back on me. "You don't have to be here, either," she says. "Why are you?"

"Because he asked me to." The answer is simple and springs immediately to my lips. There are few things in this world I wouldn't do for my husband. "Besides, it's not like I had much of a choice. He's still not fully recovered, but he'll be damned if he admits as much. You know how pigheaded he can be about these sorts of things."

"Yes, I do, and it's your own stupid fault. If you'd asked me before you got married, I would have told you that strong, willful men are rarely worth the effort."

She's unable to keep her gaze from the door leading to my father's room as she says it. I've never really thought of my dad as the strong, willful sort before, but I know better than to doubt Tara's judgment. Gauging diamond clarity and men's deepest desires—her skill sets are very specific.

"We can go see if he's in there," I offer doubtfully.

For a moment, I think she's going to take me up on it, but she gives a curt shake of her head. "Don't be silly. How your father chooses to entertain himself is of no concern to me."

The similarity of her words to my dad's strikes me as uncanny, but she prevents me from saying so with a sharp, "And I'd like to state for the record, if you so much as spill a drop on that silk, you're buying me a new romper."

Overall, the *Shady Lady* isn't a huge vessel, at least not when compared to those cruise ships that take tens of thousands of people on their dream vacations through busy tourist ports. Although the six hundred feet of length sets a more intimate backdrop for the guests, I'm happy to find that it still offers plenty of places to hide—not to mention a full squadron of lifeboats. I'm not sure what the *Shady Lady* is commissioned to do when she's not being used as a floating casino, but for the time being, she's more than doing her duty.

There are a total of ten floors, not including the sundeck at the very top. Most of them contain nothing more than row upon row of boring staterooms and utility closets, but a few are dedicated to pleasures of the flesh. Three separate dining rooms, a spa and hair salon, an enormous swimming pool surrounded by deck chairs, and even an outdoor gym with a running track make up the entertainment sector of the boat. There's also a cabaret lounge taking up half of the fifth floor, but it's closed off, so we aren't able to sneak a peek inside.

"Do you think this is where they're keeping the tiara?" I ask as Tara and I try a few of the doors to see if one has accidentally been left open. They haven't, and I wouldn't mind trying my hand at picking a lock or two, but there are several people milling around and doing some exploring of their own. "Or is there a safe or something where it's being held?"

"There's one good way to find out." Tara casts a quick look around before discreetly shoving a hairpin in the lock.

"What are you doing?" I hiss. "Do you want to get us thrown off the boat before the game even starts?"

She ignores me. "Damn. These are really strong. Do you have a credit card on you?"

"Of course not." I nudge her with my hip. "Would you please stop doing that? People are staring."

She does stop, but with a sigh condemning my lack of nerve. "Don't get mad at me for being indiscreet. I'm not the one they're staring at. You are. Haven't you noticed?"

I hadn't, so I take a moment to glance around. Sure enough, several small groups of people slow down as they walk by, their voices dropping the closer they get.

"I bet they're just admiring my outfit." I cast a glance over my clothes to make sure everything is in order. "I *do* look pretty amazing, but this romper would be nicer if it had pockets. I always wonder why more women's clothing doesn't come with pockets. I'd be able to carry lots of credit cards for you then."

"Most of us carry a purse for that exact reason, Pen. Same great features, much smoother silhouette." Her sigh this time is one of annoyance as she gives up on the lock picking. "I've never seen locks like these before — there's no way I'm getting in today. I guess we'll have to wait and see the cabaret lounge alongside everyone else. Did we miss anything on our tour?"

I shake my head, glad to call this particular job finished. Two hours spent crawling over a ship and memorizing its dark corners isn't my idea of a good time. We even explored the bottom levels, which are mostly made up of staff accommodations and a fuel-scented engine room I'd like to never visit again. Talk about confined places.

"No, I think we're good." I pause as a woman down the hallway lifts a finger and points at me, turning away just as quickly when she notices me watching.

Okay, this is getting weird. I think I preferred it when I was in cutoff shorts and everyone ignored me.

"You're right," I say in a low voice. "They *are* staring at me. Why?"

She lifts one shoulder in an elegant shrug. "I don't know. We've only been here a few hours. Did you make an enemy of someone already?"

"Not even I can work that quickly," I say, though I can't help feeling dread fill my stomach. *They know.* Word about Grant must have spread. They're searching for the traitor in their midst, and all the towel swans in the world won't be able to save him.

My rising sense of panic is cut short by a loud squeal from behind us. I turn, expecting to find a masked coalition coming to seize me, but all I find is a young woman staring at us with wide eyes and an expression of pure joy.

"What's happening?" I ask Tara, grabbing her arm. "What did I do?"

"Omigod—it's you, isn't it? It's really you?" The woman runs to greet me, stopping herself about two inches short of hitting me with a full-body slam. Not that her full body would do much damage. She looks to be in her late teens, her build rounder than mine but just as horizontally challenged. Rich, tawny skin and dark hair in a single braid down her back give her an even more youthful appearance, especially when matched by the long-lashed eyes gazing up adoringly into my own. "You're as pretty as I always imagined, but I had no idea you were so short. How tall are you? Five two? Five three?"

Her rapid-fire delivery and high-pitched, breathy voice throw me off-balance, but I do my best not to let it show.

"Uh, somewhere closer to the first one," I say. "But I always lie on forms and say I'm five three."

She laughs, showing a neat line of pearly teeth on which I swear I can see the ghost of a recent set of braces. She's *that* young.

"Do you really? Me too. Five one and three-quarters is what I write down, but it's closer to just one-quarter. Daddy says I might still grow, but I'm almost nineteen, so I don't think I will. It's hard, isn't it, being so small? No one in a place like this takes small girls seriously—especially when they have a voice like mine. Did you ever hear anyone sound so much like a mouse?"

I haven't—not in terms of tone and definitely not in terms of volubility—but I can't think of a kind way to phrase that, so I just say, "I think overly tall, deep-voiced girls have a hard time of it, too. Speaking of, can I introduce you to—"

"Oh, I know who she is," the young woman says, turning to my stepmother with the same adoring eyes. "You're Tara Lewis, right? I wouldn't miss you anywhere. Daddy says you have the body of a sinner, the face of a saint, and the heart of the damned. He means that as a compliment, even though I know it doesn't sound like it. We're big fans."

I have to laugh at Tara's expression. No one has ever summarized her quite so succinctly—or accurately—before.

"I can see he was right, too. You're so beautiful. I think you might be the most beautiful woman I've ever met."

Tara blinks a few bewildered times, but she eventually accepts the compliments as her due. Her streak of vanity runs deep.

"Well, I have no idea who she is, but I like her," Tara says. "Do you have a name, honey?"

"Oh, I'm so stupid! It's Lola. Lola Sanchez." The girl sticks her hand out, so close to Tara's chest she has to take a step back before she can shake it.

The name sounds familiar, but I need Tara to put the

pieces together for me. "Lola Sanchez, huh?" she says. "I'm guessing that would make Daddy none other than Peter Sanchez."

Ah, yes. Peter Sanchez, the smuggler currently in possession of the Luxor Tiara—the man making a financial killing on this cruise. Nowhere on the FBI dossier I read did it say he has a teenage daughter, but I accept Tara's all-knowing word for it. It still doesn't explain why the girl is fawning over us, though.

"It's lovely to meet you, Lola," I say politely. "Will you be playing in the poker game?"

She takes a wide step back, as if caught in the middle of a criminal act. "Me? Oh, no. I could never," she says. "But you're going to be in the game, right? Can I watch you play? Daddy says that under no circumstances am I to bother you with my questions and chatter, but you don't mind, do you? You're so nice in person. I never expected you to be nice on top of everything else."

On top of everything else? I look to Tara for help only to find a smile of real amusement on her lips.

"Well, well," she says, laughing. "If I'm not mistaken, I believe we've discovered your very first fangirl, Pen."

Lola giggles but doesn't seem to take offense. "It's true. I've been hearing about you ever since I was a baby. My whole life, it's been, 'Penelope Blue was helping her father break into jewelry stores when she was five years old,' and, 'Penelope Blue isn't afraid of the dark,' and, 'Penelope Blue didn't cry the first time she smashed her finger in a safe door.' You have no idea how hard I've tried to be like you."

"Er, that last one's not strictly true," I interject,

compelled to tarnish the shiny version of my reputation she's holding out. "I *did* cry the first time I smashed my finger in a safe door. For about three hours, if I remember correctly. To this day, it's still crooked."

To prove it, I lift my right hand, showing her the slightly hitched bend to my forefinger. I'd been about six years old when it happened, playing with—what else?—the safe that my father was opening layer by layer. It was a new model, and he needed to learn the mechanics of it if he ever hoped to crack one in the wild.

He did eventually learn the mechanics, and I'm pretty sure he's broken into about seven of those particular models since, but I wouldn't recommend using the door as a child's swing. No matter how bored you are and how much you wish your dad would just take you outside to play.

At the sight of my mangled extremity, Lola's eyes widen, and her whole demeanor lights from within.

"Mine too!" She holds up her left hand to show me a pinky with its own slight bend at the tip. "And he wouldn't even take me to the hospital to get it X-rayed, because he didn't want any nosy questions from the doctors. We went to the vet instead."

My heart goes out to the poor girl. Having a famous criminal for a parent isn't easy. I, too, have been stitched up alongside a kennel of dogs more times than I care to count.

"Oh, boy. When I heard you were coming on the cruise, I could barely believe it. You *will* let me watch you play, won't you?" She doesn't wait for me to answer, her sweet face crumpling. "You can say no if you want, and you can also tell me to leave if I'm bothering you. It's okay. People do all the time."

Since I can't get a word in edgewise, I have to make do with a nod of my head. I wouldn't have the heart to deny her even if I wanted to.

Her expression changes as if on rewind. "I knew it— you *are* the nicest! I feel so famous standing next to you. Everyone is staring. Did you notice? I bet you're used to it by now. I hate it when everyone is looking at me, but you just carry on like normal, don't you? Walking around as though you don't have a care in the world."

I have plenty of cares, as my current situation attests, but I'm happy to find that not *everyone* thinks I'm one small step from playing a horror movie villain. I'm even happier to find that word of my husband's undercover operation isn't the cause of my sudden notoriety.

"Why *are* they staring?" I ask. "Do you know?"

"Someone must have leaked that a woman of your vast fame and superior kindness was on board," Tara says wryly.

"Very funny."

"Oh, I'm so sorry! Did you want to be left alone? I said you could tell me to go away if I'm a bother." Lola clasps her hands in front of her and moves her head in a slight bow, as if prepared to prostrate herself at my feet.

"No, no, it's fine. I don't mind." I'm just confused. "But *do* you know what's going on? I can't imagine why people like these would care whether I'm here. I'm just a low-level jewel thief."

Lola laughs as if I've made the best joke she's ever heard. "The world's *greatest* jewel thief, you mean. I thought I knew about all your takes, but I've heard so many new ones since you got here. Paintings by the Masters, a stamp collection worth ten million dollars, an entire truck full of gold… Are you really married to an FBI agent who doesn't know you're a thief? And do you use him to get inside information on big jobs? Oh, boy. I can't even imagine what that must be like. You're so brave. It must be crazy to wake up every day next to a man who could put you in prison for the rest of your life and then kiss him goodbye like none of it matters."

She's not wrong about that. *Crazy* is one word for it.

"I hate to disappoint you, but most of those stories have been exaggerated," I say. As much as I appreciate the picture she's painting of me, I think I would have remembered stealing an entire truck full of gold. And stamps have never been my thing. Give me a clear, cold diamond any day of the week. "I'm not nearly that prolific or that talented. You know how these things happen. One person starts a rumor, it gets blown out of proportion…"

Lola isn't buying any of it. Her lips lift in a knowing smile. "Is it out of proportion for you and Tara Lewis to be trying to break into the cabaret lounge to get an early peek at the Luxor Tiara?"

"We weren't…" I begin lamely, but of course it's a lie. That's exactly what we were doing.

"It's not in there," Lola continues with the air of one sharing a great secret. "It's being guarded in my dad's stateroom until the opening ceremonies tomorrow. Daddy's not taking any chances. Are you going to try to steal it?"

"Of course I'm not—"

She giggles and presses a finger to her lips. "It's okay. I won't tell. I'd rather you have it than the others."

"But I'm really not—"

Tara stops me from asserting my innocence with a nudge of her hip—and by nudge, I mean she practically bodychecks me. Her hips are not casual observers.

"What others?" Tara asks.

"Oh, you know. Daddy's got a whole bunch of people he's watching to make sure nothing happens to the tiara. Penelope is, of course, one of his top threats." She starts ticking off names. "Then there's Two-Finger Tommy, Eden St. James, some guy I've never heard of named Hijack…"

"Hijack?" I'm unable to hold back my surprise. "He's going to try and steal the tiara?"

"Do you know him? That's a silly question—of course you do. You probably know everyone on this boat." She doesn't wait for me to confirm or deny it. "Anyway, there are lots of people on the list, and they're even starting to make bets on the thief most likely to walk away with it. You and Johnny Francis are tied for first place—you both have three-to-one odds right now."

Now it's my turn to do the staring. "I'm sorry, did you just say that *Johnny Francis* and I are tied for first place?"

She nods happily, oblivious to the way I've suddenly stopped moving.

"And is, um, Mr. Francis on the ship already?" I ask. "I don't suppose you could introduce him to me, could you?"

Her laughter dashes any hopes I had of making this the quickest and easiest case Grant's ever solved. "I wish. No one knows who Johnny Francis is, but Daddy says it's almost guaranteed he'll try to take the tiara. He's been after it for years and years, and he once even tried to break into our Munich house to steal it. This is so exciting, isn't it? I haven't had this much fun in ages. Daddy says that until I learn to keep my mouth shut and my eyes open, I'll never amount to anything, so I almost never get to come along on his business trips. But I'm so happy I did, even if nothing else happens for the whole week. After all, I got to meet *you*, didn't I?"

"Do I figure on the list of potential threats?" Tara asks, sounding slightly vexed.

If I didn't know better, I might say she sounds jealous of my new admirer. Which is ridiculous, of course. It's flattering to be the recipient of so much attention—and it totally explains the staring, if I'm such a high-ranking figure among this lot of thieves—but I'm here for one reason and one reason only: to protect Grant.

Save the husband, do the job. Those are things I've committed myself to now. In no way, shape, or form am I here to return to my life of crime. In no way, shape, or form am I going to relive the glory days of my youth.

I mean, I totally *could* steal the tiara if I wanted to, but...

"Of course you're on the list," Lola confirms happily. "Seventh place, to be exact. You weren't as highly ranked a few hours ago, but that was before we heard you part-nered up with Riker Smith. He's another one of the top favorites. Now, if all three of you were to band together, there's no saying what that might do to the odds. The relative probabilities would go through the roof. I'd have to recalculate the stake units to even get started."

I correct her before she whips out a calculator. "I hate

to disappoint you, Lola, but I'm not going to try and steal the tiara. Neither are Riker or Tara. We're here on vacation and to play poker, nothing more."

Tara coughs gently.

I turn to her, my heart sinking. "Tara, *no*."

"Sorry, Pen. I thought you'd have figured it out by now."

Lola giggles loudly, covering her mouth with her hand. "Uh-oh. Did I let the cat burglar out of the bag?"

I groan as realization sinks in, weighted, as it always is, with the exasperating truth of the people I call my own. *Of course* Tara and Riker are going to try to steal the tiara—Riker admitted as much the day I begged him to help. *I want a guarantee the FBI won't interfere with my attempts to get it*, he said. *If I walk off that boat with the tiara in my possession, I want your husband's solemn vow that no one will come after me*. It's as good as a confession. Nowhere in that statement did he promise that he planned to *win* the damn thing.

"I forbid it," I say, though it's hard to hear me over Lola's bubbling laughter. "How is this even a thing? We all paid good money to win the tiara the honorable way, not set ourselves against one another to see who could steal it first."

"Speak for yourself," Tara says. "I've never done an honorable thing in my life."

That's not true, and we both know it. Just a few months ago, she put her life and her freedom at risk to help me learn the truth about my mother, and for no reason other than a desire to right the wrongs of her past. Then again, the diamond at stake that time wasn't nearly as big as the Luxor…

"But what if you end up winning the poker game?" I ask. "All your evil plotting will have been for nothing."

"Then no one will have any cause for complaint." She tosses her hair. "Think of it as a backup plan. One way or another, I'm leaving this ship with that diamond in hand."

"I hope your dear daddy has an ironclad security plan," I say to Lola with a resigned sigh. "Keeping that tiara safe from these remorseless thieves isn't a task I envy him."

Of course, the task of trying to pin down an anonymous master criminal while simultaneously trying to keep my husband alive and my friends from making stupid, greedy mistakes isn't enviable, either.

"By the by, what *is* his security plan?" Tara asks.

I expect Lola to be insulted that Tara would try to pry secrets out of her twenty minutes after they met, but she just giggles again and shakes her head. "I'll find out when you do. He'd never tell me anything that important for fear I'd give it all away. Oh, boy. Isn't this trip going to be grand?"

THE P7LAYER

THE TRIP MIGHT NOT BE GRAND, BUT *I* CERTAINLY AM BY THE
time Jordan arrives at my stateroom to await our dinner
date with Hijack. I look amazing in a long, form-fitting
red dress with strategic cutouts in the back and side.

Jordan, unfortunately, isn't as easily impressed.

"Isn't that what you wore to steal the Starbrite
Necklace?" she asks by way of greeting. "I hope
you packed more than that. I saw about six thousand
Swarovski crystals on the walk over here. There's some
serious bling aboard this boat."

"Ha! The joke's on them," I say. "If the ship goes
down, they'll sink to the bottom while I float nimbly to
the top."

In fact, the whole reason I got this dress back when
I needed to steal the Starbrite was to facilitate nimble
action of all kinds. Not only do I look the part of an
elite poker player with oodles of cash to spare, but I
have a high rate of mobility should it come down to a

high-speed boat chase or a mad dash over the shuffle-board decks.

"Pen…"

"Yes, I have more dresses," I assure her as I let her inside. "Tara was worried I'd dishonor the family name, so she did most of my packing for me."

I take a moment to survey Jordan, who also looks pretty amazing in a sparkling emerald shift dress I swear shows more of her legs than those tiny shorts did earlier. Since she can usually be found in sweater sets, I'm finding all this a touch alarming.

"You look awfully nice," I say. "I hope it's not for Hijack's benefit. I probably should have warned you earlier, but that man is a flirt and a liar. He'll seduce your great-grandmother if he thinks it'll get him access to a score."

"Call it a hunch, but I don't think it's *me* he's coming to seduce."

Ugh. "Don't remind me. He can try to seduce me all he wants, but he's not getting anywhere. I've got far too much work to do." *And far too many men to worry about.* "If he asks you to join his crew, do me a favor and turn him down, okay? The last thing I need is for you to start blowing things up for that man."

"Pen, how could you? You know the only person I blow things up for is you."

I lean over and kiss her cheek. "You're such a sweetie. And a liar. I know Riker and Tara have already recruited you."

A knock on the door prevents her from disclaiming any intention of helping them take the Luxor Tiara, which is just as well. The arrangement between us is that I won't ask questions or interfere with their plans unless they get in the way of Grant's work—in which case I carry full veto power. I don't *think* I'll have to whip out the veto on this one, since Grant is less concerned about protecting the tiara than he is about finding Johnny Francis, but I'll need to keep an eye on them all the same. They're sneaky, my friends. It's why I love them so much.

I check over my appearance one final time as Jordan pulls the door open to reveal a tuxedoed Hijack with a bouquet of roses in each hand.

Roses and starlit cruises are about as cliché as they come, but there's something about being offered them by a handsome, muscular man in a tuxedo that makes it impossible to refuse. Bowing with mock gallantry, he presents us each with a ribbon-bound bundle. Jordan accepts hers with a murmur of pleasure, but although I take mine in hand, I sniff it with suspicion.

"What's wrong?" he asks. "You don't like flowers?"

"Not really, no."

"Penelope!" Jordan chides, but Hijack just laughs.

"No, don't make her apologize. One of the nicest things about Pen is that she's never afraid to say what she's thinking. Out with it. What do you have against flowers? Or is it me you object to?"

"It's you," I say promptly. "You want something."

"I want a lot of things," he replies just as promptly. Then, with a sly smile, "Is it working?"

"No." I toss the flowers aside. "It's going to take a lot more than a few wilty roses to get me to steal the Luxor Tiara for you."

His guffaw of laughter is all the confirmation I need. I *knew* there was no way he was that happy to see me earlier. Any and all joy he found in my arrival has more to do with the fact that he's an underhanded, sneaking thief than it does with our past romance. He doesn't remember me as the love of his life; he wants me to join forces with him.

With my suspicions thus confirmed, I feel much better about taking the arm he offers and allowing him to escort us to dinner. I *like* Hijack, but there's a limit to the amount of aimless flattery I'm willing to swallow from any man who's not my husband. As long as I know there's a legitimate reason, I can accept it with decent grace.

I can accept it, but I'm *not* stealing that tiara.

Tara and I already checked out the main dining room, which is located directly opposite the mysterious cabaret lounge. A converted ballroom done up in every shade of gold imaginable, the dining room has been blocked off so all the windows are covered and no natural light can come in. The designers have made up for the darkness by gilding every possible surface. Tables, chairs, wallpaper, chandeliers—the whole place looks like King Midas walked through, lazily trailing his hands behind him.

In other words, it's just my style. Even the forks look to be plated in gold.

"Can I get you ladies a drink?" Hijack asks, taking in the grandeur of the room with no more than a blink. Either he wasn't kidding when he said he's rich now and he's accustomed to such opulent sights, or, like me, he cased this room when he first arrived.

"None for me, thanks," Jordan says.

"Penelope?" he asks and then checks himself. "Sorry. I forgot you gave up liquor. You wouldn't come with

me to Germany, you don't drink, you're wedded to the
FBI... I swear, if you weren't aboard a ship of criminals
bound for ungoverned waters, I'd take you for a nice,
normal, law-abiding citizen."

I laugh. "You wouldn't be the first man to make that
mistake."

"Tell me about him."

I can't pretend not to know which *him* he's referring
to, especially since there's a harsh edge to his request,
uttered without preamble. I almost refuse to answer,
a tart *my marriage is none of your business* on the tip
of my tongue. But it's natural that people will wonder,
especially if Lola continues acting as if I'm the Princess
of Thieves. Hijack might be the first to broach the subject, but I doubt he'll be the last.

"What do you want to know?" I ask, as if the ring I
usually wear is a matter of supreme indifference to me.

Instead of responding right away, he places a hand
on my waist and pulls me close. Under any other circumstances, it might look like two old friends having a
cozy chat, but my dress is open in several places along
the side. His fingers slip possessively over the curve of
my waist and under the fabric that stretches down to my
hip, his skin directly on mine. It's not a feeling I cherish.

"Everything," he murmurs. "I want to know everything."

"You want to know everything about my husband
while your hand is snaking toward my ass?"

He laughs out loud, showcasing his crooked grin.
"Can you blame me? On this boat? In that dress? After
all this time? Whoever this guy is, he can't be very smart.
If you were my wife, I'd never let you out of my sight."

As I was once his girlfriend and he let me out of his

sight all the time, I don't credit this piece of gallantry with much. I also know he's not going to give up easily, so I picture my husband in his full former-quarterback-current-badass-federal-agent glory and say the exact opposite of everything I know to be true.

May Grant have forgiveness on my soul.

"He's short—maybe a few inches taller than me—and wiry." I rattle off adjectives as though I'm reading them from a list in hopes that Hijack won't notice the telltale flush that accompanies my lies. "Receding hairline, poor taste in clothes, not much in the way of a sense of humor. He's also as dumb as a post. You wouldn't believe how much confidential information he lets slip when his guard is down, how much I'm able to extract just by playing the dutiful wife. He thinks I'm visiting my sick aunt in Florida right now."

Hijack digests this information with a low whistle, though I can't tell whether he's impressed by my dedication to the job or disgusted at what, if my confession were true, would lower me to the depths of depravity.

"Damn, Pen. I may have underestimated you."

"People often do." I shrug. "It's why I get away with so much."

Hijack turns to Jordan. "Have you met him?"

"Once or twice," she says, concealing her smile behind her hand. "Most of the time, I feel bad for the guy. He had no idea what he was getting into when he married Pen."

"Hey!" I protest. "It's not *all* bad. He gets to bask in my sunny disposition. That's worth something."

"It's worth everything," Hijack says loyally, but Jordan just loses hold of her laughter. Grant would be

the last one to say that my sunny disposition outweighs
the effort he has to put in on a daily basis. According to
him, every day is a new exercise in restraint.

"What department did you say he worked for again?"
Hijack asks.

I didn't, and I have no intention of doing so in the
future. Major Thefts cuts a little too close to home for
most of the people on this boat.

"Oh, look," I say, my voice too bright in my eagerness to change the subject. "They're getting ready to
serve dinner. I hope it's something good. I'm starving."

Hijack accepts my deflection by pushing us toward
one of the tables near the back. "That, at least, sounds
like the Penelope Blue I remember."

The claustrophobia hits about the same time as the fish
course is brought out.

Unlike the airplane ride, I'm not expecting it this
time. The shaky, panicked feeling hits me like a sack
of rocks to the chest. I think it must have something to
do with the overwhelming gold of the room, the lack of
windows and open air. There are just so many people
in such a contained setting… The walls are practically
closing in.

Or, I think as the feeling of panic rises up from my
chest to my throat, *it's because you know there's no way
out. For you or for Grant.*

"Is something wrong?" Jordan asks as I begin my
breathing exercises in earnest. "You don't look so good."

"I don't feel so good," I admit, my voice weak.

"Can I do anything to help?"

Other than finding Johnny Francis in the next five minutes to end this charade, I can't think of a solution, so I just squeeze my eyes shut and will the moment to pass. "I'm feeling a little dizzy," I say. "It'll go away in a second."

Her hand covers mine and squeezes. "Take a deep breath, Pen. In and out, in and out. There's a good girl."

I try to follow her low-voiced commands, but the heat in the room seems to be rising about five degrees per second. The knowledge that I have an audience doesn't help much, especially when I was just starting to get used to my shiny new reputation. Usually when I'm combating my fear of small spaces, I do it in a dark, confined hole with only myself for company. My shame doesn't love witnesses.

"You know, maybe I just need some air." I rise from my seat, flinging out a hand when Jordan tries to follow. "No, please stay and finish eating. I'm going to step outside for a few minutes."

I can tell she wants to argue, but she lets me go as I dart toward the nearest exit. I have every intention of making it out the door alone and with my dignity intact, but my other dinner companion proves himself to be much more solicitous than I remember.

"You look like hell. Come on. I know a shortcut."

I want to tell Hijack where he can stick his interference, but as my gait is stumbling, I accept his company—especially since it turns out he really *does* know a shortcut. Bypassing the main exit for a door marked Restricted Access, a few seconds tick by before we end up on an outdoor terrace with sweeping views of the star-studded sky.

I barely see it, busy as I am gulping the night air, bent over double as I regain my calm. I'm so preoccupied that I barely register Hijack rubbing his hand in soothing circles on my bare back.

"You'll be all right," he murmurs. "Just keep your head down. Funny that I forgot about your...little problem."

Nothing could have been designed to work faster as a balm on my fears. My *little problem* has never prohibited me from taking what I want. It may be unorthodox for a jewel thief to fall prey to bouts of claustrophobia, but I always get the job done. Always.

He moves his hand to the nape of my neck, his thumb and forefinger pressing firmly against the place where spine meets skull. That action alone is bad enough, but from there, he slips his fingers into my hair and begins rubbing at my scalp in a way that feels alarmingly intimate. With one final deep breath, I force myself into a standing position and step backward.

I don't step very far. Now that my nerves are no longer intent on humiliating me, I'm able to take full note of our surroundings. This isn't, as I'd originally assumed, an empty terrace. Several linen-covered tables are set up overlooking the water, and we've drawn the attention of the dozen or so diners fortunate enough to have landed a seat at what I'm rapidly coming to realize is the VIP dining lounge I'd skipped in favor of eating with Jordan.

Before my foot has a chance to touch the ground, my back comes into contact with a fleshy wall that I could swear wasn't there a moment ago. A pair of strong hands grab me by the waist to ground me, the grip familiar for the fraction of a second it lingers.

"Whoa, there," says a low, rumbling male voice. "Take it easy. You don't look too steady on your feet."

Even if I *had* been steady on my feet, I wouldn't be now. I know those hands, and I know that voice—and more importantly, I know the body that houses them both.

"She's fine," Hijack says for me, his hand once again taking a proprietary place on the small of my back. "She's not used to the constant movement of the ship yet, that's all."

I manage a feeble smile and look up into my husband's face. It's a testament to his skills as a federal agent and a man of steel that no signs of his emotions are apparent. At least, no signs of emotions are apparent to anyone meeting him for the first time. As I know full well, that unreadable look in his eyes only appears when he's hiding something.

Amusement, if I'm lucky. Anger, if I'm not. At this point, it could go either way. I guess I'm not the only one who noticed Hijack's hands in my hair.

Grant lifts a brow. "Good thing she has you to take care of her. And to speak for her, it seems. Does she have a name?"

"As it so happens, she does." I offer him my hand. "Penelope. Penelope Blue. And you are?"

"Kit O'Kelly, at your service."

I fully expect him to shake my hand or, given the formal way he introduced himself, bow at the waist, but he lifts my fingers to his lips and drops a light kiss on the surface instead. Between the tuxedo molded to his god-like form and the dark hair that gleams in the moonlight, it's all I can do not to swoon at the contact. Especially since he lingers a moment longer than necessary, the touch of his mouth soft and warm against my skin. The whisper of his breath is a reminder of everything I want right now—and everything I can't have.

"Penelope Blue, Penelope Blue…" He says my name with the affectionate inflection he normally reserves for our private time together. "The name is familiar, but I can't think why. Should I know you?"

I struggle to keep a laugh from springing to my lips. The question is a ridiculous one. There's no man on earth who knows me better than this one; even before we were married, he had an alarming amount of insight into my inner workings.

"Probably not," I say. "I'm a pretty small-time thief. But you might know my father, Warren Blue."

He pretends to think about it for a moment before shaking his head. "No, that's not it. Were you in Prague last year?"

"Uh, no. I've never been."

"Paris in the winter of '14?"

"I'm sorry. You must have me confused with someone else."

"Impossible. I never forget a face, especially one as beautiful as yours."

I can't help it. I blush. It's the cheesiest and most overused compliment in the world, but the way Grant's eyes—no, the way *Kit O'Kelly's* eyes—are devouring me makes me feel as if I'm standing on deck without a scrap of clothing on. It's been less than two days since he and I parted ways, and already his absence has become a physical ache.

This is a man I cannot live without, I think. *And this*

is a man who's never been in more danger than he is right now.

Despite the balmy air of the Caribbean, I shiver.

He sees it, of course. The stubborn idiot is unable to hide his concern over my well-being and starts to shrug out of his jacket.

"You're cold," he says. "Let me."

I jump back, determined to put as much space between us as possible. If he touches me again, if he keeps being solicitous and caring to a perfect stranger, Hijack is going to notice. My ex-boyfriend is far too interested in my FBI husband for my comfort level. The last thing we need is him asking more questions.

"I'm fine," I state, even as goose bumps break out on my arms. "It was just a cold breeze."

Hijack clears his throat, and I turn to him with a smile, grateful for the distraction he offers. "This is Hijack," I say, nudging him forward. "I don't think you'll have heard of him either—he's even smaller time than I am."

Both men laugh obligingly.

"Hijack?" Grant offers his hand. "That's an interesting name. Am I to take it literally?"

"Not while we're on board the *Shady Lady*." He shakes Grant's hand, both their fingers gripped way too hard for a friendly greeting. "Except for the ship itself, there's nothing here for me to hot-wire. We're sorry to have interrupted your meal, but like I said, the lady needed some fresh air. She wasn't feeling well."

The lady still isn't feeling a hundred percent, but no way is she going to show it. If Grant thinks for one second that I'm not able to see my side of this job through, we're both done for. *I'm* supposed to be the one worrying about *him* out here, not the other way around.

As if to prove my fears, Grant examines me closely, his eyes sweeping over my body from head to toe. I'm suddenly aware of the bags beneath my eyes and the unsteadiness of my stance, both of which are difficult to hide under such intense scrutiny. I breathe evenly and deeply, hoping he'll let us go without further incident.

We almost get there, too. But Hijack, sensing a rival in Kit O'Kelly, places his arm firmly around my waist. "Come on, sweetheart. We'll find you somewhere to sit down."

Damn. And we were so close.

"If *your sweetheart* is feeling faint, the last thing you want to do is head back inside," Grant says, a hard edge to his voice. "The noise and heat inside the dining room are enough to overpower anyone. I have plenty of room at my table. Come. Join me."

"Oh, no. We really couldn't—" I begin, but it's no use.

"I insist," Grant says, and in such a way that neither Hijack nor I are capable of saying no. Without waiting for an answer, he leads the way toward the back of the terrace, weaving around tables as if he was born to this role.

If I'd doubted that this was the VIP area before, there's no question of it now. The first clue is when we move past a table where my father and a few of his cronies sit sipping brandy, which he raises to me with a nod and a look of fabricated surprise at my husband. From there, we keep moving until we find ourselves facing a table with none other than Peter Sanchez, who I recognize from the FBI dossiers and from the same long-lashed eyes shared by his daughter.

Well, crap. So much for Grant keeping a low profile. He's been on this boat for all of eight hours, and he's already wining and dining the owner. Someone's been keeping himself busy.

"Peter, I hope you don't mind my asking this nice couple to join us for the rest of our meal," he says. "The lady found the dining room a touch overwhelming."

Peter Sanchez, a middle-aged man with dashing salt-and-pepper hair and a white linen suit cut to perfection, rises to his feet to greet me. Knowing what I do about highly skilled criminals who are closely watched by the FBI, I'm surprised at how mild-mannered he seems. He looks like he'd be more at home dandling babies on his knee than running stolen goods over international borders.

"Of course, of course," he says. "Welcome. Any friends of yours…"

"Oh, they're not my friends. We just met." Grant pulls out a chair for me and stands, his hand on the frame, until I lower myself into it. "But I'm given to understand that she's one of your more exalted guests, so I assumed there could be no harm. Warren Blue, you said your father was?"

I stifle the groan that rises to my throat. He said that plenty loud for my dad to overhear, plenty loud for *everyone* to overhear. I don't know what his game is yet, dining with the elite and playing off these highly visible, extravagant airs, but I don't like it. He might as well walk around with a neon sign affixed to his back directing people where to stab him.

"Yes," I say tightly. "Maybe you noticed. He's sitting a few tables over."

"Of course!" Peter's eyes, black under the dimly lit

terrace, meet Grant's in a moment of shared intelligence.
"What a fortunate coincidence. Mr. O'Kelly, this is the
young woman I was telling you about."

The queasiness in my stomach is replaced by a knot
of dread. I can imagine all too well how that conversation must have gone.

*Did you hear the news? Penelope Blue is going to try
and steal my precious tiara. In fact, we consider her one
of the most likely suspects. Would you like to make her
walk the plank, or should I?*

"*That* would be why the name was so familiar," Grant
says. "Though not the face. Are you sure you've never
been to Prague?"

I stare at him for as long as I feel I can get away with,
hoping to catch some clue as to how he wants me to act.
Do I pretend to know him? Feign ignorance of any and
all past meetings? Act like an ordinary thief who's plotting to steal a twenty-million-dollar tiara from the man
seated across from me?

In the end, I decide to go with that last one. Of the
three options, it's the one I'm most familiar with.

"Never," I say with as much resolution as I can
muster. "I'm not much for traveling."

"It's true. I tried to get her to come with me to Germany
years ago, but she's a New York fixture." Hijack sits back
in his chair, one arm draped over my shoulder to make
it appear as if we're hugging. I know Grant has noticed,
because he's been careful not to let his gaze fall there
even once.

"Is that so?" Peter asks politely. "How convenient.
One will always know where to find you."

There's a thinly veiled threat in there, so I answer

with one of my own. "Yes. I can often be found staying with my dad. He moved there to be near me—to take care of me. You, of all people, must know how protective fathers can be."

"Aha. I take that to mean you've met my little Lola."

"I have," I admit. And then, because it's no more than the truth, "I like her."

At the mention of his daughter, Peter's smile grows thin. "She has her moments. She's got a good head for figures and is eager to learn. Unfortunately, she takes after my wife in all other regards—no common sense and even less discretion."

There doesn't seem to be a polite response to that, so I offer a bland, "I didn't realize you were married. Is your wife on this trip, too?"

"No. I had her killed years ago."

I choke. Not one of the three men seated with me even blinks—either at the confession or my reaction to it—though Grant unbends enough to pass me a glass of water.

"I'm sorry," I say, my hand on my chest as I attempt to swallow. "I thought I just heard you say that you had her killed."

"I did," Peter says, still with that sweet, almost grandfatherly air. He toys with the stem of his wine glass before holding the bloodred liquid up to the moon. "I told you—no common sense and even less discretion. She cheated on me with her yoga instructor."

"Um…" I look to Grant and then Hijack for help, but I might as well be flanked by statues for all they care. Am I the only one who finds this alarming? "That's terrible. I'm sorry to hear it?"

"Thank you." He bows his head slightly, accepting

my apology as condolences befitting the deservedly bereaved. "If there's one thing a man ought to be able to count on in this world, it's his wife's fidelity. Wouldn't you agree, Mr. O'Kelly?"

Grant looks at me, a flash of mischief in his sudden smile. "Absolutely."

I open my mouth to protest—hello, misogyny and double standards and, you know, *murder*—but Grant isn't done.

"When I take the leap into matrimony, I intend to protect what's mine regardless of the consequences," he says calmly. "No man will lay hands on my wife without feeling the full weight of his regret."

As Hijack is technically laying a hand on me right now, I can't help but feel slightly alarmed at this declaration.

"I couldn't agree more," Peter says. "Which is why I had the yoga instructor killed, too."

I take another drink of the water, draining every last drop and wishing I had more. So much for the nice, soft-spoken baby dandler. Peter Sanchez is every bit as ruthless as his dossier suggests.

"I'm so pleased that you and Lola have hit it off, Ms. Blue," he says, still in that mild tone. "I'm counting on you to keep an eye on her. She thinks the world of you— she always has. I'll feel much better knowing she'll have at least one friend on board the *Shady Lady*."

Considering how he treats people he's married to, I'm not sure how I feel about being his daughter's new best friend, but I can hardly refuse. "I'm happy to do what I can, of course, but I'm not sure how much free time I'll have once the game gets underway. I intend to give the cards my full attention."

"Naturally, naturally." He waves his hand, apparently done with the subject of his family. "Does that mean you're as adept at poker as your father? If so, my guests are going to be up against a much bigger challenge than they realize."

"Not at all," I admit. It feels good to be on neutral ground again, even if we haven't fully escaped danger. "I'm more of a casual player than anything else, but I *am* looking forward to catching a glimpse of the Luxor Tiara. I heard the grand unveiling is tomorrow?"

Peter inclines his head in assent. "Yes, at the opening ceremonies. It promises to be an interesting event. You'll have to tell me what you think of my little treasure."

"If I know Penelope, she'll have nothing but good things to say." Hijack squeezes my shoulder. "Diamond-mad, this one. Always has been."

I swear, it's like he's purposefully *trying* to get Grant to blow his cover.

I cough gently. "I reserve the right to be disappointed. Remember—my expectations are awfully high. I've been hearing about this diamond since I was in diapers."

"From the looks of you, that can't have been too many years ago," Peter says. "You're a mere babe among grizzly old wolves."

"Ah, that's where you're wrong, Peter," Grant puts in, all calm elegance across the table. It's making me nervous. I mean, I know how good he can be at playing a role—we were married for a whole year before he stopped playing one with me—but I still don't like it. "Never mistake youth for inexperience. These two might look like high school sweethearts, but something tells me they've seen more action than most of us can boast in a lifetime. How long have you two kids known each other?"

Unaware of the fine line he's treading, Hijack answers for us both. "Pen and me? We go way back. You could say she was my first love."

Grant doesn't so much as twitch. "But not, I hope, the last?"

"It's too soon to say," Hijack says with a laugh and another dangerous squeeze of my shoulder. "I get the feeling the answer to that might depend on whether I end up getting my hands on that tiara."

"Is that a fact? How interesting. I had no idea the lady's affection could be so easily bought."

It seems a timely moment to intervene. "The lady is getting awfully tired of hearing herself spoken about in the third person, if you want her opinion. And for the record, the answer is no. My affection can't be bought that easily. If I want a diamond, I'm perfectly capable of going out and taking it for myself."

Too late, I realize how that sounds.

"Not that I'm going to *take* the Luxor, of course," I say quickly, casting my stricken eyes Peter's way. "I just mean in the general order of things."

"Don't you worry on my account. I like a woman who shows initiative." Peter drops his napkin to his plate and rises, ignoring my faux pas and making me all the more frightened of him because of it. "No, no, don't get up. I have a few minor details to attend to before the game gets underway. Security has been a nightmare, as I'm sure you can imagine. You three enjoy yourselves. Mr. O'Kelly, I'll see you tomorrow?"

Grant lifts his head in what I assume is a nod before

Peter disappears into the night air. I'm a little jealous of his escape, actually. With just the three of us sitting here, there's every chance our encounter is about to get even more awkward. Fortunately, Grant also makes a motion to depart.

It's only a motion, though. He rises to his feet, all six feet two inches of him looming over the table, and waits there. I'm so busy trying to make out the features of his face—difficult to read under any circumstances and almost impossible now—that I don't notice right away he's holding out his hand, waiting for me to take it in my own.

Instinct warns me to play this cool and easy to avoid suspicion, which is why I'm so taken aback by how firmly he grips my hand, how deliberate he is as he helps me to my feet and once again drops a kiss to my fingers. *Cool* and *easy* are not the words I'd use to describe the intensity of his lips on my skin.

Hot. Hard.

"You're looking much better for the fresh air," he says. "Is there anything I can procure for you, anything you need to make your passage easier?"

"Don't worry. I'll take care of her." Hijack doesn't move from his chair. Normally, being in a seated position puts a man at a disadvantage, but the way he has one ankle propped casually on the opposite knee exudes a kind of laid-back power that not even Grant's impressive stature can suppress. "She's in good hands."

"You've vastly relieved my mind," Grant says in a flat tone and makes a slight bow. "Penelope. Hijack. It was a pleasure meeting you both. I look forward to facing you across the tables."

Somehow, I doubt the sincerity of that.

Hijack waits until Grant's dark form disappears the same way as Peter's before releasing a low whistle. "Well, shit, Pen," he says. "I always knew you'd done well for yourself, but I had no idea you were *famous* now."

My laugh is shaky. "I'm not famous, not really. Most of my notoriety is thanks to my dad."

"You're the one sitting at Peter Sanchez's dinner table, not him."

"So are you," I point out. "Besides, people never used to treat me like this. It's a recent development. You have to understand—my life is a lot different now that I have a father, a home. I'm not the scrappy delinquent you used to know."

"I'm beginning to see that." He doesn't attempt to rise, his head turned to me, watching carefully. *Too* carefully. "Who was that guy, by the way?"

"The tall one? He said his name was Kit O'Kelly."

It's not the answer Hijack is looking for, but it's the only one I have that doesn't give myself away, so it'll have to do.

"Yeah, I picked up that much," he replies. Then, "I don't trust him."

"I dunno. I kind of liked him."

Hijack chuffs a soft breath. "Of course you do. You like everyone. Peter Sanchez was right—you're a babe among wolves."

First of all, I *don't* like everyone—not even close. It took me over ten years to warm up to my stepmother, and I'm still not sure I'd save Simon from a burning building if it came down to a choice between him and virtually any other human being on the planet. Second,

I don't appreciate being treated like some frail wisp of a woman who doesn't know what she's doing. I might be small and I might be working for the FBI, but I can still out-steal every man on this boat—Hijack included.

"I can handle myself, thanks," I say tightly.

"Are you sure about that? You're an attractive, wealthy, well-connected jewel thief with a track record of success most of us only dream of. There are lots of men on this boat who might try to take advantage of that."

My spine stiffens at the implication—that I'm weak and vulnerable, that I can be corrupted by a handsome face and sleek manners. *Please*. If that was the case, I'd have knuckled under my husband's iron will years ago.

"You mean men kind of like you?" I ask.

"No, Penelope." He laughs and helps me to my feet, an unnerving glint in his eye. "I mean men *exactly* like me."

THE INTRUDER

THE SUN HASN'T YET RISEN WHEN I HEAR SOMEONE TRYING
to break into my room.

Even though I made an early night of it, lingering in
the dining room just long enough to excuse my lengthy
absence to Jordan before I hit the mattress, I'm deep in
the throes of sleep when the attempt is made.

Click. Clack.

I bolt upright, groggy and unsure of my surroundings,
my thousand-count Egyptian cotton sheets clutched to
my wildly pounding heart. More out of instinct than
coherent thought, I stay perfectly immobile, waiting to
determine if the intruder will try again.

Click. Clack. CLICK.

Apparently, he will. I slide from the bed and land on
steady legs, instinct and coherent thought now working
in tandem. Instinct tells me to grab something heavy and
hide behind the door so I can take up an offensive position. The coherent half of me isn't so sure. After all, it's

common knowledge on board this boat that my dad is located a mere wall and a shout away. Only a fool would come after me here.

A fool or, perhaps, a man in love.

My heart pounds again—though this time for a different reason. *Grant*.

"It's about freaking time," I mutter. There hadn't been any newly folded towels waiting for me when I got back to my room last night, and I checked the rest of the linens with a thoroughness bordering on the obsessive without finding any kind of message. I guess stealing into my room in the wee hours of the morning is as good a communication method as any.

"You have some serious explaining to do," I say as the door swings easily open. "I've been worried out of my—"

"Pen?" The man standing at my door boasts an impressive and familiar physique—not to mention the bright and annoying eyes of a morning person—but he's not my husband. "You look like hell. Don't tell me I woke you up—it's already five o'clock."

Already five o'clock? Is he kidding?

"The sun is starting to come up on the portside viewing deck. If you hurry, we can catch it. We could also go for a jog on the running track and watch from there. No one is out yet, so we'll have the whole place to ourselves."

"Is this some kind of sick joke?" I blink a few times, wondering if perhaps I'm still asleep and this is a dream version of Hijack. But he remains stubbornly in focus—and focus isn't a point in his favor, as he's dressed in what I can only presume is some kind of athletic onesie. "Why would I go for a jog before the sun is even up?"

"Because we won't get another chance today. The opening ceremony starts at noon." He doesn't wait for me to respond or invite him in, pushing his way past the door as though he owns the place. He also thrusts a steaming cardboard cup into my hands. "I come bearing presents."

"Bless your early morning little heart," I say, almost willing to forgive him. But then I sniff the cup and recoil, shoving it back into his hands as quickly as I can. "Oh, dear God. What did you do to it? It smells like death."

"I added a scoop of spirulina. Great for night vision. Who were you expecting?"

I pretend it's sleep clouding my brain for how long it takes me to process his question. "What are you talking about?"

"Just a minute ago, when you first came to the door. You were worried about someone."

"Oh, you mean Riker," I say, falling back on the first person to come to mind. It's not that much of a stretch. Of all the people I'm worried about on this ship, he *is* in the top three. "You know how he gets with gambling—he's supposed to check in with me at least once a day. But I wasn't kidding about this being way too early for a visit. For you or for Riker. I don't do morning jogs anymore. Or any jogging at all, really."

"Right. I keep forgetting. You're not the Penelope Blue you used to be." He says the words cheerfully enough, but I can't help feeling there's an underlying threat to them—especially when he follows up with, "Nice shirt, by the way. Is it his?"

I glance down, aware that I'm wearing one of my husband's FBI training shirts, used so often and put to such physical hardship that it's become a soft, Grant-scented nightgown. I rarely sleep without it and had to smuggle it in via my secret luggage compartment for fear Tara would throw it out otherwise. The fact that Federal Bureau of Investigation is blazoned boldly across the front isn't a problem—most people know that thumbing my nose at authority is as natural to me as breathing—but the way it fits me *is*. The hem dangles to midthigh, the rest of my body swimming in its voluminous cotton folds. It isn't exactly the attire of the short, wiry man I painted my husband out to be yesterday.

"Oh. Um." I tug on the hem, conscious of how bare my legs are underneath the shirt. "No, it's not his. It's mine."

"Really? You own a lot of government-themed attire?"

I can't decide if he's mocking me or testing me, but I don't like how interested he is either way. I cross my arms and glare. "Yes, actually, I do. If I'm going to do a thing, I'm going to do it right. We're very pro-FBI in our family. The shirt was a gift from my husband's mother."

Hijack's laugh fills the room. "Oh, shit. He has a mother?"

"Everyone has a mother."

"I mean, he has a mother you've met and are in a position to receive presents from?" His laugh diminishes into a chuckle as he shakes his head. "Never let it be said that you aren't willing to play along to get a score. You want me to wait in the hall while you get dressed?"

What I want is for him to go away and find a bed in his own room, but I doubt I'll be able to get back to sleep now. Besides, that algae-infused coffee is starting to stink up the room.

"Yes. Out." I put my hands on his pecs and push,

alarmed at the scope and size of the musculature under my fingertips. There's a lot more to this man than I remember, and I don't mean that in a good way. He's a threat I wasn't anticipating. "And give me whatever it was you used to break in here."

"I wasn't breaking in. I was bringing you breakfast in bed."

"Microorganisms are not breakfast. Pancakes are. Give it to me. What is it—a specialized lock-picking kit? Magnet?"

"Master key," he says and smirks. "And I'll give it to you, but only because you asked so nicely."

I stop and stare. "You have a master key to the whole ship?"

"No. You do." He hands me a key on a small metal ring, pressing my fingers as he passes it over. "But don't let anyone know you have it. If Peter Sanchez were to hear that I got my hands on a copy…"

The metal, which is warm from his fingers, suddenly feels very hot. Only by closing my hand in a tight fist am I able to refrain from throwing it back in his face. I have a pretty good idea of what Peter Sanchez would do if he found out about it, and there's not enough bleach in the world to clean up *that* bloodbath.

"How did you get this?"

He shrugs. "I have my ways. The how is less important than the why."

I don't bother indulging him by asking that question. I know the answer. "For the last time, Hijack, I'm not going to help you steal the Luxor Tiara."

"Just hold on to that for a while. See how you like the fit."

"I know how it fits—like a noose."

He laughs and does another one of those condescending nose-tweaking maneuvers. It's even less endearing the second time around. "You used to be a lot more fun, you know that? Come on. Time's wasting. I have a surprise waiting for you."

I don't know what it about my ex-boyfriends and their obsession with making me run, but I must have done something terrible in a past life to deserve this kind of punishment.

I'm clutching a hitch in my side, staggering as I draw air into lungs that would much rather be sleeping, when Hijack whizzes by for the fourth time. In my defense, the rate at which he's overtaking me isn't as bad as it sounds. The track on board the *Shady Lady* is located at the very top of the ship, wrapped around a central opening that peers down to the pool a few decks below. It takes thirteen laps to make up a mile, or so my enthusiastic trainer informs me, so he's taking them at a clipping rate.

"You used to be in better shape than this." Hijack slows just long enough to switch to a backward run, keeping an effortless pace with me. "You're getting weak in your old age."

I glare at him through the sheen of sweat dripping into my eyes. "I used to be in better shape because Riker held a pitchfork to my back and made me run. He's learned not to do that anymore."

"Your body is your temple, Pen. I did three ultramarathons last year. One almost killed me, but you don't hear me complaining about it."

Through a series of grunts and hand gestures, I manage to convey my disappointment that it failed in its task.

"Look lively! Someone's coming." Without further warning, he returns to his forward position, slapping me on the ass as he does. I'm so startled that I start jogging faster, albeit not at the demonic pace Hijack is hoping for. With a brief glimmer of disappointment, he slows his pace to match mine. "If my intel is correct, that'll be Eden St. James. She never misses a morning run. No, no, don't look. Just keep jogging."

"Eden St. James?" I hiss. *That's* my surprise, the reason he was so gung ho on my getting out here in the open air before the sun? "Isn't she…"

"The thief who's likely to steal the tiara if you don't start making plans to get to it first? Yes, she's one of them. You need to check out the opposition if you're going to pull this thing off successfully. I need you to feel her out a little, tell me what you think. You're good at getting under people's skin."

I open my mouth to remind him—again—that I have no intention of allying myself with him anytime soon, but there isn't a chance. As we round the gentle curve of the track, we come within full view of our so-called competition.

The woman herself isn't terribly alarming. Jealousy-inducing, yes, but not alarming. She's taller than me— not a difficult feat to accomplish—and built like the kind of person who spends every morning running. And by that, I mean she's wearing nothing but a sports bra and infinitesimal spandex shorts, her abs so clearly defined, I halfway suspect they're painted on. She's also incredibly fast, taking to the track with the kind of ease and skill I'm sure Hijack was expecting from yours truly.

I wouldn't mind so much—the speed or the body of a gazelle, the cute outfit that puts my black leggings and faded tank top to shame—except that she's not alone. On the contrary, she's somehow managed to find herself the only companion who can keep up with her.

A companion, I might add, who should be doing virtually *anything* except early morning sprints.

"Ugh. Is that Kit O'Kelly? I swear, that guy is everywhere." Hijack sums up my feelings on the subject quite nicely. "Step it up a little, would you?"

I do, but only because I'm half-afraid Hijack will slap my ass again to get me going. I can't tell from Grant's expression whether he witnessed the first one, but I'm not taking any chances with a second. My husband knows the likelihood of me a) running, and b) running this early in the morning of my own volition. He has to know I'm here because of Hijack—and I seriously doubt that information will please him, especially given the current hour. To an outside viewer, it looks as if Hijack and I haven't parted ways since dinner.

I regret my speed about two minutes later. I'm not nearly as terrible a runner as Hijack seems to think, but even with Grant's injury, I don't stand a chance of keeping up with the pace the rest of the runners set. I'm winded and panting by the time we make our first revolution.

Both Grant and Eden slow as they pass us by, their strides a perfect match for one another, but only the former bothers to acknowledge us. "Good morning, Penelope. Hijack," he says.

"O'Kelly," Hijack replies, as casual as my husband.

I mostly just wheeze.

Hijack continues, "This is a pleasant surprise. And here we thought we'd have the track to ourselves this morning."

"Nothing like a little fresh air and competition to get the blood pumping, that's what I always say," Grant says for what I'm pretty sure is the first time in his life.

"That's one way to do it," Hijack acknowledges. "Although this is more of a cooldown than a warm-up for us, if you know what I'm saying."

I know what he's saying, but I don't have a chance to elbow him severely in the ribs, because Grant just laughs. "I see we're not the only ones to find sleeping aboard this ship a little difficult, Eden. The constant motion is something else, isn't it? Ms. St. James and I have discovered we're both terrible insomniacs."

False. Grant sleeps like the dead. His favorite position is to throw every single one of his weighty limbs on top of me and pin me to the bed until he's ready to face the day all refreshed and ready for action.

"We indulged ourselves in a little late-night prowling," Eden confesses with a prim smile. It matches her prim voice, which carries a clipped British accent that sounds as if it came directly down ten generations of royalty. "The ocean is so peaceful when no one is around. It's a shame we have to share the boat with the hoi polloi. Quite ruins the effect."

As she's looking directly at me as she speaks, I assume the *hoi polloi* is me. I don't know what it means except that I'm really starting to dislike this woman.

"Did you find anything interesting?" I ask, my teeth clenched so tightly, I might as well be a ventriloquist. "During your prowls, I mean?"

She looks the whole two inches up into Grant's face and smiles again, this time with much less primness. "Oh, I found lots of things interesting."

Okay. I changed my mind. I'm really starting to *hate* this woman.

"Can't we run faster than this, Kit?" She makes a bow with her pouted lips. "I was hoping to get in a real workout this morning, not a quiet stroll around the deck."

Grant smiles in a disarming way I recognize and fear, but Hijack stops him before he can speak. "Actually, Mr. O'Kelly, there's something I was hoping to get your opinion on," he says. "Maybe we could let the girls run together while we…" Hijack glances over at a covered walkway next to the side railing, secluded enough for a private talk but well within view of the track.

I know what he's doing—trying to clear the field for me so I can chat up Eden, see what I can glean about her plans for the Luxor—but I'm not interested. Not in trying to eke information out of this British beauty and especially not in doing so while keeping pace with her freakishly long stride.

But I know I'm done for when Grant struggles to suppress a laugh, his lips in a tight line but his eyes crinkling in a way that betrays everything.

"There's nothing I'd love more," he says, his deep voice rumbling. Unlike my ex-boyfriends, he knows how I feel about enforced exercise. "You'll be okay without me for a few laps, Eden?"

She doesn't look pleased at being abandoned to my paltry company, but there's no way for her to say so without looking like a poor sport in front of the menfolk, so she does it. That right there tells me everything I need to know about her—as a thief and as a woman—but I doubt that will be sufficient recon for Hijack.

"I hope you can keep pace with me, love," is all she says, and she takes off at a gait that would make Olympians seethe with jealousy.

I'm tempted to wait until she makes a whole revolution before I join her, but Grant chooses that moment to *also* smack me on the ass. He knows just where to land the blow on the familiar landscape of my backside—and it carries a lot more sting as a result, though it's mostly to my pride. There's no way I can retaliate without giving our relationship away, and he knows it.

"Oh, I'm sorry," I can hear Grant murmur as I cast an angry look over my shoulder and start loping after Eden. "I thought that was a thing we were doing now."

Whatever Eden's skills as a long-distance runner, she turns out to be one hell of a sprinter. I know this because I'm *sure* that's what she's doing as she completes the first two laps, her long legs eating up the padded track and causing her neat brown ponytail to swish behind her like a pendulum keeping time. My own short legs, bless them, have to work twice as hard to catch up, my ponytail coming loose and trailing behind me like a horse's unkempt mane.

"You. Are. Very. Fast." I pant as we make our third revolution. I'm going to kill Hijack after all this is done. And Grant. And maybe Eden St. James, if I can convince her to follow them overboard. "You. Have. Nice. Form."

She looks down at me with that prim smile from before. I suspect it's the "company" smile she pulls out when the company isn't particularly welcome.

"Thank you," is her response. As we pass Grant and

Hijack, she lifts her hand in a wave, but the men are deep in conversation and don't notice. Their lack of attention is the only thing that saves me from cardiac arrest. The moment Eden realizes her audience isn't paying attention, she slows her maniacal pace to something more manageable.

Not *a lot* more manageable, mind you, but enough so I don't have to pretend to twist my ankle in order to stay alive.

"I'm not stupid," she says. "I know what you two are doing."

At first, I think the two she's referring to are me and Grant, and I feel a momentary spasm of alarm. But then she speaks again, her eyes trained on the path in front of her. "You're delving into my psyche."

That sounds like an awfully complicated task for a first meeting, and I say as much. "Or, and I'm just throwing this out, I'm trying not to trip over my own feet."

The way her breath comes out sounds almost like a laugh. "Nonsense. I've heard how Penelope Blue operates. They say no one is better at worming her way into other people's graces. Man, woman, child…no one is immune to your charm. Even our ship's host is singing your praises, and he once took a man apart with a pair of pliers."

Peter Sanchez's praises aren't something I want to hear, not when there are pliers involved, but I can't help feeling flattered by the picture Eden is painting. From the way she's putting it, I'm basically the baddest ass on a boat of badasses.

I could get used to that.

"And now you've taken up running in an attempt to

woo me into friendship and lowering my guard," she adds. "You're trying to find my weaknesses."

"If I wanted to be your friend, I would have picked a less exhausting activity," I say with complete honesty. The way I figure it, the lack of oxygen making its way to my brain gives me about five more minutes of this, and then I'm down for the count. "If you could just tell me your weaknesses and save me the trouble of finishing another lap, I'd really appreciate it."

That breath-laugh sounds again. I'm not fooled by it, because she starts running faster. "You're a cute little thing, I'll give you that much."

"Thank you," I manage.

"It wasn't a compliment. This act of yours might work with most people, but I don't want to be your friend, and I don't want a quirky sidekick to chum around with. If we have to interact, I'd prefer us to call each other what we are—enemies."

"Would you believe me if I told you I have no intention of being your enemy?" I pant. "I don't want to steal the Luxor Tiara. In fact, I'm starting to hate the very sound of it."

"Nice try," she says and promptly sticks out her leg, sending me sprawling.

Okay, I can't say for sure that she stuck out her leg to trip me, but it's the only explanation I have for what happens next. One second, I'm concentrating on my forward momentum, and the next, I'm hurtling through the air, a feeling of weightlessness taking over just before my knees slam into the polyurethane surface.

I don't feel the impact on my kneecaps at first, nor do I feel the rough scrape of abrasions on my palms. All I feel is the dizzying whir of my body coming *way* closer to the ship's railing than I'm comfortable with.

"Uh-oh." Eden's voice sounds several feet away, which, at her previous rate of speed, would make sense. "That looks painful."

As there's not much in the way of concern in her voice, I doubt my pain is something this woman cares about. The other two, however… I don't need to look up to know that the black Nikes making a beeline for my side belong to my husband.

"I'm fine. I'm good. I'm fine." I force myself to sit upright before he can do something stupid like wrap his arms around me in a gesture of comfort. "It looks a lot worse than it is. I promise. I'm a very theatrical faller."

"What happened?" Hijack drops to a crouch next to me, taking a quick and efficient survey of my limbs. "Is anything broken?"

"I'm fine," I repeat, forcing myself to concentrate on his hands as they take each of my arms and legs in turn, bending and twisting them to check for ailing parts. It's good for him that nothing *is* broken, because he's none too gentle with his medical care. "It's just my knees and hands that are dinged up."

I'm also feeling slightly woozy from the fall, but I don't mention it. From the way Grant is watching us, silent and white-lipped—and from the way Eden is watching *him*, with a sharp, narrow-eyed interest—it's best for all of us to sweep this away and move on.

"Help me up." I lean on Hijack's arm, using him to leverage myself to a standing position. The quick movement causes my head to spin, and I falter. Hijack's strong arm around my waist prevents me from sinking to the ground again.

"See?" I ask shakily, doing my best to underplay how close I am to falling into a swoon. "As good as new."

It doesn't work.

"Take her to the infirmary," Grant says, his voice thin and hard.

"No, no, I'm good. Really. There's no saying how long that could take." My own voice isn't leaving any room for doubt. "The rules clearly state that anyone who misses the opening ceremonies forfeits their entrance fee. No way am I missing out on my chance at that tiara for a pair of scraped knees."

"He's right," Eden says. "You look pretty close to passing out. But then, I wouldn't know. I've never been squeamish about blood."

That I can easily believe. In fact, I wouldn't be surprised if she outright reveled in it. This woman has tortured her share of small animals, or I miss my mark.

"I'm not squeamish either," I state and shake off Hijack's arm. "And I'm not losing my spot for being a no-show."

"There's plenty of time to do both." Grant scans the sky. I can practically see his Boy Scout antenna go up as he makes a quick assessment. "It's a quarter to eight. Go to the medic and get checked out. I'll ensure Peter doesn't start until you're there."

"You have the power do that?" Hijack asks, surprised.

"You'd be willing to do that?" Eden asks, also surprised.

I can't decide which question would be worse for Grant to answer, so I forestall both by tossing my head and glaring at Eden. "There's no need. A few bandages back at my stateroom, and I'll be good as new. It's going to take a lot more than one tiny fall to stop me."

She doesn't take the threat as it's intended. "Good to know."

I look helplessly to Grant, but if he sees anything wrong in his new flirt's sociopathic behavior, it doesn't show. He's divided between concern for my bleeding limbs and his need to keep his cover preserved.

The preserved cover is more important—about twenty million times more important, if you ask me—so I plant my wobbly legs on the ground despite the pain. I'm going to have some serious bruising tomorrow. "It was nice meeting you, Eden. Good to see you again, too, Kit. I hope you two enjoy the rest of your run."

Grant compresses his lips tightly, but he knows better than to argue further. To do so would be ruinous to us both.

"And watch your step," I add with a sweet smile Eden's way. "You wouldn't want to fall overboard. I hear there are sharks nearby."

"Oh, I'm not afraid of sharks," she replies just as sweetly. "A little blood in the water is just the way I like it."

THE DIAMOND

9

ATTEMPTS AT MY LIFE NOTWITHSTANDING, I MANAGE TO make it to the opening ceremonies with plenty of time to spare. A long, flowing tropical skirt hides my ugly bandages, but there's not much I can do about the scrapes on my hands, so I leave the raw skin exposed in hopes it will heal over quickly. Hijack wanted to put on some kind of homemade salve crafted from essential oils, but I drew the line at that. I prefer my medication to be of the unpronounceable chemical variety, thank you very much.

We take the stairs up from Jordan's stateroom, which I consider to be as good as any shipboard infirmary. Although she was happy to clean my wounds, she declined the honor of joining us at the cabaret lounge, citing a need to "freshen up first." As there was a fluffy polar bear towel folded up on her comforter, I assume that means she has some other assignments to attend to.

"You know that woman tripped me on purpose, right?"

I ask Hijack as we make our way upstairs. "She wanted me to be disqualified from the game before it starts."

Instead of being outraged at my suspicions, Hijack just laughs. "Can you blame her?"

"Um. Yes?"

He pushes through the stairwell door. "It's the laws of nature, Pen. The first thing someone like Eden St. James does when faced with the competition is try to take her out. You're lucky there were witnesses around to stop her."

"That woman is *not* my competition," I say hotly, even as I picture the way she smirked at Grant as they discussed their nocturnal activities—and the way he smirked right back. My husband has always had a thing for the spandex-clad, law-breaking type. "No. I refuse to believe it. He wouldn't do that."

"He?"

It takes me a moment to process Hijack's confusion, another to realize my error in causing it. *Of course* he's not talking about me and Eden competing for the same man. He's talking about us competing for the same piece of jewelry. You know—the thing ninety-nine percent of the people on the *Shady Lady* are after.

"Peter Sanchez," I say quickly, hoping he won't notice my slip. "I don't think he'll put both Eden and me at the same table. Not for the first round, anyway. But can I just say how much I'm starting to hate that tiara? I haven't even seen it yet, and I wish it was still at the bottom of the ocean."

"You're the only one," he says as we arrive outside the cabaret lounge doors. They're finally unlocked and thrown open to reveal the secret inner workings, but it's difficult to see anything through the teeming swell of bodies clamoring to get in. Everyone on board the *Shady Lady* seems to have arrived at exactly the same time and with exactly the same goal in mind.

"Maybe we should find another way in," I suggest, eyeing the crowd doubtfully. I don't want another repeat of last night's panic attack.

"Why?" Hijack asks. "Afraid someone will pick your pockets?"

"Well, I wasn't *before*. Now that you mention it, however..." I take a wide step back. This place is a pickpocket's paradise. Hijack's master key is secured in a hidden pocket inside my bra, but I don't relish the thought of it making its way into anyone else's hands. It's dangerous enough in my own.

"You know what they say..." Hijack looks at me askance. "The best defense is a strong offense. Maybe we should do the pickpocketing instead. How do we like the looks of that tall man with the mustache?"

As a mark, I like him very much. He's a good foot taller than everyone else, so there's a shelf of heads between his line of vision and his wallet. He'd never see us coming. However, I don't like the possibility of accidentally robbing Johnny Francis. I have enough enemies on board this ship as it is.

Fortunately, I'm saved from having to deny Hijack yet again by the sight of a dark head bobbing my way.

"Penelope! I thought that was you. I stopped by your room this morning to tell you to come find me before you arrived, but you were gone. You must be a really early riser. I knocked three times."

"Hey, Lola," I reply, pleased to see her familiar

beaming face. She looks even younger than she did yesterday, clad in a yellow sundress with her hair falling in big, loopy curls down her back. "Sorry I missed you. I, uh, went for a jog."

Her eyes grow wide. "Did you? You must be super dedicated if you're willing to exercise on vacation like that. I'd love to be more active, but I get winded so fast. Asthma, you know? Too much excitement, and my lungs close right up. I'm supposed to keep my inhaler with me wherever I go, but I forget sometimes. Who's this?"

Accustomed by now to Lola's artless chatter, I have no difficulty following along. "This is my friend Hijack. Hijack, this is Lola Sanchez."

Lola's eyes flare in excitement. "Oh, you're the one she's friends with—the thief, I mean. I know all about you. Current odds are set at ten-to-one but going steadily down. I'm afraid you're getting hurt by the parlay."

Hijack blinks at her.

"She means you're one of the thieves in the running for the you-know-what," I explain, though I couldn't tell him what parlay means. Gambling terminology has never been my forte, though Lola seems to know her fair share on the subject. I'm beginning to wonder if she isn't some kind of savant. "Apparently, people are side-betting on which one of us is going to steal it first."

"I'm all the way at ten-to-one?" Hijack says, frowning. He sounds as insulted about his standing as Tara did yesterday. For hardcore thieves, we sure are a sensitive bunch. "Are you sure you did the math right?"

"Oh, I never get the math wrong," Lola says confidently. "I'm useless at just about everything else, but numbers I can do. Don't ask me to explain how. My brain soaks them up and spits them back out again. Go ahead. Ask me anything. I'm really good at ratio determinations."

Hijack doesn't take her up on the offer. "I'd like to speak to the person in charge of those figures."

"You just did, silly," Lola says with a laugh. "Come on. We should head inside."

Unless she can part crowds as easily as she can divide fractions, I don't see how that's happening. "Is there a line we're supposed to get in or something?" I ask.

"Not for you. The great Penelope Blue never has to wait in line." Lola grabs me by the hand. The grating of her palm against my cuts causes me to cringe, but her grip is as difficult to shake as her enthusiasm. "Let's go—there's a side way in. I'll show you. You're going to want to get a front row seat for this so you can see all the security protocols up close and personal. The tiara is so beautiful in person. What are you going to do with it when you steal it?"

Give it to the FBI, probably. Those greedy bastards would never let me keep my hands on something so valuable. Not that I say as much out loud. No need to give her—or Hijack—any more ideas than they already have.

"Swiss bank account," I lie.

Lola's side way in turns out to be a hallway used to move food and plates from the dining room to the kitchen, with one small outlet for access to the cabaret lounge. The passageway is so narrow, it's almost impossible to notice the way it's slightly set into the wall. I do my best not to look at Hijack as Lola shows us the trick for jimmying the door open.

"There," she announces triumphantly as she leads us inside. "Isn't it so much nicer this way?"

It is, but the question is a rhetorical one, and my attention is caught up in surveying my surroundings. To my surprise—and dismay—the cabaret lounge turns out to offer nothing the name suggests. Although a stage at one end indicates that the room is no stranger to theatrical exhibitions, it's been stripped of almost all baubles and overkill in favor of stark, bare walls. To make room for the poker game, there are also several sets of bleacher-style seats flanking the room's exterior and seven gaming tables placed at appropriate distances from one another in the center. The bleachers must have been brought in especially for the tournament, but everything else about the room is neat and serviceable and, frankly, boring.

"What's wrong?" Hijack asks as I pause on the threshold, taking it all in with a frown.

"It's not very glamorous, is it?" I ask. Unlike all the other parts of the ship, which teem with luxury, this room is strangely stark. "When I heard we were going to be in the cabaret lounge, I envisioned feathers and red velvet as far as the eye can see. I was expecting more…"

He laughs. "Places to hide?"

Well, yes, actually. The lounge might be disappointing from an aesthetic standpoint, but when seen though a different lens—a thief lens—everything about it makes sense. The bright lights and bare walls allow few opportunities for concealment, and the clearly marked seating arrangement means anyone wandering out of place will be noticed in an instant. The exits are also visible from almost any vantage point in the room, so there will be no sneaking in or out.

"Don't you worry," Lola says warmly and squeezes

my arm. "If anyone can find a way to take the tiara out of here, it's you. Of course, the room's not very pretty, but you didn't think Daddy would make this easy, did you?"

I'm in no position to make any guesses where that man is concerned, although I wouldn't be surprised if murder is somewhere on his gambling cruise to-do list.

"Wait, you won't mind if Pen takes the tiara?" Hijack looks at Lola with interest for the first time. "You want her to get it?"

"Of course I do! I'm not supposed to say so out loud, and I can't offer any help or Daddy would just kill me, but if anyone is going to steal that diamond, I want it to be her." She adds loyally, "And she'll do it, too."

"That's not necessarily decided on yet…" I begin, but there's no point. Hijack feigns deafness with a wide smile.

The cabaret lounge is starting to fill by this time, the not-so-fortunate masses finding their way inside and looking around with the same air of expectation. Although a burly pair of men in dark suits stand off to one side of the stage, Peter Sanchez is nowhere in sight, and no one sees fit to enlighten us. The suspense is palpable. At this point, I wouldn't be surprised if someone rappelled down from an overhead access panel with the tiara in hand.

I am, however, surprised to see Riker appear as if from out of nowhere, no sign of Tara in his wake. For a couple on a half-romantic, half-criminal vacation, they sure are spending a lot of time apart.

"There you are, Pen," Riker says by way of greeting. "I've been looking everywhere for you."

"Why?" I ask suspiciously. "What are you plotting?"

"Shame on you," is his easy reply. "Maybe I just

wanted to escort you to the game. Your safety and comfort are, after all, the two most important things in my life."

The left side of his mouth is turned up in an ironic smile, which I assume means that Grant asked him to make sure I got to the cabaret lounge on time. As if a few scrapes would keep me away. I paid a million bucks for this.

"Lola, have you met Riker?" I ask and perform the introductions. "I know you're aware of him from a statistical probability standpoint, but I find he's a lot more entertaining in the flesh. Riker, this is Peter Sanchez's daughter, Lola."

Riker grunts a semipolite greeting, but I get nothing out of Lola. Not a squeak, not a squeal, not a running dialogue on how incredible our chances would be if the three of us reverted back six years and joined forces once again.

"Lola?" I ask, turning.

She's standing in the same spot as before, her lips parted and her eyes wide as she stares at Riker. At first, I think she's frightened of him—that the chip Riker wears so proudly on his shoulder has transformed him into a beast—but then she swallows. As in, *swallows*, her throat working up and down as she takes in the full glory of him standing there.

I almost ruin the moment by laughing out loud, but I manage to clamp my lips shut in time. I forget, sometimes, just how attractive Riker is to someone meeting him for the first time. The heavy brows over deep-set eyes, the sharp angles of his cheekbones, the dark scruff he wears mostly out of laziness… If you have a penchant for brooding masculinity, then Riker is definitely the man you want.

"Is something wrong?" Riker asks gruffly, unaware of the reaction he's causing in that poor girl's heart.

"No, I'm fine... You're just so... I can't even... Ohhh." She gives up. "You must be the most gorgeous man I've ever met."

I can't help it—at that, the laugh escapes. Riker *is* good-looking, but his swaggering confidence has always come from his professional attributes, not his personal ones. He'll sit and listen for hours as you outline all the ways his intelligence and leadership skills can't be rivaled, but start an ode to his dreamy eyes and he'll curse the day you were born.

"What the hell?" he demands, turning to me with an accusing stare.

"Don't blame me," I say, still laughing. "You're the gorgeous one. Most people would say thank you."

"Thank you," he mumbles, but even his poor manners aren't enough to keep Lola from gazing up at him with reverent, puppy-dog eyes. If I were as sensitive as Hijack and Tara, I might feel slighted at having been so easily supplanted in her esteem, but this is far too entertaining. I wouldn't trade Riker's discomfort for a hundred adoring Lolas of my own.

"So all three of you know each other?" Lola asks, although she looks at Riker as she speaks. I'm not sure she's blinked yet.

"Oh, yeah, Riker and I have known Hijack for years," I explain. "Actually, the three of us used to indulge in a bit of light larceny together. We were kind of a crew."

"Speaking of, you still owe me ten thousand dollars," Hijack says to Riker.

"Like hell I do." Riker doesn't sound angry—he mostly seems grateful for the change of subject. "You're the one who left us to go to Germany. As I recall, you walked out on your own two feet."

"Yeah, but you cheated me out of my share of the Tailortown job," Hijack says. "You were supposed to forward the money once I reached Berlin, but I never saw a penny. I could have used it, too. The exchange rate was brutal."

I tilt my head, trying to remember. That doesn't sound like something we would have done. Honesty among thieves and all that. "Is that true?"

"Of course it is," Riker says. "Don't you remember? He left before we finished the job. We were a man short, and you had to spend four extra hours hiding in the luggage compartment of that Greyhound bus to make up for it."

"Oh, yeah!" I snap my fingers. I *do* remember that. In our lengthy past, Riker and I have pulled so many jobs that most of them are a blur, but the unpleasant memories associated with that one linger. The plan had been for Hijack to "borrow" the bus while it was at the depot, thereby circumnavigating the usual route and driver to cut four hours off the drive. We'd gotten a hot tip on a passenger who didn't trust the TSA to turn a blind eye to the quantity of stolen Rolexes in his checked bags, so he traveled by bus rather than plane. All I had to do was squeeze into a suitcase stowed underneath, slip out while the bus was moving, take the watches, and crawl back in until we arrived at our destination.

We still pulled off the job without Hijack's help, but we'd had to rely on the regular driver and route, so the trip proceeded at its usual pace instead.

Which was slow. Very, very slow.

"I can't believe I forgot about that," I say. "I got a cramp in my leg about two hours in and had to sit there in agony until we finally arrived at our destination. Now that I think about it, it was *my* idea not to send you anything. I considered it recompense for my pain and suffering."

"The going rate for a leg cramp is ten thousand dollars?" Hijack asks.

"It was a really bad one."

At the sound of my vehemence, Hijack just laughs and shakes his head. "That's what I get for trusting a pair of thieves like you two. I'll be more careful next time."

"Wow. You guys really do go a long way back, huh?" Lola asks. "That must be nice, having friends with so much history together."

Nice doesn't even begin to describe the complex relationship I share with each of these men, but I hate to dispel her illusions. Especially when she follows up by saying, "I don't have any friends—not *real* ones, anyway."

I pat her hand. "I'm sure that's not true."

"Well, I did have one once." She wrinkles her nose, remembering. "It was this girl I used to play with when I was younger. Her dad worked for my mine, so she came over all the time. We had so much fun together. We'd dress up and splash in the fountain and share all our secrets. Regular kid stuff, you know? But our fathers got into an argument over money one day. Hers made the mistake of threatening mine and…"

I watch, horrified, as Lola gives a sad shake of her head.

"Of course I couldn't play with her after that. *You* know how it goes, Penelope. Daddy offered to get me a new friend, but I was afraid she'd have to leave, too, so I asked for a horse instead. I named him Boxcar Billie."

My first reaction is to take that poor, traumatized girl to my bosom and emphatically claim that the experiences of all criminal princesses are *not* the same, but a strange glint in Riker's eyes forestalls me.

"Did you just say Boxcar Billie?" he asks.

She nods, her long curls bobbing and eyes shining as she basks in the full force of Riker's attention.

"Boxcar Billie, as in the Thoroughbred racehorse?"

She nods again.

"Boxcar Billie, as in the freak surprise winner of the Triple Crown?"

"Oh, do you know him?" Lola claps her hands together, delighted. "He doesn't run much these days. Daddy wanted to sell him after he injured his knee, but I begged him to let me keep him. He lives at our place in Almería now, but I don't get to see him nearly as much as I'd like. He was always such a sweet horse."

"I know him," Riker says darkly. "I lost a hundred thousand dollars on that fucking horse."

"So did a lot of people," Lola confesses, laughing. I expect her to shrink from the vitriol in Riker's eyes, but she remains blissfully unaware of it. "It's how I got so interested in gambling odds in the first place. In fact, I'm using the binomial distribution for horse racing to determine the standard deviations for the tiara betting pool." She releases a wistful sigh. "Poor Bernadette."

"I thought you said the horse was named Billie?" Hijack asks, blinking in confusion.

"Bernadette was obviously her friend's name," I explain. Honestly, are these guys even listening? "And don't worry, Lola. You're not as alone as you think. You can count yourself among friends here."

I cast a stern look at Hijack and Riker, hoping they'll chime in and support her, but they refuse to acknowledge me. Hijack is busy gazing around the room with the shrewd eye of an appraiser, and Riker is still glowering over his lost investment. Lola's going to have a heck of a time getting him to notice her now. If there's one thing Riker likes less than youthful admirers, it's losing that kind of money on a fluke.

In the end, it doesn't matter, because Lola takes my offer of friendship as gospel. With a squeal of delight, she wraps her arms around me and squeezes so tight, I can barely breathe.

"Oh, Penelope, you have no idea how much that means to me. It's perfect. *You* won't be scared of Daddy, and *your* father wouldn't make the mistake of arguing with him over something as silly as money. You don't know how much I've dreamed of this day."

I swallow uneasily. In all honesty, I'm terrified of Daddy, and there's no telling what my father will do when it comes to money. And I'm hardly the ideal confidante for this sweet, trusting girl—especially once you consider the fact that my FBI agent husband is somehow tangled up with her father.

"Yes, well," I say and attempt a smile, "don't pin too

many of your hopes and dreams on me, Lola. I'm just another thief."

"You're not just a thief," she replies happily. "You're my friend."

There's not a whole lot I can do to dispel her joy after that, so I don't try. I don't have to. The entire room stops talking and buzzing as the figure of Peter Sanchez walks out onto the empty stage with a black box under his arm, the two guards flanking him.

Lola squeals again, thus confirming my suspicion that the box contains the tiara. I'd like to play it cool and pretend I'm used to seeing two-hundred-carat diamonds in real life. But like everyone else in the room, my attention is fixated on that tidy black cube.

"First, I'd like to thank you all for participating in the Luxor Tournament." Peter's voice is as soft and mild as it was last night, but there's no need for him to raise it or resort to a microphone. We're all hanging on his every word. "I had a long speech prepared to welcome you on board the *Shady Lady* and to outline the tournament rules, but my daughter urged me to throw it out. The last thing anyone wants is to hear an old man ramble about things like seating arrangements and punishments that will be meted out for anyone caught cheating. According to her, the only thing you really care about is the tiara. Lola, are you out there?"

Lola laughs and raises her hand. "Yes, Daddy. I'm here."

"Excellent. Would you mind joining me on stage?"

"Oh!" she says, eyes wide. She casts me an anxious look before returning her attention to her father. "I didn't know you needed my help."

"My beautiful daughter, everyone," Peter says. "Can we give a round of applause to get her up here?"

The crowd obliges him in that request, mostly because they're growing tense at the fanfare. Few things are more frightening than impatient thieves. I swear, if Peter opens that box and someone has stolen the tiara, he's likely to have a mutiny on his hands.

"Do you know what's going on?" Hijacks asks me in a whisper, his head tilted toward mine as we watch the crowd part for Lola's small form. "Did you know anything about this ahead of time?"

"Of course not," I whisper back. "Why would I?"

He eyes me sideways. "Just a hunch."

There's no time for me to ask what he means, because Peter chooses that moment to hand Lola the box.

"I thought about letting one of my exalted guests do the honors," he says in his mild way, "but you're an untrustworthy, thieving group, the lot of you. Besides, there's no better person to show this beauty off than my beloved daughter. Go ahead, Lola. Open it. Try it on so everyone can get a glimpse."

I don't pay nearly as much attention to Lola as I should as she lifts the lid off the box and pulls out the tiara, but I can hardly be blamed for human nature. Later, I might remember how her hands shook as she reached for the diamond or the mute, bewildered plea she cast my way, but for now, all I feel is anticipation.

Anticipation and then, when the tiara is pulled out of the box and placed on top of Lola's shining black curls, full-on laughter.

"You're kidding, right?" I ask, doing a poor job of stifling my giggles. People around me are starting to stare. "We paid a million dollars for a chance at *that* monstrosity?"

The tiara is as ungainly and unattractive as you'd expect a three-hundred-year-old piece of jewelry to be. The gold scrolls and oversized setting are too large for anyone to wear comfortably, and on Lola's sweet little head, they look even more ridiculous. It's like perching a cage on top of a baby bird and expecting it to take flight.

Of course, that doesn't make the diamond in the middle of it any less glorious. I was off in my estimation of its grandeur. It's big, heavy, simple. The facets are large and the adornments few, making it look more like a rock than a gemstone.

"That's the ugliest piece of jewelry I've seen since the Starbrite," I announce. "And that was one hideous necklace."

"I still want it," Riker says, unblinking.

"I'm going to steal it," is Hijack's contribution.

Am I the only one who realizes how dangerous it is to even say that out loud? "I think Peter Sanchez might have something to say about that," I warn.

We watch as he spins one of his fingers to get Lola to turn, almost like a dog trainer showing off his prize poodle. "Give us a twirl, Lola. Show that beauty off."

She obliges, her bright yellow skirt flaring around her.

"How does it feel?" he asks, loud enough for everyone to hear.

She laughs. "Heavy."

He smiles his appreciation and places a hand on her shoulder, gazing at her with all the apparent fondness of a father doting on his offspring. It makes me wonder where my own dad is right now. I don't see either him or Grant, which is unusual, since they both have a tendency to stand out in a crowd. Then again, they're also good at blending in when the mood suits them. Grant could be standing right behind me and I'd never hear him coming—he moves like a cat on soundless feet.

"Well, Lola, you better get used to it." Peter turns to his audience with a smile. "For the remainder of our journey, that tiara is going to remain on my daughter's head. She will not be removing it to eat, to sleep, or to bathe. She will wear it, and wear it proudly, as she moves among you. She will take it with her when she goes to bed each night. If she decides to go for a swim, it will even take a dip with her. In other words, for the next six days, she and that tiara will not be separated for any reason whatsoever."

Lola's eyes, already so oversized, look like a cartoon version of themselves as she stares up at her father.

"I know it seems unorthodox," Peter continues, raising his voice for the first time. He has to—there's no way we'd hear him otherwise. The murmured shock of five hundred people is a lot louder than you'd think. "But this is an unorthodox tournament. As I will be playing in the game myself, I can't be personally responsible for the tiara's safety, and we're already operating on a reduced crew. You've seen a handful of my personal bodyguards in the background, I'm sure, but no matter how we spread their numbers, nothing my new security advisor and I could come up with was foolproof against you savages."

We savages just stare at him.

"Which is why Mr. O'Kelly and I have decided to

put each and every one of you in charge of the tiara's security instead. For the duration of the tournament, I will have nothing to do with the Luxor. Instead, Lola will be moving around in the public eye, which means the burden is on each and every one of you to make sure no one does her—or the tiara—any harm. Day and night. Twenty-four seven. She's on your watch."

"Daddy?" Lola says, her voice small but clear. She's rooted to her spot.

I can't help but admire her restraint. My own instinct upon hearing this pronouncement is to tear through the crowd until I find my husband and kick him in the knee. This is *his* idea? To make Lola the target of five hundred hardened criminals? To put something so valuable in the hands of a child in the hopes we'll be too busy murdering one another to hurt her? I know Grant will go to unholy lengths to find his man—the fact that he's even on this boat is proof of that—but this goes beyond putting himself at risk, beyond even putting me at risk. At least I walked into this game knowing the rules, accepting them, excited and eager to play.

Lola just looks terrified.

"You'll be fine," Peter says, bestowing a fond kiss on his daughter's forehead. The fact that he presses the tiara more firmly on her head isn't lost on me—or, I note, anyone else watching the scene unfold. "I'm sure everyone here knows how precious you are to me. After all, I've entrusted the Luxor to your care, haven't I? I have no doubts they'll do *everything* they can to ensure your safety."

I could almost swear Peter looks directly at me as he says that last bit.

"You're my only daughter, Lola. You're my legacy. And now everyone on board the *Shady Lady* knows it." He turns to us with a smile so calm, you'd think he just walked in for tea. "Any questions?"

There are dozens, if not hundreds, of questions swirling around the room, but most of us are in a stunned state of shock, unable to utter them and unwilling to be the first to step up. *Where will Lola sleep? What will Peter do to her if she loses the tiara? How much force is too much force to use against the first bastard to try to wrest it from her sweet little head?*

I find myself intensely interested in that last one.

"No one has any concerns? Excellent. I knew you'd understand." Peter rubs his hands together. "Then let the games begin. You'll find your table assignment slipped under your door by morning. I expect each of you to be ready and in place at ten. Game play will continue for eight hours, with regular breaks for meals. Failure to show up at any of the designated times will result in immediate disqualification, so I suggest you set your alarms and get plenty of rest. Good luck to each and every one of you."

It's as good a dismissal as I've ever heard, but no one moves.

"Oh, and Lola and I will be heading up to the pool bar, in case any of you'd like to accompany us. You wouldn't believe how much that diamond sparkles in the sun."

With that, he turns on his heel and exits the way he came, leaving Lola to follow in his wake. I watch, blinking, as they go.

The scheme is, at once, the best and the worst security

plan I've ever heard. By placing the tiara in an easily accessible and highly visible place, Peter has almost guaranteed that one of us—if not all of us—will attempt to take it. However, by putting his own daughter in direct danger of being attacked or kidnapped or *worse*, he's also guaranteed that all of us—or at least one of us—will do everything we can to stop it.

He's essentially pitted five hundred highly capable thieves, extortionists, con artists, and murderers against one another. On a contained vessel. For six more days.

And Grant helped him do it.

Oh, man. Forget the search for Johnny Francis. Forget my being on board the *Shady Lady* to protect my husband. The next time I see that man, he's going to be in serious need of protection from *me*.

THE SEDUCTION

Riker is hot on my heels as I push my way out of the cabaret lounge to the stairwell beyond. "Holy shit. This is the best thing that's ever happened to us," he says.

"The best thing that's happened to *you*?" Hijack protests. He's also on my heels, both men close enough that I can feel the excited tension in their bodies. "You're not on her team for this. I am."

"I've always been on her team. Tell him, Pen. We never do this kind of thing without each other."

I ignore them both. The implication behind their misguided enthusiasm is that all I have to do is saunter up to Lola, ask her for the tiara, and depart the ship a very wealthy woman. In theory, I suppose that makes sense, but they're obviously not picking up on the nuances of this situation.

"If you think this is going to be another Tailortown job you can cheat me out of, you're way off the mark," Hijack says to Riker.

"I didn't cheat you out of anything," Riker protests. "You left. It was your decision."

"Well, I'm *deciding* to stay put this time. But I don't know why we're heading to the pool bar. There's not going to be any chance of grabbing the tiara now. It's going to be a madhouse up there."

"He does have a point, Pen." Riker slows his steps. "We might be better off going back to your stateroom and discussing our options first."

I pause on the landing, so angry that I'm tempted to push the pair of them down the stairs in hopes their thick skulls crack together.

"I'm not going to the bar to grab the tiara, you idiots," I say. "I'm going to see if Lola's okay. I don't know if you noticed, but she looked like she was going to pass out up there on the stage. The poor thing is frightened out of her mind."

Riker has the decency to appear ashamed of himself, but Hijack just blinks at me. "Oh, good thinking," he says. "You'll want to stay on her good side, build trust. She likes you."

I open my mouth to tell Hijack exactly what I think — that building Lola's trust is a self-serving, cruel approach only the worst kind of human would resort to — but I stop myself before the words pass my lips. He's already suspicious of my FBI husband and the fact that I've shown myself so reluctant to return to our former life of crime. Until I know what Grant's trying to do with this dangerous and highly visible Kit O'Kelly persona, I need to keep Hijack as far away from him as I can.

"She *does* like me, and I intend to keep it that way," I say. "Which is why I'm going up there alone."

"But—" Hijack begins.

I shake my head, stopping him short. "But nothing. We don't want to overwhelm her or make her think we're plotting anything. She's young, but she's not stupid, and neither one of you showed her the least bit of interest before the ceremonies. If you go up there and start flirting your heads off, she'll know something's up."

I recall the way Lola swooned at the sight of Riker's handsome, glowering face, and add, "And yes, Riker, that includes you. If you so much as bat your *gorgeous* eyes at that girl..."

The right side of his mouth pulls down in a frown. "I wouldn't do that."

I frown back. There's not a doubt in my mind that all Riker would have to do is croon a few soft-spoken words to have her eating out of the palm of his hand. She'd trust a cyclops if I said he was a friend of mine.

"Riker..."

"I *wouldn't*," he repeats, his voice hard. "She's practically a kid. I might be an asshole, but I'm not a monster."

I'm instantly contrite. Riker has his share of faults—there's no denying it—but taking advantage of people's innocence for personal gain isn't one of them. In fact, he devoted most of his adolescence to making sure my innocence couldn't be used for *anyone*'s personal gain—a thankless and tiresome job few men would have been willing to shoulder at such a young age. Or ever, really.

"I'm sorry," I say. "That was insensitive of me."

Riker tilts his head in acknowledgment of my apology.

"Yeah, well. You're an insensitive person. I'm used to it by now."

I flash him a grateful smile. Riker has never been one to hold a grudge. His anger burns hot and fast, but it rarely lasts.

"The one thing I want to do right now is make sure she's okay," I say. When neither of them moves, I make a shooing motion with my hands and add, "I mean it. You two aren't welcome. Can't you find something to entertain yourselves for a little bit? Go…play shuffleboard."

The look they share indicates that playing shuffleboard is less appealing than putting their heads together to try and figure out a way to convince me to steal the Luxor, but I can't find it in me to protest. Let them plot and plan and argue. I don't care so long as they plot and plan and argue somewhere I don't have to look at them.

As predicted, the pool area is overflowing with people by the time I arrive, though no one is in the water. Almost everyone is chatting politely and casting wary glances toward the bar at the far end. It doesn't take a genius to realize that's where I can find the tiara—and the unlucky girl attached to it.

I expect there to be an even bigger crush surrounding Lola, which is why I'm surprised to pop out of the wall of gawkers to find a wide, empty arc surrounding her. It's as if a circle has been drawn around the barstool where she's perched. Her small form shakes under the combined weight of the tiara and the pressure she's been forced to shoulder, but I'd still peg her as the bravest person out here. From the dark and suspicious glances everyone is sending each other, it's obvious they're scared out of their minds.

These fully grown adults, professionals who shoot people and steal money for a living, are scared. Of Peter Sanchez, of each other, and most importantly, of Lola.

"Oh, for crying out loud, she's just a child," I say to no one in particular. I cross the imaginary line and plop myself on the barstool next to her. She might be a child with a devil for a father and no one in a gathering of five hundred guests willing to come to her aid, but she's a child nonetheless.

"How's your breathing?" is the first question to cross my lips. "Do you have your inhaler?"

There's a glitter of unshed tears on her lashes, visible to anyone with eyes in their skull and a heart in their chest, but her lungs seem to be functioning fine.

"I'm okay," she says in a weak voice. "I don't need it."

"You're sure?" I know virtually nothing about respiratory diseases, but any ailment that could cause a person to stop breathing seems worth checking up on. "Because I can go grab it if you need. I don't mind."

And it just so happens I have the ship's master key tucked in my bra.

"No, I'm good, thank you." Once again, her voice is weak and her words short. I find I don't much care for her newfound restraint. Her bright, easy chatter was infinitely preferable to this.

"Well, this is a fine mess you've gotten yourself into, isn't it?" I ask and heave a mock sigh. Lola appears startled, but I don't back down. "I wish you'd have asked me before you decided to take up jewelry modeling, because that tiara is ridiculous on you. Your head looks like it's going to topple over at the first sign of a strong wind."

She hiccups on a laugh.

"Then again, it could prove useful if we find our-selves stranded on a desert island somewhere. With a rock that size, we could find all kinds of uses for it. Starting fires, scaling fish, slicing open coconuts…"

Her laugh turns into a giggle. "Isn't it awful?"

"Hideous," I declare.

"It's so heavy, too," she confides. "I bet when ladies used to wear it back in the olden days, they only had to keep it on for a few minutes at a time. You know, for ceremonies and stuff."

"Ten-pound weaklings, every last one of them," I proclaim. "If *I* were fortunate enough to have that sucker placed on my head, I'd never take it off again. They'd have had to bury me in it, like ancient Egyptians and their cats."

She giggles again, but with a wary smile that has me inwardly cursing my clumsiness. Reminding her of my mad love for that tiara probably isn't the smartest move while she's sitting here alone and unprotected. For all she knows, I've come up here to do exactly what Riker and Hijack wanted.

I grab her hand and squeeze it.

"I'm not going to steal the tiara from you, Lola, so you can stop worrying. You're safe with me."

Her smile is watery and fleeting, so I continue in a blasé tone, "And if you want my opinion, I doubt anyone else on board this ship will be stupid enough to try for it, either." I think but don't add, *at least while your father is watching*. "It's going to be a huge pain in your ass—and neck—to have to lug that thing around everywhere you go, but you'll be fine."

She squeezes my hand back. "Do you promise?"

I have no idea how to respond. I'm not the sort of woman to make promises easily—you wouldn't believe the kinds of persuasions Grant had to pull out to get me to agree to marry him—and I have no physical way of ensuring this girl's safety. Not only is it going to be impossible for me to follow her around when I have Johnny Francis duties to attend to, but I'm hardly an ideal bodyguard. I can't even open a jar of pickles without my big, strong husband coming to my aid.

But the words "I promise" come out of my mouth anyway. I'll have to deal with how Hijack and Riker and—oh, God, I forgot about Tara—are going to react to that bit of news later. They're not going to take this twist lightly.

"Well, well, well. I see you're being well taken care of," a low, rumbling voice says from behind us. "And here I hurried to the bar, thinking you'd be all alone."

I don't turn right away. The sound of that voice fills me with equal proportions of joy and anticipation and righteous, seething fury. Lola, however, brightens so much that I assume she and the suave Kit O'Kelly have already met.

"Mr. O'Kelly!" she cries and jumps to her feet. The quick action jostles the tiara so much that gravity takes hold, sending all two hundred of those carats tumbling to the ground.

Grant and I reach for it at the same time, the pair of us diving as if in slow motion. Just before his fingertips graze gold, he withdraws, allowing the full weight of it to land in my waiting palm instead.

Man, it feels good. Several hundred years under the

ocean mean nothing when it comes to the solid beauty of precious metals and gems like these ones. They could stay buried for millennia and never warp, never change, never bend to the ravages of time. I like how constant diamonds are. People change and circumstances get turned upside down, but a flawless gem always remains the same.

And this gem, my friends, is *flawless*.

Grant lifts the tiara from my hand. "Okay, tiger. That's enough—the rules state it has to stay on Lola's head for the duration of the tournament."

The amusement flickering in his eyes indicates that he's well aware of how mesmerized I am by the thought of taking this sucker home with me, and that he won't stop until he's wrung out as much of my agony as possible.

"I was going to give it back," I say irritably.

"Sure you were," he says and places it on Lola's head. "There you go. Good as new. Penelope and her quick hands saved you from disaster."

"Oh, do you two know each other?" Lola asks, glancing back and forth between us.

I want to admonish her to stop moving her head so much, but I manage to keep the impulse under wraps.

"Drat. That means I don't get to introduce you. And I was so looking forward to it."

Grant clears his throat. "Yes, I had the pleasure of making Penelope's acquaintance last night when she and her boyfriend joined me for dinner."

"I never said he was my boyfr—" I begin, but Lola cuts me off breathlessly.

"Oh, then you've met Hijack, too? He's awfully

good-looking, but I prefer her friend Riker. Have you seen him?" She doesn't wait for Grant to reply. "I'm sure you have—he's hard to miss. Wears all black, kind of grouchy, probably the most beautiful person I've ever met... Am I allowed to say that about a man?"

A scowl descends on Grant's previously unruffled brow. Despite the fact that I'm still annoyed with him, I laugh to see such patent jealousy taking hold. That's what he gets for taking stupid risks with his life.

"Of course you can say that," I say, my voice syrupy sweet. "Riker is one of the most beautiful people I've ever met, too. I know some women prefer a coarse kind of ruggedness in their mates"—I'm careful to avoid Grant's perfectly coarse ruggedness as I say this—"but there's something about a chiseled set of cheekbones that gets me every time."

"Attraction is a strange thing," my husband counters. "Take me, for example. I've always preferred tall, sub-servient brunettes."

I choke.

"I knew you two would get along!" Lola says with an excited clap of her hands. "Don't ask me how. I think it's because you both have such laughing eyes."

Our laughing eyes meet over Lola's head, impeded only by the impressive scrollwork of the tiara. My instinct is to back away and let a professional disinterest fall over our exchange, but Grant leans into it.

"I hate to correct a lady, Lola, but Penelope's eyes don't just laugh," he says. "They dance."

"They do, don't they?" Lola sighs. "I wish she would tell me the secret. All my eyes do is see the way people keep staring at me. I can't help thinking they're all trying to figure out how to slip into my room tonight and bash me over the head while I sleep."

The reminder of her precarious situation has me sending a glare my husband's way. He has some nerve, sauntering over here and pretending he's Lola's friend. *She* might be too innocent and trusting to understand the kind of havoc Grant can wreak on a girl, but I'm well acquainted with what can happen once he decides on a course of action.

"It does seem awfully risky, leaving you to fend for yourself with so many hardened criminals on the loose," I say. "It leaves one to wonder what kind of an imbecile was put in charge of security."

"Oh, Penelope, no…" Lola begins, but Grant cuts her off with a short laugh.

"You'll have to acquit me of such an honor," he says and bows slightly. "All credit for this scheme goes to Lola's father. I'm merely helping him with some of the more…complex details."

Complex details? Is that what he's calling this disaster? So far, he's bound himself to the owner of this ship, tied himself to the tiara's fate, and notified virtually everyone of his false name and even falser importance. If his goal was to keep a low profile on board this ship, he's earned a big fat zero points so far.

"Are you sure that's a good idea?" I ask.

He shrugs with maddening calm. "Time will tell, I suppose. We can't all of us be as famous and daring as the great Penelope Blue."

Okay, now he's goading me on purpose. "How great could I possibly be?" I mutter. "You'd never even heard of me until yesterday."

His brow lifts in a faintly mocking gesture. "Yes, but that was before I started to hear the rumors of your exploits. A whole truck full of gold, was it? I'd love to hear how—and when—you managed that."

"Oh, me too!" Lola chimes in. "Please tell us, Penelope."

As Grant knows very well I haven't done even *half* the things currently being credited to my name, I assume he thinks I started those rumors myself. Which is ridiculous. While I might have found the attention flattering at first, I've since learned that my newfound notoriety is nothing but trouble. Not only is Hijack on my case about stealing the Luxor Tiara, but I've also been brought to the attention of people like Peter Sanchez and Eden St. James.

Between the pair of us, Grant and I couldn't have pulled this thing off any worse.

"That's a story for another day," I reply with a prim lift of my chin. "Right now, I think the most important thing to do is figure out how to keep Lola out of harm's way. Or is that not part of the complex details you're attending to?"

Grant's jaw clenches tightly before he forces it to relax. "No, actually, it's not. You heard Peter. The burden of her safety rests on the general population of this boat. My assistance would interfere with his plans."

I'm unable to miss the spasm of fear that crosses Lola's face—nor the determined way she tries to stifle it.

"I'm sure I'll be fine in my room," she says, her smile wobbling. "All the locks on the *Shady Lady* are unpickable. My father had them specially installed."

My hand moves automatically to the top of my bra, where the press of the master key against my skin feels tight and hot. Unpickable the locks may be, but I have one very distinct advantage in that arena. In fact, I imagine Hijack is regretting his decision to saddle me with this responsibility—unless, of course, he has another backup key he's not telling me about.

It would be so easy for him to slip into the poor girl's room while she's unconscious, take whatever he wants and damn the consequences...

"Why don't you stay with me tonight?" I ask.

The words are out before I can stop them, and I instinctively look to Grant to see how he'll react. I expect to see another one of those angry jaw flexes, his natural protective instincts rising up and demanding I play a more cautious game, but there's no mistaking the warm regard I see there. His eyes aren't laughing, and they definitely aren't dancing. If I had to pick an action, I'd say they're *admiring*.

Flustered at the heat of that dark, liquid gaze, I quickly add, "I won't be able to do much if someone comes at us with a club, but you'll feel better knowing you're not alone. And my father is right next door—we can open the passageway so he'll be able to hear if anything happens."

"Oh, Penelope, can I?" Lola gasps. "You wouldn't mind? Really and truly?"

"Really and truly," I say. "But you should probably check with your dad to make sure it's allowed. I don't care what Kit says—I find it hard to believe that he doesn't have other plans for securing you and that tiara tonight."

She frowns deeply and shakes her head, the transition

from happiness to despair so fast, it seems unreal. "No, Mr. O'Kelly is right. Daddy isn't going to help. He told me so as we were leaving the stage. He wants me to show some responsibility and backbone for a change."

Oh, man. I'd like to show *him* what he can do with his backbone.

Grant must see some of my murderous intent, because he clears his throat. "You don't have to ask his permission, Lola, but you should probably let him know what you're up to. I'm sure he'll rest easier knowing you're among friends."

"I suppose," she says and surveys the bar for a sign of her father. He's not difficult to spot, as he's seated at a corner booth in the company of what looks like a tall, subservient brunette. I guess he and Kit O'Kelly have that in common. "I'll be right back. You won't leave without me, Penelope?"

The heartbreaking way she voices the request almost has me marching across the bar with her to give Peter Sanchez a piece of my mind, but Grant stills me with a slight shake of his head. I guess upbraiding a criminal overlord will have to wait for later.

Without Lola there to act as a buffer, a heavy tension settles between us. There are so many questions I want to ask Grant, so many things I don't understand, but this is hardly the time or the place to voice them. Even with the arc of emptiness around us, several heads are turned our way, watching us interact. If we show too much familiarity, people will start to ask questions.

"That was a good thing you did, offering to stay with Lola tonight," he says, leaning back against the bar with an air of calm assurance.

"Yes, well, someone had to. What Peter is doing to that girl is unconscionable. I find it hard to believe that anyone could be so—"

Another shake of Grant's head has me quelling my rage to a more controllable simmer. With a deep breath, I change my tack. "You and he seem awfully close," I say as neutrally as possible. "How long have you known each other?"

"We go way back," he says. "A whole day, in fact."

Gee, how helpful. "And did you know ahead of time what he was going to do?"

His sharp look contains yet another warning, which adds to my mounting frustration. I've never been great at blindly following orders, especially when they come from him, and feeling as though I'm missing an important part of the puzzle doesn't help. Especially not when there's so much at stake.

"Dammit, Kit, I know you're more involved in this than you're letting on," I hiss. "If we're going to make this work, you have to give me *something*."

He looks pained at my indiscretion, but there's not much he can do about it in a public venue. I don't care. I want answers, and I don't know how else to get them. A terrycloth swan isn't going to cut it this time.

"Lola was right, you know," he says in an overloud voice. At first, I think he's trying to cover for my slipup, but he's moving in. One of his arms is on the bar top; the other reaches for me, stopping just short of my face as he tucks a wayward strand of hair behind my ear. That small brush of his fingers against my lobe is enough to set my heart skittering.

"About what?" I ask, trusting neither his fingers nor

my heart. Both have a way of getting me in trouble where this man is concerned.

"About the two of us getting along." He leans in closer, though his voice doesn't lower any. "I haven't been able to stop thinking about the way you looked in the moonlight."

I jolt back as if burned. Is my husband *flirting* with me?

"And again this morning at the track, all grumpy and rumpled as you struggled to keep up with us. How are your wounds?"

Instead of allowing me to answer, he takes one of my hands in his. Cupping the appendage gently, he runs his fingers over the edges of the scrape. He also leans down and blows, the cool air of his breath skimming over the surface of my palm. Even though the hot afternoon sun is blazing overhead, I shiver.

"I'll live," I manage, my voice strangled. "But I hope you realize that woman tripped me on purpose."

"Who, Eden? No." He peeks up at me, dark eyes glinting. "What possible reason could she have?"

"Gee, I don't know," I say with heavy sarcasm. "To rid the *Shady Lady* of my troublesome presence?"

He doesn't pick up my lure for information. "Uh-oh. Sounds like someone might be jealous."

"Of your long night prowling the corridors with a six-foot, perfect-haired thief?" I scoff. "I barely know you. What you do with your free time is of no interest to me."

"Can I be honest with you?" he asks.

I can't think of anything I'd like more. "Please do."

He nods across the bar to where Lola is nodding contritely at her father. "I wish I was the one saddled with the tiara for the rest of this trip instead of her."

I don't. This situation is complicated enough as it is. Nor is his revelation terribly helpful in *un*complicating it.

"No offense, but I don't think it would suit you," I say. "You strike me as more of a gold watch sort of guy."

He disarms me with a full crinkly eyed smile. "You're probably right. But if *I* was the one wearing the tiara, then I'd be the one who gets to spend the night in your bed. I can't tell you how much I'd love to be under your…protection."

Oh, crap. He's flirting again.

"Of course, we'll have to get rid of that pesky boyfriend of yours first," he says leadingly.

I refuse to take his bait. "My pesky boyfriend might have something to say about that."

"A husband at home, a boyfriend on the side…" Grant makes a soft tsking sound. "You're a very busy woman, Penelope Blue. Unfortunately, I'm not a very patient man."

I gulp.

"Daddy thinks it's a great idea!" Lola lopes back to the bar with new enthusiasm and impeccable timing. "He wanted me to convey my thanks for your help, Penelope, and also to tell Mr. O'Kelly that if he's done trying to seduce dangerous beauties, he could use your input on whether you suggest video cameras in the cabaret lounge tomorrow."

Instead of taking offense at being found out, Grant laughs. "Am I that obvious?" he asks, his dark eyes boring into mine. His look is both proprietary and predatory. A flood of intense longing moves through me at the sight of it, settling heavily at the apex of my thighs.

I forgot how good Grant could be at this wooing stuff when he puts his mind—and his body—to it.

"Oh, yes," Lola says, not the least bit discomfited at finding herself in the middle of our flirtation. "Even I can tell there's something between you two, and I'm terrible at reading facial cues."

"You hear that, Penelope?" Grant says with a quirk of his brow. "Even Lola can tell there's something between us. Strange that you should be the only one so unaware."

I have no response to that, so it's just as well that Grant chooses that moment to lift my hand to his lips, his gesture similar to the one last night. This time, however, he turns my hand over and lands a kiss on my wrist. The press of his lips against my pulse point is soft and sensual, sending a ripple of delight though both me and Lola. Her gasp is almost equal to mine.

"I'll see you at the games tomorrow," he says, his voice rumbling. "Hopefully, you won't be placed at my table. I'd hate to have to ruin your chances of making it to the next round."

Yeah, right. He'd love it. That man lives to challenge me.

"I wouldn't be too sure about that," I reply archly. "After all, luck is supposed to be a lady."

"Yes, but my instincts tell me you're anything but that. A *woman*, certainly." His gaze flicks lazily up and down my body, lingering on the parts that assert my femininity the loudest. "But not, I think, a lady."

He's absolutely right. If he keeps sucking all the air from between us, filling it with an animal magnetism that pulses in my veins, all pretense at decorum will vanish.

So I laugh as naturally as I can and take my hand

back. "I think that's enough of that for one day," I say. "Until the poker tournament, Kit O'Kelly. I'm almost looking forward to it."

"That makes two of us," he says with a slight bow.

Lola and I both watch as Grant moves across the lounge to where her father sits. Grant's head is held high, and there's a whistle on his lips. And, I don't need to add, his figure is an image of masculine perfection. I swear, if I hadn't already succumbed to that man's damnable arrogance and swaggering charm, this would have sealed my fate.

"Oh, he *likes* you," Lola says in a whoosh of air.

"Not as much as he likes the idea of beating me at my own game," I mutter. "Take my word for it, Lola, and avoid men like that at all costs. They're nothing but trouble."

My advice is similar to what Tara bestowed on me twenty-four hours ago, and I sigh to think how far I've come in that time. The tides have turned, our fates reversed. I'm the master and Lola my pupil.

In other words, both of us are doomed.

There's a towel animal waiting for me when we get back to my room. Despite my many attempts to convince Lola that she wanted nothing more than to spend her day napping and getting repeat full-body massages, she insisted on making the most of our time together. Lola sitting alone at a pool bar might be a shaking, miserable heap of a girl, but Lola with Penelope Blue at her side is up for anything.

Anything, as it turns out, is code for bowling with

Riker and Hijack, getting pedicures with Jordan, helping the chef in the kitchen make five hundred chocolate lava cakes, and finally—finally—sitting down long enough to watch the sun set at the end of the day.

I've never been so exhausted in my life.

"Oh, you get your towels made into animals?" Lola flings herself on the bed, reaching for today's creation, which is a penguin balancing a pair of my sunglasses on the top of his beak. "That's no fair. Mine have just been folded and put away every time."

"No, don't open him," I cry, and leap across the room to pull him out of her arms. I want nothing more than to rip into the little guy and see how Grant intends to explain himself for that show at the bar earlier today, but not while Lola is present.

"I, uh, want to keep him intact for as long as possible," I explain somewhat sheepishly. "I have a thing for penguins."

"You do?"

Even sweet-tempered Lola finds that odd, so I do my best to move the conversation along.

"The poker game starts at ten tomorrow, so we should get to bed early," I say, and casually set the penguin on the side table. My sunglasses slide off, dislodging his beak and showing the edge of a slip of paper protruding like a tongue. "You should take a shower—I'm sure you need it after our big day."

"With this thing on, though?" she asks and touches the tiara on her head.

I'd almost forgotten it was there. It's strange to think I could get used to the sight of two hundred carats in just a few hours, but the tiara no longer has the same dazzling effect. I can't help wondering if that's part of Peter Sanchez's plan—to get us all so inured to the sight of it, it's just another twenty-million-dollar rock.

"Well, your father did say you'd have to wear it in the shower, but unless he somehow sneaked cameras past *my* dad…"

At the mention of her father, Lola's lips pull down. "No, you're right. I better follow Daddy's orders to the letter. It's the only way. If I take the tiara off and something happens to it, he'll be sure to blame you for it. We wouldn't want another Bernadette situation."

Um, yeah. We definitely don't want that.

"Just do the best you can," I say and direct her toward the bathroom. "You go in there and relax. It's been a big day."

"It has, hasn't it?" she asks, her chest rising. "I think it might be the best day I've ever had."

It takes me a moment to follow her line of reasoning. I meant the term *big day* as a euphemism for exhausting day, emotionally draining day, a day in which her father revealed himself to be the most ruthless and uncaring parent in the world. If it were me in her place and my father traded my safety and well-being for the sake of a stupid diamond, I'm not sure I would've had the strength to make it through.

To Lola, however, there's nothing but joy in the hours she spent in the company of me and my friends. Sure, there were five hundred people keeping a close watch on her, and yes, her death was a possibility at every turn, but for the first time in her hard, strange, isolated life, she got to enjoy herself like a normal young woman.

My heart, already strained with empathy for the girl, cracks.

"Take your time in there," I say roughly. "I'm not going to shower until the morning, so there's no hurry."

"Thank you, Penelope," she says.

She looks as if she wants to add more, but I turn away to prevent any additional outpourings of gratitude. There's nothing to thank me for—not really—and I still have reservations about my ability to keep her out of harm's way. Especially if, as the rumors suggest, the likes of Eden St. James, Two-Finger Tommy, and Johnny Francis are lying in wait for the first opportunity to steal that tiara.

I wait until I can hear the water running before I tear into the penguin, hoping for a long, rambling explanation of Grant's intentions and what he wants me to do next.

So of course I don't get one.

I knew I could count on the great Penelope Blue. Keep that tiara safe for me, okay?

And that's it. No mention of Kit O'Kelly's intentions or how the hunt for Johnny Francis is progressing. There's not even a hint about what he's doing in Peter Sanchez's pocket. Just some basic instructions.

It's so typical of him. High-handed mystery is his default status.

As I prepare to rip the paper to shreds so I can dispose of the evidence, I notice a postscript on the back. That, too, is so typical of Grant, I can't help but laugh.

You dated that guy? Really?

I can practically see him shaking his head at me from the other side of the boat.

I think I preferred it when I only had Riker to worry about.

THE VISITOR

11

My dad doesn't appear in his room before we're ready to turn in, which means I'm forced to leave the adjoining door slightly ajar with a note informing him that he should keep an ear out for attempts at robbery and/or murder. A note's not how I prefer to do things, but I also don't want to leave Lola alone for any length of time to hunt him down, so it has to do.

I also follow Grant's directions and channel my inner FBI agent to make a full sweep of the room. I start with the balcony—which, if *I* was planning on making a clandestine entry, is exactly where I'd get in. Several of the rooms on this side of the ship have outdoor balconies, which means a crafty thief could leap from one to another, slowly but surely making her way toward this one. Granted, hanging off the side of a moving cruise ship is a pretty strong deterrent, but given the quality of thieves aboard this boat, it's a definite possibility.

There don't seem to be any hooks or carabiners in my line of sight, but I slick the railings with a bottle of coconut-scented body oil from my bathroom anyway. It's a terrible waste of the oil, which smells quite nice under the wide Caribbean sky. I also feel slightly guilty at the thought of sending one of my peers careening off the side of the ship and into the ocean, but a girl's gotta do what a girl's gotta do.

Hopefully, anyone trying to head in this way will have a security harness on. Or at least a life raft waiting down below.

That task completed, I lock the sliding door securely and draw the curtains tight before I start knocking on the walls to see if any sound hollow.

"What are you doing?" Lola asks from the bed. She's much better at this whole girls' night sleepover thing than I am, sitting cross-legged as she braids her damp hair. The tiara is perched carefully on top of her head, glinting like a party favor.

"I'm making sure no one can sneak in while we're sleeping," I say and keep knocking. I might not be good at braiding, but this I can do. "How's the battery life on your cell phone?"

"Um…decent. Why?"

"I'd like to set it up near the door with a motion detector app. It's not the best tech in the world, but it's better than nothing. Does this wall panel sound different to you?"

She unfolds herself from the bed and places her ear against the wall. "Do it again."

I knock on that one and the panel next to it, but Lola shakes her head. "They sound the same to me." She pauses. "You're really good at this sort of thing. Do people sometimes hire you to be their bodyguard?"

"Not if they want to stay alive for very long," I say. But then I see her stricken face and regret my flippant words. "I'm sorry—that wasn't a very good joke."

It's an accurate one, though. As the bodyguard of one Agent Grant Emerson, I'm failing spectacularly. I haven't thought about Johnny Francis or the FBI in hours.

"If you want to know the truth, all I'm doing is figuring out the different ways *I* might try to get into this room undetected," I explain. "Then I'm making sure no one else can do the same."

She perks. "You'd have climbed onto the balcony from the outside?"

"I might have, yes."

"Even with the bowed grade of descent?"

I stare at her. "The what now?"

"The way the ship curves on the outside," she explains in a tone so matter-of-fact, she might be telling me about what she had for dinner. "When you rappel down a cliff, there's usually a straight or measurable angle from the top. But between the *Shady Lady*'s shape and her velocity as she moves through the water, you'd have to account for—"

"Yeah, um, I don't know what any of that means. I would have just charmed my way into a room a few doors down and jumped from balcony to balcony."

"Oh," she says, nonplussed. "I guess that would work, too."

I pause. "So…you're like a mathematical genius, right?"

"Oh, no. Not me." She laughs and shakes her head,

whipping her wet braid over one shoulder. A few droplets flick my cheek. "I can remember things like numbers and facts, but I don't know anything else. I only finished high school because Daddy got me private tutors, and even then, he had to pay someone off for my diploma. He's always telling me how useless I am. He wanted to teach me the family business so I could carry it on when he retires—kind of like you and your dad—but I couldn't do it. I don't like to hurt people."

I don't say anything. And here I thought *my* family was messed up.

"If you didn't manage to get in through the balcony, what else would you have tried?" she asks brightly.

There's nothing in her tone to indicate she's suffering from the aftereffects of a cruel and unusual upbringing, so I answer her as levelly as I can.

"I might cut through a wall panel—which is what I'm sounding for now—or find a hiding place to wait in. I looked in all the cupboards and the laundry basket, but they're clear. So are the suitcases."

"Oh, of course." She nods. "Like the Tailortown job."

"Exactly."

"Would you also try to come through the door?" Lola asks. "That's why you want my cell phone?"

I don't tell her about Hijack's master key still tucked in my bra.

"It's just a precaution," I say. "Given how secure these locks are, a door entry isn't likely. There are too many people, both staff and guests, milling around in the hallway—and thanks to your dad's threat, the last thing anyone wants is a witness to this theft. But it never hurts to be safe."

"You sure know a lot about this stuff," Lola says. "I'm glad you're on my side. I feel a lot better knowing you won't let anything bad happen to me. You won't, will you?"

I wince. "About that, Lola…"

"You're wrong when you say anyone under your protection would end up dead. I don't think that's true. I don't think that's true at all." A wobbly smile crosses her lips. "Anyone lucky enough to have you looking out for them is sure to be okay."

Even though I want to correct her misguided assumptions, words are having a hard time escaping the tight squeeze of my throat. I hope she's right. There are far too many people on this boat depending on me.

"You better secure that tiara to your head and get to sleep," I say, mostly to forestall any other emotional outpourings. "I'm going to bunk down near the sliding glass door. I'm not sure I trust that coconut oil to do the trick."

"That doesn't sound very comfortable," Lola says with a frown.

No, it doesn't. But the couch is bolted down, so I have no choice but to grab a pillow and head for the floor. It's not ideal, but since the alternative is to disappoint all the people on board this boat counting on me to keep them alive, I don't see what other choice I have.

I only get a few indifferent hours of sleep before I hear the muffled sounds of the first attempt on our lives.

Sleeping on the floor turns out to be a great way to stay vigilant and wary of intruders, because the deep ache of my hips grinding against the floor makes it impossible to get comfortable for more than a few minutes at a time. I toss and turn and wedge pillows in unlikely places, but nothing seems to do the trick. It only takes a slight scratching and a hissed whisper in the distance to jolt me to awareness.

My first thoughts are of Lola and her twenty-million-dollar burden. Clutching my bedding like a weapon, I prepare to smother and/or pillow-fight the intruder to the death. But other than the gentle and steady sound of the girl's breathing, I detect nothing amiss. The glint of the diamond on her pillow provides enough light for me to see the dark swirls of her hair that have come loose and wound their way around the tiara's prongs. Those will be awful to untangle in the morning, but she appears to be fine otherwise.

And who wouldn't be, on that cloud of a bed with all those lovely pillows padding her hips?

More furtive movements sound to my left. I force my creaking bones into a crouched position and cock my head to try and ascertain the direction it's coming from. The dark shadows of the room make it impossible to see every corner, but the blinking red light of Lola's phone at the door and the lack of movement behind me indicate that the two most obvious portals are secure.

As quietly as possible, I shift to the edge of the room and wait for the sound to return.

It comes a few seconds later, this time as a low-throated laugh and a purring sound I can't place. Unless I'm mistaken, the intruder is near the conjoining door to my father's room. I hold my smothering pillow tighter.

The unknown sound picks up again, followed shortly by a soft thump and a muted, "Oh, Warren…"

Okay. Yep. I've got a pretty good idea what's going on now, and I regret everything.

"The door to the other room is locked, right?" the female voice says, soft and indistinct. "I wouldn't want anyone to…"

Overhear the sounds of my dad having sex with some random woman he picked up on the cruise? Yeah, that would be a terrible thing to foist on a girl.

My father murmurs some kind of response, which increases in volume as he approaches the door. I can tell the exact moment he realizes it's ajar, his pause heavy as he reads the note I left informing him of my visitor.

"I'll be damned. She's either the most brilliant thief in the world or the most foolish," he says. "She's got the girl in there with her."

I can't make out the woman's reply, which I assume is delighted surprise. And why wouldn't she be delighted? My father is a remarkably good thief—there's no denying it—but it appears he's just as stupid as every other man when sex is on the line. He basically just told that woman where she can find quick and unsecured access to the Luxor Tiara.

There's another laugh and the snick of the latch closing. I also hear the telltale click as my dad locks the door from his side. The added security doesn't make me feel comforted. I'm happy my dad isn't wallowing in his loneliness, of course, but what's stopping that woman from sneaking in here as soon as his passions are sated and taking what she wants?

Unfortunately, I know the answer to that question. *Me*.

As quietly as I can, I also turn the lock from my side.

Yanking my blankets close, I abandon my post by the balcony to resume a long night of not-sleep closer to his door instead. At this rate, I *might* be able to sneak a few hours of shut-eye before dawn.

The great Penelope Blue is starting to seriously regret she ever agreed to this trip.

THE
COMPETITION

12

THE NEXT MORNING DAWNS BRIGHT AND CLEAR — AND BY bright and clear, I'm talking about the diamond on Lola's head, not my mood. Although it's a relief to see the tiara intact and us with it, I can't help but feel uneasy about any visitors still resting next door. The last thing I want to do is confront my father regarding his late-night booty call, but I fear the task lies in my immediate future.

Yay, me.

Lola, in her bright optimism, notices nothing amiss. Like so many of the people in my life, she's up way too early and with way too much enthusiasm about the day ahead. I guess it could be worse. At least she's not trying to make me drink algae.

"We have just enough time to grab breakfast before the games start," she says as she gets dressed. She's still weirdly obsessive about following her father's instructions to the letter, which means I have to help her as she tries to pull a shirt on around the tiara's prongs. "You didn't change your mind about letting me sit with you, right? I can still keep you company at the table?"

"As long as the rest of the players don't mind, I can't see why not." In fact, I think they'd prefer it that way. Nothing feeds the competitive spirit like a highly visible prize. "I'm sure they'll all agree that your safety is the most important thing."

I reach something of an impasse as I search my own bag for something to wear. While I'd like to keep up my new reputation by wearing something daring and authoritative, eight hours is a long time to sit at a table playing cards. My instinct says to go full yoga pants and forget about the rest.

In the end, I go for the middle ground—an asymmetrical top and a tight black skirt that, if you cut a few inches off the hem, might pass for something Tara would wear. I sigh as I think about the likelihood of her descending on me tomorrow and picking my clothes out for me.

Lola hears the sigh and assumes it's meant for her. "I promise not to talk any more than necessary," she says and makes the motion of a zipper over her lips. "I'll just sit quietly and observe. I can, you know, especially when people are doing something like playing poker. When my brain is busy, my mouth takes a rest."

I pause in the act of slipping a pair of flat-soled sandals on my feet. I don't like the way that *busy brain* part sounds—especially since I'm starting to understand the way her brain works. "Um…can you count cards, Lola?"

"Of course!" Her wide-eyed incredulity suggests that *not* counting cards would be a much stranger occurrence. "I mean, I don't do it on purpose, and Daddy says that under no circumstances am I to let anyone know about my abilities, but it's impossible to turn it off once the cards start flipping over. That's why Daddy won't let me play in the tournament. I always win."

I bite back a groan. As if there weren't enough problems with this girl. Of course she'd be some kind of poker whiz on top of everything else.

"I hate to say this, Lola, but if you can count cards, I'm not sure you should sit at the table with me. If word gets out, people might think I'm cheating."

"Oh." Her face falls. "That would be bad."

Yeah. *Bad* is right.

"Maybe you can find a seat in the nearby bleachers," I suggest. "I doubt anyone is going to take the tiara in such a public place. That's the whole point of your dad's security plan—you literally have hundreds of bodyguards."

"You're right. Of course you're right." Lola's smile is so sudden and pronounced, I know it's fake. "I wouldn't want to be in the way any more than I already am."

"You're not in the way," I say automatically, but we both know it's a lie. I try to alleviate some of the sting with, "I'll tell you what. Why don't we ask Jordan to sit with you so you don't have to be alone? She was planning on watching today anyway, and it might be fun. You guys can talk chemistry and math together."

"She won't mind?"

I don't say what I'm thinking—*even if she does mind, she's too nice to say so out loud.* "Of course not. She'll probably enjoy having you explain how card counting works. Next to you, she's the smartest person I know."

A flush of color spreads across her cheeks. "I told you, I'm not smart. I don't know anything about the real world."

Yes, well. A few years ago, neither did I. Since marrying Grant and plunging myself into this messy, complicated place where good meets bad, I've come to realize that I'm only as smart as the people who have my back. It just so happens that the people who have my back are pretty freaking brilliant.

"The real world is overrated," I say and grab the phone to ring up Jordan. "But the benefits of friends like mine are not."

I can't decide whether or not it's a good thing that I don't recognize any of the people at my table.

The tournament is set up with seven tables, each of which has been assigned seven players. For the first few days, we'll be playing in a process of elimination—each game will continue until there's a single winner at every table, at which point the winners move on to the final game. That's where the real competition will take place—assuming, of course, that the tiara is still around by that point.

Not everyone has arrived by the time I find my table and settle in, but the four men sitting in surly silence on the other side of the green felt aren't inspiring me with much excitement about the game ahead. I know we all paid a million dollars for this chance, but I thought it was supposed to be *fun*.

"See the older guy in the visor sitting down next to Riker?" Hijack asks from my right. He's not playing against me, but he's using this opportunity to discreetly catch me up on the competition. I'm not sure how he knows so much about these people, but his insight comes in handy. I doubt even Grant has as much information at his fingertips.

"Yeah, I see him. Who is it?"

"That's Two-Finger Tommy."

I recognize the name as one of the top contenders for stealing the tiara, which explains why Hijack is pointing him out. For him, this event is less about winning poker and more about beating everyone else to the Luxor.

I swear, he seemed almost disappointed to see me and Lola arrive this morning with the tiara in tow. Did he honestly think it was going to be that easy to steal? Even if I *was* in the market to take it, the heist would have to be an intricately planned balance of getting the goods while simultaneously defraying all suspicion so as to avoid Peter Sanchez's murderous vengeance. That's not the kind of plan a girl can come up with on the fly.

I mean, I *could* do it, but...

"You'll be interested to know that Two-Finger spent most of last night in the stateroom directly below yours," Hijack goes on to say. "It belongs to one of the spectators—that guy in the windbreaker sitting on the far right of the stands. He goes by the name of Rainier. He's not much to be afraid of, wanted for a few petty burglaries and drug possessions, but word is he's willing to trade rooms to the highest bidder. My guess is Two-Finger wants to be that man."

"Geez. You didn't waste any time, did you?"

"One of us has to be on top of things," Hijack replies.

"You're lucky he didn't tunnel through the floor while you slept."

That's a possibility? Oh, goody. This trip keeps getting better and better.

"Where are you playing?" I ask, mostly to avoid having to spend any more time looking at Two-Finger's craggy face, which seems to be growing more sinister by the minute.

"I'm at table five." Hijack jerks his head toward the middle of the room. "So far, no one of any note is playing against me, so I should take it easily. Your father will be at four, and your stepmother is surrounded by her admirers at one. They're both considered the favorites to win at their tables, but that will come as no surprise to you. Um, let's see…who else do we need to worry about?"

We notice her at the same time, though Hijack is the first to speak. "Aha—Eden St. James," he says, grinning at me. "Your new best friend."

I don't like the way that sounds. I also don't like the purposeful gait to Eden's walk, which seems to be headed straight toward us.

"Where is she playing?" I ask, my mouth dry. "Hijack, please tell me she's not coming this way. Is she coming this way?"

But it's too late. She's already here.

"Hello, gentlemen." Eden approaches the table with a nod for the four seated men and a smirk for me. Her voice carries the same clipped undertones I remember from the track yesterday, though I could swear it drops a whole octave when she adds, "And Penelope Blue. My, my. Isn't this a delightful surprise?"

"Delightful," I echo and look to Hijack to see if he

has anything to add to the conversation. I swear to all that is good and holy, if placing her at my table is somehow his doing…

I can't tell. There's a look of calculation on his face as he appraises her, but that could just be admiration for the deeply plunging neckline of her pantsuit.

The ten-minute warning bell sounds, informing us that it's time to take our places or risk immediate disqualification. I consider it both a blessing and a curse—a blessing, because Hijack finally peels himself away to settle at his own table, and a curse, because I'm now stuck with Eden St. James for the next eight hours of my life.

"How are your wounds?" she asks in a false show of concern as she sits in the chair directly to my right. "I hope they're not going to get in the way of your poker playing. Abrasions can get nasty on their second day."

So can she, apparently.

"I'm a lot tougher than I look, thanks."

"Well, you could hardly be less, could you?" she says with an evil smile. She proceeds to introduce herself to each of the men sitting at the rest of the table. There are five of them now, the last straggler just as blandly and ominously ferocious as the rest. I try to pay attention to their names, but I'm too busy noticing that everyone is in place and ready to start playing—with one notable and, to me, very important exception.

When Grant finally arrives alongside Peter Sanchez and his requisite bodyguards, it's with a mere two minutes to spare. The pair of them chat in an amiable and unconcerned way, knowing full well the game won't get underway without them. In fact, Grant takes the time to stop by our table, beaming as though nothing could make him happier than to find Eden and me thrown together again.

"Well, well, well," he says. "It looks like this is the table where all the fun will be happening."

He stands directly behind the two of us, a hand on the back of either of our chairs. I twist to peer up at him, wondering if there's a hidden meaning somewhere in there. I can't see much from this position, but the scrape of late-night stubble across his jaw does catch my eye.

I know that stubble. I *love* that stubble. I'm also aware that it means he's not nearly as rested as he'd like everyone to believe.

"A pity we can't switch seats, or I'd ask one of these men to make the trade," Eden says sweetly. "It would be fun going up against a man of your many…talents."

Wouldn't it just?

"Look on the bright side," Grant replies easily, his gaze careful not to stray in my direction. "Maybe we'll both come out victorious and meet at the winner's table."

"One can hope," she says with a purr.

"You'll have to do a lot more than hope," I grumble. "There are six other people sitting at this table, every one of whom would like a chance at that tiara."

"Speaking of, where is the pièce de résistance?" Grant asks. It doesn't take him long to spot Lola in the front row of the stands, chatting unconcernedly with Jordan. "Ah. I see you managed to keep both the jewels and the girl safe. You have my admiration."

Grant's admiration is something I tend to value pretty highly in the general order of things, but right now, I'd like to stick it in places better left unmentioned. He doesn't get to flirt with Eden and mock me at the same time. It's one or the other.

"How do you know I didn't swap out the diamond for a fake while Lola slept last night?" I ask. "We could all be playing for a two-hundred-carat counterfeit, and no one would ever know."

That gets the table's attention—and not in a good way. Six murderous glances rocket over the green felt, but Grant just laughs.

"I was warned about you, Penelope Blue," he says, reverting to the rhyming singsong of our courtship. "I was told you're adept at twisting truth and reality, that you always toy with your victims before you go in for the kill. I see my sources are correct."

Please. His sources are biased against me, mostly because his sources are *him*. I only twist truth and reality where he's concerned—and I do it because he does plenty of twisting on his own. A contortionist I might be, but that man knows how to wriggle out of a tight spot just fine.

"All the more reason not to cross me," I say. "You wouldn't want to be next on my list of victims."

"I don't know," he says and leans down so close, his lips are touching my ear. His breath is warm and intimate, but despite the spike in temperature, I shiver. "I have the feeling that falling at your feet would bring far more pleasure than pain."

I don't have a glib response for that one, not while my heart does somersaults in my throat and the rough scratch of his stubble abrades my jawline. As it turns out, I don't need one, because the starting bell sounds, stopping him short. But not short enough—Eden must have overheard our exchange, because she watches with a queer light in her eyes as Grant takes his leave.

"That's my cue," he says and lays another one of those killing smiles on us both. "The best of luck to you, ladies. Not that either one of you will need it."

I'm not so sure about that as our dealer takes his place and barks an order for us to ante, a no-nonsense expression settling on his brow. I'm even less sure when Eden crosses one long leg over the other and applies herself to her cards with an intensity that doesn't bode well for my chances.

And I have absolutely no confidence at all when Grant takes his seat at table five.

Right across from Hijack.

THE GAME

13

"THAT MAKES ANOTHER WIN FOR EDEN ST. JAMES," THE dealer says, grinning deeply as Eden rolls a blue chip— one of the expensive ones—across the felt as a tip. "The bell for last call just sounded, so get ready for your final ante of the day."

Six chips are tossed into the middle of the table with a soft clank. One of the men lost already—just a few hours in, actually. He was fine until Eden asked him if he planned to blink that rapidly every time he bluffed, because it was starting to get on her nerves. I've never seen anyone strive—and fail—so valiantly not to close his eyes. He and his dry eyeballs lost pretty soon after that.

"Are you sure you want to bet that much?" Eden asks me as the game continues and I push a stack of my chips forward. "At this rate, you won't have anything to play with tomorrow."

"I'm sure." The pair of jacks winking up at me

promise a change in my fortunes. "Even *your* winning streak eventually has to come to an end."

From the looks of it, I'm not alone among my friends and relatives in finding the first day of poker to be off to a discouraging start. Of everyone in the room, only my dad and Grant appear to be enjoying themselves—my father, because emotion of any kind is rarely allowed a chance to surface, and Grant, because I presume he's baiting Hijack to within an inch of his life. At least, that's the vibe I'm picking up from the way the pair of them keep facing off across their table.

According to my tally at the last break, both Riker and Tara are also losing heavily, which means Team FBI isn't doing so well overall—not good news. If each of us ends up getting kicked off our tables within the first few days, our access to Johnny Francis suspects is going to be severely restricted.

Of all of us, though, poor Lola is in the worst position. Long since done trying to hold that tiara high, she's curled up on the bleachers, her head in Jordan's lap. Even though her father is seated just a few feet away, fully capable of lifting her burden, he hasn't looked over at her even once.

Peter, I need hardly mention, is playing just fine.

"That's another full house for me," Eden says with a cluck of her tongue as she pulls the stacks of chips to her side of the table. "How far down does that make you for the day, Penelope? Three hundred thousand? Four?"

Worse. By my last count, I've lost about half my money so far.

"I was just lulling you into a false sense of security,"

I say. "And planting fake tells so you think you know my every move. Did you notice them?"

Her sharply narrowed eyes indicate that she took careful note of everything I said or did, though of course none of it was planted. I'm not so sophisticated a player as that.

"Is this what Kit was talking about earlier?" she asks. "Are you toying with me by playing around with the truth?"

Well, yes. It's all I *can* do, especially since an honest win isn't in the cards, so to speak. Eight hours spent in this woman's company have shown me two things: one, that I actively dislike her; and two, that she has a much cooler head than I do. Not even a threat to hunt down and eat everyone she's ever loved could cause her to misplay her cards.

These people are kind of scary.

"Kit O'Kelly is an incorrigible flirt who would say anything if he thought it would put him at the center of attention," I say as I rise from the table. "I wouldn't believe a word out of his mouth if I were you."

She stays seated, presumably to oversee the dealer counting out our money for tomorrow's game. "I don't. But then, I don't believe a word out of yours, either. You two are up to something."

We two are up to a lot of things, but I'm not about to share them with this woman.

"You think?" I say. "And here I thought he was just trying to get in my bed."

Her laughter is genuine. "That makes one of us. He certainly didn't want in mine."

"Oh, really?" I try to keep the smugness out of my

voice, but it's difficult. My husband might be a manipulative, mule-headed idiot nine-tenths of the time, but he's a manipulative, mule-headed, loyal one.

"Yes, really," she replies without looking at me. "I've never flirted so hard with a man as I did with Kit the night we prowled the ship together. He flirted back, but it was all superficial. No man has been less interested in me my entire life."

"Maybe he finds your personality off-putting. You can't tell me that hasn't happened to you before."

This time, her laugh is so loud, it takes me aback. "Why, Penelope Blue. I think you're growing on me."

I'm immediately on alert. "I thought you said you were immune to being charmed."

"Yes, well. That was before I knew you were on such close terms with Lola Sanchez. You're useful to me now."

My admiration for the woman moves up a notch, but so does my internal alarm. Between Hijack's flattery, Eden's sudden burst of attention, and all the fake rumors floating around this boat, I might be the most popular woman around, but I'm not so self-deluded as to think *I'm* the real focus. Right now, I'm the thief with the best access to that tiara, period. That's all anyone cares about.

"Being useful to you is, of course, at the top of my list of priorities," I say dryly and leave it at that. As much as I'd like to keep pressing Eden for information, I have a few more days of her company to look forward to. My super stealthy and charming interrogations will have to wait. My main priority right now is getting Lola somewhere she can rest. The next priority after that is getting *me* somewhere I can.

"How'd it go?" Jordan asks as I approach the bleachers. The sympathy in her drawn brows indicates she already knows the answer to that question.

"Ugh," I say. "I forgot how much I hate poker."

"I know. I could tell when you remembered. It was about fifteen minutes in." Jordan casts a look over my shoulder. "Hey, Riker. Bad day at the tables?"

Lola, who had been looking rather wilted until now, perks up the moment Riker appears. Although holding her neck up has to be killing her, a bright smile crosses her face, and she lifts her long-lashed eyes in Riker's direction.

"I thought you played wonderfully," she says with a burst of enthusiasm. "Oh, I wouldn't have played for that flush right before lunch, and I think you were a little too quick to get rid of that ten of spades for the chance at a straight, but I loved watching you. You hold the cards so well."

He stares at her. "I hold the cards well?"

"Absolutely. You have such nice hands. I could watch you play all day."

Jordan and I are careful not to look at each other for fear of falling into hysterics. I'm not sure I've ever seen Riker turn that shade of purple before.

"But when you sit down tomorrow, you might want to try easing up on bluffing the eensiest bit," Lola continues, heedless of the dangers. "Not that you aren't good at it, of course—though you always toss your cards around when you're trying to hide something. No, it's just that bluffing won't work against Two-Finger Tommy."

Riker's ire simmers to a more controllable level. "Really? Why?"

"He'll call every time. He always does. It doesn't

matter if he has nothing more than a pair of twos in his hand—if you're staying in, so is he. He doesn't like to back down from a challenge. He thinks it makes him look weak."

Riker's ire is now full-blown interest. "How do you know this?"

"Daddy plays against him all the time. He likes to know all the latest methods for cheating at cards, and there's no better way to stay current than to study what Two-Finger is up to."

Riker opens his mouth to continue this line of questioning, but I've got a few queries of my own. Two-Finger and Johnny Francis seem to share a few too many unappealing characteristics for my peace of mind. "What else does Daddy know about him?" I ask.

"Oh, loads of things. He says Tommy is more like a snake than a man, but good luck proving anything against him. He always covers his tracks."

With that, my suspicion that the two men might be one and the same grows, but Riker has other concerns.

"Are you saying what I think you're saying?" he growls.

Lola is instantly contrite. "Oh, dear. Was I not supposed to?" She clutches his arm. "I thought everyone knew about Two-Finger's love of cheating. It's not great news, but if anyone can beat him, it's you. I just know it."

Tara chooses that moment to join our party. A strange expression settles over her face as she notices her boyfriend being soothed by another woman. I take note of it with a sinking heart. Whereas Tara is sharp and cunning and wields her sex appeal like a knife, Lola is sweet and trusting and as unaware of her charm as a kitten. There aren't a lot of women who could incite my stepmother to jealousy, but I imagine Lola is one of them. Artless innocence is the one thing she'll never have a chance of competing against.

"How'd it go?" I ask, more out of an attempt to save Lola from Tara's anger than any real interest.

Tara shakes herself off and turns her attention to me. "It could have been worse. I broke my losing streak there toward the end, but I'm still far enough behind that I'll have to make up a lot of ground tomorrow. You?"

I shake my head. "Horrible. Eden has it out for me."

"I'm not surprised. You'll want to watch out for that one. She's been asking a lot of questions about you."

"Questions?" I don't like the sound of that. Questions lead to answers, which could lead to Grant. "What kind of questions? And who has she been asking?"

"The usual—who you hang out with, what motivates you, why you refuse to act like a normal thief who just takes things and then moves on with her life." She shrugs. "I think she might try to bribe you into taking the tiara. Don't do it for less than ten million. She's not trustworthy."

"Thank you for that super helpful tip," I say. Trustworthiness isn't an adjective I'd apply to most of the people on this boat—Tara included. "Anything else you'd like to inform me of? The color of the sky? My own middle name?"

Tara tactfully ignores me, but Lola giggles. It's nice to know at least *one* of my friends finds me amusing.

"So what's the plan now?" I ask. I know that the answer isn't *all of us should quietly return to our rooms and contemplate the day's events*, but I cross my fingers anyway.

"Observation deck. Alcohol. Party." Tara rattles off her plans with fearful efficiency. "The night is young, and so are you, my dear. If you want to keep up your reputation as the great Penelope Blue, you're going to need to put in more effort than this. There's already talk of your dismal failures at the tables today. People are starting to wonder if you made up most of your successes."

"I was never the one—" I begin, but there's no use arguing. Everyone is making plans to change and grab a bite to eat before the festivities begin.

Since I doubt my husband will miss the opportunity to present himself in such an open, crowded, dangerous place as a party full of drunk criminals, I resign myself to going along. *One* of us, at least, needs to be acting like the responsible adult in this situation.

I just really wish it didn't have to be me.

THE THREAT 14

BY THE TIME WE ARRIVE ON THE OBSERVATION DECK, THE party is in full swing. From afar, I'm sure it looks like a dream—strings of twinkle lights sparkling underneath the darkening sky, men and women dressed to impress, laughter and the clink of free-flowing alcohol lowering inhibitions. From up close, however, it feels more like mass hysteria. Diversions aboard the *Shady Lady* are scarce enough that it seems everyone came out for a chance to mingle.

I can't help but wonder if this is yet another part of Peter Sanchez's master plan—to keep us all where he can see us, corralling us like cattle from one entertainment to the next.

I'm about to declare my intention to buck the herd and go back to the room when Lola's breathless voice reaches my ears.

"Oh, isn't it lovely?" she asks, making me feel like a perfect ogre. "It's so nice to see everyone relaxing and enjoying themselves after a long day at each other's throats."

"Yes, lovely," I murmur, though I see a lot more continued cutthroat activity than I do relaxation and enjoyment. There's a woman to my right who just lost a necklace to a mustachioed man with light fingers, and if that couple over by the edge isn't careful, Two-Finger Tommy is going to gently nudge them over the side.

But then, I guess this is like one of those abstract paintings Grant loves so much. You see reflected back at you what's inside your own heart. Lola sees love and friendship; I see subterfuge and theft.

I blame my husband for that. If I wasn't so worried about *him* being the one gently nudged over the side, I might be able to enjoy myself out here.

"They're starting the music for dancing," Lola says as the strain of a tango rises above the chatter and carries out over the open sea. "I *love* to dance. Tara, would it be awful of me to steal your boyfriend for a few minutes? I'm too scared to dance with anyone else for fear they might take the tiara, but with Riker…"

Oh, dear. There's another area where Lola's point of view might be discoloring reality a little. If Riker scowls any deeper, he's going to be dragging his lips on the floor.

"I don't know how to dance," he says shortly.

"Everyone knows how to dance!" she says, laughing. "You just move your hips. Here, I'll show you."

"I don't move my hips, either," he says. "Not if I can possibly help it." He turns and moves off in what I assume is a search for silence or a stiff drink. Probably both.

Lola sighs as she watches his retreat. It's not a pained

sigh so much as a wistful one, so I don't worry too much about it. The sooner the poor girl realizes that Riker's gruff charm is more than just an act—it's ingrained in his soul—the faster her puppy love will wane. Some painful truths are better to learn from the start.

"I should probably see where he's going," Tara says, also with a sigh. Hers doesn't sound so much wistful as it does pained. I know I promised myself I wouldn't get involved in the relationships of anyone I'm related to, but I'm starting to feel like there's more going on than either one of them is letting on. "I'll come find you two later to walk you to your room, okay? Don't go wandering the halls alone."

I nod. I hope *later* means minutes rather than hours. Jordan abandoned us after receiving a furtive summons from Oz, who was not dressed as a crew member for once, so I'm back on Lola duty all by myself. Well, and all the other watchful eyes, following us like hyenas and their prey.

"So, Lola," I say with forced cheer. A duty she might be, but I refuse to make her feel like a burden. "Would you like to grab something to drink, or do you just want to hang out for a while? I think I spied an open table over on the other side of the boat."

"What I really want to do is dance…" she says.

The answer to all her hopes and dreams comes from an unexpected source. "If that's the case, then may I have the honor?" Appearing as if from nowhere, Grant makes Lola a formal bow. He's not in a tuxedo this evening— it's not *that* kind of party—but he does more than justice to the white button-down rolled up over his forearms.

I don't know what it is, but there's something about

rolled shirtsleeves that makes my heart pound faster every time. Maybe it's the way Grant's forearms flex and twist under the moonlight, but I suddenly feel a profound jealousy that it's Lola and not me who gets to feel those arms around her.

"Oh, Mr. O'Kelly, do you mean it?" she asks and doesn't wait for a reply. "I know you'd much rather ask Penelope to dance, but I'm selfish enough to take you up on your offer."

I send Grant a grateful smile. Asking Lola to dance isn't the most chivalrous thing he's done—not when we're talking about *my* white knight of a husband—but it's in keeping with everything I know about him. He's always been good at making sure people are comfortable and taken care of, a gentleman to the core. It's part of what makes his willingness to let Peter Sanchez put Lola at risk so maddening. It's not like him to sit back and let other people accept danger on his behalf. In fact, it's the one thing he hates most.

"You don't mind, do you, Penelope?" Lola asks.

"Not at all." I give an airy wave of my hand. "I'm sure Kit will have a much better time with you anyway. I'm poor company after my heavy losses today."

"Uh-oh. Did you get the pants beat off you?" Grant asks, a laugh on his lips and a dark glint in his eye.

Despite my strongest protestations, Tara wrangled me into a dress for this evening's party. It's black, which is nice, but it's also incredibly short.

He appears to have noticed.

"Not yet, but you could say I've been stripped to the waist," I admit.

"In that case, I can't offer you any condolences."

Grant allows his gaze to drop to my neckline. "There are few things I'd love more than to see you without a shirt."

"And without my dignity, apparently," I retort. "Because that's what going to happen if I have another day like this one."

"On second thought, if you have to choose between dignity and the shirt, please keep the second one. You're enough of a distraction as it is."

Lola giggles. "I don't know how you're not melting in a puddle at Mr. O'Kelly's feet, Penelope. If a man said things like that to me, I think I might die."

"*When* men start saying them to you, Lola," I caution her, "don't believe a word. Mr. O'Kelly here is just trying to get under my skin."

"I beg your pardon. I'm trying to get under a lot more than that." He offers me a devilish grin and Lola his arm. "Shall we?"

She giggles again, pausing long enough to cast a backward glance at me as if to make sure I'll be okay on my own. There's no need. I've never been so happy to see the back of my husband's head in my life. He might think it's nothing but fun and games to make sport of our relationship in front of all these people, but I'm not so easily amused.

"Fuck. I thought that guy would never leave."

Under normal circumstances, Hijack's sneaking up on me and muttering obscenities in my ear might cause me to scream. Under *these* circumstances, I can only agree with him. This is one instance where Grant's tenacity isn't doing him any favors.

Still, "What guy?" I ask, as if I'm not watching my

husband's every dip and twirl out of the corner of my eye. He's light on his feet and strong enough to lead Lola through the most intricate dance steps, making it difficult for me to feign indifference for long.

Being led by that man is a pleasure few women have gotten to experience for themselves, but let me tell you—it's a pleasure no woman forgets.

Hijack doesn't buy my indifference. "I hate dudes who show off like that, don't you?" he asks. "We get it. You can swing a human around a dance floor. No need to rub it in."

Oh, he's rubbing it in, all right. He wants me to feel the agony of each step, watch him as he laughs and enjoys himself. It's my punishment for not falling for his flirtation. *So close and yet so far away.*

"Aw, Hijack, are you jealous?"

"Of Kit O'Kelly?" he scoffs. "Please. That guy's got nothing on me."

"I don't know. It looked like he was kicking your ass at the poker table today. He must have *something*."

"Not really. That man is a lot less important than he'd like you to think." Hijack drops his voice just enough to cause alarm. He's not talking about a playful competition between men. "He's hiding something."

"What are you talking about?" I ask.

"According to word on the ship, he's some kind of big-time international securities expert, right?" Hijack's question is a rhetorical one. He doesn't wait for an answer. "Then how come I've never met anyone who's worked with him before? Believe me, I've been asking around, and no one has been able to vouch for the guy."

"What do you mean? Peter Sanchez vouches for him."

"So he claims." Hijack casts me a knowing look. "But the pieces don't fit. They've never worked together in the past, at least not according to what I've been able to discover. I can't figure out why our man Sanchez would give a relative stranger such a central role on his security team. Unless, of course, he has other plans for the guy."

"What kind of other plans?" I ask sharply.

Hijack's eyes don't leave mine. "So the rumors are true," he says. "You *do* have a thing for him."

"I don't have a thing for anyone," I say and turn my back to the dance floor. Watching the intricacies of Grant's body in motion isn't going to convince Hijack—or anyone else paying attention—of my innocence. "I'm married, remember?"

"Ah, yes. To the unimpressive federal agent whose ring you can't be bothered to wear."

I glance at the empty space on my left finger, reeling with Grant's absence even though he's literally less than a hundred feet away. "You don't have to make it sound so seedy. Lots of women get married for money."

"Is he rich, then? I wasn't aware federal agents made that much money."

"Of course he's not rich," I mutter before I realize he's fishing again. I don't know what Hijack is doing asking about my husband—or why he cares so much—but I don't like it. I transform my irritation to a bland smile. "I just meant that I use him to get information on big jobs, that's all. He's like my own personal spy."

"How do you know he's not using you right back? Maybe he just wants you for your contacts."

There's enough truth in that statement to leave my head spinning. Although I know Grant didn't marry me for the access I provide to my father, there's no denying our relationship began for that exact reason. But there's no way Hijack can know that, and even if he did, what use would that information do him now?

"He's not that smart," I say.

"Really? They must not have very strict requirements at the FBI these days."

Not for the first time, I wish I was better at keeping my true feelings from showing on my face. All Grant's safety hinges on the premise that no one will care enough about him—or me—to ask questions. It would take a five-minute internet search to pull up my marriage records and grab Grant's name, five more to find pictures of him at various ages and in various guises. From there, it won't take much to pinpoint Kit O'Kelly as my spouse—even with his shorter, darker hair, he's easily recognizable as the FBI's golden boy. Our whole mission was predicated on the idea that no one would be able to connect *my* husband and a quiet, unassuming card player who promised to blend into the background.

"I wish you'd tell me why you're so interested in him," I say. Maybe if we can get all this out in the open, Hijack will stop asking so many questions. "Why does it bother you so much that I married a fed?"

"It doesn't bother me. I'm just curious, that's all." He doesn't, as I expect, continue his line of questioning. He takes a much more dangerous path instead. "Have you given any more thought to my proposal? I gave you as much time as I could, but I'm going to need a firm answer soon. Everyone else is getting their plans for taking the tiara underway. If you're not going to help me, I'm going to need to make alternate arrangements."

Although I knew all Hijack's allusions were heading this way, I'm surprised he's willing to say so out loud. And in such a public place, too.

"What kind of alternate arrangements?" I ask.

"You know what I came here to do, Pen," he says by way of answer. "I don't care who's been pulled onto Sanchez's security team—nothing has changed. You have more skills and expertise to pull this heist off than anyone, and thanks to your friendship with Lola, you've got more opportunity, too. At this point, we're all just waiting for you to take the tiara—and I'd like to be the one to help you do it."

"Are you sure *help* is the word you mean to use?"

"I don't care what you call it as long as you agree." He shrugs, but it's a studied gesture—a dangerous one. "I can do it with or without you, but the job will go so much smoother if I have the great Penelope Blue on my side. With careful planning, no one has to get hurt."

There's not a doubt in my mind that what he's offering me isn't a deal so much as an ultimatum. If I don't help him steal the tiara from Lola, then he'll make the attempt on his own—and he won't be nearly as concerned for the girl's welfare in the process.

It's extortion, plain and simple.

"Why not ask Eden St. James?" I ask. "You seemed to be awfully interested in her before."

Mistaking my comment for jealousy, he smiles. "I'm interested in everyone on board this boat. I have to be. There isn't anyone on this deck right now I haven't studied and researched and categorized well ahead of time. Pick someone, anyone."

I stare at him.

"I mean it. Pick someone at random, and I'll tell you exactly what they can do and how well they can do it."

I don't want to get drawn into his game, but short of jumping over the edge, I don't see an immediate way out. "You've come an awfully long way from stealing cars, Hijack."

"And you've come an awfully long way from hiding yourself inside luggage compartments. Pick someone, Pen."

I indulge him. "Okay, over on the edge of the dance floor, the guy in the shiny purple shirt with the scar bisecting his face. He looks pleasant."

Hijack finds the man almost immediately. "Actually, I think you'd like him. He's big in the art circuit."

When I don't comment, he starts listing the man's credentials. "Randolph Penske, forger. He's your guy if you want an Impressionist piece done. There are about three people in the world who can tell the difference between him and Monet."

"Really? That's impressive."

"Thank you."

I make a face. "I meant *he's* impressive, not your ability to pick him out of a lineup."

"That's because he was too easy. Everyone knows Penske. Pick someone else."

Once again, I'm torn between a desire to tell Hijack exactly where he can stick his stupid game and an urge to keep playing. I'm leaning toward the first option when I spy Oz standing near the railing, seemingly unconcerned as he sips a drink and watches the dancers. I suspect he's here at Grant's request to keep an extra eye on the tiara, but I doubt Hijack knows that.

I nod in his direction. "Okay, how about that guy in the blue suit and skinny tie off to one side? I've never seen him around before."

From the way Hijack's entire body stills, I'm guessing he's never seen Oz around before either. I can't decide if I feel more smug at having beaten him at his own game or guilty at having introduced Oz to his notice.

"Huh. I'm not sure I know that one. Jerome? George? I feel like it's something that starts with a *j* sound."

"Johnny?" I suggest.

Hijack just laughs. "No, not him. *If* Johnny Francis is on this boat right now—and I'm not convinced he is— I'd assume he's hiding out in his room memorizing kill lists. A guy like that wouldn't waste his time at parties. Hey, where'd he go?"

I glance up. Sure enough, Oz has disappeared from his watchful post. Even though I know it's impossible for him to have overheard us all the way over here, I can't help feeling he knew he was being catalogued and left before the task could be completed.

"Huh, weird," I say. "Maybe he is Johnny Francis, after all." Since I'd rather not dwell on Oz's likelihood to be any number of hidden criminals, I add, "What does this have to do with anything, anyway? So you know people. Big deal."

"I know *these* people," he corrects me. "And I know that before the trip is up, one of them is going to steal that tiara."

"Yes, and then what? Where will they go with it? To a submarine they have waiting just below the surface?"

"Why not?" He shrugs. "As long as they can find a way to steal it and conceal it, there's nothing stopping any of us. Think about it, Pen—it'll be the crime of the century. Swiping twenty million dollars from under the noses of the most dangerous criminals this world has ever seen and doing it in such a way that not even a hint of suspicion falls on our heads. Tell me you didn't get a shiver just from thinking about it."

Oh, I get a shiver, all right. Goose bumps break out down my arms and rise up my neck, the tiny hairs standing at full attention. It *would* be a coup unlike any other. It would also be, thanks to Peter Sanchez's watchful eye, incredibly risky.

"You know you're going to be the top suspect if the tiara goes missing anyway," Hijack adds. "Peter Sanchez and his new errand boy saw to that when they dumped Lola into your lap. The only way you're *really* going to be safe from suspicion is if you take it and make sure the blame lands firmly somewhere else."

Is it my imagination, or do I detect another ultimatum in there?

I'm saved from having to commit myself one way or another by Lola and Grant's breathless return to my side. Well, Lola is breathless; Grant does his valiant best to hide any strain the dance put on his physique. All that twirling, though—it can't have been doing his abdomen any favors.

"Oh, Penelope, I'm sorry we were gone for so long, but dancing with Mr. O'Kelly is like flying! You should take your turn now."

"Is there a waiting list?" Hijack asks. "I didn't know dance partners were in such demand, or I would have offered my services."

"Not just any dance partner," Lola says, unaware of

the undercurrent of tension between the two men. "Just the ones as good as Mr. O'Kelly."

"What do you say, Pen?" Hijack offers me his hand. "I can't promise it'll be like flying, but it hasn't been *that* long since we were partners. I think I can remember a thing or two about what you like."

His words do exactly what they're designed to do, which is rankle Grant.

"Ah, but you had your turn with Penelope," Grant says with a soft tut. "Is it fair to punish me because you didn't use your time wisely?"

"I didn't plan on dancing tonight," I say, but it's no use. There's a playful gleam in Grant's eye I recognize all too well. Stopping him in one of his stubborn moods is hard enough; stopping him when he's toying with me is damn near impossible.

He holds out his hand. "May I?"

I cast a quick look at Hijack, hoping to gauge his reaction. It doesn't look promising, but Lola swoops in with a pretty smile and a question about the difference between ten-gauge versus twelve-gauge starter wire when jacking a car. Not even all the Kit O'Kelly hatred in the world is enough to distract Hijack from his favorite subject. And since he can hardly take the tiara with so many people standing nearby, I'm forced to slip my fingers into Grant's waiting palm.

Lola was correct in her assessment of Grant's dancing skills. He confessed to me once that he learned the ballroom basics for the sole purpose of impressing the girl he took to prom. It's one of my favorite stories, actually—I love thinking of him as a high school jock, winning trophies and setting teenage hearts aflutter.

It's so far removed from my own experience, it seems unreal. My own dancing skills are, naturally, the result of a long con.

One of his large hands grips me about the waist as he begins to twirl me to the middle of the dance floor. For a moment, I let myself fall into the music, the rhythmic steps and steady beat of his heart, the familiar scent of his sweat and laundry soap, but of course, the moment doesn't last.

He and I have work to do.

"I don't think your boyfriend likes me very much," he says, not mincing matters.

"That's okay," I reply, not doing any mincing of my own. "I don't like him very much, either."

His soft laughter shakes us both. "Uh-oh. Lover's tiff?"

"You could call it that." I try to think of a way to phrase my dilemma without actually saying the words out loud. "He's been pressuring me to do something I don't want to do. I've managed to hold him off so far, but after tonight, I don't think I can anymore."

Every muscle in Grant's body stops and stiffens, his hands on my waist tightening to clamps. I realize my error almost immediately.

"No, no, no," I say quickly. "That's not what I meant."

"I'll fucking kill him," Grant says, his voice a low growl.

The couple next to us looks over in alarm. I will Grant to keep breathing, keep dancing, keep up the pretense.

"Actually, you might be able to help me out with this little problem, seeing as how you're in charge of security." My voice is light but strained, as the clamps on my waist haven't let up yet. It's like wearing a corset made of flesh and steel. "Was it your intention for everyone on board to jump at each other's throats for a chance at that tiara, or did you expect us to create teams and go at it that way?"

"He wants you to help him steal the tiara," he says, understanding lighting his eyes. He also relaxes, my poor waist finally released from its shackle. "You had me scared for a minute."

That's what he's scared of? Not cold, callous smugglers? Not exposure in front of an angry mob?

"Well?" I ask, my eyes imploring. "Aren't you going to give me advice on how to deal with him?"

His answer is decidedly not helpful. "I, for one, am tired of talking about Hijack. What I'd really like to talk about is you."

"Too bad," I say baldly.

"Now, now." He tsks. "Consider it the cost of the dance. Why do you insist on holding me at arm's length? I'm not so bad once you get to know me, I promise. Some women find me downright endearing."

Some women obviously don't know any better. "You know, it seems an awful lot like you're trying to distract me from the job I originally came here to do."

He laughs in a way that makes me think I've hit the nail on the head—which means that I'd also like to hit *him* on the head. In case he doesn't remember, the job I came here to do isn't one either of us should take lightly. You know, saving his life and all. It would be nice if I wasn't the only one who remembered that.

"I see you've figured me out," he says. "A man should be more careful around someone like you, Penelope Blue. You make him forget everything but the joy of the game."

"Does this mean you won't mind if I partner with Hijack to steal the tiara from Lola?" I ask, annoyance lending an edge to my voice.

"Oh, if you steal the tiara, I'll hunt you down," he says, perfectly calm. He also places one firm finger under my chin, forcing my gaze to meet his. "That's a guarantee. I'll hunt you down, tie you up, and extract its whereabouts using whatever means are necessary. And I mean that literally. I can be a very determined man when I put my mind to it."

I lick my lips, which have suddenly gone dry.

"That tiara is the most important thing right now," he adds. "I thought I already made that clear."

He *has*, but that doesn't mean I like it. The tiara is important, and so is Lola, but not at the cost of his own safety. He has to know that.

"Oh, look. The music has stopped." Grant's movements across the dance floor also come to a close. "Thank you, Penelope Blue. This has been a most productive evening. I can't wait to see what tomorrow brings."

Quick—so quick I don't have time to prevent him—he holds my chin in place and drops a light kiss on my lips. It's no more than a peck, and an unsatisfactory one at that, but there's no denying my body's reaction to it. From the moment his mouth touches mine, I'm all in.

Unfortunately, I'm not the one it's meant for. That kiss was a public promise, a declaration of intent for all the world to see. It's all I can do to stand in bemused wonder as I watch Grant go.

That man will be the death of me, I'm sure of it.

I wouldn't mind so much as long as he isn't the death of himself, too.

THE
CONVERSATION

I WAIT UNTIL LOLA DRIFTS OFF INTO AN EFFORTLESS, exhausted sleep after the party before tiptoeing to my father's door.

Pressing my ear against the surface, I strain to hear any signs of consenting adult passions. There aren't any of those purring sounds from last night, and all heavy breathing and laughter seems to be at a minimum, so I decide to go for it.

Knock-knock.

No one answers. I'm not too surprised—it might be bedtime for emotionally drained eighteen-year-olds and their weary twenty-six-year-old keepers, but my father tends to keep later hours.

"Hello?" I call, trying again. "Anybody home?"

Once again, I get nothing but silence. *Damn*. I was hoping to get a chance to talk to my father—ask him to increase his own security and keep his nighttime visitors to a minimum—but it looks like I'm going to have to prop open the door again and hope for the best. With a sigh, I reach for the handle and twist.

Or attempt to twist, anyway. It's locked from his side.

"Oh, come on," I mutter and try the handle again. "Are you kidding me? He's locking his own daughter out now?"

I hate to draw parallels between Lola's father and my own, but there does seem to be a certain callousness in putting up these kinds of barriers when there's so much at stake. I mean, I know my father doesn't love that I came on this trip, and he dislikes even more that I brought Grant along, but he could be a *little* more concerned for my welfare.

With a perfunctory glance back at Lola, who's fallen into the deep sleep of the contented, I slip the master key from out of my bra. I haven't tested it yet, but from the way it slips in to the lock and easily turns, it's clearly the real deal.

"What do you think you're doing, young lady?"

To my surprise and suddenly leaping pulse, my father waits on the other side of the door. His glasses are pulled down to the end of his nose, and he's staring at me over the top of them, his dad-face impossible to ignore.

"Geez, Dad, you scared the crap out of me." I hold my hand to my chest, cleverly concealing the key in my palm. "Why didn't you answer when I knocked?"

He shifts his body so it covers most of the doorway. "That's what a man does when he doesn't want company," he says in his maddeningly controlled way. "Or is that not something you've learned in your lifetime?"

The harshness of his tone causes me to flush. I'd like to pretend that had *my* father been the one to demand

I wear the tiara, I'd have stood up against his tyranny, but I wonder if I'd have ended up as meekly compliant as Lola. Dads are a hard breed to thwart. For most people, that's a good thing, since fathers are supposed to protect their young. For people like us, it's not so easy to tell.

"Sorry," I mutter, unable to look him in the eye. "I just wanted to ask you—"

A sleek female head appears by my father's side, perfectly on level with his own. I stop, sure I must be seeing things, but when a few seconds pass and that sleek head is still there, I know I'm done for.

Eden St. James.

"Why, Warren, I thought you told me the doors between your rooms were locked." Eden smiles down at me. "Isn't this a convenient mistake?"

I can only think of one reason why Eden would be in my father's room, and it's not a good one. My heart sinks. So much for counting on my dad to keep me safe. He's let the lion into the den. Literally.

"They *do* lock," I say, my eyes narrowed in a glare. It looks like I'm going to have to protect myself around here. "And they're the same strength as the main doors, so don't even think about trying to pick them. As soon as I slam the door in your face, that's the last you'll see of me until morning."

She's not, as I hope, intimated by that show of bluster. With a tilt of her head, she asks, "Is that so? Then how did you get in here?"

Too late, I realize I've given myself away. With my hand still pressed to my chest—and the key with it—I attempt to back into my room. But my father, whether through sheer perversity or a desire to teach me a lesson, throws the door open wider.

"You might as well come in, Penelope," he says and sighs. "I trust the girl is asleep?"

I cast a nervous glance back at her. "Ye-es. But I promised she wouldn't be alone."

"We'll keep the doors propped open. She's fine."

I don't want to. I don't like it. Even though I did my thorough sweep of the room and there are no fewer than five scary-looking strangers camped out in the hall-way determined to keep an eye on things, leaving her unguarded seems like asking for trouble.

"I don't have all night."

"I guess it won't hurt," I say. At this point, retreat is probably worse. "But I really am tired, so only for a few minutes."

"How *did* you get through the door just now?" Eden asks, unwilling to let the subject drop. "I watched your father lock it with my own eyes."

Oh, dear. I cast a mute, pleading look at my father for help, but he's just as interested in the answer.

"I, um…" I can't think of anything even remotely believable, unfortunately. "It's a trick I have."

"You have a trick for getting through Peter Sanchez's impenetrable doors?" Eden asks.

Her disbelief only serves to fuel my confidence. For all this woman is aware, I know *dozens* of tricks. It's just that poker playing doesn't happen to be one of them.

"Of course. You think one tiny lock is going to stop me?" I toss my hair. "There isn't a door in this place I can't find my way through."

I push past her into my father's room, which is an

exact mirror image of my own. As my back is to them, I slip the key into my bra and let my hand drop. I can't be sure Eden didn't see me, but it's the best I can do given the circumstances.

Both Eden and my father are fully clothed, and the only signs of dissipation—or, to be honest, *habitation*—are a pair of wine glasses on the coffee table. It's hardly the stuff of scandalous sexual interludes. Still, it would be nice to hear from their own lips what kind of excuse they can come up with for their traitorous relationship, so I don't back down.

"Well," I say brightly as I turn to face them. "What are you two up to in here?"

"Nothing much." Eden seats herself on one of the beige chairs. "I was simply asking your father what he knows about Kit O'Kelly."

My mouth goes dry. "Kit O'Kelly?"

"Eden suspects he might be the elusive Johnny Francis in disguise," my father explains in an unconcerned way. He takes the opposite chair, leaving me standing in the center of the room and gawking at them both. "Apparently, she's interested in tracking the man down for…what was it, Eden?"

Eden smiles tightly. "Mr. Francis has access to certain privileged information I'd be willing to pay a hefty price to get my hands on. *You* wouldn't happen to know if there's any truth to my theory, would you, Penelope?"

"Me?" I squeak. "I barely know the guy."

"Oh, yes. I keep forgetting. It must be the familiar manner he's adopted with you that has me so confused."

There's nothing in Eden's tone or her posture to indicate she meant that as a threat, but I swear the room drops a good ten degrees as she sits there sipping her wine. And even though I know the smartest thing for me to do is beat a hasty and silent retreat, I can't help feeling a sudden curiosity about my father's guest. I drop to the couch.

"What makes you think he's Johnny?" I ask. "Did he say or do something to tip you off?"

She smiles over the edge of her glass at having caught my interest. "Oh, no. Nothing so amateur. Call it a hunch. When a man of his caliber appears on the scene and no one can recall having seen him before, it raises a few questions, that's all." Her smile deepens. "I'm sure you understand what I mean, Penelope. Could you forget a face—or a body—like that one?"

Oh, dear. There's no way around this one. "No. No, I can't say that I'll ever be able to forget that man."

"My sentiments exactly."

"So what are you going to do to him?" I ask. I'm almost afraid to hear the answer, but I'd kick myself for not putting it out there.

"*To* him?" She releases a brittle laugh. "I doubt there's much I could do—I don't have so much confidence in my combat skills that I'm willing to take a man of his…physique on single-handedly. But to *catch* him? That's easy."

"Oh?" I ask.

"I'm going to do what everyone else on this boat—including Johnny—is trying to do," she says, a cold glitter in her eyes. "Except I'm going to succeed."

My father coughs gently. "She means the tiara, of course."

Some of my confusion must show on my face,

because Eden sighs and says to my father, "Surely no daughter of yours is this ignorant?"

I bristle. I'm *not* ignorant, thank you very much. I'm terrible at jogging, lacking in poker skills, and yes, not likely to beat anyone in hand-to-hand combat, but I know dozens of things she doesn't. Including the fact that Grant Emerson is *not* a man she wants to cross—and that Penelope Blue isn't a woman she wants to, either.

"Uh-oh. That hurt her feelings, didn't it?" She crosses one leg over the other and sits back in her chair. "Darling, it's common knowledge that Johnny Francis is on this ship for one reason and one reason only—he wants that tiara."

"We *all* want that tiara," I say. I swear, those words are becoming almost mechanical by now.

"Yes, but some of us are more likely to get it than others, aren't we?" Her lips spread in a dangerous smile. "And whoever does end up the lucky winner will hold all the power. Just think what Johnny Francis might be willing to sell in exchange for a rock like that. I get a shiver just thinking about it. They say that man knows the secrets of every thief who's ever walked on two feet."

I'm not sure how to respond, so it's just as well that my father intervenes.

"Unfortunately, I haven't been of much use to Eden. I don't approve of this Kit O'Kelly's extravagant airs, obviously." He casts me a warning that's as firm as it is unnecessary. We share that sentiment. "But I have no reason to believe he's Johnny Francis. Nor am I convinced the man is here in the first place."

I stop. "You aren't?"

"He'd be a fool to be on board a ship like this," my

father says. "I know plenty of people who would like to see him at the bottom of the ocean. He knows too much and is far too willing to sell that information. It would be best if we all just forgot about him and concentrated on the game. That is, after all, why we're here."

"But—" I begin.

I don't get a chance to finish. Without a word, my dad rises and moves to the adjoining door, standing with his hand on the door until the message gets through. *It's high time little girls are in bed*.

"Good night, Penelope," he says.

"But—" I try again. I still need to warn him against letting Eden stay the night. Surely he saw that malicious, greedy glint in her eye?

"I said good *night*, Penelope. And be sure to lock your side of the door before you retire. You were foolish to leave it ajar last night."

Me? I'm the foolish one? For trusting my father to have my best interests at heart?

The door closes in my face, preventing me from saying so out loud. The click of his lock being put into place carries with it a note of finality.

Do not enter. Do not pass go. Do not trust anyone.

And most of all, do *not* let Eden get her hands on that tiara.

THE TOP DECK

16

THERE'S A NOTE UNDER MY FRONT DOOR THE NEXT MORNING.

I manage to get to it before Lola notices, which is a good thing, since I assume Grant has some instructions to issue that can't wait for Oz to make his towel rounds. Finally—*finally*—he has something concrete for me to do.

Imagine my disappointment when I find a message scrawled in an unfamiliar hand.

> Meet me in the fourth floor starboard aft supply closet at dusk. I can help you get away with the tiara without anyone noticing. Bring the girl.

There's no signature, no indication of compensation, nothing. Just an invitation to lure my charge into a dark and unattended room where the sounds of our screams would go unheard.

"Yeah, right," I mutter as I crush the paper in my palm. "You're going to have to try harder than that."

I might have considered it a fluke—and an amusing one at that—if I didn't get repeat offers throughout the day. No one else is stupid enough to assume I'll answer an unsigned summons, but the other patrons on board the *Shady Lady* don't do much to convince me their collective intelligence is very high. Two separate men accost me on the way to the cabaret lounge, offering me cuts of sixty percent and seventy-five percent, accordingly, if I'd be willing to cast all my scruples aside and join forces with them.

As they make these proposals within Lola's hearing range and in full view of the entourage accompanying us to our destination, I don't hesitate to let them know what I think of their not-so-subtle tactics.

Lunchtime finds me the unhappy recipient of three more offers, one of which is written on a napkin and slipped to me under the plate of the main course. That one makes me the angriest of all, as I find it incumbent to toss my lamb chop out. I don't *think* anyone would resort to poisoning my food in an attempt to clear the path to Lola, but it's not a risk I'm willing to take.

"Aren't you the belle of the ball?" Eden asks as she watches me ransack the bread basket. "Let me guess— they want to hire you to kill the girl and steal the tiara for them, don't they?"

"Don't start with me, Eden," I warn. Between my low blood sugar and the fact that I'm down another two hundred thousand dollars that have made their way to her stack of chips, I'm in no mood to deal with her attitude. "It's not funny. We're talking about an actual human being here."

"*I* would never ask you to harm her. I'm not that

kind of professional." The way she says the word *pro-fessional* sends a shiver down my spine. "I'm sure we could come up with a plan that's amenable to us both. And then I promise we never have to interact again—a partnership of convenience, if you will."

I swear, it's enough to make a girl scream. I can't help but imagine this is what it feels like to be an heiress thrust into some old English marriage mart. The offers just keep coming, each one a little more desperate and a little less appealing than the last.

Everyone wants a piece of the great Penelope Blue.

That's my excuse, anyway, for what happens at the end of the day's poker play. Although I'm down to about a quarter of my money by the time the final bell sounds, the other members of my family have made a pretty clean sweep of things. Both my father and Tara won, as expected, which gives them a few days of lei-sure while everyone else finishes. Riker's stormy look and Two-Finger Tommy's smug one don't bode well for his chances of making it to the next round, but Grant appears to be a few hands away from taking his table out from under Hijack.

With a few exceptions, Team FBI is back.

"Pen, do you have a second?" Hijack asks before I have a chance to join my friends off to one side of the cabaret lounge. I look longingly at Jordan, who I notice has a pastry in her hand waiting for me.

"Not really," I say, more curtly than I intend. "No offense, Hijack, but it's been kind of a long day."

"I can tell. You look like shit."

It's the last straw. I *know* I look like shit. I haven't gotten a good night's sleep since I boarded this stupid boat, and my stomach is rumbling so hard, it feels like there's an alien baby in there. I'm wearing leggings and yesterday's tank top, and Eden kicked my ass at the tables so badly today, I doubt I'll be able to recover. And to top it all off, I can see her out of the corner of my eye making a beeline for my husband's side. Thanks to the useless one-way towel communication method he devised, I haven't had a chance to warn him yet about her theory that he's Johnny Francis or that she's probably sleeping with my dad so she can slip into my room at night and kill me.

Maybe, if people would leave me alone for more than five minutes, I could work on improving my appearance. *Maybe*.

"Hijack, I swear to God, if you so much as mention that tiara to me, I will rip your heart out right here in the middle of the cabaret lounge and start playing Ping-Pong with it." My vehemence gives him slight pause. "For what is the last possible time, I am *not* going to steal the Luxor Tiara. Not for you, and not for anyone. In fact, I'm going to do the exact opposite. I'm going to guard it—and Lola—with everything I have. If you want it so bad, you're going to have to buckle down and win it the old-fashioned way."

Since it appears my vehemence is also giving pause to the rest of the people in the cabaret lounge, all of whom are standing perfectly still and watching me as one might a circus freak, I add, "And that goes for all of you. You should be *ashamed* of yourselves, behaving like cannibals. Whatever happened to honor among thieves?"

I could probably keep going in this vein all

evening—or at least until I pass out from hunger—so it's for the best that Riker makes a beeline for my side.

"Hey there, Pen," Riker says, laughter underscoring his voice. "Whatcha doing?"

Oh, you know. Not much. Just alienating five hundred people who'd like to see my head impaled on a wooden pike.

"They started it," I mutter.

"Yes, they did. And I think we can safely say that you've ended it." His arm slings over my shoulders. It's a casual movement, but I can feel the strain of his muscles as he exerts pressure to keep me from flying out. "What do you say you and I get out of here for a spell?"

"I can't," I protest. "Lola—"

"Will be just fine with Tara and Jordan," Riker says and taps on my shoulder to draw my attention to the two women in question. They've arranged themselves on either side of Lola, providing a physical barrier few would have the nerve to break. "You won't mind if I tear her away, will you, Hijack? You've never seen Penelope in this kind of mood before, but it's not easy to bring her back down again."

"I don't need to be brought down. I need—"

Riker's fingernails bite into my shoulder, which is when my anger abates enough for me to take notice of Hijack's perfectly grave expression. Gone are the smile and easy charm that have always characterized him; he's hard and cold and, I hate to admit it, a little frightening.

I realize, too late, that I miscalculated how serious Hijack was about last night's ultimatum. That wasn't him cajoling and wheedling me to do his bidding. That was him reaching the limit of his tolerance.

And I, in my anger and hunger, just took one wide step over it.

"Of all the people I know, I thought I could at least count on *you*, Pen," Hijack says.

Guilt is added to all the rest of the emotions swirling through me. Granted, Hijack's out to serve himself— and has been since day one—but he never made any attempt to hide what he wanted from me. In this place of lies and double-dealing and husbands who refuse to tell you what they're up to, honesty is a rare thing.

I open my mouth to apologize, but he's already turned away and brushed past Lola without so much as a second glance at the tiara perched on her head. His disinterest alarms me more than all the rest.

"I should follow him," I say, but Riker holds me firm.

"No, Pen. What you should do is get something to eat." Such sound logic from Riker's mouth is difficult to refute, especially when he follows it up with, "You also need to chill the fuck out. Come on. I know something you'll enjoy."

I stare at him. There isn't a single thing on this boat that would bring me more happiness than leaving it behind forever.

"Just trust me, okay? You'll like this one."

Riker's idea of a good time rarely coincides with my own, but as there doesn't appear to be much else I can do, I give in.

"On my count of three. Ready?" Riker crouches a few feet away from me, his eyes meeting mine in a moment of pure mischief. He doesn't wait for me to confirm or deny my readiness. "One. Two. Now!"

Moving together, we turn and peer through the center railing overlooking the pool area. From the jogging track, it's a mere three levels to the bathing beauties below. Riker's target is a pale, skinny man who keeps berating the waitress to bring him a fresh drink. Mine is Eden St. James, who's resting languidly on a chaise lounge in a bright-red one-piece.

Our aim, unfortunately, is off. I blame the forward movement of the ship for my water balloon splashing a few inches above Eden's head. Riker decides his misfire is the fault of the wind. Either way, the sound of broken latex and splashing water on the wooden deck below is overridden by several shouted obscenities.

Giggling, I duck out of the way, my back to the railing. "Damn. I almost had her."

"It'd be better if we could put food coloring in them, but the kitchen didn't have any." He laughs. "It's too bad. There are a lot of people who would pay good money to see Eden St. James walking around with a purple face. We could make a killing."

"I think more people would be willing to pay to watch heavy objects fall on *me*," I say. Then, before he can chime in with his own delight at such a thing, I ask, "Again?"

Riker hesitates. "Aren't you afraid they're going to come up here and murder us?"

"This was your idea. You tell me."

"One more, and then we escape down the side stairwell." He makes the decision quickly and with confidence. It's always been his way. His decisions aren't always smart ones, but there's no denying he's willing to stand by them. "Ready? Go."

We turn and take aim again. My balloon misses Eden by an even wider margin this time, but Riker's lands squarely on the man's chest. The man spills his drink and sputters up at us with so much rage, we hightail it to Riker's side stairwell. By the time we fly down one flight of stairs and make it to the deck below, we're breathless and laughing.

"Oh, man. That was way more fun than it should have been." I follow Riker to the ship's stern, where a small overlook gives us a nice view of the engine's wake. "I can't remember the last time we threw projectiles at innocent bystanders."

He grins. "Those bystanders weren't innocent. I'm pretty sure that guy I hit invents fake charities for a living."

"Guilty ones then," I amend. "Either way, it was fun. Thank you, Riker. I needed that."

Instead of acknowledging my thanks, Riker settles himself on the boat's deck, slipping his legs over the ledge and hooking his arms on the railing. It looks comfortable—if slightly dangerous—so I join him. The spray from the water isn't tall enough to make it up to us, but there's a mist in the air that peppers my skin. It feels good, looks good—*is*, by all accounts, good. This is the kind of vacation most people only dream of.

"So," he says, ruining the moment. "You going to tell me what that was about down there?"

"No." I continue staring out at sea. There's something mesmerizing about the steady hum of the engine and the sluicing of the ocean against the hull. Mesmerizing and, I can't help noting, great for hiding open-air conversations like these. Riker's no fool.

But then, neither am I.

"Are you going to tell me what's going on between you and Tara?" I counter.

"No."

"I guess that doesn't leave us much, does it? We could talk about the weather instead. Isn't this a nice breeze?"

Riker has never been great at taking hints. "Lola is *fine*, Pen. I know you're worried about her, but you-know-who ordered each of us to make sure we have eyes on her at all times. You, me, Jordan, Oz, Tara—security detail is basically all we're doing. She's probably the safest person on the boat right now."

"It's not that," I say, though of course I'm happy to hear that *you-know-who* is still capable of understanding the basic concept of danger. If only I could convince him that the concept also extends to him...

"Then is it Hijack? The dude's a hack, Pen. He always has been."

I look at him in surprise. "What are you talking about? You were the one who recruited him in the first place."

"Yeah, six years ago. When we didn't have Oz and Jordan and needed a getaway driver. I was desperate." He makes a disgusted sound. "I meant to get rid of him as soon as possible, but then you got all attached, so we were stuck. You always have had shitty taste in men."

I bump him with my hip. "Excuse me. I dated you, didn't I?"

He grimaces. "Exactly."

The grimace lingers a second too long, the downward pull of his lips tugging on my gut. In all my concern over Grant and Lola, I've been neglecting him.

"Riker, are you okay?" I ask as gently as I can. "I mean, *really* okay? With all the poker playing and bets over the tiara... You're not doing anything I need to worry about, are you?"

I expect my question to needle its way under his skin, cause him to fly out, but all he does is sigh. "For once in my life, no. I'm not. Not at the gaming tables, anyway. I don't have a chance to. Two-Finger Tommy has the dealer in one pocket and a stack of aces in the other. I was screwed before the first hand was even dealt."

As a metaphor for the rest of his life, that's pretty bleak. And accurate.

"You don't seem very upset about him cheating," I say.

"I *am* upset. I'm furious."

Never, in all his life, has Riker sounded less furious about anything.

"But this isn't the time or the place to deal with him," he says, doing little to reassure me about his current state of mind. "With the way things are situated right now, I can't give the game—or him—the attention they deserve."

"Riker..." I begin again, though I'm not sure why. To apologize? To plead?

He cuts both those options short. "Oh, stop it. For once, this has nothing to do with you. I only came in the first place because Tara—" He stops and casts me a quick glance.

"Because Tara wanted you to keep her company?" is my hopeful guess. Somehow, I don't think I'm right.

"Yeah. For that." His mouth is a flat line.

"Do you want to throw water balloons at Two-Finger

to make yourself feel better?" I ask. "We have a few left."

The short, sharp bark of Riker's laugh is one of the most welcome sounds in the world. "Thanks, but I value my skin where it is."

"I wish *other* people on this boat would care more about theirs," I say.

Riker casts me a sidelong look. "He's going to be okay, Pen. He knows what he's doing."

"You think? Then he's the only one who does. *I* certainly don't have any idea what he's up to. He hasn't sent me a message in forever."

I don't mean to be so negative, but I can't help it. It's easy for people like my dad and Riker to say that Grant is capable of seeing this thing through on his own, but that's because they don't know him the way I do. Playing complex, twisted games with dangerous men *sounds* fun—I know, because it's one of my favorite pastimes—but there's a difference between doing it on solid ground and doing it out at sea.

The fact that my legs are dangling off the edge of the deck and there's nothing but the deep blue ocean in every direction serves as reinforcement. We're as alone as we could possibly be out here. The whole ship could be taken over by pirates, and no one would come to our aid.

"You don't need a message to know what he's up to." Riker recalls me to a sense of my surroundings with a nudge. "He's finding Johnny Francis, remember? That's the whole reason you're here."

At first, I don't do more than register the fact that Riker spoke. I'm too busy dwelling on the agreeable image of pirates taking over the ship and throwing both Hijack and Peter Sanchez from the bow.

"In fact, I wouldn't be surprised if he's found him already," Riker continues. "Or at least that he has a solid plan for drawing him out. Otherwise, why would he have pulled us off the search to keep watch on Lola instead?"

I whip my head to stare at him. "What did you say?"

"Nothing," Riker says, alarmed at my sudden vehemence. "Just that I assume he's found Johnny by now — or close enough to count, anyway. That's why he's not sending you any messages. There's no need."

I groan and clutch the railing with a force that feels strong enough to snap it. "Oh, my God," I breathe. "That's it. That's what he's doing. That's why he took charge of the tiara's security."

"Um, Pen? What are you talking about?"

"I can't believe I didn't see it before." I slide my feet from the edge of the boat and stand on angry legs. The combination of adrenaline and churning water makes me dizzy. "I can't believe he'd do that to her—to *me*."

"Pen?"

"You said it yourself—he's drawing him out." I shake my head, my windblown hair whipping my face. "He *hasn't* found Johnny Francis yet. Lola, Hijack, Eden St. James…none of them have any idea who he is. They said so themselves. The only thing any of us knows for certain is that he'll stop at nothing to get his hands on that tiara."

"So? That's common knowledge. It's why we're all here."

"Yes, but what's Grant's favorite way to lure out unsuspecting bad guys?"

His lips lift in a quirked smile. "Um. Marrying them?"

I'm not amused. "No, he loves to dangle bait in front of them."

The man once tried to bait me with a diamond necklace; he succeeded in baiting my dad with *me*. It's his favorite negotiating tactic. If he has access to a tool to draw someone out, he'll use it. It's the one aspect of our relationship that's remained constant from the start.

"Think about it, Riker," I say. "What's the *one* thing Johnny Francis wants most on this boat—the *one* thing that will draw him out of his hidey-hole?"

Riker blinks. "The Luxor Tiara?"

"Exactly." I wish I could be more triumphant about my breakthrough, but my legs and arms are shaking. I can't help but remember how pleased Grant looked when I invited Lola to stay in my room with me. Of *course* he was pleased—I was playing directly into his game, helping him set the trap. "He planned this whole thing. Every part of it. Lola walking around wearing the tiara, me taking care of her, all you guys watching her every movement. She's the bait. He's waiting for Johnny Francis to strike so he can catch him red-handed."

"You think? Putting an innocent girl at risk? He'd go that far?"

"I can't come up with any other scenario that fits," I say. And it makes sense. Not content with putting himself in harm's way, he's sentenced the rest of us to doom with him. "It would also explain why he refuses to tell any of us what's going on. He knows how I'd react. He knows I'd pull the plug on this operation in a hot second."

In fact, he's been so worried I'd pull the plug anyway

that he's committed himself to distract me through any means necessary. The Kit O'Kelly flirtation, the playful way he's conducting himself—it's all an attempt to get me to look the other way. Grant knows from extensive personal experience that the best way to control me is with a pair of strong hands and a blinding smile.

And the worst part is, it's *worked*.

"Pen, where are you going?" Riker leaps to his feet. "You can't go after him. You can't say anything. He's probably surrounded by Peter's men right now."

"Oh, I'm not going after him," I say, my teeth clenched tight.

"Then what are we doing?"

"Keeping an eye on Lola, of course. Isn't that what His Majesty decrees?"

Riker releases a sound somewhere between a laugh and a sigh. "Since when have you followed anyone's decrees but your own?"

"Never," I reply tightly. And I'm not about to start now.

THE ATTEMPT

17

MY LUCK TURNS THE SECOND I START TRYING TO LOSE.

"I'll take three cards, please," I say sweetly to our dealer. It's the same guy we've had the entire time, but I don't dislike him as much today. Mostly because he's as eager for this game to end as I am. "And if you could make them all hearts, I'd really appreciate it."

"I'll do my best," he replies and proceeds to deal me exactly what I asked for. Three bright, shiny hearts—all I need to give myself a flush and a stack of chips that, at first glance, looks to contain about two hundred thousand dollars.

"Oh, fuck. She's got them." The man seated to my left tosses his cards down in disgust. "Look at her face. She can barely believe it herself."

"I don't know what you're talking about," I protest, but one by one, everyone at the table follows him. Fold, fold, outraged fold... The pot is mine for the taking.

Well, with the exception of one player.

"I'm not buying it. No one has that bad of a poker face. She's bluffing." Eden turns her head to stare at me. "I call."

I watch with a sinking heart as she pushes a stack of her chips to the middle of the table. It's so tall, a few topple over and come rolling my way.

"Sorry," I say with a wince. I flip the cards over. "I actually *do* have that bad of a poker face. I can't lie to save my life."

Her own poker face is pretty good. You wouldn't think, to look at her, that she wants to reach up and strangle me, but I know the urge is there. It's in the pulse of the vein that bisects her forehead. When she's calm, her forehead is like smooth porcelain, but the more I win, the more pronounced that vein is getting.

I'm sorry, I want to tell her. *I'm trying my very best to lose*.

In fact, I've been trying to lose for the past four hours to no avail. I'm not sure yet what my plan is for bringing this FBI operation to a grinding halt, but I do know that I can't accomplish anything when I have to dedicate eight hours of every day to this stupid table. I'd hoped to be out within fifteen minutes, but no matter how recklessly I bet or how many cards I do—or don't—take, my pile has been growing steadily larger all day.

It would be hilarious if it wasn't so annoying. I have things to do, dammit.

"A jewel thief who can't lie?" Eden asks in her clipped voice. She sounds calm, but I doubt the emotion goes very deep. "That must be a liability when you're on a job."

"Not really." I start pulling the chips my way, heedless

of the untidy piles. "Most of the time, I don't bother hiding what I'm doing. It's easier that way."

She doesn't miss a beat. "What are your plans for stealing the tiara?"

I don't miss one, either. "I don't have any. I don't need them. If I keep playing like this, I'm going to get my hands on it the good old-fashioned way."

My insult hits home. I'm so busy gloating over her forehead vein's new proportions that I don't notice the dealer trying to get my attention.

"Are you going to ante, miss?" he asks.

"Oh. Yes. Sorry." I toss a chip in the center of the table before returning my attention to Eden. "If we're exchanging truths, does that mean I get to ask what you were doing in my father's room?"

"I can't stop you from asking," is her tart reply.

"You're not going to pry any secrets out of him, if that's what you're hoping," I say. "He's much more professional than that."

"Professional? Is that what you'd call it?"

I flush. I most decidedly would *not* call his late-night activities professional, but I'm also a big fan of family solidarity, so I don't give my dad the public denouncement he deserves. "It just seems like a cheap ploy is all I'm saying. I'd have thought a woman like you could be a *little* more creative than that."

The dealer coughs gently, forcing my attention back to the table. "Ms. Blue?"

"Um, sorry. I wasn't listening."

"I gathered as much. How many cards will you take?"

Gah. Stupid poker. "I don't care," I reply with a wave of my hand. "You pick."

When the dealer coughs again, this time more insistently, I push a single card from my pile his way. "Fine. One. I'll trade this one. And I'll match whatever's in there."

"Are you sure about that?" The dealer's hand remains poised on the deck of cards.

I cast a quick glance at the table to find that the pot is much larger than I realized, the mound bigger than any I've seen thus far. It spills over like treasure. All three of the other men at the table have put the last of their small piles into it, making this their final hand. Even Eden looks slightly alarmed at the lackadaisical way in which I'm playing this—especially since I haven't looked at my cards yet.

It's not nice of me to play so haphazardly with other people's fortunes, but I can't help myself. I want to lose, and I don't mind causing Eden a minor heart attack in the process. So why not?

"You know what? I changed my mind. I'll keep my cards the way they are. And you can just go ahead and put the rest of my money in there."

A collective murmur from the crowd informs me that my theatrics haven't gone unnoticed. I wish I could say that the attention makes me blush, but I'm feeling rather maverick.

Eden narrows her eyes to shrewd slits. "What kind of game are you playing now?" she asks.

"No game," I reply, holding my smile. "Just trying a new technique."

"Aren't you going to look at your cards?"

"No need. I like the way they feel."

"You like the way they *feel*?"

I nod. "Do you want to touch them? I don't mind. Maybe my luck will rub off on you."

I start to push the cards across the felt toward her, but Eden commands me to stop showing off before shoving her own stack of chips to the mound in the center.

I sit back, almost dazed. That's it. That's all of it. One of us is going to walk away from this hand the winner.

I'm not the only one aware of the implication. The audience's gasp is loud as Eden calls the pot—almost as loud as the pounding of blood through my ears. Win or lose, this is unquestionably the most fun I've had at this table so far. If it wasn't so painful to whistle a million dollars away for no reason other than to save my husband's stupid life, I could get used to this kind of thing.

"The honor goes to you," Eden says with a lifted brow at my hand.

Since this is the last time I'm going to get the chance, I decide to prolong her agony as much as possible by flipping the cards over one by one.

The first is revealed to be a five of hearts. It's not very exciting, and the relief that washes over Eden's face at the sight is almost comical, but when I flip over the next one to reveal another five—this time with a diamond attached—her look of murderous intent returns.

"I told you I'm not so easy to bring down," I taunt as I prepare to flip the next card. I can feel all eyes on me, the drama of the moment suspended until even I can't take it anymore.

That's when the room goes dark.

I mentioned before that the dining room on this floor is gilded from top to bottom to make up for the lack of windows and natural light streaming in. The cabaret lounge is exactly the same. Because it's an interior room—and because it was chosen for its fortresslike exits and entrances—the darkness reaches a pitch-black level rarely seen in this day and age. It takes three seconds for people to pull out their cell phones and flash the screens, three seconds more for staff members with flashlights to start swinging their beams to and fro.

It's six seconds too long. I feel Lola's scream before I hear it. It ends almost as abruptly as it began, punctuated by a sickening thump before every voice in the room picks up in earnest.

My years as a jewel thief hiding in dark holes haven't given me the *full* ability to see in the dark—I still have to wear night-vision goggles for that—but I'm better at discerning shapes and shadows than most people. Driven partially by adrenaline and partially by fear, I knock over my chair and push my way to where Lola and Jordan were sitting. Several people jostle me along the way, hands grabbing at my waist and breasts, but I don't pay them attention. What's a little inappropriate groping when there's real danger to worry about?

I reach Lola's huddled body about the same time the lights come back on. Jordan sits with a dazed hand to her head, blinking at the sudden brightness, but Lola is curled up in a ball next to her.

"Lola?" I ask as I drop to my knees. "Lola, sweetie, are you okay?"

Her response is a wheezing breath that sounds almost as though it's stuck in her chest.

"Lola, I need you to talk to me. You're okay. It's over now. No one is going to get you."

Although she makes an attempt to push herself up to

a seated position, she's still not talking. Her head lifts and falls as though she's breathing, but the sucking rattle of her chest indicates otherwise.

"Oh, shit." I might not have any experience with her symptoms, but I can make an educated guess what's causing them.

Panicked, I search her body, her pockets, any fold of her clothes where she might have stashed her inhaler this morning. Nothing.

"Jordan, she can't breathe," I say, my own breath having a hard time reaching a normal pattern. "She needs her inhaler. Did you see her grab it this morning?"

"I can't remember." Her own voice is weak enough that I look over in alarm. She still has a hand to her head, a trickle of blood starting to ooze out from under her fingers. She could probably use some first aid herself, but that doesn't stop her from helping me search. A trail of bloody fingerprints showcases her efforts. "Wait. I do recall that she brought a bag with her," she says. "It must be around here somewhere."

With a hurried leap, she starts searching under the bleachers and discovers a black canvas tote, on its side and with the contents spilled all over the floor.

"Oh, good! It's right here." Jordan makes a grab for the little canister spread out among the gum wrappers and betting playbooks, but a large, angry-looking man from one of the other tables yanks her arm back before she makes contact.

"Don't even think about it," he warns in a voice like a battering ram. "If you so much as touch that tiara, I'll rip your arms from their sockets."

It's then that I notice the tiara lying scattered among

the remains of Lola's upended bag. Whoever attacked her must have accidentally knocked the Luxor off her head before he had a chance to steal it.

"She's not grabbing the tiara, you moron." I reach over Lola's body to get the inhaler. "Lola can't breathe. She needs her—"

The man gives up on Jordan and has my arm pinned behind my back before I even know he's moved. He twists the limb until my wrist is pulled up on level with my shoulder blades, the burn of muscles being stretched to their limit familiar to me in so many ways. He wasn't kidding about that whole ripping Jordan's arms from their sockets. If I were any other human being, that's exactly what he would have done. Fortunately, it just so happens my ability to squeeze into small places is due in large part to my natural flexibility. My joints have always provided a little more wiggle room than most.

"Let go of me," I demand, my voice slightly strained.

He doesn't budge. "Stay away from the tiara. That's the rule. Only she can touch it."

"She going to *die*," I say, my voice even more strained this time. I can't decide if it's pain or panic causing it. "Do you understand what that means? Breathing? Oxygen? Life?"

"I've got it, Pen," Jordan says as she maneuvers around the guy. He makes a swipe at her, but since he's busy holding me at bay, she manages to stay out of his arm's reach. Unfortunately, the additional movement causes him to exert more pressure. Fiery jolts of pain threaten to blur my vision, but I manage to hold on long enough to watch as Jordan gets the inhaler in Lola's hand and commands her to use it.

I have no idea how long she's been lying there, struggling for breath, but Jordan manages to get the device in her mouth and press it without further ado. A few seconds pass before the scary blue color drains from her lips and the labored, sticky movements of her chest resume a normal pattern, but she gets there.

Jordan flashes me a bloody thumbs-up. Only then am I able to relax enough to assimilate the sights and sounds of what can best be described as pandemonium. Chairs are upended everywhere, and people shout accusations left and right. Several fistfights have broken out on the other side of the room, and I'm pretty sure someone is being held at gunpoint by a crewmember over by the exit. No one seems to know what happened or what to do next, and the man who *should* be most concerned about this recent series of events—Lola's father—is nowhere to be seen. Nor, I note, are his private bodyguards or Kit O'Kelly.

In the absence of proper authority taking control, the man holding my arm decides he's in charge.

"I've got her," he announces in a voice loud enough to still the panicked movements of those closest to us. "No one worry. She didn't get away with the tiara."

"*I* didn't get away with the tiara? Are you as stupid as you look?" I twist my head to glare at my captor. I immediately regret it when I see the unpleasant contortions of his face. He may not be as stupid as he looks, but I'm guessing he *is* that mean. I decide not to ask any follow-up questions—which is fine, as everyone else seems to have plenty to spare.

"What should we do with her?" a woman to my left asks.

"Are we sure that's the real tiara?" the man next to her adds.

"Where is Peter Sanchez?" yet another nonhelpful bystander puts in. "Or the tall one in charge in security?"

I wouldn't mind hearing the answer to that second one, but instead, I turn to Jordan with a murmured, "Is she okay?"

Jordan looks up from her crouched position, her arm around Lola as she continues instructing the girl to inhale and exhale in a low, soothing voice. I've been on the receiving end of that voice enough times to have complete confidence in its efficacy. "She's good. Shaken up, but I think she'll be fine."

The gash on Jordan's head still flows freely, a rivulet of blood outlining the right side of her face.

"And you?" I ask.

She grimaces. "Head wounds always bleed a lot. Someone pushed me off the bleachers the second the lights dropped. I smacked it on the edge."

"Yeah, right," my captor snorts. "Someone. You probably did that to yourself."

I snap. It's one thing to accuse *me* of orchestrating this whole thing, but it's quite another to drag Jordan into it. She's spent almost every waking minute of the past three days sitting next to Lola, chatting with the girl and making her feel comfortable while everyone else treats her with a callous, cavalier disregard.

"Say that again to my face," I say, infusing my voice with a fury that's probably not wise, given my current state of captivity. "I dare you."

He yanks on my arm again. He uses enough force this time to render the edges of my vision black.

"Someone get a chair," he commands. "And rope."

The man tries to make himself sound authoritative, but I've been tied to many a chair before. His threats don't scare me.

"And hurry," he adds. "I'll need at least ten minutes to beat a full confession out of her."

Okay. That one might be a little alarming.

They manage to find a chair that hasn't been broken and get it settled in an upright position—with me on it—before I'm saved by the timely arrival of the *tall one in charge of security*.

I'm not happy to see him.

For one, he takes a single look at me being forced into a chair with my arm twisted painfully behind my back, and a grim expression takes hold. For another, he's panting heavily and favoring his right side. The slight lean to his gait might not be obvious to anyone else, but I can see what his studied nonchalance is costing him.

It's costing him severe pain and weeks of hard recovery work. It's costing him any and all physical advantage he has on this boat. *Of course* the idiot had to go chasing after the perpetrator on top of everything else. It might have been Johnny Francis. What's a little agony when the job is on the line?

My captor makes a curt command for the rope. Instead of handing over the coil that one resourceful spectator found backstage, the mob waits to see what Grant will do.

"What seems to be the problem here?" He speaks with a coolness anyone familiar with him would know is feigned. The sharp, tense undercurrent is a dead giveaway. "Perhaps I might be of some assistance?"

"I caught her trying to make off with the tiara." The man jabs a thumb in my face, dangerously near my eye socket. "She and the pretty, bloody one were climbing over the girl's body to get to it."

While I can't fault the man's taste—Jordan *is* awfully pretty, even with the streaks of congealing blood on her face—we were doing no such thing. "I wasn't trying to make off with anything," I protest. "I told you. I was grabbing her inhaler."

The man acts as though I didn't speak. "She set this whole thing up as a distraction. I was sitting one table over—I saw it all go down."

"Oh, come on. What distraction? I was playing cards just like everyone else."

"Yeah, right," the man says. "I've never seen anyone play cards like that before."

I take his words as a compliment, but the hard line of Grant's lips makes me think that might be a tad optimistic of me.

"She cheated and set it up to look like she was going to win. Then, when everyone's attention was on her... *BAM!*" The man pounds his fist into his opposite hand. "The lights went down."

"Please. I wouldn't even know *how* to cheat at cards. All I was doing was baiting the other players. Find Eden. Ask her. She'll tell you." Saying the woman's name recalls her to mind, and I cast a quick look around. "Wait, where is she? Where'd she go?"

Now that I'm paying attention, I realize she isn't the only noticeable absence from the room. Although my father and Tara never showed up this morning, since they're both on a reprieve until the next round starts,

Hijack was in his usual spot next to Grant—emphasis on *was*. Sometime during the power outage or in the subsequent mayhem, he slipped out unseen.

Oh, Hijack, no.

I bite my lip to keep from saying my plea out loud. He warned me that he meant to get the tiara with or without me. As it's been less than twenty-four hours since I publicly and unequivocally announced my unwillingness to assist him, it's possible he took matters into his own hands.

"I'm sure she's around here somewhere," Grant says with an annoying lack of concern. He could show a little more worry. She *was* the closest one to both me and the tiara.

"We should keep her tied up for the rest of the cruise," the man says with a dark look at me. "There's no saying what else she has planned. I heard she once broke into the White House and hid inside a dining cart for three days."

Despite my current predicament, a bubble of laughter rises to my throat. Honestly, these rumors are starting to get ridiculous.

"It's true," I say and do my best not to let the laughter go. "I can go into hibernation for weeks at a time if I have to. I'm just like a bear."

"Human beings don't go into hibernation," Grant mutters. "And no one is staying tied up for the rest of the trip. The situation is being handled."

"By who?" the man asks. "You?"

"Yeah," a voice calls from the crowd. "You're probably in on it. I saw you two dancing, and you looked mighty cozy."

While *I* might be easy to subdue, my husband isn't so easily cowed—a fact this group is about to learn for themselves. It's impossible to tell exactly where that voice came from, but Grant turns with a stare that lands heavily on each and every head gathered around us.

"Oh, I'm sorry. Did I make that sound optional?" His smile is hard. "It's not—unless, of course, one of you would like to take my place as security advisor. I'm sure Peter Sanchez would love to bring you into his confidence. Just say the word."

As an intimidation tactic, his offer is foolproof. As most of us have learned by now, being in Peter's confidence means being one small misstep away from death at all times.

"I didn't think so," Grant says when no one takes him up. "But don't worry. I'll get to the bottom of this. I don't intend to let her off easy."

Oh, dear. That doesn't sound promising. "There's nothing to let me off for—easy or otherwise," I say. "I had nothing to do with this, I swear."

"For your sake, I hope that's true."

He directs his next remark to Jordan. "Do you think you can get both of you to the infirmary, or should I call in backup to escort you?" he asks.

Jordan's brows fuse together as she assesses the girl in her arms. "I can get there fine, but I'm not sure about Lola. She's still so shaken up. I think it might be better if she doesn't exert herself any more than necessary."

As if to prove her wrong, Lola struggles to lift herself to a seated position. "No, I'm good," she says in a failing voice that convinces no one—even the mean guy who likes ripping people's arms out of their sockets.

"Don't worry about me. I just need another minute, and I can make it on my own."

"No, you can't." Riker's gruff voice comes from behind us. Like Grant, he's winded from what I assume was a lengthy pursuit of the person responsible for this. Also like Grant, he doesn't appear to have had much success. "And if you ask me, you'd be a damned fool to try. Stop wriggling."

Lola doesn't take offense at Riker's vehemence, which is typical for her, but she also doesn't brighten to see him. That's when I know she's a lot worse off than she looks—he's at his scowling, sweating best right now. She should be swooning at his feet.

Riker takes one look at her wilting form and mutters a violent curse. Before anyone can stop him, he scoops her into his arms with a gentleness—and an easy strength—I wasn't aware he was capable of.

"Put the fucking tiara on her head, would you, Jordan?" he asks. "I'll take her to the infirmary. And you, too, apparently. Don't you have anything to stop your head from gushing all over my shoes?"

Both Jordan and I know from experience that his gruff demeanor is a cover, but the rest of the people watching us don't, so they accept his authority with relative complaisance. Had he strolled up here full of concern, they might have fought his authority; as it is, they accept his anger as proof that he's as annoyed at me as everyone else.

He departs, Lola's head cradled in the nook of his arm and a few stragglers in his wake to keep an eye on any further attempts on the tiara. Under any other circumstances, I might feel relief at being deprived of my watchdog duties for a few minutes, but the air he leaves behind isn't one of peace.

Several pairs of hostile eyes are trained on me, willing my blood to flow and my bones to snap. I can feel the crowd surrounding me and drawing close like a snake squeezing its prey.

Lucky for me, I have a protector here to fight in my defense. Without making it look like it, Grant angles his body so that he's positioned directly behind my chair, one hand on my shoulder in a gesture of possessiveness. It feels good to have his touch.

He's my hero. My guard dog. Also the entire reason I'm in this stupid mess in the first place.

"Take her to Peter Sanchez," someone suggests. "He'll know what to do."

"Yeah, he'll eat her alive. Do it."

"We could throw her overboard," someone else offers. "Tie her to a rope and drag her behind the ship."

That seems a little dramatic, given the substantial lack of evidence mounted against me, and I say so. "You've got the wrong girl," I protest. "Think about it. Why would I bother trying to steal the tiara *here*, in front of all these people? If I wanted to take it, I'd just do it in the middle of the night when no one is watching."

There's a slight pause before someone offers, "You staged it so that someone else would take the blame."

It's not a bad theory. In fact, it's exactly what I *would* do if I wanted to actually go through with this stupid heist.

I'll never know if the crowd would have continued circling until there was nothing left but my picked-over bones, because that's the moment Peter Sanchez finally returns. Unlike Grant and Riker, he doesn't appear to be the least bit winded by his flight. Nor does he show a concern for his daughter's safety beyond asking, "Is it secure?"

"Lola's heading down to the infirmary now," Grant says. "The tiara is with her."

Peter nods once. "Excellent, excellent. It was in good condition?"

"From all appearances, yes."

I can hardly believe what I'm hearing. "Your daughter is also in good condition, by the way," I say. "She couldn't breathe for about two minutes, thanks to the angry mob that refused to let me get her inhaler, but I'm sure the brain damage will be minimal."

Peter turns to me with a hard, glittering look that lands like a punch. Before, his threats were always so mild and subversive, a casual discussion that slipped occasionally into the ominous. This time, the expression on his face is something else: a total lack of human empathy, an emptiness so dark, it hurts.

I swallow heavily.

"Thank you for the update," he says in a voice that's as mild and unconcerned as any he's used thus far. His eyes remain dead. "It does you—and my daughter—credit to know she has such good friends."

I don't know how I manage to stay coherent while the exchange takes place, but I suspect Grant's hand on my shoulder has something to do with it. It's hard to be scared when my husband literally has my back.

In fact, I suspect that showing my fear is the worst thing I could do. I draw resolve from Grant's warm presence to ask, "Then will you please tell these people to step down so I can go be with her?"

"I'm afraid not." Peter smiles in his deceptively gentle way. "Of course *I* would be delighted to let you go, but it's not me who distrusts you. It's the crowd, you see. They demand answers."

"I already gave them an answer," I say, but Grant increases the pressure on my shoulder. I close my lips accordingly.

"Do you want me to question her?" Grant asks, indicating me with a tilt of his head. "I find I can be quite… persuasive when I put my mind to it."

I don't dare move, dare even less to breathe. It's too good to be true. Being trapped alone with my husband in a small room is the height of all my dreams and aspirations right now. Especially if they pick a soundproof one. Giving that man a lengthy, voluble piece of my mind would be a veritable delight.

But then I realize that I should be terrified for my life—threats of torture are supposed to do that to a girl—and put up a protest. "Please don't," I say. "I don't have anything to confess, I swear. I'll be of much more use if you let me get back to Lola."

"Don't let her anywhere near the girl," my previous captor warns. "It's a trick. This is how she wants it."

My patience, never in abundant supply, runs out. I swivel to glare at him. "You honestly think my plan to steal the tiara was to cheat at poker to draw everyone's attention, drop the lights, have my partner knock Lola over just enough to cause her to stop breathing, only to *not* steal the tiara? At which point I'll—what?—slip into a carefully watched sickroom where I'm known to be visiting her and take it from there? What kind of heists are you planning where that level of amateur bungling is standard?"

I can tell, about halfway through, that I've crossed a line.

Grant's grip moves from my shoulder to my upper arm, the bite of his fingers sharp enough to warn me into silence. The good news is that he yanks me to my feet with such force that my wince of pain and look of fright are one hundred percent real.

"That's enough out of you," he says, his voice a low growl. "Save it for the interrogation."

Peter watches us interact with a slight smile. I get the feeling he likes interrogations.

"I knew I could count on you, Mr. O'Kelly," he says with imperturbable calm. "You'll see to it that something like this doesn't happen again?"

Grant gives my arm a tug, pulling me toward the nearest exit. I've never been so happy to see a door in my entire life. "Don't worry. You can count on me."

"And make it hurt," the angry man calls after us.

"Thank you," Grant replies with maddening calm. "That's exactly what I intend to do."

18

THE INTERROGATION

THE INTERROGATION ROOM GRANT LEADS ME TO IS MUCH worse than I expect.

To reach our destination, he leads me down several flights of stairs, each one drawing closer to the ship's fuel-scented bowels. I don't remember a lot about the *Shady Lady*'s bottom deck from my tour with Tara, but I can recall an alarming lack of fresh air.

Don't let it be the engine room. Please don't let it be the engine room.

"This is taking things too far, isn't it?" I ask as we bypass the last of the curious crew members, all of whom clear out with an alacrity that says much about the amount of authority he's been granted on this ship.

"Be quiet," Grant says, his voice filled with mock solemnity. "You'll go wherever I tell you to go—and you'll like it."

Well, the first part of that statement might be true, but no amount of Grant-imposed sternness can enforce the second one. I'll like whatever I want to like, thank you very much, and the dark hold where fuel is pumped and burned to keep thirty thousand tons of metal moving through the ocean isn't on that list.

Yet that's exactly where we end up, the pair of us standing at the dark portal to a loudly churning, steel-lined cell that would do a maximum-level federal prison proud.

I balk at the doorway. "It's awfully close in there," I say, thinking of my earlier freak-out in the gilded dining room. If a room that size with plenty of exits can cause a reaction, what is this place going to do?

Grant is alarmingly lacking in sympathy as he places a hand on the small of my back and propels me in. I think for a moment that he's going to banish me in here—alone—but he sweeps in behind me, locking the door as he does.

The click of that lock causes a constriction in my throat, so I distract myself by turning to my husband.

"Did you catch whoever caused the blackout?" I ask. I also don't wait for an answer before punching him on the arm and adding, "And what the *hell* compelled you to chase after him in the first place? I swear to God, if you've reinjured—"

"Not another word," he growls, and in such a sinister way, I wonder if I misread the depth of his anger. He doesn't really believe I caused that distraction on purpose, does he?

"But—"

"Especially not that word." Without waiting for me to argue, he starts moving around the engine room, running his hand along seams in the walls and bolts where various pieces of machinery are attached. His actions are efficient and assured, his search thorough. I realize after about thirty seconds that he's looking for bugs.

Safety. It's always safety first with this man. At least, it is where *I'm* involved.

Since the room is large enough that his search could take hours, I start at the opposite side of the room and make my own sweep. The clanking of the machinery seems loud enough to render all electronic devices null and void, but we don't want to risk anyone overhearing us. Especially since I've got quite a bit to say.

There are spots of grease on my fingers by the time I'm done, and the heat of the room has my hair curling in damp tendrils at my neck, but I come up empty.

Grant must not find anything, either, because he stops in the center of the room and turns to me. He has a wary look on his face, his brow lowered in concern. "I think we're clear."

"Does that mean I'm allowed to speak now?" I ask.

"Yes, but—"

I don't wait to hear his stipulations. "You stupid, hard-headed, careless *idiot*," I say as I march toward him. His lips twitch with laughter, but I don't let it distract me. "And don't you dare laugh at me right now, because I've never been so angry in my whole life. Take off your shirt."

"With the greatest pleasure in the world," he says as he reaches for his shirt hem. He also winces at the contortion of his body, which has me slapping his hands away so I can perform the action for him instead.

"I can't believe you're this irresponsible," I mutter as I slide my hands under the warm cotton to the even warmer skin below. "You know you're not supposed to be putting this much strain on your injury. How long did you chase after the guy?"

"Not long enough. I didn't catch him."

I peer up at him, but his expression is guarded.

"I'm okay, Penelope. A little sore, but it's nothing I can't handle."

The liar. The angry pink scar on his abdomen looks much as it always does—like an exploded starfish—but when I touch it, he winces and automatically turns sideways to favor the wound. The whole reason I developed the poke test in the first place is because his physical therapist once told me that the best way to determine if he's lying about his state of wellness is to jab a finger right in there.

His body will stop you, he said. *It's a lot smarter than he is.*

I love his physical therapist, by the way. His specialty is working with FBI agents who refuse to accept the limitations of their own bodies.

"Goddammit, Grant. It'll serve you right if you rip everything open inside and end up on the operating table again," I say. My words are stern, but the kiss I drop on his poor, tortured skin is anything but.

The action drags a groan out of him. "If you know what's good for you, you won't do that again."

"Or what?" I ask and do it again. Despite his convalescence, his abdomen is still chiseled underneath that scar. As is the case with mountains and rocky monuments, eroding a form like his requires more than a few months. "You'll lock me in an interrogation room? Torture me until I confess to trying to steal the Luxor?"

"Of course not." He pauses long enough to sigh. "I know this room is a lot smaller than you prefer, but I couldn't think of any other way to be alone with you. Not without tipping anyone off."

"Yes, well. Maybe if you weren't cutting such a conspicuous figure on board this ship, it wouldn't matter." I drop his shirt and jerk my head toward a metal chair off to one side. "Grab that, would you?"

He casts a wary glance at it. "I'm okay, Penelope. I don't need to sit down."

Yes, he does. He needs to rest, relax, or, better yet, sleep until next week. But, "It's not for you," is all I say. "And stop arguing. I don't know how long an interrogation is supposed to take, but I, for one, would like to get out of this room sooner rather than later."

He goes to retrieve the chair while I start rummaging in a toolbox, gingerly favoring the arm that had been mauled by the angry man upstairs. I don't stop until I find what I'm looking for.

"Why do you want zip ties?" Grant asks when I turn to face him. No explanation is necessary, though. He picks up on my intention after only a few seconds, laughter crinkling his eyes. "You think?"

"I *know*." I plop onto the chair and hold the restraints aloft. "And you'd better make them good and tight. We'll need there to be marks, or no one is going to believe I've been properly questioned. Kit O'Kelly strikes me as a man who likes to take his time with these sorts of things."

When he hesitates, I add, "*One* of us is going to have to leave this room looking vanquished. I hate to point out the obvious, but I believe it's my turn to take the bullet." I cast an obvious look at the hard lines of his abdomen, now tucked away behind his form-fitting shirt. "Don't wimp out on me now, Emerson."

He doesn't blink for a full thirty seconds, determined, I'm sure, to out-stare me. But I'm right, and he knows it. If we're going to make this look convincing, there needs to be at least some torture taking place inside these walls.

"Fine," he finally agrees, taking the zip ties from me and beginning the process of binding me to the chair. "But you know I'm more of a handcuff sort of a guy."

It's impossible to mistake his meaning. He's not talking about the kind of handcuffs he uses to bring down bad guys.

"And I won't make them very tight," he promises as he wraps his arms around me in a move that's much more embrace than stronghold.

Even though the engine room is sweltering and the confines of it alarming, I bask in the hot-bodied press of him. Oh, how I've missed this man's touch, his voice, the low-rumbling way he laughs with his entire body.

His head dips to mine, his voice whispering over my ear. "And I won't give you anything you can't handle."

A pang of liquid longing hits me deep in my gut. Those words might sound like a threat, but I know from long and excruciating experience that they're also a promise. Grant has always had a way of knowing exactly how to push my buttons.

"I can handle anything you throw at me," I say with a toss of my head and a flippancy that's mostly feigned. This room might have been tolerable while I was free to prowl and explore at will, but being pinned in place causes the rattle of the engine and the closeness of the air to magnify tenfold. Only by focusing on the brush of Grant's fingers against my skin and the glint of his strangely dark hair under the engine room lights am I able to accept my confinement with anything approaching ease.

He'll look out for me. He won't let me come to any harm. These are the things I know to be true.

"So do you want to ask the questions first, or should I?" I say as he eventually steps back to survey his handiwork. My arms are behind my back, secured to the chair frame at the wrist. Even though the bindings are tight, my limbs are loose. I'm about as comfortable as a person can be while bound.

Not that I expected anything less. Grant is good at this sort of thing. It's not his first time tying me to a chair, and given the strangeness of our relationship, I doubt it will be the last.

"I warn you, I'm not going to take it easy when it's my turn," I add. "You may want to conserve your energy."

He stands in front of me, feet squared and arms crossed, looking every bit as intimidating as his fake reputation suggests. At least, he looks intimidating until you get to his face. His lips are pulled up in a smile with the crinkles around his eyes to match.

"What's your name?" he asks, dropping right into the role of interrogator.

I guess he's going first. "Penelope Marianne Blue."

"Occupation?"

"World's greatest jewel thief."

The crinkles around his eyes deepen. "Who's your husband?"

"An obstinate brute of a man I'm rapidly coming to regret marrying."

"That's fair." He pauses a beat. "Who's Hijack?"

I jolt in my chair. It seems he's not going to be making this easy, either.

"You already know," I say. "He's my ex-boyfriend back from when he and Riker and I used to run together. He wants me to help him steal the Luxor Tiara."

Wordlessly, he scrapes a second chair along the floor until it rests opposite mine. He lowers himself into it using the kind of caution necessary when your body is in agonizing pain you refuse to admit to, sitting so close, our knees bump.

"You're going to have to give me more than that," he says, his expression gentle but firm. "Who is he really?"

"I don't understand the question. I told you—he's a car thief, a getaway driver, a wheelman. That's all I know."

Grant leans forward in his chair, causing his knees to press more firmly against mine. "I've spent the past three days sitting across the poker table from him, and every word out of his mouth is something about you. The jobs you used to pull together, how happy he is to have this opportunity to reconnect—to hear him tell the tale, you're a paragon of every virtue known to mankind."

My lips spread in a wide grin. Grant is *jealous*.

"I can't help it if I inspire men to madness," I say.

He rests his hands on my legs, his palms hitting me just above my knees. Despite the fact that I'm tied to a chair in order to convince a murderous smuggler that I've been questioned within an inch of my life, I'm comforted by those hands. Comforted and, if I'm being honest, turned on. Grant has a way of making even captivity pleasant.

"Madness is a much nicer word than I'd use," he says with a sigh. "I mean it, Penelope. If Hijack was such a large part of your life, why haven't you said anything about him before?"

My answer pops out automatically. "Because he wasn't a large part of my life—not really. We hung out for a few months, pulled off a few jobs. I didn't think he was worth mentioning."

When Grant's expression doesn't lighten, I say, "Besides, it's not like you've told me about every ex-girlfriend you've ever had. *Not*," I'm careful to add, "that I want to hear any stories. Keep the subservient brunettes of your youth where they belong."

He laughs obligingly, but it's a short reprieve. "Has it occurred to you that Hijack is far more interested in getting his hands on this tiara than anyone else on this ship?"

"You're only saying that because you don't know about the guy tunneling up to my room from below," I joke, but his meaning penetrates a few seconds later. "Wait a sec—what do you mean he wants it the most? You think *Hijack* is Johnny Francis?"

His only answer is a carefully lifted brow.

"Impossible," I say. "Most of the time, Hijack is more interested in admiring his own reflection than anything else. He's lazy. He never follows through. He's—"

"—the exact type of guy who might sell his secrets to the highest bidder rather than earn money the hard way?"

"Well, yes," I'm forced to admit, but only because Hijack is the sort who will take any shortcut that's offered him. That doesn't make him a criminal mastermind—in fact, it makes him the exact opposite. "It can't be him. I mean, he's a lot stronger and more persistent than the guy I used to know, but he lacks finesse. Even Riker agrees with me—he called him a hack."

Grant's brow comes down. "I've always thought Riker a man of good sense."

Now I *know* things are getting twisted. "You have not. You're just trying to distract me from all this other crap you've been doing."

"What *I've* been doing?"

"Yes, Kit O'Kelly, international securities expert," I say with heavy emphasis. "Remember that time you convinced me to come along on a dangerous undercover mission by swearing a solemn oath that you'd keep a low profile?"

Instead of answering me, his hands slide further up my legs. I jerk against the soft friction of his palms on my bare thighs, but there aren't a whole lot of places I can go.

"Don't you dare try to distract me right now," I warn. "I have a lot of questions for you. Especially regarding your use of Lola as bait to draw out Johnny Francis."

His hands halt their upward journey. "Is that what you think I'm doing?"

"Isn't it?" I don't fail to note that he neither confirms nor denies my accusation. "What other explanation can you have for standing by while that poor girl is put in so much danger?"

He glances away. "I already told you that wasn't my idea."

"That's not an answer. What's going on, Grant? Why won't you tell any of us what you're doing?"

"I have my reasons," he says.

Oh, man. It's a good thing I'm tied down right now, because that might be the most arrogant comment to ever leave his mouth—and that's saying something. "Not good enough. Try again."

"There have been...complicated developments," he says. "What I need most is for you to keep playing poker and keep watching Lola. I've got everything else handled."

"Oh, really? Does *handling things* include injuring yourself to the point where you can't even walk in a room without limping? Does *handling things* mean flaunting public relationships with people like Eden St. James? She suspects you of being Johnny Francis. Did you know that?"

"Does she?" A wry grimace crosses his face. "That's going to come as a disappointment."

"It's going to come as an attack in the dead of night," I counter. "*Talk* to me, Grant. Tell me what's going on. You're the one who begged me to come on this trip with you, remember? Backup? Support? The pair of us working as a team? How can I help you if you won't tell me what's going on?"

His hands tighten reflexively. The response is one he can't control—I can tell because his fingers dig deep into my bare legs.

"Talk to me," I repeat, softer this time.

Something about the earnest entreaty in my voice finally penetrates, because he draws a deep breath and shakes his head. "I know you're not happy with the way things are set up, but the situation on board this ship isn't what we hoped it would be."

"Oh, really?"

"Johnny is proving more difficult to pin down than I thought."

"No kidding?"

A reluctant chuckle shakes out of him, but he quickly sobers. "And Peter Sanchez is more dangerous than we realized, too. I don't like it, Penelope. When it comes to how far he's willing to go, this stuff with Lola is just the tip of the iceberg."

Titanic again. I'm starting to get tired of that ship. This one, too.

"So tell me what you want me to do," I say, leaning forward—or as much as I can lean, anyway. "Your Hijack theory is questionable, but I can play along with it for now. What else? Do you want me to throw Eden off your scent? Try to convince my father to lend his aid? Steal the tiara?"

There's no mistaking the way my voice grows hitched with anticipation at that last one.

"No, no, and most definitely no," he says, his hands moving upward on my thighs. "I already told you what I need. I wasn't kidding about that. The best thing you can do for me right now is play poker and keep a close watch over Lola. *Not*," he adds when my legs flex convulsively, "because I'm using her as bait, but because I have reason to believe Peter is."

"You think he'd go that far?"

Grant grimaces. "I think we have to consider the possibility that we aren't the only people on this boat with a hidden agenda."

I can't help but agree. It's starting to feel like everyone we've met wants something more than just a twenty-million-dollar piece of jewelry. *What a bunch of greedy bastards.*

"Okay," I say. "If that's what you need, then that's what I'll do."

He hesitates. "But?"

"But nothing. You asked, and I shall provide. That's the whole point of this, right?"

He stares at me for a long, drawn-out moment. "That's it?"

I incline my head in a majestic nod. Even though I'm in a highly undignified pose, seated and bound and at my husband's mercy, I've never felt more powerful. "I don't like a lot of things about this mission. I think you're playing a dangerous game making Kit O'Kelly such a public figure. I think being so close to Peter Sanchez is going to end up hurting you in the end. And I most definitely wish you'd spend more time sleeping and less time gallivanting about with Eden St. James."

A slow smile spreads across Grant's face at that last one.

"But—" I say, refusing to let that smile turn my limbs to liquid. It's a close thing, though. "We work best when we work as a team. If you need me to watch Lola, then that's what I'll do. Let's finish this, Grant. Let's find this guy so we can go home. Alive. *Together.*"

His coffee-black eyes, always so dark, turn even darker. "Together," he echoes.

"And I think you can go ahead and cut me loose now," I say, straining against my bonds. "I'm plenty interrogated now."

Grant must not agree with me, because he doesn't,

as expected, let me go. He stays exactly where he is instead, those dark eyes never leaving mine.

"Why are you looking at me like that?" I ask, a slight waver in my voice. "We're done now. We should head back upstairs."

"But Kit O'Kelly is a man who likes to take his time, remember?" he asks with a quick glance at his watch. "By my estimation, we have a good fifteen minutes before anyone starts to ask questions."

"Oh, no, you don't." I jerk against my bonds again, but it's no use. "You're supposed to be doing *less* activity, Grant. Not more. Not—*Ohhh*." The moan escapes before I can stop it, and I jump as one of his fingers slips underneath the hem of my skirt. The legs of the chair give a small leap from the ground with me.

"You're the one who said we need to make this look convincing," he taunts.

And I regret it. I regret everything. "Maybe you should just rough me up a little instead."

"I'm going to have to do a lot more than that." His voice is a low croon. "Nothing but torture will satisfy this bloodthirsty crowd."

"Grant, you sneaking, traitorous—"

"And nothing but torture will satisfy this bloodthirsty man," he adds with a deepening grin. "Unless you want me to stop? It could be days before we're alone together again…"

The firm and insistent movement of his hand up my skirt stops as he awaits my answer. Which is silly, because we both already know what I'm going to say.

Touch me, tease me, take me.

Grant Emerson, FBI agent and mule-headed guard

dog, always has been and always will be my biggest weakness.

Fortunately for us both, he's also my greatest strength.

"I hope you have a lot more in mind than just tying me to a chair and smirking at me," I say, tilting my chin up in a gesture of defiance and acceptance. "You won't break me that easily."

"Don't rush me," he says. "There's a fine art to intimidation. It's all about the anticipation, the slow reveal of the intended instruments of torture, the promise of what's to come—"

"Yes, well, I've just been given a very important top-secret assignment," I say. "So if you could speed things along…"

He doesn't.

He begins by slowly rolling up his shirtsleeves. That man's forearms are a gift to womankind, all ropey sinew and hard swells of muscle that he reveals one glorious inch at a time. He also loosens the tie at his collar, completing a look of dishevelment that has me breathing harder.

"You don't have anything I haven't seen before." Since it's the only movement I can make, I give a disdainful sniff. "You're going to have to work harder than that."

"I haven't even warmed up yet," he warns as he kicks off his shoes.

That part I *do* find slightly alarming, mostly because the second his shoes come off, all chances of me tracking his movements disappear with them. This room is loud, and he moves so silently when he walks—rob him of that piece of rubber between sole and floor, and it becomes virtually impossible to know when and where he'll strike next.

As if to prove this, he slips behind me.

That's when the slow reveal of torture instruments starts to happen. The first is a breath of warm air on the nape of my neck. There's something haunting about that sensation coming from a virtually undetectable source, especially since the pattern of his movements is familiar. Up and down over the gentle slope of my shoulder, lingering painfully long over the sensitive spot behind my ear. I twitch but don't move, though at considerable cost to my self-control.

"Bo-ring," I claim in a singsong voice. "It's just air."

His lips are the second torture device. They land unerringly on my pulse point, the soft pressure sending my heartbeat into overdrive—especially since he follows up that first gentle kiss with a succession of decreasingly gentle kisses. Each press of his mouth against my skin is its own kind of agony.

"You won't leave here until I get what I want from you," he mocks in a low voice as his lips reach my ear.

He doesn't wait for a response before continuing his assault. Under my chin, down my neck, along the delicate ridge of my clavicle... By the time he reaches the upper swell of my chest, I'm breathing heavy and seeing stars.

"Is it a confession you're after?" I manage to ask. "Because I have nothing to confess. For the first time in my life, I'm completely innocent."

"No, not a confession." He continues moving further downward, landing more of those kisses on the line of my bra. Inadvertently, I arch closer, mentally willing him to flick a tongue inside the fabric. He anticipates my desire and stops himself short.

That's the first rule of surviving an interrogation, I guess. Never show your captor your weaknesses, or he'll use them.

"Do you want my secrets?" I ask, a low moan escaping my lips as he continues ignoring my body's pleas for more. He opts instead to stroll casually in front of me, pure masculine arrogance glinting in his eye.

"For the first time in my life, I don't have any of those, either," I add. "I've been too busy trying to ferret out yours."

"No, not secrets." His lips lift in a smile that crinkles all the way up to his hairline. "You've never been as good at keeping those as you like to think."

Rude. There's plenty about me that he doesn't know yet. Just this morning, Lola showed me a trick for converting decimal points to fractions in my head. I'm a trove of hidden mysteries.

"Well, out with it, then," I say. "We don't have all day."

I try not to let his stare intimidate me into saying more, but it's hard—mostly because his stare is concentrated a little too closely on the spread of my legs. His gaze has the ability to turn my insides to fire under almost any circumstances. In *these* circumstances, the fiery feeling is rapidly taking over every other sense I have.

"What I want is for you to beg."

I laugh. In all the time we've been together, that's the one thing he's never been able to get from me. "No way," I vow.

His smile deepens until I swear it's the only thing in the room. "We'll see about that."

That's when he breaks out the third and most effective torture device in his arsenal—his hands. I knew it was coming, all his playful manipulation leading to this, but the reality is so much worse than I expect.

He begins, as he so often does, by landing his palm on my cheek, cupping my face in a gesture of affection. He's so sweet, so loving, so tender.

The sadist.

From there, he moves his hands over my body in a manner than can best be described as an assault. I've never had acupressure before, but I know the basics— there are certain points in the body that, when pressed, restore balance to the body. What Grant does is the exact opposite. He knows all the points of my body that, when pressed, makes me lose control. Face and shoulders and breasts. Calves and knees and thighs. He moves slowly and with deliberation over some parts, quick and efficient over others.

It's when his hand starts snaking a very careful upward path between my legs that I really start to worry.

"Are you ready to beg yet?" he asks. He *looks* to be in control of himself, eyes dark and movements assured, but I can tell from his labored breathing that he's not as much a master of this situation as he'd like. "I can make this quick and painless on you, but you have to say the words."

"Never," I manage once again, but I don't know how much longer I'll be able to hold out. I can't help it. I *miss* him—miss our playful lovemaking, this give-and-take battle that defines our life together.

I also can't help but think about what awaits us on the decks above. If anything were to happen to this man, this other half of me, I don't know what I would do.

Yes, I do. I'd take down this ship and all the people on it. I'd seek vengeance on every last person who put him at risk.

I might even beg.

"Suit yourself," he says in a singsong voice that does dangerous things to my heartbeat. "Just know this is going to hurt you a lot more than it's going to hurt me."

He means every word. The stroke of his fingers up my thighs and between my legs is an agony. He hits all the spots that drive me to distraction but none of the ones that push me over the edge. The slick slide of his thumb and forefinger against my core has me growing hot and biting down on my tongue, but I don't give him what he wants.

Nor does he give me what I want. I can't remember the last time I've been so close to release, every nerve ending straining for him to move a fraction of an inch and end my miseries, but I don't do it.

"Sorry, my love," I say, throwing his favorite term of endearment right back in his face. "I'm sticking to this one. You can deny me all the orgasms you want, but this girl doesn't beg for anything. Or anyone." I can't help feeling inordinately proud of myself for holding out. "Turns out I'm pretty good at this secret spy stuff, aren't I?"

Grant releases a shaky laugh, looking none too comfortable himself over there. The tight pants he's wearing outline every inch of his lower half, including the part of him that has been enjoying this torture session in ways I should probably worry about. "The problem with you, Penelope Blue, is that you live to thwart me."

"And the problem with you," I retort, "is that you love it."

It's true, and he knows it—a fact proven by the movement of his thumb the necessary fraction of an inch to bring all my agonies to a shuddering, spiraling halt. The delayed gratification—of my orgasm and of us finally being alone together—work in tandem to send my head whirling and my body screaming.

I don't think I actually scream, though—or if I do, the sound is swallowed by the engine room's constant clanging. Funny that I ever thought this room was unpleasant. I think I could grow to love the scent of marine fuel oil.

It takes a moment for my head to clear, another to realize that the clanging appears to be coming from the door. Alarmed, I glance at Grant and am immediately reassured by what I see. He doesn't look scared for our safety; he bears the frustrated look of a man interrupted with his panting, sated wife. This is borne out when Riker's voice sounds through the thick metal.

"Sorry to interrupt, but Lola's asking for you, Pen," he calls. "Are you done being tortured yet?"

Grant's groan clearly indicates what he thinks of Riker's not-so-timely arrival, but I can't help laughing. This is what he gets for trying to get the best of Penelope Blue. No one beats me at my own game.

"Not a single word out of you," he says with a raised finger in my direction. "And try if you can to look at least a *little* less pleased with yourself."

"I'll do my best," I promise and try for a frown. "How's this?"

"Terrible," he says and drops a quick kiss on my mouth. He lingers just long enough to press his forehead against mine, the gesture familiar and comforting and, because I honestly have no idea when I'll be able to feel it again, heartrending. "Thank you, Penelope."

"For what?"

"For not begging. For never giving in. For being you." His breath is warm on my lips. "I'm afraid things are going to get worse before they get better."

"I figured as much."

"But you understand that it has to be this way," he says, his words not so much a question as a plea. "I don't like it any more than you do, but it's just for a few more days. You know how much I love you, right?"

The answer is, as always, "I do."

THE VILLAIN

19

THE LAST PERSON I EXPECT TO FIND AT LOLA'S BEDSIDE IS her father.

As soon as I round the corner into the infirmary where she's resting, I catch sight of that perfect salt-and-pepper head bent as if in prayer. Since I highly doubt that's what he's doing, I stop and prepare to step back, bowing out unseen and unheard.

"Come in, Penelope," Peter says in his mild voice.

"Oh, um." I swallow and hesitate in the doorway. I've suffered enough torture today—I lack the stamina to confront this man, too. Especially since I doubt his methods are quite so...satisfying. "I don't want to intrude. I can come back later."

"There's no need to worry yourself. She's asleep."

And therefore can't serve as a witness to my death. It's not a comforting thought, but I don't see what other choice I have. When Peter Sanchez summons you, I get the feeling you follow, even if it's over the side of a cliff.

Resigned to my fate, I step inside the dimly lit room. I allow my eyes a moment to adjust before asking in a soft voice, "How is she?"

"Better, now that I've had her tranquilized." He pats the seat next to him. "Keep me company a while."

"Tranquilized?" That doesn't sound like good medical care for someone who needs to focus all her energies on breathing.

"It's a very light sedative," Peter says.

It's also a very *convenient* sedative, but I don't say so out loud. If Lola was asking for me, I presume she had something she wanted to say. She may have even seen her attacker. Forcing her to lie in a sickbed all day would be one way of keeping her mouth shut.

I shudder to think of the others.

Some of my fears must show on my face, because Peter adds, "It's not what you think. My daughter has always been high-strung in moments of stress. I felt it would be best if she got some rest." His smile, if you can call it that, appears wistful. "She's not like you."

I sit perched on the edge of a nearby chair, poised for flight. "Like me?"

"Naturally." He bows his head in a brief acknowledgement. "There aren't many people who would so calmly share a room with just me, my daughter, and a twenty-million-dollar piece of jewelry everyone already suspects you of having attempted to steal."

"I wasn't aware I was being given a choice."

Peter's laughter is surprisingly soft. "You're not. But I appreciate that you're willing to play along."

"Yes, well." I shift in my seat, relaxing enough to put one whole cheek on the cushion. It's not that I'm comfortable being in a dark, secluded room with a man like him, but he doesn't appear to have any murderous intentions toward me. *Yet.* "I have my father to protect me."

"Do you?"

I don't care for his implication. "Of course I do. My dad and I try not to get in each other's way, especially when it comes to things like enormous diamond tiaras"—and late-night visitors by the name of Eden St. James—"but I know he'll come to my aid the second I need it. All I have to do is say the word."

"It's such a comfort, isn't it?" Peter asks. "The father-daughter bond?"

As he doesn't look down at his daughter even once, I find myself bristling. I resent the implication that my father and I are *anything* like these two. I mean, he didn't show up to watch me play poker today, and he hasn't unlocked the adjoining door between our rooms yet, but that's hardly evidence of villainy. He's just trying to enjoy his vacation, that's all.

"The father-daughter bond?" I echo. "Is that what you call putting your daughter at the mercy of five hundred malicious thieves?"

Peter's eyes flash a warning. "No one will cross me. They wouldn't dare."

I scoff. "Someone did. Just because they weren't successful today doesn't mean they won't be tomorrow."

Peter smiles an empty, chilling smile, and I find myself wishing for the warning flash of anger instead. At least it sprang from a place that's human—a place that's *real*.

"That's why I have the great Penelope Blue to assist me," he says.

"I'm not the great Penelope anything. Most of that stuff you've heard is made up."

"I know," he says with a slight bow. "Clever of me, wasn't it?"

"*You* spread all those rumors?" I cry before slapping my hands over my mouth and casting an anxious look at Lola. She stirs but doesn't wake. I lower my voice. "That was your doing? But why?"

"I had to. You're very accomplished for your age, but I found that in order to build up your reputation to where I wanted it, it was important to expand on your exploits. I hope you don't mind."

I do mind—very much, in fact—but of course, I can't say so. "But why?" I ask, eyeing Peter warily. "What do you want from me?"

"Your help in protecting my little one, of course," Peter says in a soothing tone. He pats Lola's hand, causing her to stir once again. "I told you once that my daughter thinks the world of you. She always has. More than anything else, I wanted her to be comfortable."

I'm not buying it. A man whose primary concern is for his daughter's well-being wouldn't even allow her on a boat like this in the first place, let alone place her in the crosshairs of every villain on board.

"If you really want her to be safe, you'll let her stop wearing that stupid tiara," I say. It's a risk, speaking so bluntly to this man, but I have to do it. If even Grant's most powerful persuasions can't get me to crack, then a violent threat or two from this man won't do the trick, either. "I'm sorry if you're not used to people talking so disrespectfully to you, but you need to hear it. She's the nicest, most unassuming, sweet-tempered—"

Peter holds up one hand. "Spare me a litany of my daughter's virtues, I beg you. I'm fully aware of them and have had many an occasion to lament their existence."

"You'd rather she be ruthless, like you?"

"I'd rather she be fearless, like you. But she's not, and I've done my poor best to work with what I've been given. I was serious when I said that security on board the *Shady Lady* has been a nightmare. Can you imagine what it's like to prevent five hundred determined thieves from stealing something of so much value?" He doesn't let me answer. "No, of course you don't. No one does. If I'd have realized…"

I hold my breath, waiting for him to tell me everything he's realized and why, but all he does is shake his head.

"No. Even knowing what I do, I'd still arrange things this way. It's not easy to get someone like Johnny Francis into the open."

Grant hadn't been kidding about that, it seems. Peter *isn't* above using his daughter as bait.

"You want Johnny, too?" I ask.

"My dear, we *all* want Johnny. You didn't think I threw this little gathering for the sake of making money, did you?" His laughter is faint but mocking. "Don't be ridiculous. I could buy the Luxor Tiara twenty times over."

"So this whole thing is an elaborate trap to catch him?"

"But of course." His eyes open in the wide, doe-eyed way of his daughter. I find it much less endearing on him. "Johnny's been after my diamond for years. I wasn't inclined to let him have it, but he knows too much about a few of my business ventures, so I decided to cast a lure. This cruise was the only way I could draw him out of his hole."

I release an inward curse. Peter isn't telling me anything I don't already know thanks to the conversation below deck, but hearing the words straight from the devil's mouth has a way of turning my blood cold.

"When I heard Penelope Blue would be joining my little game, I rejoiced at the possibilities. Especially when I discovered that her husband would also be coming on board. You understand how it is. I saw at once what I had to do."

I stare, unmoving, his words making little impression on my brain.

He tsks. "Such a brave effort, sending a federal agent undercover on a cruise like this. Just imagine what my guests would say if they knew. *I* find it vastly amusing, of course, but I doubt my old friend Two-Finger would feel the same. A keen mind, but he's never had much in the way of a sense of humor." He laughs in a way that carries a sinister sort of soundlessness. "Oh, dear. I see I've frightened you, which isn't at all what I wanted to do."

Like hell he didn't. He feeds on fear, a soulless parasite sucking at other people's emotions.

"You know?" I manage.

"Of course I do. Do you take me for a fool?" His voice carries a hard edge. "I could have had him killed the moment he set foot on this boat, but out of respect for your father, I didn't."

I have to warn him. Every instinct I have warns me to fly out of this room, find Grant, and get him out of harm's way before Peter even knows I'm gone. But his next words stop me short.

"Which is why I recruited his assistance instead."

Like Lola, I'm finding it suddenly difficult to breathe, the closeness of the room and the danger of our situation working together to set my adrenaline in direct opposition to my respiratory system.

"He didn't like it, of course, but once I outlined what would happen to your pretty little head if anything happened to my tiara, he came around. You have to admit it's an even exchange—his help in securing the tiara in exchange for your life and the life of everyone you hold dear. Alas. Men who love their wives unconditionally are one of the worst liabilities out there. I never employ them myself."

I hear but don't hear his rationalizations. I'm too busy dwelling on the fact that Peter Sanchez *knows*. He knows everything—about what my friends and I are really doing here, about all our secret communications, probably even about what went down in the interrogation room. Grant's cover is blown and has been from the start.

While all that is alarming enough, the most important point is that Grant *wasn't going to tell me*. All that stuff about complicated developments, about the situation getting worse before it gets better... He was talking about this. Grant has every intention of letting me and my friends walk off this boat at the end of the tournament without him, leaving him to whatever tender mercies Peter plans to employ to bring his usefulness to a close.

My husband has always suffered from superhero syndrome—it's one of his worst flaws—but this is taking things too far. If we get off this boat alive, I'm going to *kill* him.

"What do you want from me?" I ask again.

"I told you. Protection for my daughter."

Yeah, right. "You mean protection for the tiara."

"At the moment, they're one and the same."

His words, calculated to put me in my place, stir something—a thought, an idea, a feeling so dangerous, it leaves me shaking. On any other day, I might sit here and listen to him outline his nefarious plans, playing along for the sake of the game. Today, however, I've just about had enough.

No one puts my husband in danger and gets away with it. Not even my husband.

"Then let me wear it," I say, the words out before I can stop them. "Give it to me instead."

Peter's interest is visible as a slight lift of his shoulders. "*Give* it to you? You want me to hand over the one plan I have to find Johnny?"

"Why not?" Now that I've put the idea out there, I plan to hitch everything I have on it and watch where it goes. With any luck, it will fly high enough to extract not just me, but all my friends and family members from this boat. "Your only concern is that no one steals it before the poker game is over, right? That it stay out there long enough to catch Johnny in the act?"

"I wouldn't say it's my *only* concern, but yes. That has been my primary motivating factor."

"Then there's no reason why I couldn't take Lola's place," I say. "As today's events have proven, people aren't nearly as scared of your wrath as you'd like them to be. It's just a matter of time before someone tries again. Instead of putting your daughter in danger, let me be the one to assume all the risk. Same great security plan, no asthmatic complications."

Now it's not just his shoulders that are up—his eyebrows are as well. "You'd do that for Lola?"

Not just for Lola—for everyone I love. "I would. I'll protect your stupid tiara and accept responsibility for its safety, but you have to promise me that no harm will come to Grant. You have to let him go as soon as all this is over."

"Such devotion. It positively warms the heart." He nods once. "I like it. The Luxor is yours."

The speed with which he accepts my proposal doesn't fill me with much in the way of confidence. I like this man as much as a pit full of spikes, trust him as much as a politician in an election year. I have no doubt that he'd send my husband overboard with bricks tied around his neck if he thought it would help him reach his goals.

Still, I can't help feeling a flutter of satisfaction as he reaches down and extracts the tiara from the silken strands of Lola's hair.

He bought it. I did it. I'm in.

"I'll go make a formal announcement now, but you should plan on showing yourself sometime this evening." He hesitates. "I can't promise this will go down easy, coming as it does so soon on the heels of your interrogation. They'll be out for your blood."

"Just tell them it's my punishment," I say. "That's believable enough. At this point, putting this tiara on my head practically guarantees my death."

He chuckles. "Fearless, just as I said."

He sets the tiara in place. Once again, the heaviness takes me by surprise, all that gold and all those precious gems carrying the weight of its previous bearers. Instead of feeling buried by it, however, the tiara feels natural, an extension of myself. My neck comes up, and my shoulders straighten. I rise to the task ahead of me, to the responsibility imbued in all these impressive scrolls.

In that moment, I can almost see why Johnny Francis is so keen on getting his hands on it.

"It looks good on you." Peter steps back to survey his handiwork. "Better than it ever did on Lola. Unlike my daughter, you have the confidence to pull it off."

That's easy for him to say. He's not the one carrying the full weight—pun intended—of his actions.

"I'll expect that to be ready and waiting for me at the end of the poker tournament," he adds. And with that, his apparent interest in the tiara is gone. "Now, if you'll excuse me, I'll hand the bedside vigilance over to you. Sickrooms have never been my forte."

"By all means," I say and gesture for him to find the door. The sooner this evil villain of a man is out of the room—and our lives—the better. "I wouldn't want to detain you from your duties as host."

He doesn't take note of the heavy sarcasm in my voice, but he does pause in the doorway, lingering just long enough to look back at me with an ironic, almost grandfatherly air. "By the by, I hear congratulations are in order."

The last thing I want is this man's congratulations. "What for?"

His eyes widen in mock surprise. "For making it to the next round, of course. Word came in while you were detained. They salvaged the gameplay at all the tables, and you've been declared the official winner at yours. Four-of-a-kind to Eden St. James's paltry three jacks."

He tsks. "Poor Eden. That loss is going to be difficult for her to bear."

I can't find it in me to be excited about the happy news. "Not quite as difficult as bearing twenty million dollars on your head, though, huh?" I ask.

Peter laughs out loud. "You're worth a hundred of my daughters, Penelope Blue. I hope you don't live to regret this day's work."

I don't answer him. *Living* to regret this day's work is exactly what I intend to do.

THE PLAN

I FIND HIJACK PROWLING THE SIDE CORRIDOR LEADING TO the cabaret lounge. At this time of the afternoon, with gameplay at a grinding halt and so much drama to wind down from, it's deserted—an empty passageway leading to even more emptiness inside.

"Don't bother," I say, leaning on a wall as I watch him sound panels and inspect cracks. "It's a red herring."

"What the—" He whirls to face me with a look of guilty surprise. "Fuck, Penelope. I didn't hear you come in."

"I wouldn't be much of a jewel thief if you could, would I?" I push off the wall and approach him. "But you're wasting your time in here. It *looks* like a good access point, but it's too restricted. There's only one exit at either end. You'll need more mobility than that—I think Peter set it up because he wants people to try to get in and out this way."

"How do you know—" he begins, but that's when he notices I've dressed up for this meeting of ours. His gaze zeroes in on the top of my head and stays fixed there, unblinking. "Pen. Um. Is that what I think it is?"

I give my head a toss—or as much of one as I can muster, anyway. Peter might think his daughter is a fragile weakling, but the fact that she wore this tiara for three full days without a murmur of complaint indicates otherwise. My neck aches something fierce, and my temples throb from the pressure of the prongs that hold the crown in place. That girl is some kind of tough.

"What do you think? Can I pull it off? I think it looked better contrasted against Lola's dark hair, but that could just be my massive headache talking."

Hijack takes me by the arm and leads me toward the far end of the hallway—like I said, one of only two exits in here—his grip unyielding. A flicker of alarm moves through me as I recall Grant's theory about Hijack being Johnny, but I shake it off. I have to. At this point, I'd gladly hand the tiara over to the guy if it would mean our safety.

"We've got to get you out of here," he says. "If anyone sees you…"

I grind my heels into the carpet, bringing us both to a halt. "They *have* seen me. Well, a few people have, anyway, as I was walking over here. I'm also supposed to make an appearance after dinner so everyone has a chance to see my new look for themselves, but we've got a few hours before we need to worry about that."

A gleam of interest fills his eye. "We?"

"We," I confirm.

The gleam deepens, but Hijack is too smart to ask what he's thinking: does that *we* extend to future plans for the Luxor? It does, or at least it *will*, but I'm not about to say the words out loud in a public hallway that may or may not be wiretapped.

Hijack is also too smart to let go of my arm. All that super fruit and protein powder have imbued my old friend with a strength that might, in another lifetime, have frightened me. But I'm wearing a twenty-million-dollar target on my head, and Peter Sanchez knows the true identity of my husband. Few things will be able to scare me after this.

"That must have been some interrogation you went under," he says as he continues dragging me out the door.

I'm not sure where he plans on going, but I hope he realizes that kidnapping me won't be easy. I'll soon have five hundred people watching my every move.

"I figured you had a fifty percent chance of being tossed overboard after that stunt you pulled at the table. Only you would end up not just alive and well, but alive and well and with one of the world's most valuable diamonds in your keeping."

Yes, well. I do have a way with frightening, powerful men.

"That wasn't a stunt," I say. "It was fate. I really did get dealt all four fives—Peter confirmed it. I won."

"You think?" he asks.

"Of course." I speak without thinking, but it takes about three seconds for Hijack's doubt to become contagious. "At least, that's what Peter told me. Oh, God. He was lying, wasn't he? I didn't win—he just wants to me to be stuck somewhere he can keep an eye on me."

"You're a terrible poker player, Pen, but you're not stupid. I'll give you that much."

"Gee, thanks," I say. "Any other compliments you'd like to lay on me while I'm in my weakened state?"

"Yeah. You can be a real bitch when you put your mind to it." Hijack frowns. "You hurt my feelings yesterday."

He wants me to care about his *feelings*? After he all but threatened to kill Lola in pursuit of the tiara? When the man I love most in this world is being held at Peter's mercy? I swear, if I didn't need Hijack's help in order to get my husband off this boat alive, I'd shove the diamond down his throat.

"Where were you when the attack happened, by the way?" I ask. "I looked for you as soon as the lights came up, but you were gone."

We pause at the hallway's end, which also brings Hijack's arm dragging to a close. Even though I'm not thrilled at being cornered in dark places with this man, I'm glad for the moment of reprieve. As soon as we open the door, there are going to be mobs of curious and outraged people following me around.

"I was chasing after the bandit," he replies.

"Funny. That makes you, Riker, and Kit O'Kelly on his tail—and not one of you managed to catch him. He must have been awfully fast to evade *all* of you."

"Or he was one of us. I told you I don't trust that Kit guy." He notices my wrists and pauses. "What did he do to you, anyway?"

"Oh, nothing much," I lie. "Asked a few questions, made a few threats. The usual. Those security types are all the same. They're mostly talk."

And action. So much action.

He runs a finger over the raw, reddened skin. "Did he hurt you?"

I hesitate before answering, which turns out to be a good thing, since he takes my silence as a confirmation of the agonies I was forced to endure for the sake of the secrecy. Nothing builds up a criminal's reputation quite like well-timed reticence.

"I'll kill him," Hijack says and drops my wrist. "Say the word, and it's done."

In that moment, I think he will, too. I can't decide whether his willingness to fly to my defense is further proof that he's Johnny or a complete denial of it. It doesn't matter either way, since he won't have a chance. Kicking Grant's ass is something I'm looking forward to doing myself. "Please don't. I have other plans for him."

"Oh, yeah?"

"I also have other plans for you," I add. "That's why I'm here."

"I knew I could count on you, Pen!" He leans in and lands another of those quick and friendly smacks on my lips. Accustomed as I am to Grant's long, lingering kisses, it's hard to feel anything but disgust. "Please tell me those plans include the words *steal* and *tiara*."

"I'm not telling you anything where we can be overheard," I reply. "But don't worry—I think you're going to like what I have to say."

Hijack takes to my instructions about as well as I expect—with enthusiasm and excitement and, I'm pleased to say, admiration—but the next part of my plan isn't so easy. In order to successfully extract Grant *and* all my loved ones *and* the tiara from this sinking mission, I'm going to have to coordinate a carefully balanced sequence of events—events that, unfortunately, include my father.

He's not a man to take orders, and he's especially not a man to take orders from a daughter he's none too pleased with right now.

Still, I lift my hand and knock on his front door mere minutes after leaving Hijack. The sooner I get this part over with, the sooner the rest of the plan can get underway. I have a lot of work to do and less than two days in which to do it.

My dad doesn't answer at first, leading me to fear he's not there. I think about sneaking inside and lying in wait for him to return, but considering the likelihood that he won't be alone when he does, I decide to knock again.

There's a quiet shuffle and the sound of a slamming door, but my father eventually appears.

"Penelope," he says, his voice dry. He glances at my tiara and blinks. "Oh, my. I see you've been busy in my absence."

That's one way to put it. "Can I come in?"

He stills, his hand on the doorknob. "Must you?"

There's enough quelling disfavor in his voice that I'm tempted to turn around and do this without him. Asking for favors is hard enough; asking for favors from an unwilling, disapproving paternal figure is so much worse. And the terrible part is, I can't blame him for being disapproving. Everything about my situation is clumsy, messy, and fraught with human emotion—all things he despises in a heist.

But that's me, unfortunately. That's the daughter he raised, the person I've become. Clumsy and messy and an emotional wreck—and determined to get us all out of this if it's the last thing I do.

"Yes, Dad," I say and shove my foot in the doorway. If he wants to force me out, he's going to have to crush my bones to do it. "It's important, and if you don't let me in, there are about fifteen people out here waiting for a chance to push me down a dark stairwell."

"Then perhaps you should avoid dark stairwells," my father says, but he lets me in.

His room appears as it almost always does, devoid of life and activity, tidy to the point of obsession. I imagine an entire team of FBI agents could sweep through here with every technological advance they have, but they wouldn't find a single fingerprint or DNA sample anywhere. Except, of course, for the wine glass with a ring of lipstick he failed to fully hide behind the television set.

Oh, Dad. Not again.

"Does my friend Peter know that you've, ah, confiscated his daughter's tiara?" he asks as he extracts a water bottle from the minibar and hands it to me.

I drink the water gratefully. I hadn't been aware of my thirst, but between all the torture and evil plotting I've been doing today, I haven't been hydrating properly.

"He's the one who gave it to me."

"I see," he says, even though there's no way he can possibly see anything. "That was a bold choice."

"He knows who Grant is."

No flicker of emotion crosses my dad's face. "I was afraid he might."

"You knew?" I ask and deflate onto the nearest chair. I don't know why I'm surprised—omniscience is kind of my dad's thing. I also don't know why I'm hurt—he's never pretended to love my choice of husband. "Why didn't you say anything?"

"Let's just say I suspected it," my dad amends. He remains standing, his upright stature putting me neatly in my place. "It's not like Peter to take an ally so publicly without reason. A reason, I might add, that rarely bodes well for the ally."

The churning sensation that's taken over my stomach since my conversation with Peter solidifies into cement.

"That being said," he continues, "I fail to see the connection between your husband's folly and that tiara on your head."

Yes, well. He would. My dad is incredibly smart and even more dangerous, but he's never been very creative.

"I convinced Peter to let me wear it in Lola's stead," I explain. My voice shows an alarming tendency to waver, so I clear my throat and force my gaze to meet my dad's. "It's the only thing he really cares about, which means it's the only way out of here."

"There's rarely just one way to accomplish something, but go ahead. I'm listening."

I dig my fingernails into my palm. I won't let him do this to me—turn us into another Peter and Lola, the man who knows everything and the girl who will never be good enough for him. I might not be perfect—there's no denying that fact—but neither is he. At least I'm willing to do something about it.

"Where is she?" I ask.

He doesn't blink. "Where is who?"

"Eden St. James. Is she hiding in the bathroom, or did you shove her in the closet?" I don't wait for him to reply. "Or is it the balcony? You should have warned her not to try and swing to mine. I reoiled the railings this morning. She'll plunge to her death."

Now my dad blinks—several times, in fact, his steely eyelashes fluttering in feigned disbelief. "You think I have Eden in my closet?"

"Or the bathroom," I remind him. "It's okay. I'm resigned to it by now. I heard you guys enjoying…relations the first night. I think you have terrible taste in women, and I'm pretty sure she's using you to get to me, but I'm not here to judge. I just need her to go away."

My dad clears his throat. At first, I think it's a warning to stop talking about his *relations*—even if I do overhear them—but he does it again almost immediately, louder the second time.

"You'd better come out here," he says. "She knows."

"Yeah, she totally knows," I echo. "And she's not about to let you ruin her father's life, so be prepared to grovel. I have a blunt object on my head, and I'm not afraid to use it."

She's not, as it turns out, in the bathroom or the closet. She's hiding in my room—a turn of events I find so upsetting that I whirl on my dad in anger.

"Are you kidding me, Dad?" I cry, hands on my hips. "You let Eden into my room, just like that? What if Lola had been napping in there? What if she decided to plant a bomb or saw through the floor so she could sneak in later?"

"Honestly, Pen. You always make everything sound so dramatic." The feminine voice behind me is full of exasperation. "The only thing I did in there was tidy up your clothes. You have to hang silk up or it gets crushed. I wouldn't have given you my favorite blouse if I knew you were going to wad it up with the rest of your crap. That's a five-hundred-dollar print."

"Tara?" I watch as my stepmother enters the room and gives my father a peck on the cheek. He accepts the salute with a warm smile—the kind of warm smile he almost never gives me.

I'd like to take a moment to express my outrage, but Tara notices the tiara and lets out an almost inhuman squeal.

"You got it? You actually got it?" She runs for me, arms outstretched. "How much does it weigh? Does it feel good? Can I try it on?"

She doesn't wait for an answer. Lifting the tiara from my head, she transfers it to her own platinum locks.

She looks amazing in it, of course. Without waiting for anyone to invite her, she saunters over to the nearest mirror and preens at her own reflection. The gold scrollwork with the imbedded sapphires sets off her hair to perfection, and not even the enormous rock in the center looks out of place next to her immaculate white dress.

"You never cease to surprise me, Pen," she says, taking in her image with satisfaction. "I thought for sure you had no plans to take it—you were very convincing. What are you going to do now?"

"First of all, I'm going to call up Riker and let him know where you are." I take turns glaring at both her and my father. "You should be ashamed of yourselves, both of you. Sneaking around like horny teenagers, betraying a man who's done nothing but support you. How long has this been going on?"

They share a guilty look. "It's not what you think,"

Tara says, at the same time as my father speaks up with, "I don't have to explain myself to you, young lady."

Since it appears I'm going to get a lot more out of Tara than my traitorous parent, I start there. "It's going to break his heart, you know. He really likes you."

"He really likes *you*, Pen," is her tart reply. "I'm just a temporary distraction. It's all I've ever been, and it's all I'll ever be."

Her words sting, mostly because they carry an element of truth. Riker and I haven't been romantically involved in a long time, but he never fully got over my choice of Grant over him. Even though I know our friendship will always be a huge part of my life, it's shifted these past few years. That's why I liked his relationship with Tara so much—it was evidence that he was moving on, that he was healing.

"You can throw blame around all you want, but I'm not the one he's currently sleeping with," I say.

"Well, neither am I, so you can stop looking at me like that."

When I stare at her in confusion, she lifts the tiara off her head and returns it with a sigh. "He and I are just friends, Pen."

I stare at the tiara and then back at her. "But you came on this cruise together. You've been hanging out almost nonstop for the past few months."

She turns a light shade of pink. As she's not one to be shamed by much, I can't help feeling alarmed. "He was helping me out with a little dilemma, that's all," she says.

A slow, creeping smile moves over my father's face.

"What kind of dilemma? Riker's not good at anything but looking broody and ordering people around."

She flushes darker. "He does more than look broody, Pen. He also looks…handsome. A man like that comes in handy every now and then."

That's all I need to hear to put the pieces together. "Oh, my God." I take a step back, desperate to put distance between me and my wayward parents. "You were using Riker to make my dad jealous, weren't you? You were only pretending to like him. You were running a sex con."

"It was *not* a sex con!" Tara protests.

"I don't approve of that language," my father adds.

I groan. This suddenly explains so much—the way Tara and Riker have been spending so much time apart, Tara's interest in my father's room, the late-night sounds that will forever be burned in my brain. "Then you brought him on the cruise to—"

"To nudge your father in the right direction?" she asks, sending me a quelling glance. "Yes. You'll be happy to know your father and I have fully reconciled. We're going to try and make a real go of our marriage this time."

"And that is all we're going to say on the subject," my father adds in a firm voice. "What happens between your stepmother and me is of no concern to you."

"Does Riker know?" I ask.

"Of course he knows," Tara says. "He's been in on it from the start—in fact, he's the one who convinced me to give it a try in the first place. He was feeling restless and thought a project would give him something productive to do. If you ask me, that man's talents are going to waste. He shouldn't be stuck in New York, dancing attendance on you. He could be running a huge criminal enterprise of his own."

I'm far too relieved to hear that Riker isn't about to have his heart shattered into a million pieces to feel angry at her implication. Besides, I don't *make* him dance attendance on me. He's in New York because it's his home—it's where he belongs. He's as much a part of it as I am.

"Then what was Eden St. James doing in here?" I turn my attention to my father. "The other day, when she was asking about Kit O'Kelly?"

"Exactly that," he says. He loses some of the stern, unyielding look I've seen on him so much of late— especially when his gaze lands on Tara. It's almost sweet, the way he turns all soft and gooey when he looks at her. "She thought I might have some insight into the identity of Johnny Francis and stopped by to ask. Also to try and sneak some information on you, but I hope I'm not *that* obtuse. I told her you had your whole room wired with explosives and that not even I dared to go in there without your knowledge."

"Really?"

"Yes, so if she asks, you have paramilitary training and pyromaniacal leanings. I also told her that I tried institutionalizing you when you were younger, but it never took. My intention was to convince her that you're as unstable as you act, but I'm not sure she bought it."

I laugh out loud. The idea of my father coming up with such a ludicrous lie—and for me—is too much. "So you're not disregarding my safety and well-being for your own selfish ends? You've been looking out for me this whole time?"

"What did you just say to me, young lady? My *what* ends?"

I gulp. "I thought maybe you were distracted, that's all. She is awfully pretty, and you have been lonely lately, and…".

My dad strides over to where I'm standing, the hard lines of his face solidified to stone. I fear for a moment that he's going to strike me or—worse—rake me down with one of his harsh verbal cuts. But when his arms come up, it's to pull me into an embrace that crushes the air right out of my lungs.

As the tiara is wedged between us, it's a necessarily brief hug. Having prongs that size stabbed into one's sternum isn't exactly comfortable.

"For Christ's sake, Penelope. Since the moment you told me you wanted to come on this damned cruise, I've been looking out for you and that meddlesome team of yours. It's the only reason any of you are still alive."

"But—"

"But nothing," he interrupts. "You're not alone out here, baby doll. You never have been. I wish you would rid yourself of this idea you have that I'm your enemy."

His moment of soft accessibility lasts for all of five seconds before he adds, "And for the record, I have never been, nor will I ever be, lonely enough to let a woman like Eden St. James come between me and my daughter. I resent any implication to the contrary."

At that, I can't help glancing at Tara, who is similar to Eden in many ways and who comes between him and his daughter all the time. If it came down to one or the other, I'm not sure he'd pick me over Tara.

I can't find it in me to be upset. Tara just looks so *happy*.

"Now. Are you going to tell me what you're really

doing with that tiara?" my dad asks, reverting back to his paternal airs almost immediately. "If you want my opinion, you should give it back to Peter Sanchez as soon as the first opportunity presents itself. His motives for letting you have it—whatever they are—can't be good."

"I know." I return the tiara to my head, standing patiently while Tara tuts and tucks everything in place. I'm pretty sure she takes an extra ten seconds or so to fondle the diamond, but I don't hold it against her. "Which is why I have a favor to ask you."

"What kind of favor?" Tara asks, instantly alert. She knows me well enough to realize that most of my favors include life-or-death risks at considerable expense to her personal well-being.

"Do I have a choice?" my father asks warily.

"I think I have a plan that will get us all safely off the boat," I say to whet their appetites. Then, when that doesn't do enough to excite them, I add, "*With* the tiara in our possession."

"I'm in," Tara says without delay.

"Do I have a choice?" my father repeats.

"Can you come up with another way to get Grant out of here alive?" I counter.

His heavy sigh is all the confirmation I need. The countdown on my husband's head began the moment this trip started, and his time is rapidly running out. My dad's influence might be enough to keep me safe from Peter Sanchez—and it might, in one of his more generous moods, even extend to cover my friends—but not even a man like Warren Blue can protect an FBI agent from a group like this one.

"I didn't think so," I say. "Which is why I need you

to punch Riker so hard in the face, he has no choice but
to fight you back."

"Penelope Marianne Blue—"

"Don't worry." I grin. "We'll let him know it's coming
ahead of time."

THE BAIT

21

I ASK RIKER, JORDAN, AND LOLA TO MEET ME POOLSIDE TO put the final touches on my plan. Jordan's part is relatively easy—and right up her alley. I need her to set a few things on fire.

"Do you mean it, Pen?" she cries, her face lighting up as though I just told her she won the lottery. Her exclamation isn't discreet, but then again, none of us are. Not only am I wearing the requisite tiara on my head, showing myself to all and sundry in accordance with Peter's directive, but I'm also wearing the white bikini.

The suit isn't technically a bikini—the top and bottom portions are attached by a metal ring in the center of my stomach—but there are maybe five inches of fabric on my body right now. They're five very strategically located inches of fabric, but I don't dare make any sudden movements. Some of these body parts have never seen the sun before.

"Yes, Jordan," I say with an imploring look. "I was

just wondering if you still have that recipe for *chocolate chip cookies*."

"Oh, I never use recipes for cookies," she says. She pulls her sunglasses down her nose and casts me a speaking glance. "You know I like to throw a pinch of something in here, a dash of something there. It's all about adapting to the ingredients you have on hand. But don't worry—you'll get the results you want."

Jordan is seated on the lounge next to mine, soaking up the evening sun in a skimpy yellow one-piece. Once again, it's a much more daring outfit than I'm used to seeing her wear—I can't decide if it's the vacation setting or something else that's causing her to give up her usual sweater-set levels of modesty, but it's a jarring experience either way.

"Just make sure the cookies don't burn," I warn. "I mostly want them for the smell. There's nothing like freshly baked cookies to bring people running."

"You got it." A look of rapt contemplation smooths the lines of her face. "Cookies. Lots and lots of cookies. I haven't whipped up a good batch of those in forever."

Content that Jordan now has more than enough information to keep her busy—that woman and her love of cookies is the stuff of a firefighter's nightmare—I turn my attention to Riker and Lola instead. Although I wouldn't go so far as to say he's being *solicitous* of the poor girl, he has kept his sarcastic remarks limited to one every ten minutes or so. It positively warms the heart.

"I like cookies, too," Lola says with a happy sigh. "Especially oatmeal raisin."

Despite Peter's heavy hand with the medications, she looks none the worse for her imposed rest. In fact, the longer she goes without the weight of the tiara on her head, the more relaxed she looks. I assume that the exact opposite is happening with me, especially given how little sleep I've gotten as of late. By the time this thing is over, I'll be a haggard old crone.

I don't care, so long as I'm not a *widowed* haggard old crone.

"Believe me, you don't like this kind," Riker mutters from the lounge on my other side. "When Jordan starts cooking, it's time to get out of the kitchen."

I smack him, my hand striking his bare chest. The sight of all that glorious nakedness almost caused Lola to suffer another asthma attack when we first arrived, but she managed to get control of herself by thanking him for his help in taking her to the infirmary. Nothing turns that man unpleasant faster than heartfelt thanks.

"Are you *sure* you don't mind wearing the tiara, Penelope?" Lola asks for what must be the fifteenth time in as many minutes. "I feel so silly causing all this panic and trouble for nothing. If there's anything I can do…"

I don't bother explaining to her that being attacked and almost killed isn't a thing she should have to apologize for. For one, I've tried already, and she keeps telling me she's sorry anyway. For another, I need to leverage her guilt for one *teensy* favor.

"It's no trouble," I say and smile at her. "In fact, I'm enjoying the attention. If I squint my eyes and tilt my head like this, I can pretend it's my cleavage they're admiring."

Lola giggles obligingly, so I continue while I have her in a conciliatory mood.

"Although I do wonder if there isn't something you can do for me…" I begin.

Riker and Jordan come to attention at once, but Lola isn't so well versed in my machinations to suspect anything untoward.

"Anything," she breathes. "Say the word, and I'll do it. You've been so kind to me, so understanding, so—"

"You haven't heard what I want from you yet," I say wryly, "or you wouldn't be so quick the use the *k* word. I was, um, sort of hoping you could take Riker back to our room and give him a few pointers."

"Pointers?" she echoes.

"If you don't mind," I say. "See, the thing is, I really want him to be at the final table. So far, we have my dad, Tara, me, Kit O'Kelly—"

Jordan picks up on that last name in a heartbeat. "Kit hasn't won yet, has he? Last I heard, he and Hijack are pretty close."

"Yeah, well." I try not to squirm in my seat. I forgot that not all the details of my plan have been aired yet. "I think Hijack might be further down than you think." Not to mention, he has explicit instructions to throw the game tomorrow. I didn't tell him why, of course, but I *need* Grant to be at that final game. It's the one way I can be sure he'll stay where I want him.

"Anyway, I thought Riker could use your help—"

"Like hell I do." By the time Riker finds his voice, he's sitting up and scowling at me. "You want me to take poker-playing advice from a teenage girl? That's where we are now, Pen? Really?"

I can't help but laugh at how affronted he looks. You'd think I just asked him to undergo a head transplant.

"Not advice, exactly," I say and send Lola an imploring look. "Remember that thing we talked about the other morning in my room? About how amazing you are at cards?"

Her eyes widen and she nods, her skin flushed. I assume the color is there because of the prospect of spending some quality one-on-one time with Riker rather than embarrassment at being able to count cards.

"The thing is, I feel like he could really benefit from some of your knowledge," I say. "I mean, considering who he's up against and all. It's only fair that the playing field is even."

Lola catches my meaning almost immediately. "I told you Two-Finger is more like a snake than a man."

"Exactly. So if you could find a way to help Riker out a little, step up his game… He could win, if he had you to help him."

Riker glares at me anew. "I don't need anyone's help."

Yes, he does, and for so many more reasons than he's aware of. For now, however, the most important one is getting him a seat at that final game—and Lola is the ticket to make it happen. "All I need you to do is listen to her, okay?" I ask. "You might be surprised what kinds of tricks she knows."

His glowering face indicates that he's not happy about this turn of events, but he gets to his feet with a sigh. He also extends a hand to hoist Lola out of her seat. He jerks way too hard and could have easily sent her flying, but she clings to him with a tenacity that would make her father proud.

Aw. The poor girl is plenty strong. She just needs something worth holding onto.

"Oh, and don't be surprised if Tara and my dad are next door," I say as a parting shot. "They've been spending a lot of time together recently, but I guess that won't come as much of a surprise to you, will it?"

If Riker's sharp intake of breath is any indication, he's none too pleased to discover that I know the truth. Too bad. I'm glad it's out there now. I don't know if he had real feelings for Tara or what, but at least now he knows I'm here in case he needs to talk.

Not that I think he will, of course. Riker talking about his feelings is like Grant behaving with circumspection. Some people never change.

As if aware that I'm lamenting the day I met him, the day I married him, the day I agreed to come on this god-forsaken mission, my husband appears on the other side of the pool. Jordan takes one look at him and decides she'd like to follow Riker and Lola to the relative safety of a room five floors down.

Before she abandons me, Jordan leans down and kisses my forehead with a laugh. "If he kills you, Pen, please know that I've enjoyed every minute of being your friend."

I don't rise to meet my foe.

Not because I'm scared or anything, but because I'm afraid that getting up will cause gravitational shifts inside my tiny swimsuit. Grant is angry enough at me without an accidental nip slip. I'm not taking any chances over here.

Instead, I tip my head back and feign sleep. It's not a very *long* sleep, however. I sense a shadow falling within seconds.

I open one eye. As Grant is standing directly between

me and the sun, he appears as a dark, looming, ominous
form.

"Excuse me," I say as sweetly as I can, but it's difficult with so much looming, ominous darkness nearby.
"You're blocking my light."

"I'm surprised you need any. With that rock on your
head, you're practically making your own."

My other eye pops open. "That's weird. You don't
sound angry."

"Angry? What makes you think I'd be angry?"

With each repetition of the word, some of his casual
facade slips.

"Call it a hunch," I say and indicate the seat recently
vacated by Riker. "Care to join me?"

I doubt he *cares* to do anything except hoist me
over my shoulder and return me to the engine room,
but since he can't do that without giving himself away,
he's forced to lower himself to the seat instead. Like
me, he's dressed for poolside activity, a pair of way-
too-tight swim trunks doing distracting things to his
lower half.

His upper half is also plenty distracting. It's weird,
but you'd think that the angry pink scars he carries on
his front and back would render him *less* attractive than
before, mar an otherwise perfect physical specimen.
They don't. There's something about the juxtaposition
of fragility and strength, the reminder that he's a man
who bleeds hot and fights hard, that makes him appear
infinitely appealing.

Grant is the best, strongest, and most virile man I
know. But he's just a man.

I'm not the only one to have noticed his manifold

virtues. Even if I do squint and tilt my head, there's no pretending anyone is looking at me anymore.

"I'm happy to see you don't hold any grudges from before," he says.

"What? You mean that silly little episode in the engine room?" I laugh and hold out my hands, where my various injuries are fading to distant memories. "Unlike some people I know, I heal quickly. I think it's because I take such good care of myself."

The fact that he doesn't answer right away shows that I've needled him. Usually, there's no one faster with a witty rejoinder.

"Ah, but even the great Penelope Blue won't be able to survive a knife wound to her back." When I don't say anything, he points at the tiara. "I assume that's how you'll go. Pity. Just when things were starting to get interesting between us."

"Better me than an eighteen-year-old who's unable to fight back," I reply lightly.

"No."

I pause, waiting for him to expand on that harsh, guttural syllable, but nothing more crosses his lips. I want to let it sit there, let him stew in it for a while, but I can't. I've always been way too curious for my own good.

"What do you mean, *no*?"

Now it's his turn to tilt his head back and feign relaxation with the close of his eyes. He doesn't even bother answering me first.

"What do you mean, no?" I repeat.

When he still doesn't answer, I decide to let gravity have its way. Rising to my feet, I do my best impersonation of a woman scorned—not a difficult feat considering how callously my husband is treating me right now. Doesn't he realize *I'm* the one with the right to be angry? He's the one who hid the truth despite our promise to work as a team, who put himself at risk when he knows he's the most important thing in my life.

He's the one who could die out here.

"What. Do. You. Mean?" I ask one last time.

I must finally sound angry enough, because his eyes flip open. They're hard at first, dark and cold, but they melt to something much more dangerous when he sees me in the full glory of my bikini. I can't help but preen a little, giving my ass a shake.

Grant's sharp intake of breath convinces me that despite my sleep-deprived state, I'm not without my charms.

"I mean," he says between his teeth, "that it is *not* better for you to be wearing that tiara. In fact, it's the worst possible outcome. Lola might not have been able to fight back, but at least she had the protection of her father. I told you I had everything under control. I told you to leave things well enough alone."

Yes, well. He also told me that next to Simon, I'm the one person he trusts enough to take care of him out here. Maybe it was all a lie, a way for him to woo me into agreeing to this plan in the first place, but this is one time I'm taking him at his word.

Grant Emerson is my friend, my husband, my *partner*. He brought me along because he needed a support team he could trust. And I'm going to extract him from this boat if I have to render him unconscious and drag his unwilling body by the feet.

"I'm sorry if you don't like it, but I'm in charge now," I say. "Whoever wears the crown calls the shots."

"This is not a monarchy. That's not how these things work."

On the contrary, a monarchy is exactly what this ship is. As long as Peter Sanchez is in charge, he's the one everyone looks to for guidance. He decides who plays poker and who's confined to the sidelines. He decides who lives and who dies.

Too bad he didn't count on the great Penelope Blue. Okay, so maybe most of the stories of my infamy are exaggerated. I've never stolen a truck of gold, and I didn't take a ten-million-dollar stamp collection, but the one thing I've been successful at since the day I took to a life of crime is looking after my own.

Peter Sanchez's reign is over. The mutiny starts now.

"Would you like to detain me again?" I ask, loud enough for people to overhear.

"I'd like to do a lot of things to you, but detainment isn't one of them."

"I'll bet you would." I give my ass another shake. This time, his sharp intake of breath is accompanied by a look of anger so intense, I worry I might have miscalculated.

But then he rises out of the chaise lounge, whether to grab me or to stalk away, I'll never know. All I can say for sure is that he almost doesn't make it. The sudden flex of his abdomen, the stress of chasing down the tiara thief, the fact that he's had to pretend for almost a full week now that there's nothing wrong with his poor, battered body—it's all too much. He stops and grunts, bent over double as pain finally gets the better of him.

I release a soft cry and jump to his aid, but he growls and flings out a hand, holding me at bay.

"I'm fine," he says and forces his body back to a standing position.

He doesn't *look* fine, a sheen of sweat covering his face and torso, his lips clenched so tight, they've lost all color. Still, I fight the impulse to run to his side and hold him up like a human crutch. To do so would not just give our relationship away but would also highlight his weakness to a crowd that feeds on it.

Oh, man. He has to get out of here—the sooner the better.

"It's okay," I say in a low voice. "I've got a plan." My words are meant to soothe him, to reassure him, but he just directs a grimace at me.

"That's exactly what I'm afraid of," he says and walks away.

No, he *hobbles* away, each step slow and deliberate, the walk of a man on his way to the guillotine.

That walk is everything I need to convince me I'm doing the right thing. He may not like it, and he may not be able to ever forgive me, but I'm pulling rank on the FBI. The great Penelope Blue is setting her foot down on this one.

THE MISSING PIECE

My plan to oust Two-Finger Tommy works like a charm—and by charm, I mean there's a good chance I've just equipped a gambling addict with a card-counting sidekick who adores the very ground he walks on.

When I returned to my room last night, Riker and Lola were sitting on the floor, guessing numbers and flipping cards. When I woke up this morning, they were putting the finishing touches on a series of signals they intended to use as communication. Lola wasn't able to pass her mad math skills directly on to him, so they're relying on a combination of card-counting tricks and clandestine gestures to give Riker an edge.

"You're not going to get caught, are you?" I ask anxiously as we prepare to head out for the day. "Maybe this wasn't such a good idea. What if Two-Finger Tommy catches you and kills you?"

"He won't," Riker says with a confidence I find difficult to share. "Everyone at that table knows he's been cheating since day one, but none of us dares to say so without proof. He can't accuse someone else of foul play without getting the microscope turned back on him."

"But—" I begin.

"Besides, it turns out I'm really good at counting cards." Riker grins, looking happier today than I've seen him this entire trip. "Lola promises to keep teaching me after the cruise is over."

I groan, all too aware that I've introduced a gambling addict to the one person who could make his problem worse. A pang of guilt fills me at the thought. After all, I'm supposed to be the person who keeps Riker *out* of trouble, not the one who introduces him to new and innovative ways to find it.

Despite the urge to say something along these lines, however, my mouth stays firmly shut. I'm not that person for Riker anymore, and the sooner I can accept it, the better. As the situation with Tara has proven, there's a side to Riker I don't have access to—a side to him where other people help to prop him up. I'll just have to trust that this new independence of his is more than a fluke, hope that he'll be able to remember how far he's come when he's back on dry land.

If we all get back on dry land.

There aren't many people in the cabaret lounge when we arrive, and since I plan on leaving as soon as I see everyone settled, I doubt it will remain busy for much of the day. As expected, the majority of the ship's guests go wherever the tiara is. I already won my table, which means I have nothing but free time on my hands, so they'll be spending the day watching me get my much-needed massages and nap time.

What? There's not much more I need to do to put my plan underway, and I'm really sore. Being bound and at the mercy of Grant's expert touch took a much bigger toll on me than I expected.

I'm still in the spa, an angry Swedish woman pounding my muscles into oblivion, when word hits that Kit O'Kelly took his table in a sweeping victory. Although my masseuse claims responsibility for my sudden and overwhelming relaxation, the real cause isn't difficult to figure out. *One down, one to go.*

Of course, by the time Riker's game ends, it's much later in the day—he had a lot more ground to catch up and a lot more work to do to accomplish it. I'm on the outdoor terrace with Jordan and Tara, our dinner being served by an efficient Oz, when we finally hear the news.

"You should have seen the look on Two-Finger's face when he lost," a man says as he takes a seat at the table next to us. "I'm glad that young, angry-looking one beat him—Two-Finger's been a cheat for as long as he's been alive—but I wouldn't trade places with him for anything. He's made a lifelong enemy of that one."

I look anxiously at my dinner companions, but they don't appear unduly concerned.

"Guys, I'm worried—"

Tara shushes me by plopping her dessert, a quivering pile of custard covered in caramel sauce, in front of me. "If you think Two-Finger is the first enemy Riker's made in his lifetime, you're a fool," she says and hands me a spoon. "Eat. He'll be fine. In fact, he's probably over the moon right now."

She turns out to be correct. He and Lola join us on the terrace not too much later, the pair of them grinning and flushed with their first foray into victory. Riker is so used to losing—at cards, at love, at life, at everything—that being in the winner's seat transforms him. He's always at his best when he's in the middle of a big job, boyish and grinning and, well, *happy*.

"Did you see the look on his face when—"

"Oh, yes. It was wonderful. I thought for sure we would get caught after—"

"Are you kidding? No one at the table suspected a thing—"

"Everyone hates him, you know. They loved seeing an underdog finally beating him at his own game. Besides, you're so sweet and handsome and—" Lola cuts herself off and casts a flushed, anxious look at Tara. "I mean…"

Tara takes pity on her and pats her hand. "He's the sweetest and most handsome man I know. You two did great today."

It's true—they did. All my pieces are set exactly where I need them to be. The final game begins tomorrow, and there's literally nothing more standing in my way.

Which can only mean one thing: *there's no turning back now*.

I realize the master key is missing as soon as I get ready for bed.

I'm not sure what prompts me to look for it, but it might have something to do with the fact that I'm packing my bags for a hasty departure. I doubt we'll have time to come and collect our things before we leave, but I like to know the option will be there. All my wadded-up clothes return to the hard-shell case where they belong, with Tara's precious silk prints laid lovingly on top. As soon as my fingers hit the metal ring in the center of the fated bikini, however, I'm recalled to another metallic object that once lived nestled close to my naked body.

"Oh, shit," I say, rifling through my pockets and checking my bra pouch, even though I can't remember the last time I thought about that key. "Where did I put it?"

"Where did you put what?" Lola asks as she emerges from the shower. Even though there's no reason why she can't return to her own room now, she's decided that just as I protected her when she was saddled with the tiara, so too will she protect me.

Mostly I think she likes having the company, poor thing. As far as I can tell, she hasn't talked to her father at all since she was in the infirmary. Even though my own father wasn't around when I was her age, I still had my friends to count on. Lola is literally all on her own.

"Um, nothing," I lie. "Just a memento I might have lost."

Not one to take a hint easily, Lola comes over to help me in my search. "What kind of memento?" she asks. "I'm really good at finding things since my memory holds on to stuff for so long. When was the last time you saw it?"

"It's a key," I admit, though I don't tell her what it's capable of. "I know I had it with me the morning of your attack, because I was careful to put it in my bra pocket."

Lola will probably never win an award for being the most astute girl in the world, but she doesn't miss how odd that sounds. "You carry a key in your bra?"

I think fast. "Yeah. It's a good luck charm."

More like a *terrible* luck charm, but who's counting?

"Oh, that makes sense." She pauses, lips pursed. "You say you had it before the attack?"

"Yes, I'm sure of it. I remember because I scraped it on my skin as I was tucking it in." As if to prove it, I lift the edge of my neckline down to show the tiny red scratch it caused.

"And afterward?"

"I can't remem—" I begin, but of course I do remember. I remember very well. Afterward, Grant dragged me down to the engine room, where he wreaked havoc on every part of my body. A considerable portion of that time was dedicated to my bra and all that's contained within it, but not once did either of us notice a key.

That's when I recall the wayward hands in the plunging darkness of the cabaret lounge—and how odd I found it that someone would use that moment to cop a feel.

"Oh, no. No, no, no." I start tearing through my bags anew. "It can't be missing. It can't be gone."

But of course it is. Ever the trooper, Lola helps me work my way systematically through every item of clothing I have and every pocket in them. It's no use. I know, in the depths of my heart, that the key isn't there. It's only after we've exhausted all possible hiding spaces that I allow myself to admit how badly I've screwed up.

I slide to a sitting position against the wall adjoining my father's room, Lola beside me, all four of our short-girl legs out in front of us.

"Is it really so terrible if it's gone?" Lola asks in a small voice. "I mean, you say you lost it two days ago. That means you didn't have it yesterday, and Riker still won his poker game. Your luck held just fine."

I stifle a groan. Unfortunately, *my luck* has little to do with that. Neither did Riker's. That was good ol' cheating and manipulation.

Lola hesitates in that meaningful way people have before they start speaking again. I wait for it, sure I know what's coming.

"You're planning something tomorrow, aren't you?" she asks. "That's why you wanted Riker to win against Two-Finger—it's why you need the good luck key now. Are you going to steal it?"

Thanks to our intensive search, the *it* in question sits askew on my head, poking me with its prongs and making me long to take up a nice, quiet life of embezzling instead.

"Yes, Lola." I'm careful not to look at her. "I'm going to steal it."

"Oh. Okay. Cool."

I can't help but laugh. "That's it? Cool?"

"I told you that if anyone is going to have it, I want it to be you," she says. "It's what I thought the first time I met you, and it's what I think now. It's what I'll think forever. You're the only person on this boat who likes me, the only one who cares whether I live or die."

"That isn't true, and I don't want to hear you say it again," I snap.

Just as she never winces when Riker grumbles, never cries when her father's cold look settles on her, so too does she accept my harsh words with a nod.

Dammit. How did her father ever think she could follow in his footsteps? Why would he want her to be more like me? Can't he see that she's way too good for this life we lead?

I snatch her hands in mine, softening my tone to say, "There are so many people here who care about you, Lola. I mean it. Do you think Tara accepts just anyone in her inner circle? Did you notice how Jordan always makes sure you're eating well and getting rest? Even Riker smiled at you yesterday—I saw it with my own two eyes. And he smiles, like, three times a year, max."

Her lips quiver. "Do you promise?"

"That Riker only smiles three times a year? Oh, yeah. I counted."

Her laugh is mostly a sob. "Does that mean you'll let me help you steal the tiara tomorrow? I won't get in the way. I swear, Penelope, I won't. Please let me help you. It's the least I can do after everything you've done for me."

I don't know how to respond, my heart heavy in my chest.

"Oh," she says and brushes a tear from her cheek. "I see. You've already made your plans."

"You'll be safe," I say. "We won't leave you behind. And you *did* help by getting Riker to the next round. We couldn't have done any of this without you."

"Of course." She nods and gets to her feet, doing the worst impersonation of a happy person I've ever seen. "You know what you're doing. There's no need for me to be involved. There's no need to take me into your confidence."

I watch her move around the room and tidy up my things, her gaze never straying to mine. I wish I *could* take her into my confidence—assure her that not only are Tara and Jordan and Riker looking out for her, but the suave Kit O'Kelly, as well. Unfortunately, there's still too much danger involved to let her know about my relationship with Grant.

That truth will have to wait until I have him safe and back home again.

"I hate to do this, Lola, but you can't stay here tonight."

She looks up from the act of folding a skirt. "What?"

I think about that master key and what it means now that it's missing. Almost *anyone* could have taken it from me in that panicked flight to Lola's side. That it hasn't been used yet to steal the tiara is no comfort whatsoever. A good thief bides her time, waits to strike at the best possible moment.

Like, you know, the night before the final game begins.

"Being with me is too dangerous right now," I say. "I think it might be best if you stay with Jordan tonight."

She recoils as if struck. "You're kicking me out?"

"Of course I'm not kicking you out," I say, prepared to assuage her hurt feelings and draw her into my arms. Unfortunately, a look of optimism replaces the injured kitten look, and I realize that the only way to get rid of her—for both our sakes—is to rip the bandage off as quickly as possible. "Actually, yes, I am. I haven't gotten a good night's sleep in weeks, and I need to rest up before the big game tomorrow. You'll be a distraction if you're here."

If I'd said that to any of my other friends, they'd have laughed and berated me for being a grump. We've been through way too much to take offense at the occasional need for solitude—like a family, we're stuck together whether we like it or not. But Lola isn't used to good-natured ribbing, and she's emotionally fragile enough that rejection hits her hard.

"Oh. Okay. I understand."

She doesn't understand—at least, not yet—but she meekly submits when I call Jordan to come collect her. Jordan doesn't demand an explanation, but I know she's curious, especially when I add that I'm going to bunk down with my dad for the night.

"Whatever you say, Pen," is her reply, but I can tell she thinks I'm being needlessly cruel to Lola.

I don't disagree. Considering that I'm about to rob Lola's father blind and endanger the lives of everyone I care about in the process, needless cruelty is just the start.

THE
EXTRACTION

MUCH TO MY DISMAY, I MAKE IT THROUGH THE NIGHT WITH
all my body parts—and the tiara—intact. Not once
during the long night did anyone attempt to break in
and rob me; at no point did I feel the need to flee to the
safety of my father's side.

It sounds strange, I know, but I'd been half hoping
someone *would* use the key to try and take the Luxor. At
least then I'd know who had it, feel the relief of knowing
the worst had already happened.

As it is, I'm forced to accept the possibility that
the key simply fell out of my bra during the scuffle.
Maybe it got kicked to a dark corner. Perhaps someone
threw it overboard. And if someone does still have it,
hoping they can strike tonight...well, they're going to
be disappointed.

By tonight, I have every intention of being as far
away from this ship as possible.

In honor of the final seven sitting down to play the

last game of the tournament, the cabaret lounge is teeming with spectators settling down on the severe metal bleachers. While the suspicious glances they send my way aren't what you'd call *welcoming*, my plan's success hinges on as public a spectacle as possible, so I can only be glad to see that so many people have come out to witness this final game.

Extra seating has been put in the empty spaces where the seven tables used to sit; this time, a lone table is set up in the middle of the room for gameplay. The names are clearly marked on the chairs so we all know our places. I, naturally, am at the head of the table—a position chosen by Peter to ensure that everyone will be able to keep an eye on me at all times.

From there, most of the names are familiar ones: Warren Blue, Tara Lewis, Riker Smith, Kit O'Kelly, Peter Sanchez. If this wasn't a matter of life or death, and if I didn't fear that every bite of food I've eaten over the past few days is poisoned, this would have been an ideal outcome. The game is strongly stacked in favor of my friends and family—I like the odds of one of us actually being able to win this thing.

"Good morning, everyone," Peter says as we approach the table. In honor of the day's events, he's worn his whitest, crispest linen suit. "I'm happy to see you looking well rested. The day promises to be an eventful one."

His comments are spot-on. With the exception of Riker, who's scowling and smells of fuel, we all look incredibly calm at the prospect of one of the most intense, challenging games of poker ever to be played. If Peter knew us better, he'd be aware that nothing is more alarming than this particular group sitting down amicably together. Most of the time, not even Grant and I can sit down to dinner without one of us turning the meal into a competition.

"How's my tiara this morning?" Peter sends a questioning look my way.

"She had a difficult time waking up, but I bathed her in coffee, so she should be perking up any time now," I say. "Oh, and a man tried jostling me as I left breakfast, but the man behind *him* was carrying a fork and stabbed him in the forearm. I suggest plasticware the next time you do this. People are getting desperate."

The story isn't exaggerated—that really did happen. From the look of it, the stab went all the way down to the bone.

Peter chuckles. "With any luck, we'll wrap things up either today or tomorrow, and we'll get that tiara in safer hands. I can't thank you enough for volunteering to wear it in my little Lola's place."

"Anytime," I say with a grand smile.

Next to me, Grant is so angry, I can feel his emanations reaching out to strangle me. He didn't try to make contact with me at all yesterday, and my towels have been sadly message-free, but he's walking easier today. If nothing else, at least I have that to be grateful for.

"Are we going to stand around and chat all day, or are we getting this game going?" Tara asks as my father pulls out her chair and hands her into it. He also leans down and murmurs something in her ear, which causes her to fall into a trill of laughter.

I have to hand it to him. Never, in all my life, have I seen my father give in to public displays of affection.

That he's willing to play the role of provocative lover for my husband's sake imbues me with some much-needed confidence. Together, we *can* do this. We have to.

"That's *my* spot," Riker says as my dad begins to lower himself into the chair next to Tara. "You're on the other side."

My father's brows raise a fraction. "Why, so I am. How remiss of me not to have noticed." He turns his attention to Tara. "Do you need anything else before the game gets started?"

She lifts a fond hand to his cheek. "Aren't you sweet? Just send me a few extra aces, and I should be fine."

"I've had more than enough cheating for one tournament, thank you very much," Riker mutters as he drops jerkily to his chair.

Peter pulls a similar routine with me, helping me to my chair and making sure I'm comfortable before taking his own seat. Nothing could be more catastrophic in upsetting Grant, who bristles to see me on good terms with the man trying to kill us all. He sits in mute anger, watching my every movement as though I'm going to run away with the tiara at any second.

I'm not—at least, not for a few hours—so I sit back in my seat and wait for the game to begin.

It becomes clear after about twenty minutes that I'm outpaced and outplayed on every hand. If there was any doubt that Peter cheated me into the finals before, there are no more questions on that now. There's no way I'm even close to the same caliber of player as the rest of the table—I'm being systematically destroyed by all those I love. In fact, Grant is more intent on getting me out than all the rest, betting heavily and taking the pot almost every time. He must assume that any plans I have require that I be in the game and is therefore trying to remove me from it as fast as possible.

The poor man. If he knew how close we are to things getting underway.

"You're playing awfully conservatively, Warren," Tara says in her sultriest, most cloying voice. "I thought you were planning on going bold or going home. I was counting on you."

"Were you, my dear?" he asks mildly. "My apologies. Let's double this bet."

Riker watches their proceedings with a deepening frown. Only the playful light in his eyes indicates that he's not nearly as annoyed as he's letting on, and he's keeping his gaze concentrated on his cards for that very reason.

Next to me, Grant stiffens even more.

"Wonderful!" Tara says as I toss my cards down in disgust. I actually have a nice pair of kings and would like to see if they can stand on their own legs, but that's not part of the plan.

"Oh, great. So now you two are going to ruin the poker game, too," Riker says in a disgusted voice. "How nice for the rest of us."

My dad lifts a cold brow. "Is this too steep for you? I should have warned you that I play to keep. Maybe you should fold while you still have a chance."

Riker sets the line of his mouth. "I call."

"Your mistake," my dad tuts. "I have a straight."

Tara laughs as my father takes the hand. "Sorry, Riker. You should have seen that one coming."

It's the first of many such interactions to come. With each hand, Riker postures more and more, challenging my father and coming up short every time. Tara and I feign indifference, but both Grant and Peter Sanchez have taken note of the table dynamics with rising alarm. In fact, after Riker enjoys a lengthy outburst on the wisdom of allowing traitorous, lying women at the table in the first place, Peter decides to call an impromptu break to defuse tensions.

There's a dark look on his face that makes me fear for my own safety—he knows I'm up to no good. I see it, Grant sees it, and most importantly, Riker and my father see it.

It's showtime.

No one is able to say exactly how the altercation starts. One moment, we're all getting up from the table, stretching our limbs and discussing what we intend to do with our luxurious thirty minutes of freedom. The next, Riker is up in my dad's face, telling him to step down or risk his fury.

"She's made her decision, young man," my father replies. "I suggest you step away before you make this situation any worse than it is."

"And I suggest you stop colluding. Has that been your goal all along—the two of you working together so one of you wins? Whatever happened to fair play?"

My dad stares at Riker with a look that would have any man, woman, or child trembling in fear. "Did you just call me a cheater?"

"Why not?" Riker laughs bitterly. "You're no better than Two-Finger Tommy. The wonder isn't that you cheat. It's that Peter Sanchez would allow this kind of thing to go on under his roof."

That barb has the power of being true, since Peter did

know of Two-Finger's tendency to cheat and did nothing about it. Peter is drawn into the argument against his
will, and with that, all attention is fixated on them.

Well, all the attention except for a select few. Although
I try very hard not to watch as Jordan slips through the
side passage and out into the relative safety of the hallway, I'm happy to see her making her rounds.

The flames start about thirty seconds later. I'm not one
hundred percent sure how she does it, but she gave me a
long, rambling explanation yesterday about the ethanol
she was cooking up in her stateroom from—I kid you
not—the sugarcane she confiscated from the kitchen.
Apparently, ethanol is the one fuel that has no real scent,
so you can slip it in an air-conditioning unit and spread
it throughout the ventilation system without detection. It
also burns very hot and very fast, which means that as
soon as she lights the fuse, flames begin spouting out the
vents in the ceiling in a way that reminds me strongly of
a rock concert with an overly enthusiastic pyrotechnician.

It's not strictly a bomb made from her dinner, but it's
close enough to count. Oh, how I love that woman.

Jordan's fire ends up being quite beautiful in that
dangerous, people-are-going-to-trample-each-other-to-
death sort of way. I enjoy a moment of calm stillness,
a silent appreciation for the wonders of her chemist's
brain, before I see the panic begin in earnest. There's
also a moment in which I hear a deep groan and Grant
says, "Goddammit, Penelope. You and I are going to
have a serious talk when we get home."

My husband has me behind his back in a matter of
seconds.

It's a lovely gesture, but it's not what I need to happen

just yet. The plan is definitely *not* for me to get caught in the middle of the mass hysteria with the tiara still on my head. Oz is supposed to be around here somewhere, ready for the grab that will get this rock as far away from me as possible.

"Stay behind me, and don't say a word," Grant says as he begins to back up toward the far wall. "And I hope you're prepared to swim, because that's the only way we're getting out of here now."

On the contrary, I have no intention of leaving this boat along with everyone else. I'm rather looking forward to staying behind, actually.

See, that's the whole point of this exercise. Sitting in that infirmary with Peter the other day was one of the most frightening experiences of my life, yes, but it was also one of the most illuminating. It was when Peter mocked Grant for putting my safety first that he showed me his one true weakness, the one thing that no amount of money and no amount of power can buy.

Loyalty. Affection. *Love*.

Peter Sanchez can hire all the bodyguards he wants, surround himself with criminals he can manipulate into fighting one another, but as he walked out the door and left his daughter behind, he also showed me the chink in his armor.

Without the tiara, without his boat of criminals, he has nothing. He *is* nothing.

Unlike me. He could take literally everything I own, rip the tiara from my head, and I would still be surrounded by the most valuable possessions in the world. They go by the names of Grant and Riker, Warren and Tara, Jordan and Oz. *And Lola*.

Which is why I'm doing all this. I'm going to take everything away from him and let him see how it feels to be truly alone. We'll see who has the power then.

"Not now, Grant," I say, knowing full well he won't listen. If there's one thing I can count on from that man, it's that he won't leave this ship without me in tow. Unconditionally loving your wife might make a man vulnerable, but it also makes him predictable.

And valuable. So much more valuable than anything Peter Sanchez has to offer.

"I have one more thing to do first, and then you can come find me." Without waiting for a response, I duck underneath his arm and make my escape.

"Penelope—" he calls, but it's too late. I'm using the distraction of licking flames and panicked people to get the hell out of here.

As expected, I'm a target the moment I step away from Grant's protection. Two men notice me and step forward, cracking their knuckles and tilting their heads in an ominously foreboding way. I dart to my right, but a woman is waiting there with her shoes in hand, which she chucks with so much force, I barely manage to duck in time. As Grant is also hot on my tail, I'm not left with many choices for retreat.

So I don't. I don't need to.

In all my preparation, only two names popped out as people I genuinely feared might try to wrest the tiara from me in the aftermath: Eden St. James and Two-Finger Tommy. The former because she's evil incarnate, and the latter because he's just plain mean. So far today, I haven't seen Eden at all, which is a circumstance I find both unusual and alarming. However, as much as I'd like to guess where she is and who she might be pushing overboard to get to safety, Two-Finger is the more immediate threat.

He spies me almost at once. He also does me the favor of disposing of the two men cracking their knuckles, shoving one into the side of the bleachers and tossing the other at the woman with the shoes. His path thus cleared, he nods once. It's an oddly generous gesture, this declaration of intent, but the extra second he takes is a mistake.

Riker makes a sudden appearance twenty feet to my right, just as we planned. It was too risky to have him walking around, goading Two-Finger into revenge, so he hid out in the engine room until today's game. From the look of him—and the smell of him—it can't have been a comfortable night, but the outcome is well worth it. All he has to do is stand there, looking like the handsome, cocky bastard that he is, and Two-Finger halts. His craggy face turns back and forth between us, the decision he faces an unenviable one. He can go after me and *maybe* get his hands on the tiara, but he has to know that I'm small and quick and won't make his pursuit easy. Or, should he so choose, he can attack Riker, the man who cheated him out of a win and made him look like a fool.

I have no way of knowing for sure which path Two-Finger will take, but I've got a pretty good guess. Warring sensations of greed and revenge will do funny things to people, pit two dark sides against one another in an epic internal battle. However, if there's one thing I've learned on this trip, it's that for criminals like us, reputation is all the currency we have.

After all, the great Penelope Blue might not be anything but a figment of Peter Sanchez's imagination, but just look at what she's been able to accomplish with a little fear and admiration on her side.

Predictably, he chooses revenge.

The second I see Two-Finger head in Riker's direction with a muttered curse, I'm off and running. I don't need to look over to know that my father is making a timely intervention on Riker's behalf—if intervention you can call it. My dad intends to claim precedence over Two-Finger, falling back on the age-old rights of a man to avenge himself on his not-yet-ex-wife's lover. It has a very Peter Sanchez flair to it, if you ask me. Of course, my father's not *actually* going to murder Riker, but he's going to make a convincing case for it. Not even Two-Finger can pretend that cheating at one game of poker trumps that kind of betrayal.

With any luck, my dad and Riker will take their argument—and themselves—as far away from this room as possible. They'll do it with Tara and Jordan and Lola in tow and head for the extra lifeboat waiting for them at the ship's stern. I had Tara do a little more flirting with the captain, and it turns out the rules for a fire evacuation require the captain to stop the ship and ensure everyone is safely unloaded before they can try and investigate the cause.

If all goes according to plan, Peter will be so busy trying to catch *me* that the entire lot of them will make for the nearest coast with Oz and the tiara, free and clear.

Speaking of... I move along the edge of the room, where I've pressed myself as flat and small as possible.

Scanning for any sign of my dear old friend, I nudge the tiara off my head and prepare for the handoff.

Oz turns out to be an officiously loud employee directing people to the nearest exit. He pauses in his duties just long enough to take the tiara from me and tuck it under his uniformed cap before resuming his post and continuing the evacuation. To look at him, you'd think he'd never so much as heard of a diamond before. I don't doubt that he'll remain in place until every last person is off the ship—though whether he's doing it because he genuinely cares about the safety of the passengers or because no one commits to a cover story like he does, I'll never know.

Nor do I particularly care right now. The tiara is as good as gone. I'm free.

Well, almost. Despite Oz's best intentions, the evacuation isn't an orderly one. Because ethanol offers a smoke-free burn, the sprinkler systems aren't coming into effect. Everywhere I turn is mass hysteria and none of the regular security protocols are falling into place—all the things my friends and I love in a heist.

In fact, instead of an orderly progression in which the weakest are encouraged to lead the way, people push and shove their way to the lifeboats. Even several of the crew members and Peter's private bodyguards are caught up in the swell, forgoing their duties to save their own skins.

I'm happy to see them go, since the fewer scary people with guns there are on the *Shady Lady*, the better, but I also hope they don't get too violent in their eagerness to evacuate. Yes, almost all the people on this boat are criminals, but that doesn't mean I want to see them get caught in the crossfire.

There is one person in my plan who *isn't* a criminal, however, and keeping him out of the crossfire is the entire purpose of this. My escape was too good, though, and I can't seem to find him. I scan the crowd trying to catch a glimpse of the familiar wide shoulders, but my short stature isn't doing me any favors. I crawl up onto the cabaret lounge stage to get a better view. I find him almost immediately—or, rather, I should say that he finds me. Grant is behind me just as I get one leg up on the stage.

"Oh, no, you don't," he says and catches me around the waist. "You're staying right where I can see you."

"*There* you are," I reply, unmoved by the way he holds me aloft, my legs suspended in midair. "Come on. We don't have much time before Peter descends upon us in all his wrath."

"Oh, good. You *do* realize that you've just pissed off one of the most dangerous men in the entire world."

I smile sweetly down at him—my husband, my love, my favorite highly dangerous man to anger. "Of course I do. One might say it's my true calling."

"Penelope…" he warns in that tone I know so well. It's fifty percent outrage and fifty percent laughter. And, most importantly, one hundred percent on my side.

"I'm sorry," I say and mean it. "I know you wanted to get Johnny Francis, and I respect that—I really do—but I can't allow you to do it at the cost of your own safety. Don't worry. I have a plan to get us out of here, but I need you to—"

I don't get an opportunity to tell him what I need. Just as Grant finally lowers me to my feet, one of Peter Sanchez's two main bodyguards comes up on him from behind. I shout a warning, but it's too late. A loud, sickening blow to the back of my husband's head has him crumpling in a heap at my feet.

"Grant!" I fall to my knees to try and catch him, but it's no use. Before I even manage to wrap my arms around him, trying to shield him from another strike, the second bodyguard leaps down from the wings.

After that, I know there's nothing more for me to do. We're caught. We're trapped. The plan now rests in Peter's hands. With a sharp breath and a wince for what I know is coming, I wait for the second punch to land.

Thank goodness I'm not wearing the tiara anymore, I think as the back of a gun catches me behind my ear. *Better my skull than that horrible, ungainly, twenty-million-dollar masterpiece.*

THE ESCAPE
24

WHEN I FINALLY COME TO, MY HANDS ARE BOUND TIGHTLY behind my back and I can't move.

At first, I don't bother trying, since movement of any kind causes a wave of nausea to move through me. My head aches sickeningly, and it doesn't feel as though there's a single muscle in my body that hasn't been stretched beyond the limits of human endurance. Opening my eyes and taking stock of my surroundings drains all the energy I have.

Fortunately, my surroundings are more or less what I expect them to be. I'd assumed Peter would be upset at having his boat evacuated without his consent; I also expected him to do whatever he could to get that tiara back. Being tied to a chair on the middle of the cabaret lounge stage seems pretty reasonable, all things considered.

Nor am I all that surprised by the warm, solid wall at my back. That's *my* wall. I'd know it anywhere.

"Shut your eyes again and pretend to be unconscious," Grant commands me in a low undertone. My straining movements must have tipped him off that I'm awake. "He won't do anything until he knows you're conscious."

I ignore his advice. Grant no longer gets to call the shots on this mission. I've officially taken it over.

"Are you okay?" I ask instead. "How's your stomach holding up?"

A muttered curse escapes him. "It'd feel a lot better if you listened to instructions for once in your god-damned life."

"No way. You don't get to blame this one on me. You had your chance to run this mission, and all you ended up doing was almost killing yourself. It's my turn now." Louder and to the man standing off to one side of the wings, I call, "Hey! You! I'm awake now and ready to negotiate with your boss."

"Penelope, for God's sake, at least tell me what it is you plan to do."

I nudge Grant with my ass. It's the only real action I can perform while so tightly bound. "I'm showing Peter that we aren't afraid of him."

"But you *should* be afraid of him," Grant says. "Do you have any idea what he's going to do to us?"

"Not a damn thing," I say with a light laugh. "He can't."

There isn't a chance to explain how I know that, since Peter chooses that moment to saunter in.

"The Sleeping Beauty awakens," he says with all the mildness I've come to expect from him. "That must have been some blow to the head. You've been out for over an hour."

Good. That means everyone else has had ample time

to get away—with the tiara. "Sorry," I say, not sorry at all. "I haven't been sleeping so well on this trip. I needed the rest."

Peter walks around to stand in front of me. He looks, to put it simply, *pissed*. His linen suit is rumpled, and there's a huge scorch mark up one arm, leaving him looking almost like a love letter that's been tossed into the flames.

"Don't worry," he says, his voice ominously controlled. "A long, enforced period of unconsciousness can be arranged. All you have to do is say the word."

"Touch her, and you'll regret the day you ever heard the name Penelope Blue," Grant growls from my back.

"I don't think you're in any position to make orders, Mr. O'Kelly. I believe our deal was that I'd keep your wife alive only as long as the tiara remained secure."

"Oh, the tiara is plenty secure," I promise. "In fact, I'd argue that it's now in the safest place it's been since this whole thing started: as far away from you as possible."

The blow comes from out of nowhere. To be honest, I didn't think Peter had it in him—he always struck me as the sort to hand the physical violence off to someone else for fear of staining his clothes with blood. As it turns out, he's more than capable of landing a punch, even on a woman half his size.

I've never been hit like that before, so it takes a moment for the shock to wear off and the pain to settle in. It's a strange combination—the dull thud of blunt force trauma to my jaw and the fiery sting of his ring cutting my lip open. A metallic tang fills my mouth, and I do my best impersonation of a Bond villain spitting blood out of the side of his mouth.

But my lips are numb, and I mostly dribble. I'm glad Grant's back is to me so he doesn't witness the attempt.

"If you feel the need to hit anyone, I'll ask you to extend the honor to me," Grant says in a voice I barely recognize. "I promise you aren't going to like what I do to you if you touch my wife again."

Peter doesn't blink. "You're tied up on *my* boat, surrounded by *my* bodyguards. Are you sure that's the tone you want to take with me?"

"Absolutely."

I know the blow is coming this time. I'm not sure if it's the growing bruise that makes the second one hurt so much more or if it's because I can see the incoming fist before it lands, but my head whips back and cracks against the back of the chair, leaving me reeling.

"Any more witty comebacks from you two?" Peter asks.

My head still rings from the blow, so his voice sounds distant and tinny. Grant's furious silence, however, is easy enough to interpret. I can *feel* how much he wants to speak—how much it's costing him to sit idly by while I take the beating for him.

Triumph shouldn't be my primary emotion, but I can't help it. *See, husband dearest?* It's not so easy to stand back and let the love of your life undergo physical trauma. One might even argue that it's worse than the pain itself.

Something, in that moment, shifts between us. Maybe it's the feeling of ineffectiveness, which neither one of us has ever been good at, or maybe it's just his exhaustion and pain finally catching up. But for what feels like the first time in our relationship, I can sense Grant handing over the reins.

It's a scary sensation, that kind of responsibility. It's also a powerful one. As the recent events on board the *Shady Lady* have proven, my husband's complete confidence and trust is a thing that doesn't come easy. It's taken me years to earn it—and I don't mean to squander it now that it's mine.

"Now." Peter hitches his slacks and squats to my level.

I'd like to attempt another one of those badass blood-spitting moves, but I restrain myself.

"I appreciate the effort you've gone through to steal the tiara and clear the boat of your competition, but you appear to have forgotten that I don't take being crossed lightly. You've made me appear foolish in front of a lot of people."

"Yeah, I thought that part might sting," I say and wince as he lifts his hand to punch me again. He doesn't, though, which is almost worse. I don't like the uncertainty.

"Call your father or that angry one Lola likes and have them bring the tiara back." He extracts what looks like a walkie-talkie from his jacket. "I want that diamond returned to my ship by nightfall, or you'll see what happens to those who make a fool out of me."

"Sorry," I say. "I'm not going to call anyone. And they're under strict instructions not to release the tiara to anyone but me. If you want to see it again, you'll need to keep me alive."

And intact, I think, grateful for small favors.

"You may think your father will protect you, but he's not here right now. You, however, are." Peter's lip lifts in a sneer that he directs over my shoulder. "As, I might add, is your husband. It would be terrible if anything were to happen to him in your stead."

I laugh. Amused is the last thing I'm feeling toward

a man who just basically threatened Grant's life, but I like the way Peter reacts to the sound, like it curdles his blood. "Except that my husband is the only man on this ship who knows who Johnny Francis really is," I say—or, I guess it would be more appropriate to say, I lie. Johnny Francis remains the loose end in all this, the person no one was able to identify.

But Peter doesn't know that, and the one thing he wants more than the tiara is Johnny. Much as he will be loath to admit it, he needs the pair of us. *Both* of us.

And we're always strongest together.

Now it's Grant's turn to laugh. His is a genuine sound—meant, I know, for me. "She's got you there, Sanchez. I don't know where the tiara is, and she doesn't know Johnny's identity. If you want to win this round, you're going to have to let us both walk."

Peter's jaw ticks, but he doesn't lose his cool veneer. "On the contrary, I don't have to do anything of the kind. Let me assure you that there's nothing either of you can do to force my hand while you remain captive on my ship. There are enough supplies for the *Shady Lady* to stay in operation for weeks. You and your husband are at my mercy until I decide otherwise."

"But *is* it your ship?" I ask. "Is it really?"

"You tell me," Peter replies. "You're the one who's tied up and surrounded by my men. Maybe, if you're very good and do exactly as I say, I won't resort to torture."

I smile, the sore side of my mouth burning at the attempt. "And maybe, if you're very good, I'll dock *my* ship somewhere there aren't dozens of U.S. agents lying in wait for you."

The quick narrowing of Peter's eyes is all the indication

I need to know I've made my point. "What are you talking about?" he demands.

"You may not have noticed in all the screaming and panic of the fire," I say, "but by now, the ship is heading for the nearest Florida port. I hate to be the one to break it to you, but your boat has been…ah, how can I put this delicately?"

I laugh, as there's no other word for it.

"It's been hijacked."

As I'd hoped, Peter leaves us with his two favorite gun-wielding bodyguards while he goes to investigate my claims. I can't be a hundred percent certain that Hijack accomplished his goal of forcing his way onto the bridge and taking over the captain's controls, but I feel pretty confident overall. The old Hijack used to be able to commandeer just about any kind of vehicle out there—if it had a motor and a steering wheel, he was in. Even then, the steering wheel was optional. I once saw him drive off with a BMW using a screwdriver.

"You have some serious explaining to do, Penelope," Grant says in a low voice the moment Peter disappears from sight. "You *stole* Peter Sanchez's cruise ship?"

"I think one of my front incisors is loose," I say by way of reply. I run my tongue over the front line of my teeth, but other than an alarming amount of blood, my teeth appear to be intact.

"You deserve it," is his prompt reply, but then he hesitates and his voice lowers to a harsh, "I'm sorry I antagonized him. I didn't think he'd retaliate like that. Did he hurt you?"

"Not enough to make a difference," I reassure him. "And he won't do it again. Not while we hold all the cards."

"We?" he asks ruefully. "I sure as hell don't have any cards, at least not while I'm tied to this chair and can't strangle him. Can you reach the rope from where you are?"

I strain my fingers toward his bound hands. Although I can technically reach them, my fingers grazing the edge of the rope, it doesn't do either of us much good.

"What if we tipped over on the side?" he suggests. "How contortionist can you get in a situation like this?"

"Do you mean, can I lift my legs over my head and underneath my tied hands without drawing the attention of the two armed guards over by the door?" I shake my head. "No. If I had that kind of skill, I'd have escaped the *last* time I was tied to a chair like this."

"I did *not* tie you like this," he says and struggles anew.

It doesn't do him any good. In addition to his skills at decimating human bodies with pliers and murdering unfaithful wives, Peter Sanchez is quite adept at tying people up. We have nowhere to go and nothing to do until he returns.

"If we're going to die like this, I want you to know—" Grant begins, but I stop him with a nudge.

"Would you relax?" I say. "This is all going according to plan."

"Your plan was to get tied up and beaten by Peter Sanchez?"

"Well, no," I admit. "I'd hoped we'd sit at a table together and have a rational conversation among adults. But this works, too."

A soft chuckle escapes him. "What exactly is the endgame, if you don't mind my asking?"

"Our lives. The tiara. Peter Sanchez in handcuffs— preferably Simon's." I pause. "I know he's not Johnny Francis, Grant, and I'm sorry, but he's all I can offer you as an alternative."

"Did it ever occur to you that I might not want him as an alternative?"

"Yes, it did." Even though Grant can't see me, I put on my most resolute expression. "But you know what he did to Lola—know what he *will* do to her the second he's off this ship. That girl deserves way more than to be used as a pawn in her father's evil games. There's no way I'm letting him walk away now."

"Good."

With that one word, everything in my world clicks into place. Grant and I might not always agree about who gets to call the shots, but when it comes to the things that matter—the *people* who matter—we're always on the same page.

"Just be ready to act on my signal, okay? I promise to let you get your hands on Peter without interruption, but not just yet. We've got to get him away from his henchmen first." I hesitate before adding in a voice that mimics the one he used in the engine room, "I'm afraid things are going to get worse before they get better."

He heaves a mock sigh. "They always do."

"*Psst.*"

The sound comes from the wings of the cabaret stage. From where I'm sitting, it's impossible to see much except a dark panel and a few dangling ropes. At first, I think the sound is a figment of my imagination or the result of repeated blows to the head, but it sounds again.

"*Psst. Penelope.*"

It's louder this time—and much more frightening because of it. With increased volume comes recognition. I recoil against my bindings in a renewed attempt to free myself.

"Oh, Lola. No." My words are little more than a moan. I will her to stay where she is, out of sight and out of mind. The guards can't see the backstage area from where they're standing, but the second she walks out to where we are, she's going to be at their mercy.

But my warning is no good. She skulks out of the wings with a look of determination. Her delicate jaw is set, and her wide eyes are zeroed in on where Grant and I sit in full open view.

"Get back in there," I call, but it's too late. She's close enough now that I can see the penknife in her hand. She's coming to free us, and nothing could be worse for my plans.

Taking his cue from me, Grant orders her back to the wings. His tone is firm and commanding in ways mine will never be, but Lola doesn't stop her forward momentum.

At least, she doesn't stop until she notices the two men. "Octavian? Laurie?" Her voice sounds small but resolute. "You're still here?"

The larger of the two, a man with such a large gut, it looks like he's gestating twin elephants, takes a step forward. "Lola, what are you doing here?"

Instead of being afraid of him, she lifts her chin. "I came to rescue my friends."

My heart sinks. Lola was supposed to be long gone by now, safe in the keeping of my friends and father.

"You gotta get out of here, honey," the other man says. Like Gut Guy over there, he's wearing an almost softened expression as he looks at Lola. "Your dad isn't going to like this."

"Not without my friends," she repeats.

For a moment, I think it's actually going to work. Whatever loyalty these men have for their fearless leader is nothing compared to their feelings for this sweet, brave girl he somehow sired. I don't know why it didn't occur to me before. If she was able to win a man like Riker over in less than a week, how much more effective would she be against men she'd probably known her whole life?

But, "He'll kill us," Gut Guy says with a shake of his head. "You know we can't let them go."

Her crestfallen expression turns to one of outright dismay as the door is thrown open and her father returns to the lounge. Peter bears the lowered, angry look of a man who tried—and failed—to force his way onto the bridge, but that look changes almost instantly. The sight of his daughter coming near his captives with a knife in hand seems to afford him great pleasure. He doesn't even seem to mind that his guards are almost as upset by his untimely return as the rest of us.

"My sweet little Lola," he says in a faintly crooning way. It sounds like an army of spiders marching up and down my spine. "What a fortunate occurrence. I'm so happy to see you safe and returned to my arms."

In her sudden alarm, Lola drops the knife. It clatters to the stage, spinning far enough out of reach that neither I nor Grant can grab at it with our feet.

"Daddy?"

"I knew you would come back like a good girl," he says. "Did you bring me the tiara?"

"N-no." Her eyes open wide. "I don't have it."

"Who does?" he asks.

"I-I don't know."

"I think you do." He draws forward, lulling her with his calm voice and assured air. "I think you know *exactly* where Penelope has hidden it. If you know what's good for you, you'll tell me."

"But I don't," she protests. "I just came to…"

"Yes, Lola? What is it you want to tell me?"

If Peter had yelled or cursed, revealed himself to be the true villain he is, I think Lola might have been able to make a run for it. Fleeing from visible evil is easy. It's the kind that hides—in the people we love, the people who are supposed to love us back—that catches us unaware.

"Just tell me where it is, and no one has to get hurt," Peter adds.

Lola begins shaking uncontrollably, her fear so strong, it's a palpable presence standing on its own two feet. My chest aches to see it. There's no way that girl can withstand her father's particular brand of torture, quiet and complete. She's spent her entire lifetime being victimized by it.

"You can tell him if you want to, sweetie," I say. "Go ahead. I won't be mad."

"Penelope is right," Grant agrees. "Don't be a hero for us, Lola. We'll be fine. You don't owe us anything."

Our words have the opposite effect from the one we intended. Lola's jaw sets at the same time her shaking stops. She even ranges herself in front of our chairs, putting herself physically between us and her father.

"I'm not telling you anything until you let them go." Thanks to her position on the stage, Lola's small voice carries throughout the entire room. "I'm sorry, Daddy, but they're my friends. I can't let you hurt them."

Heroism of this sort—the kind that bucks parental decrees and topples every hierarchy a young girl has ever known—doesn't come easy, I know. I can't help watching Peter to see how he'll react to what, in my mind, is true fearlessness.

He should be proud of his little girl for standing up to him, for taking a side and believing in it so strongly that she's willing to sacrifice everything she knows.

He shoots her instead.

Because the cabaret lounge is designed to carry sound, the sharp report of the gun seems supernaturally loud. So does the cry Lola releases just once before crumpling to the ground like a paper doll folding in on itself. I can't see where the bullet hit, but I can see Peter standing some distance away, his expression empty as he takes in the sight of his daughter's inert form. The two guards have almost become statues, staring at the fallen girl in alarm.

"Well, now." Peter holsters his gun and approaches us, perfectly at his leisure. "That's a fortunate circumstance, isn't it?"

"If you've killed her, you asshole…"

Peter turns his mild gaze my way. "You'll what? Steal both my boat and my tiara? Nice try. That only works once. I might have to keep you two alive to get what I want, but Lola is expendable. She has nothing more to offer me."

He reaches down to grab the knife Lola dropped,

flipping it open and closed several times in succession. "I think what's going to happen next is that you'll accompany me to the bridge and inform your friend Hijack that you've had a change of heart."

"No."

"I think you'll also find that the tiara has become a burden you no longer wish to bear."

"Never."

Peter nudges Lola with his foot. Her body gives a shudder before slumping once again into inertia. "I shot her in the shoulder, but I doubt her lungs will be able to keep up with the shock of the injury for much longer. Decide quickly, Ms. Blue. She doesn't have much time."

"She's your *daughter*," I say. "What kind of monster are you?"

"The kind who doesn't like to lose. What do you say? Are you willing to trade in all your chips for one miserable little girl's life?"

Of course I am—and he knows it. He knows it and I know it and even his horrified-looking henchmen know it. The only person who has no idea how much she's worth is lying there, bleeding out and unable to breathe.

"Grant?" I ask. I know which way I'm going to vote, but it's not just my life that's at stake here.

"I'll follow your lead, Penelope. Just say the word."

It's the moment I've been waiting for. For what might be the first time in our lives, Grant and I are in complete solidarity. We're unified, we're a team, and nothing can tear us apart.

Too bad we might have to die before we can enjoy it.

"Untie us," I say to Peter. My heart feels both heavy and light, a rock in the seconds before it slowly sinks to the bottom of the ocean. I'd always planned on getting Peter to the bridge, where Hijack has a gun taped to the underside of the captain's chair, but not yet. And definitely not like this. "I'll take you to Hijack, but I'm leaving Grant here to tend to Lola."

"Not on your life. You'll all stay exactly where I can see you. Your husband is free to carry her along with us, but we'll make that trip to the bridge together."

It's not an ideal outcome, but I don't see what else I can do. I agree with a slight nod.

Peter makes short work of cutting through our bonds, life returning to my limbs in a prickle of painful sensation. I have only to glance at Grant's grimace to know that my face looks as bad as it feels, but there's no time to worry about my appearance. There's just enough time for Grant to scoop Lola into his arms before Peter shoves the gun in his back and commands him to start walking.

It's the most depressing procession I've ever been in, this gun-propelled march to the bridge. Lola is way too limp, and her trailing arm leaves drops of blood with every careful step Grant takes. The ship is eerie, empty as it is, the halls ringing with silence. Even worse is when we arrive at our destination and I knock, calling to Hijack with a voice that's almost as heavy as my heart. "Let us in, Hijack."

"Pen?" he calls. "Is that you?"

"I'm sorry." My voice cracks. "But there's been a change of plans."

THE END

25

THE CAPTAIN'S BRIDGE, LIKE MOST OF THE ROOMS ON BOARD the *Shady Lady*, is neat and efficient. Located at the ship's bow, the huge window overlooks the water, providing a long, clear view of the ocean ahead. There are also an alarming number of buttons and panels, but Hijack is nothing if not good at his job. He oversees them all with an almost joyous look on his face, the captain's discarded hat tilted at a jaunty angle on his head.

I might admire the picture it makes—my old friend commandeering a multimillion-dollar cruise ship—if it weren't for Peter transferring his gun to Hijack's back instead. He also issues a curt command to the four henchmen he's managed to round up—two posted outside the door and the more familiar Octavian and Laurie following us inside. "Lock the door and don't move from it," he tells the pair of them. To us, he adds, "Don't even think about trying to escape. We'll all stay right here until the ship turns around in the other direction."

From a purely logistical standpoint, this situation is close to what I'd been trying to accomplish from the start. Neither Grant nor I is currently tied up. The good guys in the room technically outnumber the bad guys. And the ship, instead of heading for Florida like I told Peter it was, is actually headed on an express route to Cancun. With nothing but cerulean sea surrounding us, I doubt Peter will notice until too late that in turning the ship around, as he demands, he's playing right into my plans to head for U.S. soil.

In short, these are good odds. They're the exact odds I was playing for.

But I'd been figuring without Lola. I'd *especially* been figuring without Lola bleeding out all over my husband.

"Penelope, it looks like there's a first aid kit mounted on the wall over there." Grant casts aside a nautical map laid out on a table and places Lola down in its stead. She's gone limp, and her lips have turned blue. "Will you grab it?"

I take it down and hand it to him. My first aid skills might not be top-notch, but I know they're part of his regular field training, so I give myself over to the task of assistant. "What can I do?"

"Hand me the bandages so I can get her shoulder bound, and then look for an epinephrine pen."

"An epinephrine pen?"

He doesn't look up from his patient. He's too busy ripping the shirt from her shoulder so he can better examine the wound. "Yes, or something like it. It should be with the allergy stuff—anything with adrenaline will do."

"Got it." I hesitate. "Grant, is she—"

"Alive." His voice is grim. "For now."

Up until that point, Peter and Hijack were content to stand back and watch our ministrations, one with disinterest, the other with a dawning realization of just how screwed we are. At the sound of Grant's name, however, Hijack's interest suddenly picks up.

"You called him Grant."

Oh, geez. That's what interests him right now? "Yeah. So?"

"This man's name is Kit O'Kelly."

I'm still frantically searching the medical kit for the pen Grant asked for, so the comment doesn't register at first.

"And Grant is the name of your husband," Hijack adds.

That gets me to look over. "You know his name?"

"Of course I know." He glances at Grant with sharp interest. "Or at least I thought I did. Everything is suddenly starting to make sense."

"Nothing is going to make sense if you don't take this boat off its current trajectory," Peter says with a snarl of irritation. "You have five seconds to turn us around, or I'll shoot you where you stand. Don't worry—I'm good for it."

I nod without looking up. "He's not kidding, Hijack. Do it. He's the one who shot Lola." I find the yellow cylinder underneath a rolled piece of gauze and release a shout. "Aha! Got it. Here."

Grant doesn't pause from his work. He extends his hand for the pen, accepts it, and jabs it into her thigh without once losing his concentration. I know it's a terrible time to dwell on how much I love that man, but *damn*. He's always at his sexiest when he's hard at work. As if in evidence of this, Lola's color starts to return, her chest moving up and down in a painful wheeze that's music to my ears.

The ship lurches sharply to the left, almost sending Lola and the medical kit flying to the ground. Grant catches her before she falls, but the momentum of her weight hits him in the stomach and causes him to stagger.

In that moment, any hopes I'd had that he'd be able to take out the two guards while I grab Hijack's gun disappear. As much as I'd love to rely on my big, strong, capable husband to save the day, he's just not in the physical condition to do it. Especially not while his attention is so taken up with Lola.

Which means, of course, that *I* have to take out the two guards. Who are twice my size. And armed.

"Okay, now what?" I ask Peter. I also edge toward the door, though what I think I'm going to be able to do to Octavian and Laurie in our current predicament, I have no idea. Octavian keeps casting worried glances at Lola, his face almost as pale as hers, but I'm not sure how far to trust him. He is, after all, still blocking our only escape route. "You have the boat, but I have the tiara. Shall we make this an even trade?"

"Nice try. Nothing less than your death will satisfy me now."

"You'll have to get in line," Hijack says with mock outrage. "How could you, Pen? You told me your husband was short."

I shake my head in warning, hoping to get Hijack to back off. I know what he's doing—he's trying to create a distraction. It was a failsafe built into the Tailortown job, built into all our jobs, actually. If ever I got stuck in a tight spot—literally—it was up to the wheelman to draw the attention so I could wriggle my way out.

Unfortunately, what I need is for Peter to focus less on Grant and more on literally anything else. From the looks of it, Lola is starting to show signs of life. With any luck, soon she'll be stable enough that Grant won't have to keep attending to her.

"And *you*," Hijack says to Peter, still in that injured tone. "Letting federal agents wander around on your ship like that. I never would have come if I'd known how lax security was going to be. I thought this was supposed to be the safest place to surface."

Peter stiffens. At first, I think he's annoyed at the insult to his safety procedures—which, considering how easily we *did* take over his ship, is fairly ironic—but he's watching Hijack with burgeoning interest.

"What did you say your name was, young man?" Peter asks.

"Hijack," he says with a wink. "But it's only a nickname. I've had it for just about ever, haven't I, Pen?"

Peter ignores the question and leans forward. "Hi, Jack…short for John, perhaps?"

Oh, no. I cast a panicked look at Grant, who's showing signs of both satisfaction and alarm. Satisfaction, because he tried to warn me about Hijack's motives days ago; alarm, because if Hijack really is Johnny Francis, then the one thing keeping Grant alive—my lie that he's the only person in the room who knows Johnny's true identity—is, if you'll pardon the pun, *shot*.

"Oh, my." An evil smile curls Peter's lips as he turns to us, his gun raising once again—this time in Grant's direction. "Talk about a timely revelation."

I dive.

Tucking and rolling is a skill that has served me well many times in the thieving circuit, and it doesn't fail me now. I reach Peter's gun just as he manages to get a shot off, nudging his aim enough to miss my husband.

"I am *not* sitting by that man's bedside, watching him recover from another gunshot wound," I say with a low, almost feral growl. I mean it, too. The first one almost killed him—and by extension, me.

The bullet lodges somewhere in the wall behind Grant's head, but his safety is of a short duration. Octavian and Laurie are finally moved to action, propelled forward by the need to ensure their boss's protection.

For a moment, I think their sudden movements are going to work in our favor and finally tip the power in the room toward our side. The hope doesn't last long. Before I can even blink, Peter yanks me to my feet by the hair. My already sore temple protests the sudden, unyielding force, and my vision blurs. I try to kick and lash out and do *something* to make him loosen his grip, but it doesn't work. By the time I'm fully on my feet and my nerve endings have stopped screaming, Peter is holding me against his chest as a shield. He even goes so far as to place the gun to my temple, the metal still hot enough from the last shot that it burns a scorching ring into my skin.

The scent of burnt hair mingles with the smoke, making the entire bridge smell like a fireworks show gone awry.

"Not another move," he warns Grant and Hijack, both of whom are on the balls of their feet, fists up and seemingly determined to each take out one of the henchmen.

"If you so much as twitch, I'll shoot her where she stands."

I want to say something brave—something like *don't listen to Peter* or *sacrifice my life for the greater good*—but no words come out. Mostly because I don't particularly want to die, but also because I doubt either of them would obey my orders anyway.

"Subdue them through any means necessary," Peter tells his henchmen with a nod at Grant and Hijack. "You'll have to leave Johnny's hands free, but I doubt he'll need all his toes to pilot the ship."

"But I'm not J—" Hijack begins before Peter cocks the gun and presses it even harder against my skull. Something like a whimper escapes my throat, but I don't have time to be ashamed of it. I'm too busy scouring the room, looking for some kind of weapon that will allow me to gain the upper hand.

Penelope Blue is not going down without a fight.

Peter yanks on me, dragging me backward. I'm not sure where he's heading, but I dig my heels into the carpet to render his journey as hard on him as I possibly can. I'm struggling to find any kind of handhold to make his way even more difficult when a loud bang sounds.

I jump, sure that I've just been shot and killed, when the now-unguarded door slams against the interior wall. That feeling of detachment from my surroundings only increases as a tall, elegant female form fills the doorway, a gun in her hand.

"Eden?" Hijack cries.

All attention—including that of my captor—turns to the door. In his sudden surprise at seeing Eden standing where there should have been a locked door guarded by two of his henchmen, Peter's grip on me slackens. It's not much, but it's enough for me to go limp. I learned it as a self-defense move to use when cops and security guards think they've got you. It turns out it also does the trick just fine in life-or-death hostage situations. Peter's gun hand comes down, so I use the only weapon I can find—my teeth—and sink them into his meaty forearm.

His yelp of pain doesn't last long. After another resounding thud, he falls to the ground in a heavy slump. I whirl, confused at what could have caused his sudden stumble. I mean, I know I bit him hard, and the salty taste of skin and flesh will linger in my mouth for a long time, but Grant and Hijack] are busy taking out a now-bewildered Octavian and Laurie, and Eden continues standing in the doorway with what I swear is a smirk on her beautiful face.

Which is why I'm only slightly surprised to find Lola standing with the metal first aid kit in hand, her breathing hitched and her posture stooped, ready to strike her father over the head again.

"I told you already, Daddy," she says, perspiration beading her upper lip. I don't know what it's costing her to stay standing, but I imagine it's a lot. She's strong, this girl. I knew it from the start. "I'm not leaving here without my friends."

THE WILD CARD

26

THE SCENE THAT FOLLOWS SAYS A LOT ABOUT OUR RESPECTIVE roles in the takedown.

As soon as Octavian and Laurie are subdued, Grant assumes his natural air of authority. I can't help but be grateful for it, as I'm still not a hundred percent sure what happened.

And who can blame me? My face throbs, and my temple burns. My arm is wrapped around Lola's waist as I try to hold her aloft.

Yet through it all, I can't stop staring at Eden St. James's impassive face, which seems to be growing more impassive by the second. Her timely arrival may very well have been the thing that saved us. I'd kiss her if I didn't hate her so much.

"Would it be asking too much for you to have a pair of handcuffs on you?" Grant asks her as presses his knee hard into Peter Sanchez's back. From all appearances, the man is knocked out cold, but my husband isn't the sort to take any chances.

I think, at first, that he's talking to me, but Eden replies in her cool, clipped voice. "Not on me, no. You'll have to forgive me, but I was in something of a hurry to find you."

"Hijack? Penelope?"

"I have gauze," I offer doubtfully, looking at Lola's dented first aid kit.

"Clipped to my belt," a gruff voice says.

As one, we all glance over to the source of that voice. It's Octavian, sitting against the wall next to Laurie, the pair of them bleeding profusely from the mouth and nose. Hijack has them covered with a gun in each hand, but I don't know how necessary his vigilance is. From the state of their hanging heads, I've never seen a pair less likely to rise up in arms.

"On the right side," Octavian adds. "But be careful. I think Mr. O'Kelly broke a few ribs."

I hesitate, wondering which of us gets the dubious honor of frisking the giant. Before anyone can volunteer, Lola detaches herself from my grasp and moves haltingly toward him, dropping to her knees with an expression of sympathy. "Oh, Octavian. Are you okay?"

He winces, though not, I think, from physical pain. "I'm sorry, Lola. You know how it is. We were just following orders."

I have no idea what she whispers to him, but it must be something kind, because he doesn't look quite so miserable by the time she extracts the handcuffs. I mean, he's still bleeding and has a gun pointed at his head, and I doubt he's going to walk away from this room in anything but federal custody, but the hangdog look is gone.

I almost feel bad for the guy, honestly. Working for a man like Peter Sanchez can't be a pleasant task.

"I was trying to kill him, you know," Lola says as she passes the handcuffs to Grant. "I wanted him to die." It's difficult to tell if she feels guilty at her own daring or sad that she didn't accomplish her goal.

"It was a good strike," Grant replies with a warm smile. "It landed right where it needed to knock him out cold."

"You're the heroine of the day," I add.

Eden coughs gently. "This is all very touching, I'm sure, but can we please tone down the theatrics?" She turns to Grant with a tight smile. "Unfortunately, you seem to have made a terrible botch of this, O'Kelly, as I suspected you would. It's a good thing I was able to take out those two guards before you all managed to get yourselves killed."

Although impressed by the sight of the two huddled forms outside the bridge door, a prickling sense of annoyance takes over. "Excuse you," I protest. Where does this woman get off, putting the blame on my husband? This was *my* terrible botch, thank you very much.

Predictably, she ignores me. "This is what I get for trusting in American intelligence, I suppose."

American intelligence?

"I didn't know you were still on the boat," Grant says to Eden, showing neither outrage nor surprise. "When you didn't come at the sound of the first gunshot, I assumed you'd evacuated along with everyone else. How did you get in here? I thought all the locks were unpickable."

"They are." She holds up a metal object and tosses it to him. "But it just so happens I have a master key."

I squeak.

Eden hears—I can tell from the smirk that lifts her lips—but she doesn't acknowledge it. Hijack does, though, swiveling his head to glare at me.

Dammit. I *knew* that woman was up to something when she so conveniently disappeared after that failed attempt on the tiara. She groped me and stole my key. I wouldn't put it past her to have orchestrated the whole thing just so she could get her hands on it.

"That's strange," Hijack says with heavy emphasis. "I get the feeling I've seen a key like that somewhere before."

Since I'd rather not fall into apologies and explanations for how I got pickpocketed by the oldest trick in the book, I turn away to focus on the more important issue at hand—Eden and my husband working in collusion.

"You two know each other?" I demand. "This whole time, you've known each other? Is that why you tripped me?"

"You think I tripped you?" Eden asks with a trill of laughter. "Darling, you fell over your own two feet. If I were you, I'd take to jogging somewhere you can't plunge two hundred feet to a watery grave."

"And to answer your question, Penelope, no," Grant puts in much more gently. "We don't know each other. I suspected she was British intelligence after our night searching for Johnny Francis, but I couldn't confirm it. I didn't want to say anything in case it turned out to be false."

My head whirls at the thought. Eden St. James is one of the good guys? And she saved us?

Eden chuckles. "I can see she's having a difficult time digesting it all. Do you need me to slow down, darling? Shall I use smaller words?"

Nope. I don't care whose government she's working for—Eden is definitely one of the bad guys.

"But you thought Kit O'Kelly might be Johnny Francis. I heard you say so."

"It was a working theory. He fit all the markers. I figured it was either that or CIA."

Grant shakes his head. "FBI, actually."

I ignore him to focus on the more important issue at hand. "And you were practically begging me to steal that tiara for you," I add. "You said you wanted to be partners."

She casts her eyes up to the ceiling. "Of course I did. I wanted to draw Johnny out. I thought we'd covered this already." A flicker of annoyance crosses her face as she turns to Grant. "Speaking of, did you find him?"

Grant glances at Hijack, who shakes his head with vehemence. "It's not me, I swear. Hijack isn't short for anything. My name is actually Sam."

Irritation rises to my throat, mingled with a sense of satisfaction that's wholly inappropriate to the time and place. Now is not the moment to gloat to my husband that I was, in fact, right about Hijack. I *knew* he wasn't smart enough to be Johnny Francis.

I focus on the irritation I feel instead. "If you're not Johnny, then why did you let Peter think you were? You idiot. That's why he shot at Grant. You could have gotten us all killed."

Hijack glares at me. "I didn't do it on purpose. I was trying to help."

"Great job with that. Any other lives you'd like to endanger while we're here?"

Eden's smooth voice breaks in before I can tell Hijack what I think of his mishandling of the situation. "Is she like this with all her ex-boyfriends?"

Grant's lips twitch. "Yes, actually. You get used to it. I assume this means you didn't find Johnny, either?"

"Alas, no. I'm starting to suspect he never planned on going after the tiara at all. Poor Peter went to all this work to catch a ghost." She gives the inert man a soft kick. "It's a pity, but I suppose I can always take both him and these four miscreants to my superiors in Johnny's stead. You don't mind, do you? After all this, I can hardly show up empty-handed."

Grant clears his throat. "One might argue that I have an equal claim on them."

She cocks her head. "One might, but then, I did save your life, didn't I? Besides, in staying on board to track you down, I've blown a cover I spent three years investing in. Consider it my fee."

That seems awfully expensive to me, but Grant just nods. "That's fair."

"Thank you," she says and sighs as she sizes up the five bound and fully grown men she's somehow going to cart to England. I wish I could say I feel bad for the task ahead of her, but I don't. "You know, I think I might actually miss being Eden St. James. She was fun."

"No, she wasn't," I protest. "She was awful. Who are you really?"

"Tiffany Thistlethwaite, at your service." She tilts her head to the side. "I suppose I should thank you for clearing the boat to make all this possible. That *was* you, wasn't it?"

"Yep."

"Hmm. Sloppy."

I flush. "But effective."

"Oh, dear. You're one of those 'ends justify the means' types, aren't you? Your kind always make everything ten times more expensive than it needs to be. My bosses would hate you."

At that, Grant laughs out loud. Looking around at the carnage of the bridge, I can't help but join him. In terms of failed missions, we could hardly have functioned any worse as a team. In addition to the blood and damage all over the *Shady Lady*, the FBI is out a million dollars for Grant's entry into the game, we've just handed Peter Sanchez and four of his thugs to British intelligence, and even though we have the tiara in our possession, we're no nearer to knowing Johnny Francis's identity now than we were a week ago. All I've managed to acquire is a beaten-up face, a thieving ex-boyfriend, and an injured girl with a hole in her shoulder.

Not to mention the lives and safety of everyone I hold dear. I don't care what Grant's bosses say—I'm calling this one a win.

"I don't suppose I could offer you safe passage back to Germany in exchange for your help with this lot?" Eden—Tiffany—whatever—turns to Hijack, one brow raised. "Since we're both headed that direction anyway…"

Hijack is instantly interested. "By *safe*, you mean I don't have to go through customs?"

"Naturally."

"I'm in." Hijack shrugs at me. "Sorry, Pen. I never was all the way sure of you, so I grabbed a few, um, souvenirs that I'd like to see safely home. I hope you don't mind."

I don't mind in the least. There's no denying that we couldn't have pulled off this final escapade without him, but the last thing I want is for that man to follow us back to New York. It's hard enough keeping *one* of my ex-boyfriends out of jail. "What? No inviting me to come with you this time?" I tease. "All that old money, all those old buildings?"

He casts a wary glance at Grant. "No offense, Pen, but you've always been a lot more trouble than you're worth."

"You can say that again." Grant grins and offers him his hand—and, by extension, his blessing to flee the country with his ill-gotten gains in tow. "Thanks for your help, Sam. We won't forget it."

I can't say that I'm sad to watch them go. The back of Eden's sleek head as she and Hijack push and prod their captives to the top deck to await her helicopter escort is a sight that fills me with intense satisfaction.

Of course, there's still our own evacuation to plan, a task Grant settles down to with cool efficiency as he takes over the ship's radio. I'm so impressed by his ability to rattle off coordinates and make sexy boat commands that I don't notice right away that Lola has crept up behind us.

I whirl, prepared to admonish her back to the table where she's been resting. The poor thing might be stable enough to support a last-minute Hail Mary to save the day, but that doesn't mean she can stand around chatting with a bullet lodged in her shoulder.

"Um, Penelope?" Her voice is as small and whispery as always, but something about the determined look on her pale little face has me stopping short. Other than a weary pallor and a limp arm, she seems to be holding her own. In fact, there's something suspiciously like a smile on her face.

To make matters even more bizarre, she extends her good hand and holds it there. It doesn't waver, doesn't move, until I slip my palm against hers. She doesn't shake my hand, as I expect, but holds it—holds *me*. With a grip like that, I know she's going to be okay.

"I probably should have introduced myself earlier, but I had to make sure of you first." She smiles shyly up at Grant. "I had to make sure of you both. But I was hoping the FBI would show up to find Johnny Francis—I don't think I can keep being him for much longer."

"Lola!" I cry, dropping her hand like it's on fire.

"Oh, boy," she says with a shake of her head. "I can see I better start my story at the beginning. You guys have no idea how much stuff I have to tell you."

THE 27 REPORT

THE EVACUATION OF SEVERAL HUNDRED PEOPLE FROM A FIERY
cruise ship is the kind of thing that makes the news in a
big way, even when the people involved in it aren't all
that keen on being made into international celebrities.

For days, all anyone can talk about is the heroic
rescue, an effort generously coordinated and funded
by several government organizations interested in the
various passengers aboard the *Shady Lady*'s life rafts.
I *should* feel bad for sending so many of my peers into
the arms of law enforcement, but considering that most
of them would have happily tied me to the ship's bow
to be pecked by birds and fish alike, I'm managing my
guilt just fine.

Fortunately, five people managed to escape without
scrutiny. From all accounts, Riker and my father only
refrained from killing each other thanks to Jordan's
diplomacy, but they made landfall with both their lives
and the tiara intact, which is good enough for me.

"I *still* don't see why we don't get to keep the tiara," Riker grumbles as the pair of us sit inside a conference room at the FBI building back home. Apparently, after a job like that one, the FBI requires us to be debriefed. It's all very official and boring. "It's not as if it was easy, sitting in a life raft with your dad and Tara for eight hours. I'd like to see *you* do it."

"Poor dear," I say with mock sympathy. "If it makes you feel better, Grant says it's going to a museum."

"A museum?" He perks. "Which museum?"

I know that perk. I don't trust that perk. "One with a really good security system," I warn. "So don't even think about it."

"You can't stop me from thinking," he says, but his attention quickly turns to more important matters. "And that's another thing. I'm also still having a hard time wrapping my head around the idea that our Lola is the infamous Johnny Francis."

Me too. *Our* Lola, as Riker so endearingly puts it, is turning out to be a lot of things none of us saw coming. I knew she was smart—her eidetic memory and penchant for statistics more than proved that—but to have master-minded an entire personality under her father's watch-ful, vigilant eye speaks of a level of bravery I don't think I've encountered before.

It makes me a little nauseous to think of it, to be honest. Had her father caught on to her at any point, his revenge would not have been merciful.

"I'm halfway convinced she made it all up," Riker adds. "She had to have been, what, twelve when she started tracking her father's activities?"

"Thirteen, actually," Lola says from the doorway.

She's breathless and youthful in a white summer dress, her hair wrapped around her head in a crown of braids. She looks barely above thirteen now. I'm curious what all the dark suits around here make of her. "Hi, Riker. Hi, Penelope. I sure am glad to see you two."

I leap up from the table and take her into my arms for a gentle hug. It's probably silly—coddling a girl capable of the feats of daring Lola has managed in her lifetime—but I can't help it. Even daring, highly capable girls need a hug every now and then. It would have done me a world of good at her age.

"Are they done with you back there?" I ask.

"For now. I've been asked not to leave New York for a while, but I don't mind. It's not like I have anywhere else to go." Her smile wavers, but she doesn't let it go easily. "I haven't been here before. Daddy came once or twice, but those were the trips I wasn't allowed to accompany him on."

"How many of his trips *did* you go on?" I ask, curious. I also pull out a chair so she can take a seat. Her shoulder is healing nicely, but it's early days yet.

"One hundred and forty two," she says matter-of-factly. "He always said I was too stupid to understand the business, so I didn't get to go on the dangerous missions, but I came along whenever I could. To try and learn, you know?"

I reach for her hand. I *do* know how it feels to strive so hard to earn the respect of a father as skilled and dangerous as hers or mine. I also know how it feels to have it—something Lola will never accomplish, especially now that she's laid information on virtually every crime and connection the man has.

"He didn't deserve you," I say.

"No, he didn't," she says, and with such a firm little voice, I raise a silent cheer. "And Mr. O'Kel—I mean, Grant—says it was a smart thing I did, putting out the word that my Johnny Francis alter ego would be on the cruise to try and get the tiara. He says there were French and German agents on board, too. One of the governments would have eventually picked me up."

"Why *did* you do it?" Riker asks, leaning across the table. "I mean, rather than just running away from your father when you had the chance?"

"I didn't know who to go to, who I could trust. I'd always heard about Penelope growing up, so I thought she might be a good place to start—especially since she was married to a federal agent." She turns to me with a hesitant, almost wistful smile. "When I finally met her, I knew I was on the right track."

I'm about to puff up in my own vanity when she keeps going.

"But I couldn't be sure, you know? Then I met Mr. O'Kelly. And Tara. And Jordan and Oz." The smile becomes less hesitant, less wistful. "And *you*, Riker."

Riker jerks back from the table, almost knocking over his chair in the process. Although it would afford me infinite amusement to watch him worm his way out of this one, there's no chance. Grant appears in the doorway, casting a shadow over us all. I look up, pleased to see him in a T-shirt and jeans, his hair back to its normal color. He wanted to go full suit and tie before he headed in today, but I begged him to take it easy. Being all laced up like that has always made him stiffer and sterner.

I need him to unwind. I need him to unbend. I need him to put his own health above the job for once.

"Riker, Simon is waiting for you back in his office. Lola, Cheryl has ordered me to send you to her at the front desk. I believe she's taking lunch orders and is hoping you'll lend her a hand."

"Oh, is she?" Lola asks. "That's so nice of her. I told her I didn't have any plans this afternoon, so she promised to let me help her answer phones. I think I could make a good receptionist, don't you?"

From the glance Grant and I share, we both think she could make one hell of a good federal agent, but we don't say so out loud. There's time enough for her to make decisions about her future. For now, what she needs most is a safe place to land.

"What's Simon going to do to Riker?" I ask as Riker and Lola head out the door. As far as I can tell, the debriefing requirement extended to the three of us but no one else. The rest of my friends and family were thanked and dismissed hours ago.

"Nothing much. Just a few follow-up questions."

My husband doesn't look me in the eye, an action that has always filled me with a sense of foreboding. Add both Riker and Simon into the mix, and nothing good can result.

"Grant…" I warn.

"He'll be fine. It's just a small project Simon wants his help with. It'll be good for him. A sight better than teaching card-counting tricks to a gambling addict."

"Fair enough," I'm forced to say. It's not the worst idea I've ever heard. With Riker, the best way to keep him out of trouble has always been to keep him busy.

Maybe a few buddy cop missions with Simon is just what he needs to get his head straight.

Grant must agree, because he shuts the door and says, "I didn't come here to talk about Riker. I want to talk about you. More specifically, I want to talk about what happened on board the *Shady Lady*."

Hearing the ship's name aloud brings a wash of emotions over me—not the least of which is anger commingled with fear, the last vestiges of this man's obstinance in putting himself in harm's way.

Never mind that being in harm's way is where he thrives. Never mind that he eventually came around and put his trust in my hands. He has to know by now that nothing is more important to me than he is.

He has to know by now that danger is only acceptable when he lets me share it.

I push out of my chair and cross the room until I'm right in front of him. "Oh, yeah? Well I want to talk to *you* about what happened on board the *Shady Lady*." I poke my finger in his chest. "You were supposed to be my partner out there, Grant. We were supposed to be working as a team. Instead, you abandoned the plan and left me in the dark from the first day. That's not how partners work."

"I know, and I'm sorry."

I'm so taken aback by the apology, my hand drops. He catches it and weaves his fingers through mine.

"Yeah, well." I try to find the thread of my argument so I can pick it back up again. *Ah, yes.* Stubborn stupidity. That's where we were. "And you shouldn't have even been on that mission in the first place. You weren't fit to return to duty, and you knew it. You went against protocol and against common sense and, in the process, put every single one of my family members and friends in danger."

He brings my hand to his lips and drops a kiss on the surface. It's a very Kit O'Kelly thing to do, and I can't help being thrilled by it. "I know, and I'm sorry."

Gah. What is he doing? Doesn't he realize I'm full of righteous fury over here?

"He would have *killed* you, Grant," I say, pulling my last card. "Peter wasn't about to let you walk off that ship alive. The second the game was over or he found Johnny Francis, your usefulness would have ended. Not even my dad could have saved you from that."

My throat catches as I picture all the ways in which Grant might have been torn from me.

"I know you didn't like the way I pulled things off," I manage, "but it was the only way to get you out of there in one piece. I did what I thought was best for the mission, and I stand by it."

"I know," he says one final time. "And I'm sorry."

By now, I've officially run out of steam. All my arguments and all my defenses are gone. "That's all you're going to say? That you're sorry?"

"If you don't mind, yes. I know I owe you a lot more than that—my gratitude, for starters—but I've spent enough time today explaining myself to the director. I took on too much, too soon. I should have never attempted the mission. I was wrong."

I goggle at him. He was wrong? My husband—*mine*—is admitting to being wrong?

"I was wrong," he echoes, as if he knows I need to hear it again to believe it. "And the only person on my entire team to do anything about it was you. I told you there was no one I'd rather have my back out there, and I meant it. You're the only one willing to call me out when I need it. You make me a better agent, Penelope." His smile is soft as he brings my hand to his lips once again. "You make me a better *man*."

I open my mouth and close it again, unable to think of anything to say.

"And as my punishment, I've got a long road of desk work and physical therapy ahead of me," he adds. "Frankly, my love, I'm exhausted just thinking about it. Can we go home now?"

It's all I need to hear. In the entire time we've been together—dating and engaged, married and coworkers—Grant has never admitted to physical weakness of any kind. I'm under his arm and supporting his weight in seconds. Even though I doubt he needs me to hold him up, he lets me stand there a moment, pretending I'm the strength he requires, promising to carry him anywhere he needs to go.

"Does this mean you want me to drive?"

"Yes, please. I feel like I could sleep for a week."

I sneak a peek up at his face. "Just sleep?"

"For starters." His voice drops to a low rumble. "But then you have some more interrogation to undergo."

"Interrogation?" I echo, my knees growing weak. It hasn't been long enough since the last one—even the word has me flushing hot and cold, my body primed in seconds.

"Oh, yes. Lots of long, painful interrogation. For starters, I'd like to know what the *hell* you think you were doing setting a cruise ship's ventilation system on fire."

"It was Jordan's idea, I swear!" I squeal and try to dart out from under his arm, but he holds me fast.

"And then we can move on to the sheer *audacity* of you sauntering around in that bikini with a twenty-million-dollar tiara on your head."

"I had to make sure everyone saw me," I protest, but it's no use. Despite his professed exhaustion and the prospect of many long, boring weeks of sitting behind a desk, my husband wraps his arms arounds me and lands what can only be described as a punishing kiss. It's nothing but teeth and tongue and desperation, the intensity of his mouth pressed against mine all I need to confirm that Grant is fully capable of seeing his interrogation through to the end.

I'm not surprised. No matter how exhausted my husband might be, he always finds strength for the things that matter.

EPILOGUE

"ARE YOU REALLY, TRULY SURE YOU GUYS DON'T MIND?" Lola tiptoes into our living room, looking around her as though she's never seen a suburban house full of old-lady antiques and sports memorabilia before.

"I'm really, truly sure," I say, propelling her forward as gently as I can.

So far, she's proved herself to be a much better gun-shot wound patient than my husband ever was, but she still has a few weeks of doctors' visits and therapy ahead of her. It's going to be a long time until I stop feeling worried about the physical state of either one of them.

"The guest room isn't very pretty right now, but you can pick out any color paint you want, and we'll get you some pictures and things to brighten the walls."

I grab Lola's bag, a sad, half-empty duffel that contains all her worldly goods, and lead the way down the hall. Technically, she owns several houses throughout the world—the Munich house and the Almería ranch and several underground bunkers in locations best unmentioned—but they're currently being held by the British government pending her father's investigation. We offered to send someone to collect her clothes and personal effects, but she said she'd rather start fresh.

I push open the door and gesture at her surroundings. Like most guest rooms, ours used to be a catch-all for exercise equipment and piles of unfolded laundry, but Grant and I spent all day yesterday clearing it out in anticipation of our new houseguest. I swear, he's almost more excited about it than I am.

"It'll be great practice for when we have kids of our own," he'd said with a laugh and his arms wrapped around me from behind. "Like a teenager test run."

"*What* did you just say to me?" I'd asked, whirling on him.

"Oh, nothing. Do you think she'd prefer the mirror on this wall or on the one by the window?"

The mirror almost ended up smashed over his head after that, but I'd already had enough vacuuming for one day. No way was I cleaning that mess up, too.

The result is a neat, tidy—if sparse—room that could use a little love. Since Lola is probably accustomed to palatial manors, I'm a little scared to offer such humble accommodations, but it's the best we have.

I needn't have worried.

"Oh, Penelope." She enters the room behind me, her voice barely above a whisper. "This is all for me?"

"I know it's not much, but—"

I don't have a chance to finish. Her good arm wraps around me, those bouncy curls of hers tickling my nose. "I know I shouldn't accept it, not after all the trouble

I've caused you and Grant, but I think it might be the best room I've ever seen. Your house is so pretty and cute and inviting. I don't deserve to be a part of it."

"Hey, now." I brush her hair away from her face, my heart aching at the glittering tears she refuses to let fall. "That's not a very nice way to talk about my friend."

"Is that what I am?"

I pretend to think about it. "Well, I thought you were, but that was before."

Her lower lip wobbles. "Before?"

"Before," I echo. "But now that you're finally here, I can tell you're going to be a lot more than that. From here on out, Lola Sanchez, you're family."

ABOUT THE AUTHOR

Tamara Morgan is a contemporary romance author whose books combine fast-paced antics and humor with heartfelt sentiment. Her long-lived affinity for romance novels survived a BA in English literature, after which time she discovered it was much more fun to create stories than analyze the life out of them. She lives with her husband and daughter in the Inland Northwest, where the summers are hot, the winters are cold, and coffee is available on every street corner.

STEALING MR. RIGHT

First in a new romantic suspense "heist"
series, Penelope Blue brings you fast-paced
antics and a compelling caper romance

Penelope Blue has the perfect life, and the perfect husband.
Well, except for the fact that he works for the FBI...and
she's a jewel thief. It turns out that the only thing worse
than having a mortal enemy is being married to one.
Because in this game of theft and seduction, only one will
come out on top.

Good thing a cat burglar always lands on her feet.

*"A sexy, fun, cat-and-mouse chase that
hooked me from page one!"*

**—Jennifer Probst, *New York Times* and
USA Today Bestselling Author**

SAVING MR. PERFECT

Second in the Penelope Blue series

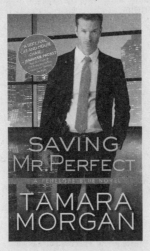

Without the thrill of the chase, life's been pretty dull. But what's that old saying? When one thief closes the door...a copycat jimmies open a window.

Set up to take the fall for thefts worth millions, Penelope have no choice but to help her FBI agent husband track the thief. Grant might not think he needs a partner, but this is one case only a true professional can solve. Let's just hope curiosity doesn't kill the cat burglar.

"A sexy, fun, cat-and-mouse chase that hooked me from page one!"

—Jennifer Probst, *New York Times* and *USA Today* Bestselling Author

For more Tamara Morgan, visit:
sourcebooks.com

BAD BACHELOR

First in the Bad Bachelors series

If one more person mentions Bad Bachelors to Reed McMahon, someone's gonna get hurt. Reed is known as an "image fixer" but his womanizing ways have caught up with him. What he needs is a PR miracle of his own.

When Reed strolls into Darcy Greer's workplace offering to help save the struggling library, she isn't buying it. But as she reluctantly works with Reed, she realizes there's more to a man than his reputation. Maybe, just maybe, Bad Bachelor #1 is THE one for her.

"Sizzling, sexy, and so much fun!"

—Sarah Morgan, *USA Today* Bestselling Author

For more Stefanie London, visit:
sourcebooks.com

ONE SUMMER NIGHT

First in the At the Shore series by *New York Times* and *USA Today* bestselling author Caridad Pineiro

Everyone knows about the bad blood between the Pierces and Sinclairs, but Owen has been watching Maggie from afar for years. Whenever he can get down to the shore, he strolls the sand hoping for a chance meeting—and a repeat of the forbidden kiss they shared one fateful summer night.

When Owen hears that Maggie's in trouble, he doesn't hesitate to step in. She has no choice but to accept Owen's help. But what's he going to demand in return?

"One Summer Night *is the perfect escape!*"

—Raeanne Thayne, *USA Today* Bestselling Author

For more Caridad Pineiro, visit:
sourcebooks.com

COLLISION COURSE

Fourth in the Body Shop Bad Boys series from *New York Times* and *USA Today* bestseller Marie Harte

Florist Joey Reeves is working overtime to stay away from Lou Cortez, the ace mechanic with a reputation for irresistible charm. She's a single mom with enough on her plate—the last thing she needs is entanglement with the hottest guy in town…

"High-octane chemistry keeps the pages turning and your engine revving!"

—Gina L. Maxwell, *New York Times* and *USA Today* Bestselling Author

For more Marie Harte, visit:
sourcebooks.com

LOVE GAME

First in a new contemporary series
from author Maggie Wells

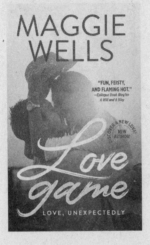

Kate Snyder is at the top of her game. So when the university
hires a washed-up coach trying to escape scandal—paying
him a lot more than she earns—Kate is more than annoyed.

Danny McMillan gets Kate's frustration, but her pay grade
isn't his problem, right? When Kate and Danny finally see
eye to eye, sparks turn into something even hotter...and
they need to figure out if this is more than just a game.

"Will steal your heart...romance at its finest."

—Harlequin Junkie for *Going Deep*

SURVIVE THE NIGHT

Third in the thrilling Rocky Mountain K9 Unit series

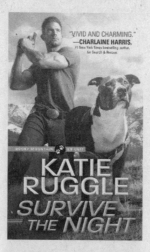

K9 Officer Otto Gunnersen has always had a soft spot for anyone in need—but for all his big heart, he's never been in love. Until he meets Sarah Clifton

All Sarah wants is to escape, but there's no outrunning her past. Her power-mad brother would hunt her to the ends of the earth...but he'd never expect Sarah to fight back. With Otto by her side, Sarah's finally ready to face whatever comes her way.

"Vivid and charming."

—Charlaine Harris, #1 *New York Times* **Bestselling Author**

For more Katie Ruggle, visit:
sourcebooks.com

EVERY DEEP DESIRE

First in a sultry, swampy romantic suspense
series from author Sharon Wray

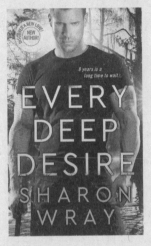

Rafe Montfort was a decorated Green Beret, the best of the
best, until a disastrous mission and an unforgivable betrayal
destroyed his life. Now, this deadly soldier has returned
to the sultry Georgia swamps to reunite with his Beret
brothers—as well as the love he left behind—and take back
all he lost. But Juliet must never know the truth behind
what he's done…or the dangerous secret that threatens to
take him from her forever.